A Wartime Ch

Betty Firth grew up in rural West Yorkshire in the UK, right in the heart of Brontë country... and she's still there. After graduating from Durham University with a degree in English Literature, she dallied with living in cities including London, Nottingham and Cambridge, but eventually came back with her own romantic hero in tow to her beloved Dales. Betty Firth also writes romantic comedies under the pen name Mary Jayne Baker and Lisa Swift, and wrote *Edie's Home for Strays* as Gracie Taylor.

Also by Betty Firth

Made in Yorkshire

A New Home in the Dales
War Comes to the Dales
A Wartime Christmas in the Dales

Betty Firth

A Wartime Christmas *in the* Dales

hera

First published in the United Kingdom in 2024 by

Hera Books
Unit 9 (Canelo), 5th Floor
Cargo Works, 1–2 Hatfields
London SE1 9PG
United Kingdom

A CIP catalogue record for this book is available from the British Library.

Print ISBN 978 1 80436 196 2
Ebook ISBN 978 1 80436 195 5

Look for more great books at www.herabooks.com

Printed and bound in Great Britain by Clays Ltd, Elcograf S.p.A.

I

MIX
Paper | Supporting
responsible forestry
FSC® C018072

For Rohen, Hudson, Emmie, Hayley, Eleanor, Niamh, Cleo, Joshua, Noah and George. With much love from your aunty
xxx

Dialect Glossary

Afore = before
Allus = always
Any road = anyhow
Aye = yes
Backendish = autumnal weather conditions
Badly = ill
Bairn = child
Beck = stream
Blumming = minced oath for "bloody"
Bonny = pretty
Brass = money (but in military jargon, also used to refer to high-ranking officials)
A brew = pot/cup of tea
Canny = sensible
Capped = pleased
Clout = a slap (or a cloth/item of clothing)
Dale = valley
Doy = darling
Favver = father
Fell = hill or mountain
Fettle = to fix or put in order
Flayed = afraid
Frame = to work hard
Frame thissen = get to work
Gang = go

Grand = excellent
Happen = perhaps; possibly
Herssen = herself
Hissen = himself
Lad = boy/man
Laiking = playing
Lass = girl/woman
Lig = lie
Lish = nimble; strong
Lug = ear
Mam = mother
Missen = myself
Mithering = fussing or complaining
Mournjy = moody; sulky
Mun = must
Nay = no
Nesh = prone to feeling the cold
Nithered = feeling the cold
Noan = none; not
Nobbut = nothing but; only
Nowt = nothing
Oss = horse
Ovver = over
Owd = old
Owt = anything
Sin = since
Sithee = goodbye
Snizy = bitingly cold
Spice = sweets/candy
Summat = something
Swadi = Swaledale sheep
T' = the
Tha/thee = you

Thi/thy = your
Thine = yours
Think on = watch what you're doing; be careful
Thissen = yourself
Thrang = busy
Tup = stud ram
Tyke = someone from Yorkshire
Us = our
Yon = yonder/over there
Yow = ewe

Chapter 1

October 1941

Bobby Bancroft rubbed her hands together, trying to get the blood flowing, before turning her attention back to the job in hand. The mess of a hedgerow stretched out before her, tangled and knotted like a bird's nest, jewelled with the fruits of autumn – fruits that were fast disappearing as a tribe of Silverdale residents plucked the plump rosehips and blackberries and tossed them into baskets hooked over their arms.

Bobby picked one of the ripe red rosehips and squeezed it between her thumb and forefinger, testing it for firmness. Finding it satisfyingly unyielding, she placed it in her basket with the others. Rosehips were the real prize in today's foraging expedition, and the Ministry of Health had issued strict instructions on the best berries to harvest: red, firm and not too soft, so they would survive the journey they were going to be making down south.

'It's come to summat when even the fodder God sends us for nowt is to go for the war effort,' Bobby's friend Mary Atherton grumbled at her side. 'Bad enough the shop shelves are empty. Now the Ministry's even begrudging us a bit of bramble jam for our Christmas table.'

It had been a long Sunday afternoon of fruit-picking and Bobby knew the older woman's joints would be feeling the chill. If there was one thing that could dampen Mary's usually irrepressible good humour, it was the effect of the cold weather on her rheumatism.

The best time to harvest rosehips was directly following the first frost of the year. The morning frost had disappeared now, apart from a little sugar crusting on the grass in shady patches, but there was a keen wind coming down from the high fells – it was 'blowing backendish', as the Dalesfolk were apt to say. The weather remained dry, however, which meant the hips needed to be collected speedily before the ever-reliable Dales rainfall returned to plague them. Wet fruit quickly went bad when stored, and this fruit would have a long way to go.

In spite of her prickled fingers, juice-stained skin and numb toes, Bobby had rather enjoyed her first experience of hedgerow foraging. However, for Mary's sake she tried to sound sympathetic.

'I know but it's for a good cause,' she said. 'There's been talk of scurvy and all sorts breaking out now orange juice is so scarce. I read in the paper that there's as much vitamin C in six rosehips as a whole orange. The Scoutmaster told me they're to be turned into vitamin syrup by some big chemist down near London, then sent out to schools and evacuees' homes.'

'Well, if it's to keep bairns healthy then I suppose it's not such a hardship to go without,' Mary said, somewhat mollified. 'They might remember we've a couple of young 'uns at Moorside who need their vitamins too though. Not to mention my Reg, who likes his bit of sweet stuff in the winter months when his leg's giving him grief.'

'The girls will be given vitamin syrup at school with the rest of the children, I suppose.' Bobby gently squeezed another rosehip. It was too ripe and burst a little, sending a trickle of juice over the kingfisher-blue sapphire ring on her wedding finger. 'Here's another for the reject basket. Since the Ministry only want fruit that can be stored a while, I don't think we need feel guilty about dividing the softer berries amongst ourselves, do you? It'll only spoil and go to waste otherwise. We ought to get at least a jar out of it for Christmas.'

'Happen even a couple if we can scrape together enough sugar.' Mary looked rather wistful. 'Oh, but poor Reg will miss his crystallised fruit this year. He's always had a weakness for crystallised fruit.'

'I suppose we must make the best of what we do have. Everyone here is in the same boat.'

'Aye, they are.' Mary glanced around at the villagers collecting fruit. 'I must admit, it's nice to see so many folk pulling together today. Patriotism seems to be all the fashion in Silverdale just now, doesn't it?'

'People want to do their bit while their men are off fighting. You're right, it is nice to see.'

Mary smiled. 'You seem to be brimful of silver linings this morning, young Bobby. I expect the prospect of a night on the town with our Charlie is behind that.'

Bobby flushed slightly at the mention of her fiancé: Mary's brother-in-law, Charlie Atherton. Twenty years younger than his half-brother Reg, Charlie was really more like a son to Mary and her husband than a sibling. Reg and Mary had lost their only child Nancy as a baby, and Charlie had lost his mother while still a young boy, so it was natural that he would have grown close to the kind, motherly woman who had come to love him as her own.

3

Bobby had grown close to the Atherton family too – ever since that fateful day a year ago when she had first arrived on the doorstep of their home at Moorside Farm to attend an interview with Reg for the position of junior reporter on his magazine *The Tyke*. And despite her best efforts to resist, she had grown more than close to Charlie.

They had been so happy, for a time: Charlie living at the farmhouse with Reg and Mary with Bobby just a hop and a skip away in the converted barn on the grounds known as Cow House Cottage, where she kept house for her father. The days had been long, the air fragrant, the fells endless and theirs to explore. But then the war had come to call for Charlie, and he had left her as Bobby knew he must to do his duty with the RAF.

Mary was right: Bobby was excited about seeing him. Although her fiancé was stationed at an RAF training centre on an airbase only ten miles distant, the squadron leader in charge was strict and leave of an evening hard to come by. Charlie had told Bobby he'd had to plead the sudden illness of a non-existent aunt to have the pleasure of seeing her last time he'd been granted a pass out, and no doubt this imaginary relative had been banished to her sickbed once again to allow for tonight's few stolen hours together.

Unbeknownst to Mary, however, Bobby and Charlie's 'night on the town' was likely to go little further than the bandstand in nearby Settle. The summer had been for stolen kisses on the back row of the picture house and nights at the dance hall swaying in one another's arms. That had been the cuckoo time, before Charlie had left to begin his training, when carefree youth had felt like it would last forever. Since Charlie had left for the RAF, the young lovers much preferred to spend the scant hours they were in each other's company quietly alone together, holding each other in the stillness of the blackout while they made plans for when the war was over. Bobby felt like they uttered that phrase now more than they ever had. When the war is over... when the war is over. It can't be long. Surely it can't be much longer now...

And yet the changing face of the village Bobby now called home showed her this was likely to be a vain hope. She glanced around the people picking fruit. Women, children and a scattering of old men made up the bulk of those out today, and what young men were present were mostly in uniform.

There was a troop of Boy Scouts from neighbouring Smeltham, who were nominally in charge of the fruit-picking operation – uniformed but not men yet, although some must only be a year or two from call-up age. Would they be called on to serve their country, these young boys? Would they come back home when it was all over? They seemed so much children still, in their short trousers and knee-high socks, that the maternal part of Bobby's heart couldn't bear to dwell on it. But with the war raging on and no end in sight, who knew what tomorrow might bring?

The other uniforms she could pick out easily among the crowd were the bright blue tunics and red ties of the patients from Sumner House, a nearby stately home that had been requisitioned as an auxiliary hospital for wounded RAF airmen. Her Polish friend Piotr Zielinski was among the convalescents out picking fruit today, with his wife Jolka and their little boy Tommy – although it wasn't long now, Jolka had told Bobby, until Piotr would be well enough to resume his training and could throw off the hated hospital blues for good. Three-year-old Tommy had a ring of dark juice around his lips, which suggested far more of the blackberries he was helping his mother and father to pick had gone into his mouth than into their basket.

Piotr was one of two Polish airmen that a rescue party led by Bobby had brought down from Great Bowside when their plane had crashed into the mountain that summer. The pilot – Teddy – was also present, although as he was confined to a wheelchair, he could help only a little with the picking. Instead he supervised Florence and Jessica Parry, the young evacuees from London whom Mary and her husband Reg had taken in, smiling as he watched them select the best blackberries. His nurse, Topsy Sumner-Walsh, sat beside him on a blanket, dreamily attempting to make a garland from hardy autumn hawkbit in lieu of daisies, and occasionally glancing fondly up at her charge to check he was well and comfortable. The four of them formed a serene domestic scene, and Bobby couldn't help but smile as her gaze settled on them.

There were women in uniform too: the long socks, brown breeches and bottle-green jerseys of the Women's Land Army. Several Land Girls were now working on the local farms as more men left for the armed forces, arriving every morning in a tilly truck from the Land Army hostel in Skipton before going home again in the evening. They were a jolly bunch, with thick Newcastle accents almost as hard for Bobby to understand as the conversation between Piotr and Jolka, who were chattering together in their own language. The girls joked and whistled while they picked, looking as though they were having the time of their lives in their work. Bobby was rather envious of them.

The only other uniforms in the crowd were worn by just three men, all new arrivals to the village. They were airmen too, but not attached to the airbase where Charlie and Piotr were training. These were fully fledged bomber crew, their cap badges marking them out as being with the Royal Canadian Air Force. They were part of a Canadian squadron stationed just over the border in Lancashire, and had been billeted with a couple in the village with whom one of them shared a family connection.

These young men had caused quite a stir in Silverdale since arriving some three weeks ago. They were quiet enough – at least, they didn't kick up a riot at the Golden Hart every night or try to sweep away the farmers' wives as the Silverdalians were apt to think 'foreign types' were prone to doing. Nevertheless, they were all tall, broad and dark, and at least one was strikingly handsome. The men were smart in their uniforms, with Brylcreemed hair and perfectly straight, white teeth, and to a Yorkshire ear their accent sounded pure Hollywood. Whenever Sandy, Chip or Ernie – for such were their names – stirred from their billet, a throng of giggling village girls instantly followed in their wake.

Still, they seemed like pleasant, clean-cut lads, over here to fight the fascist oppressor alongside their Commonwealth allies, and there'd been no scandals or rumours of anything untoward. Bobby had had no acquaintance with them so far but she had seen them around the village. She was fond of listening to their exotic – and yet to a regular film-goer, oddly familiar – accents, and observing differences in the way they behaved compared to the boys she knew. If the opportunity arose, she would be keen to have some talk with them and learn more about life in their homeland. All were single,

7

however, and Bobby was an engaged woman. It didn't do to appear too eager for their acquaintance.

'It's a good thing Charlie resigned as Silverdale's leading eligible bachelor when ye two got betrothed,' Mary observed as she followed Bobby's gaze to the Canadian airmen. 'I think those three have supplanted him completely in the favour of the lasses round here. I don't suppose any local lad can compete with them flashing white teeth and American accents.'

'Canadian,' Bobby said. 'Not that I can tell the difference, but I doubt the men will think it very good manners if we seem to mix them up.'

'They sound like they're straight out of the talkies to me. Look like it too. Makes the village seem almost glamorous, having them around.'

Bobby knew what her friend meant. There was something unreal and larger than life about the three Canadians, in a way that was different from her friends the Polish airmen. It felt like they didn't quite fit – as if they'd been cut out of a film magazine and pasted into Bobby's familiar world here in Silverdale.

'We're becoming quite international around here, aren't we?' Mary went on. 'It seems like I can't go anywhere in the village nowadays without hearing an accent from some far-flung place. I don't think I met more than one or two folk who didn't talk like me my whole life before this war, and now I'm serving all these gents from foreign parts cups of tea at the chapel jumble sale.'

'When Reg interviewed me for my job on *The Tyke*, he told me the war would bring the whole world into our parlours,' Bobby said, rather dreamily. 'I thought he was talking about the wireless. I didn't realise it was going to be the literal truth.'

'There was a time the fells shut us off from the outside world here in the Dales, and from one another an' all. Even folk from a few villages over felt exotic when I were a lass.' Mary stopped picking rosehips to glance at one of the Canadians, who was chivalrously pressing a chilly Land Girl to take his greatcoat. 'The youngsters now are growing up in a different sort of world than the one I knew. Still, happen it's good for us to learn what ligs beyond our doorsteps.'

'I think so. I can see why people here miss the old ways, but there's a whole world out there that I'd love to see more of if ever I get the opportunity – I mean, once all this madness is over.' Bobby absently tossed another hip into her basket. 'If it ever is over,' she murmured to herself.

'They seem nice enough lads anyhow, the young Canadians,' Mary said. 'Always polite and gentlemanly to the ladies, even those of us old enough to be their mothers. Molly Craven got quite giggly when one of them insisted on standing up with her at the last charity tea dance, though she's sixty-three. Have you had much talk with them?'

'Only a "good morning" when I pass them in the village or see them at church. I bump into them in the Hart sometimes when I go in to warm up after my ARP patrol, but they only touch their caps to me and then keep to themselves. I suppose it must be daunting, being in a strange country among people different from those at home.'

'Well, I approve of them leaving you be. They're better off keeping to themselves than running around with all those young lasses keen to flutter their eyelashes at them. Then again, we want them to feel welcome here. Make friends among other lads their age – what's left of them after King and Country's taken most for army and navy, any road.'

Bobby smiled. 'I think the other lads are too jealous to want to make friends. It's quite unfair really. The Canadians haven't done anything to encourage the girls who follow them about.'

'It's only the novelty of them. That'll pass as folk get used to seeing them. If they're still here come Christmas, I'll set our Charlie to introduce them around a bit.' Mary glanced at her. 'Still saving up your clothing coupons, are you?'

'I'm not saving them as such,' said Bobby, who suspected she knew what direction the conversation was going to turn in. 'There just isn't anything I really need at the moment. It's not as though I go out very often, now I've no young man around to take me dancing.'

'I'm sure you'd like to give Charlie's eyes a treat when he comes home for Christmas though. How about summat new and fresh for the festive season? There'll be dances galore to show a new frock off at then, and plenty of lads home on leave to appreciate it.'

Bobby laughed. 'Where would I get something new and fresh? All that's in the shops is drab utility wear; nothing I'd want to go dancing in. My old blue crepe can do me for a while yet.'

Mary shook her head. 'It's a sad thing for a lass in her courting years to be tied to just one or two new dresses a year. I should think for someone your age, that would be the biggest hardship of all.'

'I'm not much of a one for fine clothes. My sister complains of the clothing ration in every letter I have from her though. Lil told me that some of her Wren friends have started using dyed butter muslin for their frocks to make their coupons stretch.'

'Necessity has ever been the mother of invention,' Mary said with a smile. 'As long as we can get new material then we can make it nice for you. I'll help you trim it up bonny with a few frills, and the girls will be keen to help. I'm not averse to cutting up some of the lace gathering dust in my linen cupboard.' Mary quirked an eyebrow. 'But happen you're saving your coupons for summat else, are you? If so, I'll keep my old lace for that.'

Bobby smiled. Her friend was many things, but subtle wasn't one of them.

'Keep it for what?' she asked.

'Oh, I don't know... to trim up a trousseau, perhaps? Reg and I would be happy to pool our coupons with you and your dad to get you everything you need. And you must have new things, Bobby. It's terrible bad luck for a bride to wear a second-hand gown to be wed.'

'That's very kind of you both but I told you: Charlie and I aren't going to be wed just yet – perhaps not for a long time. Long engagements are hardly unusual these days, are they?'

'I thought you'd be champing at the bit wanting to set up home,' Mary said. 'I know the perfect cottage sitting empty over the way in Smeltham that the two of you could rent, and not too dear neither. There's a room for you and Charlie, one for your father and a little room that would be just perfect for a nursery. I'd love to hear wedding bells ringing for you in 1942, Bobby.'

'Well you won't, will you? Not unless the Germans invade while we're in church.'

'All right, clever dick. It's only a figure of speech.'

Bobby turned her face away. 'It isn't the right time for marriage. Not with all the uncertainty there is in the world.'

'You're not fixing to wait until the war ends? At the rate things are going on you could be old and grey by that time.'

Bobby winced. 'Please don't say that. I feel like I'll go mad if this war just goes on and on, all the men away and no one knowing what tomorrow will bring. It has to end soon. Please God, it has to.'

'And if it don't?'

Bobby was relieved when Florence and Jessie, the young evacuees who lived at Moorside Farm with Reg and Mary, came running up to interrupt the conversation. Florrie's cupped hands were filled with rosehips.

'Lieutenant Teddy says we've to bring you and Mary these, Bobby,' she said breathlessly. 'They're to go with the red ones, not the black ones we've been picking. There were lots of good ones so even though we're on blackberries, we picked them to bring for your basket.'

'Thanks, girls, that was very helpful of you.' Bobby held out her basket for them to contribute their spoils.

Mary smiled, nodding to Teddy a little distance away in his wheelchair. He was smiling somewhat dreamily as Topsy placed a limp garland of hawkbit over his head. The young airman was prone to spells of depression since the plane crash that had cost him the use of his legs and right eye. Today, however, he looked quite serene and content.

'I reckon I can guess why he wanted a little time free from bairns' prattle,' Mary said in a low voice to Bobby while the two girls hunted among this new patch of hedge for more treasures. 'I've never seen such a smitten expression. You don't think he's got a question to ask her ladyship, do you?'

Bobby laughed. 'I swear you won't be happy unless you've trimmed up at least one trousseau by the time Christmas comes around.'

'Ah, well, I'm an old romantic at heart. I like to see young people happy and set up in life.' Mary smiled. 'I think yon Topsy might be almost as bad as the young man. See how she leans close to him pretending to fuss with them flowers.'

'Well, you know how Topsy is. She has to make pets of people.'

'Not this time. She's had her heart snared at last, I'm sure of it. Mark my words: we'll be throwing rice and pennies outside the church before spring comes around.'

Bobby wondered if Mary was right. It was easy to see that Teddy had fallen deeply in love with Topsy, and she was certainly fond of him in return. But Topsy Sumner-Walsh was such a butterfly of a person, so demonstrative and affectionate with the friends she took under her wing, that it was hard to tell how deep her true feelings might be. And then there was the difference in their situations: Topsy's wealth, rank and family connections; the fact that Teddy was a foreigner, a poor man and a cripple, not to mention the disfiguring burns on one side of his face which had so altered his appearance. Bobby hoped that Tadeusz Nowak, so broken in body after the accident that summer, wasn't shortly going to find his heart broken as well.

Chapter 2

'You did definitely, definitely set your alarm clock for tomorrow morning, Mary,, didn't you?' Jessie asked anxiously, looking up from the hedge she was hunting through. She looked a little like a hedge herself following her afternoon's work, with twigs and even a ladybird tangled in her curly red hair. Bobby didn't envy Mary trying to comb it all out later.

Tomorrow was Monday and an important day for Jessie, who had been selected for the great honour of ringing the large brass bell that signalled the start of lessons at Silverdale Primary School. This was a terrific respons-ibility, a favour highly prized by the village children, and conferred only on those whose behaviour and class work had been deemed exceptional by the exacting but kindly schoolmistress. The girl had talked of little but 'ringing the bell' for days. This task required her to arrive at school a full fifteen minutes early, and her biggest fear at the moment was that some terrible catastrophe would occur to make her late.

Mary smiled. 'Now don't you fret, Jess. I set the alarm to ring good and early, I promise. You'll be at school in plenty of time to ring the bell.'

'Is it a very old custom, this ringing the bell?' Bobby asked Mary. 'We never had it at my school. I mean we had a bell, naturally, but only teachers ever rang it.'

'Long as I've been alive,' Mary said. 'I well remember the day it was my turn, when I was nobbut as high as your ankle, Bobby.'

Jessie's eyes went wide. 'You rung the bell too?'

'That's right, when I was a little girl. Three times I was deemed worthy by old Miss Wright, who was school-mistress then.' Mary smiled. 'I remember the first time. Mam had me in my best setting-off clothes, just as proud as Punch that I'd been picked, and all the family came to watch. I was a tiny thing and had to hold the bell in both hands to ring it, but I wouldn't have Miss Wright help me. Wanted to do it all myself. I was so smug and pompous about it the rest of the day that I wonder the other children could bear to laik with me.'

'I'm the first evacuee ever to be picked to do it. Ever,' Jessie announced proudly.

Florrie shot her sister an envious look. 'Jessie still has to do her chores though, don't she, Mary? She can't not do 'em just 'cause she's ringing the bell when I have to do mine the same.'

'Oh yes, I've set the alarm to include chore time too. I'll be making bacon and egg pie for tea tomorrow so I'll need all the eggs you can find for me, Jessie.'

The little Londoners were starting to become quite countrified after five months in Silverdale, even picking up some of the local accent, and had quickly learned the ways of their new home. Both now had their own special chores to do at Moorside before school every morning. Florrie was responsible for feeding the gang of semi-feral mouser cats that roamed the former farm, as well as the three dogs – Reg and Mary's elderly wolfhounds Barney and Winnie, and Ace the border collie pup, who had been a present to the girls from Charlie. Jessie, meanwhile, was expected to feed the biddies in the henhouse and collect up their eggs. The residents of both Moorside and Cow House Cottage – the converted barn in the grounds that Bobby occupied with her father – had all agreed to exchange their egg allocation for a ration of bran, which was mashed up with boiled cabbage, potato peel and other leftovers to feed the four hens. Until recently, the family had been repaid handsomely for their sacrifice, but now the cooler weather was upon them, some of the hens seemed to have very unpatriotically decided to go on strike. These days, they were lucky to get ten eggs a week between the six of them.

'All right,' Jessie said. 'There was none this morning though, and Henrietta still ain't laying.'

'That's a full fortnight she's not given us a single egg,' Bobby observed to Mary.

Mary sighed. 'That's a shame. She's been a right good little layer for us the past few years, but she's getting on a bit now, I suppose. We'll get a cockerel in next spring so we can hatch a clutch of chicks from the others, see if we can't raise up a replacement for her.'

'At least it makes for an easy decision about the Christmas table.'

'Aye, that's true. She won't be as tender as one of the younger birds but we can't afford to lose them as are laying. I'll start fattening her up.' Mary stood up straight, putting her hand to her back as it creaked into an upright position. 'Oof. I'll tell thee what, Bobby, it's young folks' work, this. I think we can say we've done our part now. We'd better take these young terrors home and get the tea on before Reg and your father set the place alight trying to fend for themselves.'

The rosehips deemed good enough for the Ministry of Health were handed over to the Smeltham Scoutmaster to be put with the rest of the collection, and Bobby entrusted Florence with the basket containing soft or damaged fruit that Mary intended to turn into jam for Christmas. After saying goodbye to their friends who were still fruit-picking, the four of them began the walk home, pulling their coats tight around them to keep out the biting wind. Florrie and Jessie were little more than wool and eyes, so swaddled up were they in hats, scarves and other knitted items that Mary and Bobby had made for their winter wardrobes.

But it was a bright day, though it was 'snizy', as the Dalesfolk called it when the air was raw – the people here had as many words for weather as they did for sheep, and that was saying something. Bobby breathed the scents of autumn deeply while they walked home through the village, lifting her nose like a Bisto Kid as she filled her lungs. Fallen leaves in all the glorious colours of autumn – russet, amber, orange and gold – crunched underfoot. The breeze that came down from the fells carried a rich, moist, earthy smell now the frost had thawed, mingling with the perfume of smoke in the distance as a farmer hurried to burn up a pile of raked leaves before the blackout arrived to curtail such activities. It reminded Bobby of the thrill of Guy Fawkes Night, before the war when such celebrations had still been permitted. She could imagine the taste of sweet, sticky ginger parkin on her tongue, and the joyous explosion of colours as fireworks lit up the sky. She hoped the day wasn't too far away when the sky would once again be lit only by innocent fireworks, with the bombs of war a distant memory.

Mary and Florrie were walking a little ahead together. Mary, no doubt, was keen to get her aching limbs back into the warm, while Florrie was anxious to deposit her treasure safely in the kitchen at Moorside. She was holding on to the precious basket of rosehips with both hands, as if worried a thief might appear to steal it away. Jessie hung back, however, and Bobby felt a little mittened hand slip into hers as they walked.

She glanced down at the girl. Hardly any of her face was visible between the muffler that came up almost to her nose and the pompom-trimmed hat pulled down over her forehead, but nevertheless Bobby could see the child looked anxious.

'What's wrong, my lamb?' she asked gently. 'Are you still worrying about being late for the bell tomorrow? If you like we can all inspect Mary's alarm clock together so we can test it's working properly.'

Jessie pulled down her muffler so she could speak. 'It ain't that. Bobby, when Mary said about Henrietta not laying no more... did that mean she'd be... you know, that she'd be killed?'

'Is that what's upsetting you?' Bobby squeezed the hand in hers. 'I'm afraid so, sweetheart. People have to eat to keep strong and healthy, and if a hen stops laying eggs... well, that's what happens, you know. People can't afford to keep animals these days except for food.'

'They can. We keep Barney and Winnie and Ace and the cats that live outside, and Boxer too. They ain't for food, are they?'

'No, but they are working animals as well as pets. Ace is learning to be a sheepdog, the cats catch mice and Boxer pulls the trap so we can get to places.'

'Barney and Winnie don't work. They just sleep all day.'

'That's because they're old. Reg got them to be guard dogs but they're retired now, just like people do when they can't work any more. Now they can rest for what's left of their lives, and be friends to their humans for their keep instead.'

'Then why don't Henrietta get to retire, if she's too old to lay eggs? She's our friend too. Leastways, she's my friend. I take care of her and give her her chicken food.'

Bobby felt a little out of her depth trying to think of an answer that would be acceptable to an eight-year-old's view of the world. She tried a different tack.

'You have chicken to eat all the time, don't you?' she said. 'At least, perhaps not nowadays, but you still eat it when Mary can get it.'

'I know, but it ain't *my* chicken. It ain't Henrietta.'

'Henrietta's had a good long life for a hen, Jess. It won't hurt her at all – she'll die straight away, without pain, if it's done properly. Reg knows the right way. All animals have to die one day, and it's a mercy to them if we can make that happen without it hurting them.'

'But if she starts laying eggs again, then will Mary let me keep her and we'll eat something else at Christmas?'

'Well yes, if she's providing eggs then Mary won't want to lose her. But she's quite old, my love, and it's weeks now since she laid for us. It might be that her egg-laying days are over.'

'She will lay more eggs,' the child announced determinedly. 'I'll stroke her and give her the best food, and I'll sing to her and tell her she's just *got* to lay eggs.' The farmhouse, and its satellite Cow House Cottage, were in sight now. 'I'm going to the henhouse right this minute, soon as we get home, to tell her she's got to.'

Chapter 3

'Dad?' Bobby called when she opened the door to Cow House Cottage.

There was a chill in the air inside the draughty converted barn, and her father was nowhere to be seen. Bobby cast a worried look at the ashy white remnants of the fire she'd lit that morning in the grate. Had her dad been out this afternoon? He hadn't said he was going anywhere, but if he'd been at home then he must have been very far inside his own head to let the fire die out on this cold day.

She approached the fireplace to stoke up the embers and get the flames roaring again, then hesitated as her gaze drifted to the door that led into the barn's adjoining extension. It had been Charlie's surgery when he had run his veterinary practice from the place as a civilian, and it contained several lockable cabinets where he kept the drugs he used for his profession.

Leaving the fire embers for the moment, Bobby made her way to the surgery and crouched down to try the door of a little cabinet where she had locked various items she wanted to keep safe — not least of which was the cheap potato-peel spirit she gave her father to help him sleep after a nightmare.

The handle wiggled but the door didn't budge, and Bobby smiled with relief to find it locked still. Then she frowned.

There were some marks, around the little lock. As if someone had used a tool of some kind to try to force or break it...

He'd been in here. He'd tried to get in. And if her father was experiencing alcohol cravings again, feeling the same need for oblivion that had led him to try to take his own life back in the winter... that meant things must be worse than she thought.

Where was he? Had he gone to the pub? Was he drinking with one of the local men there – Pete Dixon perhaps? If her father had felt the urge for a drink stronger than the Golden Hart's watered-down beer then Pete was the man who could get it for him. He had fingers in every slice of the pie that was the black market.

Bobby almost sighed with relief as she heard the door to the cottage open and her father come in. She sprang to her feet and went into the living room to meet him.

'What were you doing in there then, lass?' he asked gruffly as he took off his boots.

'Just a little cleaning. Charlie won't be happy if I let his precious instruments gather dust while he's away.'

'Practising your wifely duties, eh?' he said with a some-what forced smile.

'Something like that. I'll fettle the fire for us.'

She went to the fireplace and started feeding it with coke, glancing at her father from the corner of her eye as she tried to subtly examine him for any sign of drunkenness. He didn't look intoxicated at all – she knew what that looked like well enough – but he did look weary, with a glazed, distant expression in his eyes. He hadn't woken her with one of his familiar screaming nightmares last night, but all the same, he looked as though he'd barely slept.

'Been out?' she asked, as casually as she could manage.

'Just to t' outhouse. I'm a bit nesh to stir outdoors today. Not getting any younger.'

'You ought to have wrapped up and come berry-picking with us. Mary was asking after you, and the girls too.'

He gave a harsh laugh. 'This the latest nonsense, is it? Berries for Britain. You'd think Churchill and his cronies would be putting their time into figuring out how to end this thing instead of cooking up jam like a bunch of housewives.'

'I hope they are, but they have to keep people fed and healthy in the meantime. It's bairns who suffer when there isn't enough.'

'Aye, well. Summat in that, I suppose.' He put on his slippers and took a seat in the armchair by the fire. 'What're you giving us for fodder this evening then, Nell?'

Bobby winced. It was a sure sign of a bad day when he called her by her late mother's name. It meant he was at least as much in the past as he was in the present.

'Bobby, Dad,' she said gently.

'Oh, aye.' He rubbed a hand over his forehead. 'Bobby. That's right.'

'We're having cheese pudding, bacon and mash,' she said in answer to his question. 'At least, we are if there are enough eggs for the pudding. One of the hens has stopped laying completely and the others seem to be taking it in turns. I'm sure Mary has a plan though.'

'Cheese pudding,' he said in disgust. 'What sort of a Sunday dinner is that? A man can't hod his back up wi' cheese pudding, lass.'

'It's all there is, Dad. We can't have meat every Sunday; not now.'

'Aye. Aye, I know. You and Mary do your best for us.'

'Anything in the paper today?' Bobby asked, nodding to a newspaper on the arm of his chair. It had been folded back at the Situations Vacant column, which her dad painstakingly went through every afternoon in his hunt for a new job.

'Nowt your old man can do, any road.' He rubbed his head again, then turned his face away so he wasn't meeting her gaze. 'Couldn't fetch us a glass o' that stuff, could you, our Bobby? Keep the chill out, give me an appetite for my tea.'

Bobby took her time tending to the fire before she got slowly to her feet.

This was the first time her dad had asked her to bring him a drink since they'd moved out to the Dales, seven months ago now. He still relied on it to send him to sleep after another nightmare about his time in the trenches, and he relished a beer with friends at the Golden Hart of an evening, but his practice of steadily drinking himself to oblivion every day – commonplace when they'd lived in Bradford and his problems were at their worst – had ceased.

But since August, when his part in the sale of black-market meat had come close to exposure and he'd been forced to give up what he thought of as his job, his mental state had been growing worse and worse. Bobby knew that if there was one thing her father couldn't abide feeling, it was useless. When he wasn't contributing to the household, he felt himself to be a burden on his family – to be less than a man. But there were few jobs on the local farms for a man of fifty-one with no experience except in the mills, and all his attempts to find honest work in the area had so far proved bootless. The stygian gloom of the long blackout hours as days shortened had only made his depressed spirits worse.

Bobby and her twin sister Lilian had always made it their policy not to refuse their father a drink when he asked for it. Refusal, they had learned at a young age, only humiliated him, which exacerbated his depression and led to him seeking relief through alcohol via other sources. At least this way, they were able to monitor when and how much he was drinking. But this time… Bobby wished he hadn't asked. Not today. She had been so buoyant about the prospect of seeing Charlie tonight, and now the pleasurable butterflies in her stomach had all been drowned by worry and fear.

'You're sure you wouldn't rather have a cup of tea?' she asked, as brightly as she could. 'That'll keep out the chill as well as the other, and we've fresh leaves in so it'll be new brewed.'

'Best save them since they've to last us the week, eh? A little tumbler ought to do me good, I reckon. Just one.'

Bobby suppressed her sigh. 'Very well. I'll bring you a glass.'

–

'And was it just one?' Charlie asked as they sat on the edge of the Settle bandstand in the moonlight later. He had one arm around her. Bobby pressed against him, drawing comfort from his warmth.

She rested her head on his shoulder. 'Of course not. It never is. He had three tumblers before tea, and he wouldn't come over to Moorside to eat at the table with the rest of us. I had to bring his food to him on a tray.'

'You locked the bottle up again?'

'I did, but I know from bitter experience that if he wants it, he'll find a way to get it.' She sighed. 'The only time he stops drinking like that is when he feels content and useful. Hiding the bottle doesn't help with the problems that are at the root of it. All it does is condemn him to a night trapped in his own head. Trapped in the trenches, with all that horror around him. I felt dreadful leaving him alone.'

'I wouldn't have wanted you to come out if I'd known. I'd have come to you and we could've spent the evening round the piano. That always cheers him up.'

'I couldn't ask you to do that. You'd have had to leave almost as soon as you got to us to get back to your barracks by lights out. Besides, I don't think a sing-song would have helped him today.'

'No?'

'After the third drink, he was only half present in the real world. I left him in bed with a mug of hot milk. I only hope that's where he stayed.'

'He'd have been better off going to sit with Reggie and Mary at Moorside, keep him out of his head,' Charlie said. 'My brother likes to have another chap around to share a smoke and talk war with of an evening.'

'I told him he ought to go over but he wouldn't. I think he was ashamed to have them see him like that. He can't hold it like he used to.' She swallowed a small sob. 'I'm so scared, Charlie. So afraid he'll... that it'll be like it was back in the winter, when he nearly died.'

He tilted her face up to look into his. Bobby could only see him dimly in the moonlight, but she could smell him: that combination of tobacco and soap flakes that always meant Charlie Atherton to her. And his eyes... when they'd first met, Bobby had reflected that Charlie's creamy brown eyes were full of lazy fun and mischief. They were different now. Sadder; more soulful.

'What did happen in the winter, Bobby?' he asked gently. 'You never did tell me. Did he have an accident while he was drunk?'

Bobby winced. She and Charlie had few secrets from each other these days. She trusted him completely; enough to tell him all about her father's struggles with liquor and shellshock, subjects she rarely spoke about with anyone other than her twin sister Lilian and her old friend Don Sykes. But this was one thing she had never been able to bring herself to discuss with him.

Charlie seemed to sense her reluctance. 'We don't have to talk about it if it's going to upset you,' he said in the same soft tone.

'No. No, I want to tell you. It's time I did.' She met his eyes. 'What's happened to you, Charlie? You seem so different.'

'Do I? When I look in the mirror I see the same old me.'

'But you aren't the same old you. You seem so solemn and sort of… sort of gentle. You hardly ever tease me like you used to.'

'Do you wish I did?'

'I don't know. It was a lot of fun, but it's nice to know you can be serious too. Why do you seem so changed?'

He paused for a moment before answering.

'It's going away to war, I suppose,' he said. 'I don't want to tease you now, Bobby; not when I see so little of you. I want to do this. To hear what's worrying you and see if I can make it better. It won't be long until my training's done, and then who knows when we'll have the chance to be together? They might send me anywhere, and for heaven knows how long.'

'Oh, please don't say that. I hate thinking about you joining the fight. I mean I know you must, and it's important and all that, but it doesn't make it any easier. I just keep hoping and hoping the war will end before you have to go.'

'If it did, would we have won?'

'I wish I knew.'

Bobby snuggled closer to him. So many times in their courting days, she had wished that Charlie would be at least a little serious and sensible sometimes. She had never known, in those early days, whether his attentions to her had been genuine or just in fun. But now… he was changed, there was no doubt about it. The war was changing him already, before he'd even made it to the fight. How much more would he change before she had him back again – back forever, safe in her arms?

Her brain tried to push her towards another thought: one that lurked always in the back of her mind like the shadow of death, and which she daily tried her utmost to ignore. The thought of that most dreadful alternative – that the day would never come when Charlie would be safe forever in her arms. That he would be one of the many men who wouldn't come home. Bobby closed her eyes while she tried once again to smother the evil whisper.

She couldn't help thinking of her father though. Bobby hadn't known the boy he was before the last war had taken him, but she had seen a photograph: a bright-eyed lad looking proud and smart in his uniform, with no thought of the horrors that awaited him in the trenches. Bobby had seen flashes of that young man sometimes, when her mother had been alive and the demons could be banished temporarily: a laughing, boyish, carefree soul. She thought he had died when her mother had, but since moving to the Dales, she had come to realise that the boy her father had been was still in there – somewhere.

Charlie had been just such a carefree soul when she had met him: boyish, full of youthful fun. It had been his natural, vigorous, free-spirited approach to life that had first attracted her, and infected her with a little of its joy. Would Charlie, too, come home from war changed and unrecognisable, as her father had? Would his eyes be forever haunted by the ghosts of what he had seen – the friends he had lost and the men he'd been forced to slaughter?

It made her shudder. Charlie, feeling her tremble, held her tighter.

'When will I see you again, love?' she asked softly. 'Not until Christmas?'

'Unless I can wangle a way to see you for a few hours before that. I've got simply dozens of aunts at death's door for your benefit, Bobby.'

Bobby smiled at hearing him sound a little like his old joking self, and pecked his cheek.

'It sounds like your CO's got you locked up at that place like POWs,' she said. 'It must be dreadful for the men's morale, never being given a pass out to go into the towns for some fun. Surely he oughtn't to be allowed to keep you all shut in.'

'Whether he is or not, I don't see what we can do about it. Whenever anyone asks for leave, Hunt just gives them the same line about the war being in a "critical phase" and needing every man on hand. Of course that's just an excuse for keeping us where he can see us. God forbid we might be having fun somewhere.'

'Is he very strict then?'

'Believe me, he's an absolute horror.'

Bobby frowned at the suppressed anger in his tone. 'You dislike him that much?'

'I do.'

'He's the one, isn't he?' she said slowly. 'The one who didn't ground the Wellington that Teddy was flying the night of the crash, when there was all that terrible fog.'

'That's him. Squadron Leader Hugo Hunt. I wish I could tell you what I really think of him but there are some words I don't think it's proper to use in the presence of ladies.'

She looked up to examine his face again. 'Is that the reason for the change, Charlie? Is he too harsh with you?'

'Not with me,' he muttered. 'Let's not talk about it tonight, eh? I don't want Hunt ruining the few precious hours I've got to spend with my girl.'

'I'm worried about you though. You look like you've been losing sleep.'

'I'm all right, honestly I am. Training hard, that's all. The blighters sent us on a fourteen-mile hike in full kit yesterday.' Charlie smiled at her in the moonlight. 'I'll tell you what this reminds me of. That song, "They Can't Black Out the Moon". Do you remember? They were playing it the first time you let me take you on a real date, at the dance hall in Settle. I was so proud to show you off that night, all pretty and blooming in your best blue dress.'

Bobby smiled. 'I remember. It seems a long time ago now.'

'Whenever one of the boys puts it on the gramophone in the NAAFI, I think of you. I mean, I always think of you. But when I hear it, I remember what it felt like to hold you in my arms that night and know you were finally mine.' He sighed. 'You're right, it does seem a long time ago. I feel so much older now than I did then.'

'Do you?'

'Strange, isn't it?' he said with a sad smile. 'When I was a boy, I dreamed of war. Played at it in my nursery with the toy soldiers Reggie had whittled and painted for me, and later in the fields with my gang – wooden swords aloft, colanders on our heads and dustbin lids for shields. War seemed so glamorous, so heroic, that I thought there was nothing I could want more than to be there in the fray. And now, all I wish is that the war could be over and the world of my boyhood will have survived long enough for me to see it again. I didn't know, then, that war could mean the end of everything. Everything feels changed, Bobby. Everything except you.'

Bobby didn't speak for a moment. She just held him close, stroking his hair. She wasn't used to hearing Charlie talk this way.

'Are you sure you don't want to tell me what's worrying you, love?' Bobby asked gently. 'I can tell it's something more than just the war.'

'Never mind about me; my problems can keep. We were talking about your dad. Do you want to tell me what happened when he ended up in hospital?'

'All right. But kiss me first.'

He smiled. 'I think I can manage that.'

His lips found hers in the darkness, and Bobby surrendered herself to the kiss and the arms that wrapped tight around her body. This part of Charlie, at least, hadn't changed.

She always tried to laugh off Mary's heavy hints about trousseaux and imminent wedding bells, but she couldn't deny it was getting harder to resist the prospect. Charlie's long absences from her, and her fears for him when he eventually went to join the fight, added a heat and urgency to their kisses that came at least as much from her as from him. She thought about him constantly; about being close to him, waking up with him, the life they could have together. If they were married, Charlie wouldn't be spending his Christmas leave in the cold comfort of the little box room at Moorside. He'd spend it with her at the cow house, or even in a cottage of their own. Every night they could lie in each other's arms, their bodies pressed together, falling asleep side by side. Could Bobby really wait the months or even years until the war was over to make Charlie Atherton her own at last? Didn't her lover, who would soon be out there putting his life at risk for a higher cause, deserve the warmth of a marital bed to come home to?

But marriage led to children, and a world at war was no world to bring children into. Not to mention the loss of the job she loved – the reporter job she'd worked so hard for – which Reg had made clear would no longer be available to her as a married woman and a mother. No matter what her feelings were, she had to be strong. If they at least knew what path the war might take… but everything was still so uncertain. There was so much propaganda being fired at them from all sides that Bobby genuinely had no idea who was winning. No one did.

'I've missed that,' Charlie said breathlessly when they broke apart again.

'I'll bet you have.' She smiled. 'I missed it too.'

'Well? Now that I've thoroughly kissed you, may I hear the secret?'

'Yes. All right.' Bobby pressed her eyes closed. 'Dad did hurt himself while he was drunk,' she said quietly. 'But… it wasn't an accident.'

'You don't mean—'

'He did it to himself. He lost his job at the mill and he… I suppose he couldn't bear it any more. Living with the pictures in his head; feeling useless and broken. He took all his sleeping powder and washed it down with a bottle of spirits. It was lucky Don found him in time for his stomach to be pumped.'

'Bobby…' He held her tighter. 'Why didn't you tell me before?'

'I didn't know what you'd say. People don't understand about… about suicide. They think it's cowardly and shameful. Unchristian.' She looked up at him, suddenly fierce. 'My dad isn't a coward, he's the bravest man I know. After the things he saw, it's no wonder the balance of his mind is disturbed at times. How many more are there like him, so haunted by war that they're barely living at all? I'll bet it's hundreds – thousands.'

'I know. I know.' He pressed his lips to her hair. 'You could have told me. I wouldn't have been that way about it.'

'It felt so hard to say the words. And I'm terrified, Charlie. Terrified that now he's drinking again, he'll go back down the same path – and this time I'll be too late to save him.'

'It won't come to that.'

'It will if he can't find work. That's what's behind it all. When he was poaching with Pete, or even working at the mill, he still felt like he had a purpose – that he was the head of the household. It's emasculating for him to have to be supported entirely by his daughter.'

'What work could he do?'

'That's just it – in Silverdale, nothing. He's a wool-comber; at the end of the day that's the only work he knows. And at his age he'd struggle even to get work doing that, especially after his last place gave him his cards for being drunk on the job. He's too old for a farm labourer.'

'He's not exactly in his dotage. I'd have thought someone would take him, with so many lads away fighting.'

'No one's wanted him so far. There's a WLA hostel near Skipton filling most of the labour gaps. The Land Girls are less than half his age, they've had training and they're cheap. The farmers would have to pay my dad the men's rate.'

'Cheap wages would be the way to a Yorkshireman's heart all right,' Charlie said with a wry smile. 'He doesn't have anything else he can do?'

'Just hunting and trapping, the way Pete Dixon taught him, but if he goes back to poaching then it's only a matter of time until he gets caught. With the clampdown on black-market meat, that could mean a big fine – maybe even a prison sentence.'

'I suppose so.' Charlie was silent for a moment. 'Bobby… what if there was a legal way he could use those skills Pete taught him?'

'Trapping animals? What legal way is there?'

'Have you ever heard the saying "a case of poacher turned gamekeeper"?'

'I don't think so. What does it mean?'

'Well, in your father's case it could mean exactly what it says. It's talking about someone protecting things they once threatened using their inside knowledge. A little like "you have to set a thief to catch a thief".'

'All right, I understand you. What of it though? There aren't any jobs for gamekeepers in Silverdale, even if my dad could get them.'

'There's one. I had a letter from Topsy a couple of days ago. She's on the hunt for a new keeper to manage that little patch of woodland she owns – asked if I could recommend anyone locally.'

'Really? She never mentioned it.' Bobby was silent for a moment, thinking it over. 'What does a gamekeeper actually do, Charlie?'

'Traps pests – weasels, rats, foxes; anything predatory that might target the game. Looks after the habitat, runs shoots and fishing parties for the landowner; all that sort of thing. Your dad could do that, couldn't he? He might not be as young as he used to be but he's strong and healthy for his age – in body, at least. And he loves the land here almost as much as if he was a Dalesman born and raised. That's a qualification in itself.'

'Yes, but he's got no experience of that type of work. No legal experience anyhow. Old sayings are all well and good, but he can hardly tell Topsy that the reason he knows how to trap pests is because he spent most of the summer stealing her rabbits.'

'Perhaps not, but Topsy's got a good heart, and she's grown attached to you,' Charlie said. 'If you asked it as a favour…'

Bobby shook her head. 'I couldn't do that. Dad would be so humiliated if he knew I'd had to beg a job for him.'

'Well, don't tell him then.'

'It isn't only his feelings. *I'd* be humiliated. Having to go cap in hand to Topsy as lady of the manor and beg favours like some poor relation… no, Charlie.' She pushed her chin out. 'I've got my pride too.'

'You're certainly your father's daughter,' Charlie said with a smile, tapping the jutting chin. 'What will you do though? You said you don't think his mental state will improve until he's working.'

'Keep my eye on the Situations Vacant column in the paper, I suppose, then cross my fingers and say like Mr Micawber, "Something will turn up."' She took Charlie's hand and held it against her cheek. 'I just hope it turns up soon, before things get any worse.'

Chapter 4

The next morning, Bobby got up early as usual so she could light the fire before her father arose. Fuel was expensive now – coal was hard to get, and even coke had gone up to one and six a hundredweight – but they needed to keep a fire blazing. Even in the summer, the old stone barn was draughty and cold. Now that they were into autumn, Bobby invariably woke to find her nose and fingers numb and her bedroom mirror often crusted with ice.

She wondered how Charlie had coped, living here in the winter. If she hadn't been so preoccupied with her father's problems the evening before, she might have thought to ask him. Now she would have to include it in her next letter to him, and the thoughts she expressed in them were always curtailed by the knowledge that Charlie's barrack officer would be reading first so he could censor anything he felt might jeopardise the war effort. Her efforts to keep warm at night were innocuous enough when it came to the war, she supposed, but she didn't much fancy the officer smirking at her musings to her fiancé on the benefits of thermal underwear.

She wondered if Charlie was very unhappy at his station. He'd seemed jolly enough at his previous station, somewhere out in the East Riding, but ever since he'd transferred to nearby RAF Ryland Moor to finish his training as a bomber pilot, he'd been different. His letters were less buoyant and nowhere near as frequent, and he seemed so serious on the rare occasions they could see each other in person. While it was reassuring in some ways to discover her impulsive, fun-loving fiancé could take life seriously when he needed to, Bobby did find herself missing the old, teasing Charlie she'd first fallen in love with.

Before last night, she had ascribed the change in his moods to his fears about joining the fight in the near future. Now, she had started to wonder if something else might be behind it. Was his harsh CO, this Squadron Leader Hunt, making life difficult for him? Charlie said not, but he clearly had a strong dislike of the man. Or was it conditions at his barracks, perhaps? Charlie had been to a boarding school so he'd be accustomed to that sort of communal living, and it was hard to believe he was struggling to make friends – Charlie Atherton, who seemed to make them without trying wherever he went. Still, she supposed it was possible he was feeling a little lonely. Perhaps she ought to have pressed him further. Their time together was so short and so precious, it was hard to fit in everything they wanted to say – or as many kisses as they would have liked.

The fire was crackling nicely and the kettle singing when her father emerged from his bedroom. Bobby had been relieved to find him still in bed when she had arrived home from her date with Charlie the night before, snoring throatily, and no further signs of tampering around the cupboard lock where his spirits were stored. Perhaps things hadn't gone quite so far as she was worried they might have.

'Morning,' she said brightly. 'I'll have some tea brewing in a minute. You can have a cup to warm you up while I get dressed, then we'll go over to Moorside for breakfast.'

Her dad yawned, taking a seat in his armchair. 'Young Jessie's ringing the bell today, isn't she? Them two will've been up wi' t' lark, no doubt.'

Bobby treated him to a big smile. If he'd remembered Jessie's important task today, his mental state couldn't be as bad as all that.

'Yes, she was talking about nothing else yesterday at the fruit-picking,' Bobby said. 'I'll get dressed quickly so I can wish her luck before she leaves for school, and you can join us when you're ready.' She glanced at him. 'What are your plans for today?'

'Nowt much. Meeting Pete in t' village.'

'Oh.' She paused. 'Are you going… walking?'

Her dad had always employed the word somewhat euphemistically when he'd been accustomed to spending his afternoons poaching game with Pete Dixon.

'Aye, happen I might later.' He smiled at her concerned expression. 'No need to worry. Pete's got some tobacco to sell me, that's all, then he's off into Skipton for summat. I was going to take that little pup of the girls out for some laik. They need a lot of exercise, these young sheepdogs.'

'You ought to. It's warmer today, and fresh air will do you good.' Bobby felt her spirits lift, and the worry that had plagued her since the day before began to dissipate. 'If you want to stop in the pub later then there's no need to hurry back on my account. I'm on duty tonight at the ARP hut so I've made a tea you can warm up in the oven whenever you get home.'

'Aye, I wouldn't mind a little visit to the Hart, see who's about. Been a while since I had a game of dominoes.' He patted her shoulder. 'Better get ready for work, eh? You're a canny lass, our Bobby.'

—

Bobby hummed to herself as she headed to Moorside for breakfast, to be followed by another day of work at *The Tyke*. The little scene with her father had cheered her immeasurably. He'd sounded in infinitely better spirits than he had yesterday. Perhaps it had just been a bad day, and things were not so desperate as she had been worrying they were. She felt almost guilty for bothering Charlie with her fears, and wasting their precious hours together on what now seemed no more than a trifle.

'Hullo, Bobby,' Florence mumbled through a mouthful of food when Bobby entered the farmhouse kitchen. The little girl was tucking into a slice of toast at the table, Ace at her feet looking hopeful for scraps, but there was no sign of her sister.

Mary tapped the girl on the shoulder with a wooden spoon. 'No talking with your mouth full, young lady.'

'Morning,' Bobby said. 'Where's Jessie, Mary? I came over early so I could wish her luck before school.'

'Oh, Lord knows where that little monkey's got to,' Mary said impatiently. 'She knows we're in a hurry this morning so we can pack her off in time to ring that blumming bell. I sent her to the henhouse to pick up the eggs more than quarter of an hour ago. She's going to have to take some toast to eat on the way if she isn't here soon.'

'Do you want me to go find her?'

'Nay, you sit down and get yourself round some break-fast. She knows we're waiting on her.'

'It's all right, I can wait for my breakfast. I'd hate for her to be late for her important job. She's been so looking forward to it.'

Bobby left the farmhouse by the back door and went into the garden, where the little shed and wire run that served as a home for the Athertons' four hens was located. She poked her head through the henhouse door, which was open, and smiled at the sight that met her.

Jessie was on her knees in the straw next to one of the hens – Henrietta. The old biddy looked plump and content as Jessie ran her fingers over her speckled brown feathers, earnestly singing the words to 'Hey Little Hen'. The other hens – Hetty, Hannah and Harriet – looked on in serene puzzlement.

'Jessie, Mary's waiting for you to have your breakfast,' Bobby said. 'You don't want to be late to ring the bell, do you?'

Jessie stopped singing and looked up with eyes filled with elation. She held up an egg from her basket.

'Bobby, look!' she said. 'I told you, didn't I, that I could get her to lay again? I come and sung to her when I got home yesterday and stroked her, and this morning there was this egg. Henrietta laid it all her own self. So now she won't get eaten after all, will she?'

'Let's hope not,' Bobby said with a smile. 'What about the others? Any presents from them today?'

'Hetty laid one as well but Hannah and Harriet didn't lay none. That's all right though, 'cause Hannah laid one yesterday and Harriet on Wednesday. I don't think Mary will want to eat them.' She knit her brow into a worried frown. 'But I'd maybe better sing to them a bit as well. I don't want them to stop laying eggs and get killed for Christmas dinner.'

'After school you can sing to the hens all you like, Jess, but right now you need to go have your breakfast. You don't want to be late for your big important job this morning.'

–

When Bobby went into the parlour to start her day's work, her editor Reg was already there at his desk with his walking stick leaning against it. Sometimes she wondered if he went to bed at all.

'Jess get off to school all right, did she?' he asked in his usual gruff tone.

'Yes, she left with Florrie quarter of an hour ago.' Bobby took a seat at her desk. 'I practically had to drag her out of the henhouse this morning. She was very nearly late.'

'Eh? Thought she was right looking forward to it.'

'She was, but since yesterday she's had something else on her mind. Henrietta had stopped laying and Mary was talking about fattening her up for Christmas dinner. Jessie sounded quite upset when she spoke to me about it.'

Reg grunted. 'That's life out here. Can't give food and board to beasts who give us nowt in return. Hens aren't pets. Daft giving the things names at all.'

'I know that, but Jessie isn't from the country, is she? She's only eight, Reg.'

Reg's habitually grumpy expression lifted a little. 'Truth in that, I suppose. Jess is nobbut a bairn yet, and it's still new to her how we do things here.'

'I wish there was something we could say to make her feel better about it. But if it isn't Henrietta it'll only be one of the other hens, and Jessie's attached to them all.

One of them has to furnish the dinner table if we don't want corned beef on Christmas Day.'

'She'll come around. It's a hard lesson to learn for a soft-hearted little thing like Jess. Still, it needs to be learned if we're going to make a proper country lass out of her.' He smiled slightly. 'She's got a tender heart. There isn't an ounce of malice in those girls; nowt but love and compassion. It can feel like there's little enough of that going around these days. We ought to be right proud of them, I reckon.'

Bobby smiled too, although she busied herself with feeding a sheet of paper into her Remington typewriter so as not to embarrass Reg, who hated attention to be drawn to his 'talking soft'.

She had believed Reg to be gruff and surly when she first took up residence at Moorside. There were reasons for his ill moods – the pain in his lame left leg, his memories of the last war, and the still-fresh grief from the loss of his and Mary's only child twenty years ago – so for the sake of her job and her growing affection for Mary, Bobby had made excuses for Reg's grumpy spells as best she could. Since the Parry girls had come to live with the Athertons, however, Bobby had seen a new side to her employer that she would never have suspected. He'd become almost a second father to the children in their time here, joining in their games, teaching them the ways of their new home and spoiling them with treats whenever he thought no one would notice. They were abnormally fond of both him and Mary. It made Bobby wonder what would happen when the war ended. The Parrys had been so happy here, become so much a part of the place, that the idea of ripping them from their new home and sending them back to London felt… well, monstrous.

'I think we have made country lasses of her and Florrie,' Bobby said as she mechanically started filling envelopes with back copies of the magazine: always her first job of the day. 'This place seems to agree with them, although they miss their father. Even their accents are starting to change.'

'Aye, Silverdale's done them the power of good. They've colour in their cheeks and some life in their eyes now.'

'Do you think Captain Parry would ever consider moving here to the Dales? I mean, after the war. After all, the family has no home in London now. With their house destroyed there's nothing to tie them to the place, and I know the girls would hate to be taken far away from you and Mary.'

'That's for him to decide. A man with his family to support has to go where the work is.'

'Master tailor,' Bobby said thoughtfully. 'Plenty for him here in textile country, surely. There must be dozens of establishments in the towns where he could find employment.'

'Getting rather ahead of yourself, aren't you? George Parry's a Londoner, through and through – you've heard the way he talks. Loves the place with his heart and with his bones. Much as we'd like to keep them little girls close by for our own selfish sakes, it's a lot to ask a man to leave the city that bore him and bred him when he's no experience of country living.'

'But the girls love it here, and it's so healthy for them.'

'I know. And if owt'll persuade him, it'll be that. Not a decision anyone can make on his behalf though, is it?'

Reg was quiet for a moment. 'Still, I hope he'll consider it. He's a deep-thinking man, and a fond father. He'll do what's best for his daughters at the end of the day, I reckon.'

'You'd miss them if they went,' Bobby said softly.

'Aye. My missus has got right fond of them since they've been here. Mary was made for the mothering business.'

'I said *you'd* miss them, Reg.' A year ago, when she'd first come to work for *The Tyke*, Bobby would never have dared speak her mind to her stern, taciturn employer so freely, but they understood one other now. 'Wouldn't you?'

'I can't deny it. It's been another life since that pair came to turn everything topsy-turvy around here.'

'I know.'

'Stopped it getting too quiet after our Charlie went to war, any road.' He glanced up from the proofs he was correcting to look at her. 'How is the lad? Mary tells me he begged a spot of leave last night, which I'm presuming he chose to spend with you.'

Bobby flushed slightly. 'He's all right, although he seemed a little thoughtful and quiet. Not his usual daft self.'

'Not surprised. How long till he gets his wings now – four months? He could be in the sky over Germany come the spring.'

Bobby shuddered. 'Please don't remind me.'

'Was that what was on his mind then?'

'I don't think so, no – not only that, at any rate. He didn't seem to want to talk about it, but I wondered if there might be something up at his barracks.'

'What's to worry him at his barracks? He seemed happy enough in the last place.'

'I know. He never mentions friends he's made though, or anything much about life there. He's always been a social sort. I'd have thought life in the forces would agree with him rather well.'

'Aye, he made plenty of friends away at school.'

'He's unhappy, I can tell. Clearly there's no love lost between him and his commanding officer, although he told me that wasn't what was behind it.'

Reg laughed. 'Commanding officers aren't meant to be popular, lass. If they are, they're not doing the job right.'

'I don't know. This sounded… different. Has he said anything in his letters to Mary?'

'Nowt she's thought to mention to me.' Reg looked up at her as she stuffed another envelope. 'I wouldn't worry yourself too much. Only natural at times like this: all these big things happening and no choice but to be part of them.' He glanced at the walking stick against his desk. 'Changes a man, war.'

'I know that,' Bobby said, thinking of her father and the flashbacks that plagued him. 'But Charlie isn't rightly at war yet. I'm sure there's something more on his mind. You'll tell me if he mentions anything to you, won't you? I know he hates me worrying but I want to be able to help if I can.'

'If he don't mention it to you, he certainly won't be telling me about it. Young men don't confide in brothers when they've got sweethearts to write to.' He noticed her fretful expression. 'But aye, I'll tell you. Now let's have some quiet while I finish correcting these, eh?'

'All right. But oh, actually, there was one other thing,' Bobby said as she remembered a notion that had come to her while she was picking rosehips.

'About our Charlie?'

'No, for the magazine. I had an idea for an article. It was Mary made me think of it, while we were picking fruit yesterday.'

'Go on then, let me have it.'

'I was thinking about how much the village had changed since I came to work here. So many of the men gone, and all these new people – the Polish airmen and the others from the hospital, the Canadians billeted with the Cloughs, the Geordie Land Girls, the London evacuees at the school. Mary was talking about how the fells used to keep the Dales villages isolated and yet now, thanks to the war, we've got the world on our doorsteps – just like you said when I first came here for an interview. That's interesting, isn't it?'

'Hmm. Half our subscribers these days are serving in the forces. Those men and women don't want to hear about how the war's changing life here in the Dales, Bobby. They want to remember it as it was when they left – to believe there's a world worth fighting for waiting for them when they come home.'

'I understand that, but the Dales are changing, all the same – perhaps forever. Anyhow, this would be a positive article, about the war giving us the opportunity to make friends we would otherwise never have met and learning more about the world beyond our doorsteps. Change doesn't mean there won't still be trees and flowers and buttered crumpets for tea when the war's over, but it does mean a few new horizons might be opened up for the people here. I hope it would be optimistic rather than frightening, if the tone was right.'

'Well, happen it might be worthwhile,' Reg agreed cautiously. 'You can set to work on it tomorrow. Mind,

I don't say I'll print it. Let's see what you can make of it first.'

Even now, after a year of working with Reg, Bobby still felt as though she had to do battle for every story she was given permission to write. As frustrating as it was that the editor still didn't trust her judgement, it did mean she valued his praise all the more highly when she delivered an article that met with his approval. And it meant that every hard-won byline was precious to her.

'Thank you,' she said. 'I thought I could speak to some of the newcomers and ask what they make of life here. I'm sure Jessie and Florrie would be thrilled to have a quote in the magazine, and I can talk to Piotr and Teddy and some of the other convalescents at the hospital, and the Canadian airmen if someone can make an introduction for me. Maybe even the Land Girls, as long as I can find someone to translate their Newcastle accents.'

'Aye, all right. You can take tomorrow afternoon to go gathering your quotes. Meanwhile, get them envelopes filled and down to the post office.'

Chapter 5

There were two letters on the mat at Cow House Cottage when Bobby arrived home after work. She was on duty at the ARP shelter on the village green in an hour, which left her just enough time to change into her bluette warden's uniform, pack up some corned beef sandwiches and make a flask of something warming to keep her going through her shift.

'Dad?' she called, but there was no answer. She guessed he'd been out all day, since he hadn't picked up the letters. He'd taken Ace out straight after breakfast, and Bobby had heard him return the little dog an hour ago while she was working with Reg in the parlour.

She hadn't seen him, but she'd heard him speaking with Mary by the door. He'd sounded merry enough, asking after Jessie and the important task she'd performed at school that morning. Bobby presumed he'd gone from there straight to the Hart, as he'd told her he was planning to.

That was good. The beer in the village pub was too weak to have much effect on him, and the social side of it, playing dominoes with the few friends he'd made here, always improved his mood. In Bradford he'd rarely gone out, spending his evenings at home with the only company he'd cared about then: a bottle of whisky, or whatever spirit he could get hold of on the black market. If he was still interested in seeing friends, that was definitely a positive sign.

Bobby picked up the letters and scanned the envelopes. Both were addressed to her.

She had only seen Charlie yesterday so one couldn't be from him. Her only other regular correspondents were her sister Lilian, who was serving with the Wrens down in Greenwich, and her friend Don Sykes back in Bradford. Occasionally, when they remembered, there might also be a letter from one of her brothers.

Both envelopes were military: one satisfyingly fat, the other very flimsy. Bobby didn't need to look at the service numbers written on the back to figure out that the fat envelope was from Lil, who always had lots to tell about life in her Wren barracks, while the flimsy one must be from her habitually terse youngest brother: twenty-year-old Jake. She tucked the fat envelope into her pocket to savour during the long, cold hours she would be on duty, glad to have something to look forward to. Jake's she tore open at once, knowing it would take very little time to read.

As usual, her brother came straight to the point. His news was rather more interesting than the usual thinly worded accounts of army life, however.

> Dear Bobby and Dad,
>
> Hope both well. Things are shifting a bit here and you'll never guess what they've got planned for me. CO says they're to train me for technical work since I've shown 'aptitude with machines' — them are his words. Royal Engineers — how about that then, Bob? Bet you feel daft now for saying all the hours I spent on the bike were a waste of time. CO

says they're going to have me dismantling bombs when I'm finished training as a sapper. Reckon the new job might actually be something I'll be good at. Wonder where they'll send me. I hope it's London. Anyhow, see you at New Year.

Love,

Jake

PS Bringing someone to meet you when I'm home on leave. Her name's Bea, she's a dispatch rider for the Wrens. Met her at a dance. She used to ride in races when she was a civvy. You should see her bike! Don't be all Mam about it when she comes, Bob.

Bobby stared at the letter, then sank into a chair as she took a moment to absorb its contents.

Her brother was clearly excited for this new role he'd been selected for, and it seemed to be an honour of sorts – at least, it sounded like he'd impressed his CO with his technical skill. Jake had obviously learned a thing or two while tinkering with his beloved Triumph motorcycle. His love of all things mechanical would no doubt make a job as a sapper sound like a dream come true.

But bomb disposal! To think of her little brother, who she and Lil had stepped into a mother's shoes for after their own mother had died when they were in their teens, being sent to one of the blitz-hit cities and set to work dismantling unexploded bombs – that was at least as terrifying as him joining a front-line unit. By the time the summer of 1942 arrived, Bobby would have one brother serving with the army in North Africa, another dismantling bombs God knew where and a sweetheart in the skies over Germany. She didn't know if she would ever be able to get a wink of sleep again.

She looked once more at her brother's letter, and her lips twitched with a reluctant smile. Of course it was pure Jake to tuck the important news that he was walking out with a new girl into a postscript. It must be serious between them though, if he was bringing her home to meet his family. It sounded like this dispatch rider, Bea, might be nearly as mad about motorcycles as her brother, which was some feat. Bobby was glad Jake had found someone new after the disappointment of losing the girl he'd been seeing when he was called up to someone else.

–

Thanks to Jake's letter, Bobby was almost late to the ARP shelter. However, her old bicycle got her there just in time to beat the blackout, which started today at 6:24 p.m. How dark the nights seemed after the long days of summer!

The ARP hut was a draughty, dismal little building: a temporary construction of corrugated steel on the village green. As soon as Bobby got inside, she set to work lighting the old paraffin lamp on the table. It didn't give much light, since the blackout forced her to keep it dim, but it was better than sitting in complete darkness. Besides, she would need it to read Lil's letter.

With one notable exception – the night a Vickers Wellington from the nearby airbase had crashed into Great Bowside – there was little for an air-raid warden to do in sleepy Silverdale. Bobby was glad she could say she was doing her bit, but she didn't feel like she was making much of a contribution to the war. All she did was sit in her hut waiting for bombs that wouldn't fall, occasionally patrolling the village to make herself unpopular by telling people their blackout coverings needed adjusting. Still, what else could she do? There wasn't much civil defence work suitable for women out here in the sticks.

When the lamp had been lit and Bobby had poured a cup of tea from her Thermos, she took out Lil's letter. She had barely skimmed the first page when she let out an exclamation.

'Bloody hell!'

Bobby clamped a hand to her mouth, glancing around as if someone might have been there to hear.

It couldn't be! She read Lil's words again.

> Bob, I know this is going to sound strange when the last time we spoke I hadn't even been on a date with the man, but I can't possibly keep it quiet. John wants to wait until we announce it officially but I'll burst out of my corset if I don't tell someone. Lieutenant Cartwright and I are engaged to be married! Can you believe it? I'm so thrilled and happy and… well, I don't have the words to tell you. Just imagine me there with you, squealing like a madwoman and hugging you until you can't breathe because I'm so happy.
>
> And now I'm going to imagine the Bobby side of the conversation, and all the questions I know my ever-cautious little sister would ask me if I were there.
>
> Do I love him? With all my heart and all my soul. I told you when we saw each other at Bowling Tide how incredibly fond I'd become of him, and how worried I was that he was too shy to ever ask me for a date. In fact I had to take matters into my own hands in the end, and conspire with his mate, who's walking out with a girl I'm pally

with, to entice John out as part of a foursome. I ought to have told you, I know, but I was so fond of him even before our first date that it made me feel quite superstitious, worrying I might curse the whole thing. I decided to wait a little while before breaking the news, then before I knew what was happening, I had the biggest news of all to break!

Isn't it rather sudden, asks Bobby? I suppose it will seem so to you, but it's seemed an age to me, waiting for John to make his move. He proposed in the sweetest, quietest way possible, just the two of us sitting on the bank of this lake in the grounds of the Wren barracks. Honestly, you don't need to worry at all. He's been such a model of caution and gentlemanly behaviour that he'd get even the Bobby seal of approval. I know when you meet him that you'll fall nearly as much in love with him as I have − although for my sake and Charlie's, not quite as much, I hope.

And finally, you're going to ask me when the wedding is to be, I suppose. John is to move to a new base after Easter so of course we want it to be as soon as possible, then we can stay together. I'll miss the Wrens, but you know this is all I ever wanted, Bob. Romance like you see in the pictures, you used to say, and think I didn't notice how you rolled your eyes at your silly big sister and her dreams. Well now I have my dream, and I don't intend to ever let him out of my sight again. John is everything I ever wanted in a husband − handsome, noble, brave, wealthy and kind.

I do hope you'll be happy for me, darling, and I hope you have some coupons left yet, for of course you're to be maid of honour for us. Do try to keep it secret for now though, although it's hard. I give my permission to tell Dad, however, as he'll need to be prepared for the letter he'll shortly be receiving from John. My fiancé − do you see how I wrote that? My fiancé, so proud! − is the old-fashioned sort, so he doesn't feel right about our engagement being considered official, so to speak, until Dad has blessed it. I think for the first time, I'm going to be bringing home a young man our father is going to approve of. Oh, I just can't think for excitement! I wish I could see you and we could talk it all through together, just like the old days sharing secrets in our bedroom. I don't know how long it will be until I'm able to get some leave.

There was a lot more to the letter: pages and pages of Lilian's euphoric rambling, worries about bridal clothes and the ration, pondering on where she and John might set up home and what the future would hold. Bobby put it down on the table, feeling dazed.

Lilian engaged! Of course she knew her twin had been on the lookout for a potential husband, and Lil had talked to her about this handsome Lieutenant Cartwright who had caught her fancy, but Bobby hadn't expected things to rush along as quickly as all that. She probably ought to worry, but it was hard when her sister was so happy and excited. Certainly Lil's officer fiancé sounded like an upright, gentlemanlike sort, and a good influence when it came to her twin's tendency to be impulsive and head-strong. The suddenness of it was a worry, but then a lot of people were forced into making snap decisions about love and marriage these days, weren't they? It seemed to be one extreme or the other: long engagements had become commonplace, but very short engagements rarely raised an eyebrow either. If a couple were walking out and one of them learned they were about to move posts or ship out overseas, it was natural they'd want to arrange a speedy wedding.

'Good thing I did save my clothing coupons,' Bobby murmured, then laughed softly to herself. She felt rather light-headed. A sister engaged, a brother preparing to train in bomb disposal... what a difference two little letters could make!

—

Bobby often went to the Golden Hart after an ARP shift to get warm by the fire before cycling home, but tonight she was anxious to get back to the cow house and speak to her father. She had left Jake's letter on the table, so no doubt Dad was aware of her brother's news by now, but she still had the news of Lilian's engagement to break. For all she knew, John Cartwright's letter could be in the post tomorrow, and her dad would cope with it better for being prepared. Besides, she was bursting to talk with someone about it and Lil had forbidden her to share the news with anyone other than their father.

When she opened the front door, she found the old barn in darkness apart from the dim glow of a dying fire. There was music playing on the wireless, however: some sort of swing band.

'Dad? Are you up?' She flicked on the light.

Bobby felt her stomach sink at the sight of the unexpected, yet depressingly familiar, scene that greeted her.

Her dad was awake, slumped in his usual chair, but there was no expression in his glassy eyes. On the occasional table by him were three things: his son's letter, a partially empty bottle of something and a drained glass.

'Oh… Dad.' Bobby blinked hard to push back the stinging tears. 'Did you really have to?'

There was no reply. Her dad was far away now, back in the past with his dead wife, before Bobby and her siblings had even existed. Or worse, back in the trenches with all that mud and smoke and the sickly stench of death, unable to escape. Bobby went to him and knelt by the arm of the chair. She rested her forehead on his arm and pressed her eyes closed.

'I'm so sorry,' she whispered. 'I should have known. I should never have left you.'

Her dad continued to stare. Bobby knew he couldn't hear her. Only the otherworldly buzz of tinny jazz from the wireless broke the silence.

'I had a letter from our Lil tonight,' she said, hoping her sister's news might be able to break through to him. 'She's engaged, Dad. A young naval lieutenant. She sounds very happy.'

There was a grunt, but her father didn't look at her. He continued to stare straight ahead.

Bobby glanced at the bottle on the table. It wasn't the potato-peel spirit she bought cheap from Don Sykes, which was clear like water and came in unmarked bottles. This stuff was emerald green, with a strong smell like aniseed and a label in some foreign language. Her dad's lips were stained green from it.

She picked up his glass and swallowed down the small amount that had pooled in the bottom, then coughed as it burned her throat. This stuff was strong. Really strong. It probably hadn't taken much to get him into this state.

Bobby guessed this was what her dad had bought from Pete Dixon when he'd met him that morning. She ought to have known better than to have believed his story about buying tobacco, since her dad rarely smoked a pipe. So that had been the reason for his good mood earlier.

'I see you read Jake's letter,' she said, a note of desperation in her voice now as she tried again to pull him back into the world of the living. 'He sounds excited about his bomb disposal training.'

There was another grunt, and then her dad's words came: thick, slow and heavy, as if from somewhere deep within him.

'Bombs,' he slurred deliberately. 'Knew a sapper once. Jack Hebblethwaite. Manchester man. Liked his football. Loved his bairns. Blew hissen sky high one day. We found him in bits.'

Bobby winced. 'Dad, don't.' But, his little speech over, he had already retreated back into his head.

Someone had started speaking on the wireless. Bobby recognised the clipped, sneering tone of the announcer. Her dad must have tuned it to the Bremen station, which was broadcast from Germany.

'Germany calling. Germany calling,' the plummy voice announced nasally, pronouncing the first syllable to sound like 'chair'. Bobby instantly identified the voice of William Joyce, known to all as Lord Haw-Haw – an Anglo-Irish fascist who had defected to Germany, and was now tasked with undermining the morale of British people through English-language propaganda broadcasts.

The *Germany Calling* programme was nothing more than a mouthpiece for Goebbels, but it was widely listened to. While some saw tuning in as unpatriotic, there were twice as many again who listened eagerly every night.

Some said it was because they found Haw-Haw's nonsense entertaining; others because they didn't want to be out of the swim, since it was one of the most discussed programmes on the air. Others were keen to hear a different account of the war than they were being given by the newspapers and the BBC – people knew they were being fed propaganda by their own government too and wanted the opportunity to make up their own minds. They also listened because the programme gave out lists of recently captured POWs, and read messages from prisoners to their loved ones. Despite newspaper claims that people had become bored of Haw-Haw's bile, Bobby knew plenty who listened to the Bremen broadcasts still. She often tuned in since her eldest brother Raymond had been sent overseas, hoping not to hear his name in the lists of the captured.

Lord Haw-Haw had been a figure of fun back in early 1940, in the days of what had been called the Phoney War. People had tuned in in droves simply to laugh at the man, who was mocked and lampooned by every music hall comic, newspaper satirist and radio comedian in the land. His tone then had been conciliatory, endeavouring to convey to the British people that he was on their side as he informed them that their government had betrayed them, their Jew-loving politicians – and of course Chamberlain, Churchill et al were all in the pay of the powerful Jewish financiers who Haw-Haw claimed were secretly running things – had declared war for self-gain only, and Germany, which had only friendly feelings towards the British people, had done nothing to deserve this aggression. However, as the war progressed, Haw-Haw's tone changed. He had become sneering and hawkish as the Nazis goosestepped their way across Europe, taunting the

British, warning them that German might was unstoppable and the best thing they could do was to persuade their government to surrender. Bobby could think of no single figure who attracted more public odium – perhaps not even Hitler himself.

Her own lip curled as she listened to the man speak. She ought to turn it off, she supposed, but still she knelt with her head resting against her father's senseless arm.

Haw-Haw talked about the British evacuation programme, and then of the RAF offensive over occupied France. The evacuation programme had been a shambles, he said. Parents had trusted their children to the British politicians, believing they were sending these most precious of possessions away for their own good, but again the upper echelons had betrayed them. Children had been sent to live among people by whom they were mistreated, beaten and starved. Thousands had already run away from these new homes and put themselves in danger trying to find their way back to their parents. And as for the air offensive over France, which the British government had presented to their people as such a success, it had been nothing. The gnat that bit the eagle's tail and was swatted away unfelt. Hardly a single bomb had found its mark, while the Luftwaffe had shot down so many British bombers that they could declare it confidently an Axis victory. German troops in Russia, meanwhile, were only days from capturing Moscow and knocking the Soviets out of the war. Germany was mighty. Germany was unstoppable. Germany would see them very, very soon.

Bobby finally shook herself free from her trance-like state and jumped to her feet. She turned the knob of the wireless violently, and Haw-Haw's voice faded into nothing.

Families would be listening to the programme together and laughing, no doubt. Laughing at this jumped-up, posturing, comical little traitor who tried to frighten them with the false words and half-truths put into his mouth by his master Joe Goebbels. Yet as amusing as people found Lord Haw-Haw, he knew how to get under their skin. He knew where the chinks were in their armour – their fears for their evacuated children and loved ones out in the fight. He knew what words to choose to stir up a put-upon working class against what he called Britain's 'upper nation'.

In the summer of 1940 – the days following Dunkirk, when invasion had seemed imminent – his lordship hadn't seemed so clownish. He'd been transformed, then, into a sinister bogeyman with almost God-like knowledge of British military manoeuvres. Yes, people would laugh at the man, then after the broadcast they'd go to bed and wonder… could any of it be true? Were evacuee children wandering the British countryside, unable to get back home? Were British bombers lying on the ocean bed, their crews having died for nothing after failing to make a dent in the German defences? Was Moscow about to fall? Were they going to lose the war?

Bobby thought back to that day two years ago when it had been announced on the wireless that they were at war with Germany for the second time in most people's lives. The prime minister's statement, the government broadcasts about how they would be notified of air raids and poison gas attacks, the banning of public gatherings, the closure of the cinemas, the King's speech. How it had felt like the end of the world. Her dad had held his head in his hands and sobbed, right there in front of her, as Jake had run excitedly outside to shout the news to neighbours who didn't have wireless sets. Her father had drunk until he passed out, that night...

Bobby jumped, startled from her thoughts by a sound from her dad. His head had slumped forward, and a little gurgle was emanating from his throat.

Well, here was something that it was within her power to help with. After all, her pride was a small price to pay to save her father from a hospital bed – or worse. The course of the war might be outside her control, but she could still fix this. She hoped she could still fix this.

'Come on, Dad,' she said gently. 'Let's get you to bed, if you're still able to walk. Then tomorrow after work, I'm going to speak to Topsy Sumner-Walsh.'

Chapter 6

In fact, Bobby was able to speak to Topsy rather sooner than she had planned. She had forgotten that Reg had given her permission to go out and collect quotes the following afternoon for the article she had pitched to him, which she was tentatively planning to title 'Finding Friends in Unexpected Places: A Dales Village in Wartime'.

When she arrived at Moorside, she discovered Reg was already on the telephone to Topsy arranging for her to visit the hospital at Sumner House and speak with the airmen. After finishing her morning's work, Bobby duly mounted the old boneshaker of a bicycle she used to get around and set off to see her friend.

It was while cycling through the village that she spotted Pete Dixon coming down the snicket between the pub and the bakery. He was whistling to himself, his hands in his pockets and a very suspicious hunchback under his coat. No doubt one of the local landowners would find themselves missing a couple of hares or pheasants later today. Bobby stuck out her feet to stop the bike, whose brakes were long past their best, and glared at him.

'Morning, lass,' he said in his usual warm, jovial way. 'How's your old man?'

'Sick as a pike, thanks to you,' she told him in a low voice. 'I couldn't get him to bed last night; I had to leave him to sleep by the fire. What was that stuff you sold him yesterday?'

Pete shrugged. 'Some foreign muck, French or summat. I had boxfuls of it left from afore the war. Couldn't sell it then but folk're biting my hand off for it now. Say what you like about the Jerries but it's a golden time for us businessmen.'

'"Businessman", that's a laugh. Did you have to, Pete?'

'He asked me for it. What was I going to say? If money's what you're worried about then you should know I only charged him half price, him being a mate. Bargain at seven and a kick.'

'It certainly isn't what I'm worried about. And if you think you were doing him a favour, you're very wrong.'

'Rob served his country for nigh on four year. Don't see as it's for us to begrudge the old warhorse a drink after what he must've gone through.'

'But it never is just a drink,' she murmured, glancing over her shoulder to make sure no one was around to overhear. 'Not for my dad. It's all or nothing for him.'

'Well? Better a sore head this morning than a head full of bitter memories the night before. Got him to sleep, didn't it?'

'Pete, please.' She reached out to rest a hand on his arm. 'I'm sure you're trying to help him but the booze doesn't fix anything. It just makes him feel even worse when he sobers up. Leave him be, eh? You nearly got him into enough trouble with that meat raffling business.'

'Your dad's a big lad. Won't much care for the women-folk making his decisions for him like a bairn, I reckon.'

'I'm not making his decisions for him. I want to help him find his place again, that's all. If you really are his friend, just… give me a few weeks, all right? Tell him you've run out or... or anything you want. Come mid-November, if he asks you for it you can sell it him with my blessing. I just want to see if I can find another way.'

Pete's expression softened a little. 'Right worried about him, aren't you?'

'If you were me, you'd know why. Will you do it?'

'All right, lass. If you think you can help him some other way, give it your best try. I won't sell him more for now, even if he asks.'

Bobby flashed him a smile of relief. 'Thanks, Pete. I appreciate that.'

—

When she arrived at Sumner House, Bobby took the little path that led around the lake and followed it to the cottage in the grounds that Topsy and her former nanny, Mrs Hobbes, were occupying for as long as the government were going to be using her home for the war effort. Bobby didn't want to go directly to the airmen's hospital; not without Topsy, who was employed as a nurse there, to accompany her. The matron was stern, and hostile to outsiders. Besides, Teddy was now convalescing at the cottage so that his bed could be given to another patient, and Topsy had been assigned to his particular care. That meant Bobby could get a quote for her article from him before she interviewed the men in the hospital dormitory.

When she arrived at the cottage, she was surprised to discover what seemed to be a party in progress, although it was barely 1 p.m. There was laughter within, and the sound of a tinkling piano playing the mile-a-minute melody of 'Sweet Georgia Brown'. When Mrs Hobbes answered her knock, Bobby discovered her wearing a newspaper hat and holding a small glass of wine.

Bobby tried to suppress a smile. Mrs Hobbes looked so serious and solemn, in a way that was entirely at odds with her funny hat and the dance music coming from inside. She always did look solemn, although Bobby knew she hid a dry wit behind the stern facade.

'Is Topsy having a party, Mrs Hobbes?' she asked. 'I wouldn't have interrupted if I'd known. I was supposed to have an appointment with her this afternoon.'

'Don't you worry, lassie. The more the merrier, I'm sure.' She called into the house in her light Scottish lilt. 'Topsy! Your young friend is here for you.'

Topsy came darting out in her blue and white nurse's uniform, moving as ever as if she had no time to waste. She, too, was wearing a hat made of newspaper in lieu of her service cap. Mrs Hobbes disappeared back into the parlour as Topsy dragged Bobby inside and gave her a hug of greeting.

'What's happening, Topsy?' Bobby asked. 'It isn't your birthday, is it?'

Topsy giggled. 'Oh, Birdy, it's too funny. We're having an engagement party.'

'An engagement party! Not for—' Bobby just bit her tongue in time before she asked whether Topsy and Teddy might be the couple in question. 'Who is engaged?'

'Oh, someone you know very well,' Topsy said with a grin. 'Now you must come through and give your regards to the happy couple. We're having ever such a jolly time.'

'I didn't realise you'd have guests,' Bobby said as she followed Topsy into the parlour. 'I was actually hoping I might have an opportunity to talk to you alone before we went up to the hospital.'

'Oh? Are you making wedding plans too?'

'No. This is about… something else. We can discuss it later.'

Topsy ushered her into the parlour, and Bobby blinked at the odd little scene that met her there.

Teddy was there in his wheelchair and hospital uniform, of course, looking rather out of sorts despite his paper hat. He was casting resentful looks at another uniformed young man who was playing the jolly dance tune at the piano. On closer examination, Bobby recognised him as one of the Canadian airmen – the handsome one, who she was pretty sure was named Ernie. She hadn't realised Topsy was acquainted with him.

Her friend Jolka, Piotr's wife, was in the room too, talking to a pleasant-looking young man with pale, delicate features and flaxen hair. The only others present were Mrs Hobbes, her cantankerous pet goose Norman and another goose who sat companionably with him in a basket next to the fire.

'Do you know everyone?' Topsy asked as she divested Bobby of her coat and pushed her towards a chair beside Jolka.

'I… no, I don't think so. Not everyone,' Bobby said dazedly, sinking into the chair. She was trying to puzzle out who in the room could be engaged. Could it be Topsy and Teddy, after all? Or… the Canadian and Mrs Hobbes? No, surely not. Was the pale, boyish young man a suitor for Topsy?

'Well, Jolka you know already, of course, and Teddy and Maimie and Norman,' Topsy said. 'At the piano is Flying Officer Ernie King. He's with the Canadian Air Force.'

Ernie, who Bobby had never exchanged more words with than 'good afternoon', nodded chummily as if they were old friends. 'We've met. Hey, Slacks.'

'And on the other side of Jolka is my cousin, Archibald Sumner,' Topsy went on, gesturing to the flaxen-haired man in civilian clothing. 'Lord Archibald Sumner, in fact, but he gets frightfully annoyed when anyone uses his title. He and his mother are staying at Woodside Nook, the old porter's lodge, for a while. Archie's tremendous fun, when he isn't being a complete pain in the neck. We used to have some ripping games here when we were children. Didn't we, darling?'

Archie smiled. 'Steady on, old thing. You'll have your charming friend dragging me away for a game of Hide-and-Seek before I've finished my madeira. Not that that sounds so bad, but when there are pretty girls at a party then I'd far rather play Postman's Knock.'

'Nice to meet you, Mr Sumner,' Bobby said, her head spinning. They certainly seemed to be an eclectic little group – a strange collection for an engagement party. Also, was that flirting? Never having been flirted with by a young man of Archie's background before, she wasn't quite sure.

'Um, who is the happy couple I'm to give my congrat-ulations to?' she asked Topsy as a glass of something strong and sweet was pressed into her hand, determined to put an end to the mystery. This was not at all how she had predicted her day was going to unravel.

Topsy giggled and nodded to the fireplace. 'Right in front of you. Maimie's ever so proud.'

Bobby stared for a moment at the two geese snuggled together by the fire. Then she burst into laughter.

'I don't believe it.' She turned to Mrs Hobbes. 'He's not selected a mate at long last?'

Mrs Hobbes's matchmaking efforts on behalf of her stubborn pet were legendary in Silverdale. For as long as Bobby had known her, she had watched Maimie Hobbes trying to find Norman a mate from the female geese who frequented the beck in the village. Geese mated for life, but Norman's selfish and cantankerous nature meant the ladies of his species clearly didn't see him as husband material.

Mrs Hobbes gave Norman a look both fond and proud. 'He has. Jemima here has deigned to receive his dubious attentions. And about time too, I must say.'

Bobby smiled. 'Well, congratulations, Norman – and Jemima too. I'm sorry I didn't bring a gift. I had no idea I was coming to a party.'

'No more did any of us,' Ernie said, leaving off piano-playing as he finished his tune. 'You must have a hat though, Slacks. Here, take mine. I can make another.'

He plucked the newspaper hat from his head and stood up to place it on hers.

Bobby laughed. 'Thanks. I'm sure it matches my eyes.'

'You see, Birdy, I wasn't so rude as to not invite you. Maimie brought Jemima home to be introduced to me, Archie came over with the gift of a bottle of madeira from his mother and then the party just seemed to sort of happen around us,' Topsy said. 'Actually this is only half a party. It's really a meeting I arranged about something terribly important – an act of charity. I was telling Ernie and Jolka all about it when you arrived.'

Bobby glanced at Jolka. 'Charity? What is it?'

'Topsy has an idea she believes we can help with,' Jolka said in her thick Polish accent. 'It sounds rather strange to me, this tradition she speaks of, but of course I am not English. Perhaps to you it will make sense.'

'What is it?'

'Do you have plans for Christmas, Birdy?' Topsy asked eagerly. 'You're not going home to wherever it is you come from, are you?'

'Bradford. No, not this year. Our house is being let as a billet for soldiers, and none of my siblings can get home until New Year anyhow. Besides, Charlie will be here on leave and I want to be near him. My dad and I are spending it with the Athertons. Why do you ask?'

'Because this amazing idea of mine can only happen at Christmas.' Her eyes sparkled. 'The men at the hospital have been in such gloomy spirits lately. The days are so short now and their ward so dismal from the blackout shades, and then it's awful for them knowing that they must spend the festive season away from their loved ones. I've been longing to do something to cheer them up. I suppose all those war refugees in the village who aren't able to go home for Christmas feel the same – the evacuees and the Canadian airmen. Then last night I had just the most perfect notion.'

'It's a pantomime,' Archie said lazily, reaching for the bottle of madeira on the table to top himself up.

Topsy scowled at him. 'Oh, Arch. Now you've ruined my big announcement.'

'You do go on, Tops. It was about time you got to the point before your friend died of boredom.'

'I'm not sure I understand,' Bobby said. 'You want to take the injured airmen to a pantomime?'

Topsy shot her cousin a last glare before turning her attention back to Bobby. 'No, silly. I mean, we could perform a pantomime! Maimie used to write scripts for the little theatre group she was part of in Aberdeen a million years ago and she said she could dust one off for us. I'm sure lots of people in the village would want to help, and some of the airmen who aren't confined to bed could be involved too. We could perform it in the dormitory at Sumner House for the bedridden men and bring all the children from the village to watch. So many of the men are fathers that I think it would do them all kinds of good to hear children's laughter around them. I spoke to Matron about it and she was thrilled with the idea.'

'Why ask us to help with this pantomime, Topsy?' Jolka asked. 'I don't believe I have ever seen such an entertainment. Certainly I could not act in one, I'm sure.'

'Oh, but you must, Jolka. I know you'd be darling at it. You're too beautiful not to be on the stage at least once in your life.'

Jolka smiled. 'By all means try flattering me, but it will make no difference.'

'Tommy would be so excited to see his mother performing though, and it will be cheering for you to have a new project when Piotr leaves you to go back to his station,' Topsy persisted. 'I'm relying on you to help with the publicity too, with your art skills.'

'You do run away with these madcap schemes of yours, old girl,' Archie said, sipping his madeira. 'Pantomimes can't be organised in a wink, you know. How about some more tunes, eh, King?'

Ernie obligingly shuffled his sheet music and struck up 'In The Mood'.

'Any news of the war?' Archie asked him. 'We're waiting for those neighbours of yours to wake up and give us a hand. Second time they've been late for one of these shindigs.'

Ernie shrugged. 'Uncle Sam does what's best for Uncle Sam. They'll come in if Hitler gives them a reason.'

'Oh, never mind the stupid war,' Topsy said impatiently. 'What about my idea? You will help, won't you, all of you? Not you, Archie. You can go back to Woodside if you're going to keep being beastly about it.'

Archie smiled good-naturedly. 'Sorry, Tops. You oughtn't to get carried away, that's all. I didn't say it wasn't a nice thought.'

'I think it is a wonderful idea,' Teddy said loyally, breaking his long silence. 'I would love to watch a real English pantomime. It is something I too have never seen.'

Topsy squeezed his arm. 'Thank you, darling. I knew you'd be behind me.'

'I only wish I could help bring it about.' He cast a listless look down at his wheelchair. 'I can be no help to you, Topsy, I am afraid.'

'Nonsense. You're to be my right-hand man for the whole thing, and help me to direct it. I couldn't do it without you.'

'Well, I will do what I can.'

'And I'm certainly happy to help,' Ernie said. 'I figure I owe the village a debt for being good enough to put me and the boys up for a spell.'

'Do you have pantomimes in Canada?' Bobby asked.

'Not the same as the ones here, perhaps, but I saw one or two as a kid. Girl with nice legs playing the hero, young man dressed up as old woman, a lot of rhyming and cackling – is that the kind of thing?'

'Yes, that's it,' Topsy said, with an approving smile at finding him so cooperative.

'I am not sure I quite understand,' Jolka said. 'It is a type of play?'

'That's right. They're fairy tales performed for children,' Bobby said. 'There's always a wicked demon and a good fairy, and a dame who's a man in drag, and a hero played by a girl in a short tunic. They're put on at Christmas, with music and jokes and a lot of slapstick silliness. The British have been doing it for a couple of hundred years now, I think, although I read once that they really began in Italy.'

Ernie laughed. 'We ought to keep quiet about that. It could count as enemy propaganda.'

'My father used to take Archie and me to the pantomime at the London Palladium every Christmas when we were children,' Topsy said, her eyes hazy with nostalgia. 'Do you remember, Arch, how you used to come down from Ludgrove or Eton on the train? We'd meet you at Paddington and Father would take us to Hamley's to see the big toy displays, then we had tea at Claridge's before the show. I remember one year you nearly fell out of your seat laughing like a lunatic at the man playing Mother Goose.'

'I did fall out of my seat,' Archie said, rubbing his thigh. 'I'm sure I still have a bruise.'

'OK, Topsy, count me in,' Ernie said, flashing his white teeth. 'Anything for a lady.'

Topsy beamed back at him. 'Thank you, Ernie, that's much appreciated.'

Teddy shot the airman another resentful glance. There was clearly some jealousy at work. Bobby wondered if there was anything behind it. Could the Canadian be keen on Topsy, or was it only Teddy's fancy? It seemed odd that Ernie was here, and so very eager to help.

Topsy looked at Bobby. 'How about you, Birdy? I think you'd make a heavenly Cinderella.'

Bobby stared at her. 'You want me to *act*?'

'Of course, you'd be perfect. Your eyes are just right – so pretty and thoughtful, and sad too, sometimes. Jolka can be your Prince Charming, and Ernie can be Buttons. You see, I have it all planned out in my head already. It will be fun, won't it?'

Archie laughed. 'You really ought to give your friend some time to think it over, Tops. You can't spring a career on the stage on her just like that.'

Norman had got to his feet and was fussing impatiently around his bride-to-be, who looked quite comfortable by the fire. She hissed at him as he pecked at her tailfeathers, demanding attention.

'Just two hours engaged and already there's trouble in paradise,' Ernie said with a smile.

'He's getting restless,' Mrs Hobbes observed. 'Would anyone mind if we took this party outdoors? It isn't so very chilly today, and there are plenty of blankets and things in the airing cupboard for those who want to wrap up. We can take the future Mr and Mrs Norman to the lake for a swim.'

'Oh, yes, and have jam sandwiches on a blanket,' Topsy said, clapping her hands. 'Archie, you can light a little campfire. It'll be just like when we were children and we used to roast sweet chestnuts by the lake.'

'I really can't stay long. I'm supposed to be working,' Bobby said, but as usual, Topsy paid her no attention. She had already started collecting things together for their impromptu campfire picnic.

Still, at least taking the party outdoors would make it easier to take Topsy off to one side to discuss in private what Bobby needed to discuss with her. She stood and looked around for her coat.

'Here it is,' Archie said, reading her thoughts. He scooped it up from a pile. 'Allow me, Birdy.'

Bobby laughed. 'It's just Bobby. Only Topsy ever calls me Birdy. She says the way I cock my head makes me look like a budgerigar.'

'Well you make about the prettiest budgie I ever saw, I must say.'

'Um, thank you.'

He was still holding her coat open for her. Not knowing how to politely decline his assistance, Bobby allowed him to help her into it, making sure her engagement ring was nice and conspicuous. He offered her his arm, with Ernie offering to escort Jolka while Topsy pushed Teddy. Mrs Hobbes took charge of the picnic things and the two geese, and they headed outside to the lake.

Bobby couldn't work out if this cousin of Topsy's was flirting with her or just being chivalrous. His manners were so different from the other boys she knew. Bobby had never been flirted with by someone from Topsy's class before, or mixed with them much at all beyond the single titled friend she had made here in Silverdale. But while she wasn't quite sure what to make of him, there was something pleasant and frank, if a little languid, in Archie's face that meant she couldn't help liking him. She wondered if there was a reason for his visit, and what his mother, Topsy's aunt, was like.

Chapter 7

'Birdy, would you be a dear and push Teddy the rest of the way?' Topsy asked after ten minutes' walking. 'The chair feels terribly heavy when I have to take it across grass.'

'What, you'd rob me of my escortee, would you?' Archie said with mock petulance.

'We're perfectly able to escort ourselves, Arch. It isn't King Arthur times, you know,' Topsy said, waving a dismissive hand at him. 'Escort Maimie if you're so concerned about having a lady on your arm.'

'I'd escort you if I didn't think you'd deliberately trip me up and send me flying head-first into the lake.'

Topsy giggled. 'I say, that is a fun idea. But I shan't, or you may not light the fire for us.'

'What a lot of nonsense you young people talk,' Mrs Hobbes said. 'You might all learn a lesson from my wee Norman, walking respectfully beside his Jemima. Come along now.'

Bobby took the handles of Teddy's wheelchair while Topsy ran off ahead to look for kindling.

'You see, Bobby, already she grows bored of me,' Teddy said glumly as they walked a little behind the others.

'That's not true. Her arms are tired, that's all.'

'Topsy is too young and full of life to be tied to invalids. She ought to have left me behind and enjoyed her young friends without the sight of me to make her gloomy.'

'What's brought this mood on, Teddy?' Bobby asked gently. 'You seemed so happy at the fruit-picking, even with Florrie and Jessie prattling at you the entire time.'

Teddy summoned a smile. 'They are two happy little girls, those. They talked to me of their father. After half an hour, I could believe there was no greater hero in the British Army.'

Bobby laughed. 'I suppose every child with a father in the forces believes he's winning the war single-handedly. Still, Captain Parry is truly a brave man. He was wounded in the shoulder by a strafing Messerschmitt at Dunkirk.'

'Their talk did me much good that day. It must be pleasant to have children who love and admire you,' he said, somewhat wistfully. Bobby knew that one of the consequences of the horrific injuries Teddy had sustained in the plane crash was that he may never be able to father a child.

The party had reached a likely looking spot by the lake now. Topsy was building a fire from twigs and kindling she had collected while Archie stood by, idly flicking at a petrol cigarette lighter. Bobby didn't wheel Teddy to join them, however, but stayed a little back. Having someone to listen to his problems seemed to help him, and as far as she knew, she was the only person to whom he had confided his feelings for Topsy.

Bobby crouched beside him so they were level, and Teddy, grimacing, turned his face from her. The right side of his face, which had been badly burned in the accident, was now white and mottled where new skin had been grafted on. Bobby knew he was self-conscious about how it had changed his appearance. However, from her position she could only see the other side of his face: the side that showed a handsome, pensive young man with sadness in his expression.

'Are you comfortable with me here?' she asked softly.

'Yes. I am sorry. It was only instinct that made me turn away. Please, stay where you are.'

'You're jealous of Ernie King, aren't you?'

Teddy scoffed. 'He is a peacock, that man. He struts and preens and grins like a gigolo. Once I would have laughed at such a man, but it is hard to laugh now when I am stuck in this chair while he bathes in Topsy's smiles. And the other one, who presses his presence on her uninvited.'

'Her cousin?'

'The relationship is not of first cousins. I believe it is rather distant. It has always been the dearest wish of their families that they would marry and unite two branches of the family, I understand.'

Bobby blinked. 'Topsy and Archie are to be married?'

'So the boy's mother would have it, and Topsy's father wished it greatly before his death. The young man was the successor to his title in the absence of a direct male heir, so their union would ensure the peerage was passed to this Lord Sumner-Walsh's own grandchildren. I hear all this from Maimie, who likes to gossip when she has had a glass or two of her favourite beer. Topsy would care about duty. She would want to do what was right by her family.'

'Oh, I don't think Topsy gives a fig about all that sort of thing.'

'You are wrong. I believe she cares more than she would ever admit.' His gaze drifted to the impressive sandstone front of Sumner House. 'She loves this big house and all its history, and she loved her father very dearly. She would have done anything to please him.'

Bobby watched as Topsy pushed Archie in retaliation for some bit of teasing. 'They hardly look deeply in love.'

'Well, what has love to do with duty?'

'I can't believe she would marry without love. Not Topsy. She's so affectionate by nature, I don't think she could bear to be trapped in a loveless marriage.'

'Perhaps she is not in love, but all the same she is fond of this pretended cousin. He might persuade her to love him as a husband, in time.'

'They seem more like a brother and sister to me, teasing each other and bickering all the while. I can't see how they could ever be lovers.'

'Huh. Then perhaps she may take the preening young Canadian as a lover and keep this milk-complexioned cousin for a husband.' He sighed. 'No, I am being bitter. I do not believe she would do so. But this man King, look – he talks to Maimie but he looks at Topsy all the while. I can see what thought is in his mind. Neither of them are worth the dust from Topsy's shoes.'

Bobby turned to look at him. 'You're still determined not to tell her how you feel?'

'I cannot. It is harder since I was sent to the cottage to convalesce. Now I must see her constantly, and it is pain and pleasure in equal parts. But I could not ask her to tie herself to such a block, who must be a burden to her always. To give up her chance of being a wife – a true wife – to be forever a nurse.'

'I wish you would reconsider. She doesn't think of you that way.'

Teddy shook his head, closing his eyes to avoid her gaze. 'It would not be right. She could not be content with me. Her family would be angry, and cast her off, perhaps, if she were to marry a man not of her kind who they knew could never give her an heir.'

'But if she loves you—'

'She could never do so, I am convinced of it. For me she could feel only pity. Besides, love is not the only thing that makes a happy marriage, although the films might have us believe so. There are many things to consider. In all respects, it would not be right.'

'What will you do?' Bobby asked quietly. 'When the doctors say you're healed enough to be discharged from this place?'

'As soon as I no longer need to be in the constant care of specialists, I must go. Leave Topsy to be happy and no more torture myself with the sight of other suitors making love to her.'

'Where will you go?'

'Where can I go? Not back to my mother and father in Poland, who must live under the Nazi yoke until this war is ended. I have no one else. Some charity will, I hope, have a bed in the sort of bleak hostel that men like me find themselves in. But if I can know Topsy is happy, I shall try to be satisfied.' He glanced at Topsy, who was elbowing Archie out of the way as he tried to rearrange her kindling for her. 'I am sure, though, that her happiness does not lie with either of these two. I am jealous, Bobby, I cannot deny it. Perhaps I would never think any man worthy of her. But still, in my heart I believe I am right.'

Topsy was beckoning to them now, looking impatient. Archie was lighting the fire and little flames had started to appear.

'We had better go over,' Bobby said. 'She'll be cross with me for keeping you to myself.'

'You are kind to listen to such unhappy ramblings.' He fixed the side of his mouth that was still fully mobile into a smile. 'There. And now having told you my woes, I am prepared to be better company at this goose betrothal party.'

Bobby laughed as she wheeled him towards the group around the fire. 'What a typically Topsy idea, to hold a party for them. What do you think of her pantomime scheme?'

'Oh, I am sure it will be a success.' They reached Topsy, and he smiled fondly at her. 'Nothing Topsy plans could ever fail.'

'Teddy, I really oughtn't to speak to you,' Topsy said, frowning at him. 'You're very cruel to neglect me. Whenever Birdy comes to tea, she wheels you off somewhere so she can have you to herself and then I hardly see anything of you.'

'She seeks to put me in a better temper, Topsy. You see, now I am all smiles. Your friend Miss Bancroft knows how to soothe my bad moods.'

'And I only know how to cause them, I suppose,' Topsy said, laughing. 'Maimie tells me the same thing.'

Mrs Hobbes didn't respond to this. She was distracted by her geese, kneeling on the bank of the lake and flapping at them as she tried to encourage Jemima into the water to join her fiancé. Norman was floating placidly, but his future wife looked nervous of wading out into unfamiliar waters. Jolka, meanwhile, was talking animatedly to Ernie King about a painting she was working on. The fire was blazing away now, and Archie, at Topsy's request, was spreading a picnic blanket on the ground for them.

'Um, Topsy. Could I possibly have a word with you?' Bobby asked.

'Of course, darling, go ahead.'

'I mean, in private. It's a little… I shouldn't like to discuss it in front of other people.'

'Oh.' Topsy looked surprised. 'Well, all right. We'll take a little stroll around the lake.'

She slipped her arm into Bobby's and they began a circuit of the water.

'I suppose you're going to give me a lecture about tricking you into coming to one of my parties when I promised Charlie's grumpy brother I was going to get you into the hospital so you could interview the airmen for your magazine,' Topsy said. 'Don't worry, I won't keep you here all day. We'll just make merry for another half an hour so Maimie can say we've sent Norman off into married life with all the luck he deserves, then I'll take you over there.'

'It isn't that. I mean, I do need to get on so yes, I'd appreciate it if you could get me past the matron. But this is about… something else.'

'Is it Teddy? I saw him talking to you, looking all earnest. He's been much better since we brought him to the cottage but he's in frightfully low spirits today. I'm not sure if he's depressed about his situation or worrying for his family in Poland. It must be ghastly, not being able to write – not knowing if they've been deported to Germany as forced labour, or even if they're dead or alive. He tells me terrible things of how the Nazis see Slavs like them. They believe they're less than human.'

'I expect he's terribly worried about them, but I don't believe his family is the reason for his glum mood today,' Bobby said. 'I think perhaps he's feeling a little neglected while your cousin is visiting.'

'The poor love, of course he is. I'd far rather spend time with Teddy than have Archie teasing me, but I must please Aunt Constance or I shall never hear the end of it. Still, I'll try to make sure Teddy has his part in the conversation. Archie and I are too fond of talking over old times, I suppose.'

'Has he not been called up yet, your cousin?' Bobby asked.

'He enlisted early in '39 with an old chum from Eton. RAF, naturally: Volunteer Reserve. He was invalided out of active service eighteen months later though. He only got to fly a couple of missions.'

'Why, was he injured?'

'No, this was something else,' Topsy said vaguely. 'I don't know all the details. Something in his blood – not life-threatening but I suppose it could be a problem if he were to need a transfusion.'

'How long will your aunt and cousin be staying?'

Topsy pulled a face. 'I was hoping it would be just a few weeks, but Constance is threatening to hang about until after Christmas. Archie's no happier about it than I am. He hates to be away from London, holed up in the country away from his jolly young set down there, but he must follow his mother's whims occasionally or she may decide to cut off his allowance.'

'Shall you mind having them stay so long?'

'Well Archie is fun to have around, even when he's being a stinker, but his mother is the most awful bore. She's always going on at me about the great and glorious traditions of the family, my duty as a Sumner and all that rot.'

'That does sound tedious,' Bobby agreed. She knew she ought to bring the conversation back around to the favour she needed to ask for, but after what Teddy had said about this Aunt Constance's matrimonial ambitions for the two cousins, she couldn't help being interested in what Topsy had to tell her.

'She isn't even my real aunt,' Topsy said. 'Father was close to her and her husband though, and the title went to their branch of the family, so now she believes she has carte blanche to come and stay whenever she feels like it and harangue me to within an inch of my life.'

'If she isn't your aunt, what is she to you?'

'Well, nothing really. She isn't a blood relative – only by marriage, and then pretty distantly. Her late husband was my grandfather's half-brother's son – I think that was it. My father would always have me call them Aunt and Uncle, but really they're some degree of cousin. Archie and I were always together as children though, so he does feel like family, even if we aren't all that closely related. I was glad Father's title went to him.'

'What does this aunt-cousin harangue you about?'

'Everything she can think of. Letting the government have my house, as if I had any say in the business when they'd a perfect legal right to take it, and all these horrid vulgar commoners treading the ancient halls of Sumner House. Consorting with the low types I hang around with, like you and Charlie – oh, no offence, darling. That's just how she is – you'll see for yourself when you meet her. She's the most awful snob. And then her favourite thing of all is that she'd have me make a match of it with Arch, of all the ridiculous notions.'

'Why would she have you make a match if it isn't what you want?'

'Family, blood – all that nonsense she cares so much about. Secure Sumner House for future generations of

Sumners. It was my father's dearest wish too. Apparently that was why Archie was invited here so frequently when we were children, in the hope we might form an attachment. Unfortunately it had rather the opposite effect than the one Father intended, because now Archie's the last person in the world I could ever see as a husband. We're far too much like family, and besides—' She stopped herself. 'Well, it just wouldn't be right.'

'How does Archie feel about it?'

'The same as I do. He must have told his mother a thousand times that it isn't meant to be, but she won't take no for an answer. I've a good mind to up and marry someone else, just to shut her up.'

'That would be one solution.' Bobby glanced back at the group by the fire. 'I didn't know you knew Ernie King.'

'I don't, really,' Topsy said, looking at the man with mild interest. 'He was making himself charming to me at the fruit-picking and I took the opportunity to get him involved in my pantomime idea. Lots of the girls there were gazing besottedly at him, and he is very handsome. I thought if he agreed to be involved, it might lure in some of the village ladies to help. Perhaps that was rather devious of me but it is for a good cause.'

'Do you think he's handsome?'

'Of course. That's just a fact, you know. He's charming too – a little flirtatious, just in fun, but not pushy. I rather like him.' She smiled fondly back at Teddy. 'But he can't compare with my pilot for handsomeness. No one has eyes to equal Teddy's.'

'You think a lot of Teddy, don't you?'

'He's the best thing in my life,' Topsy said simply. 'I wish I was able to keep him. When his spirits are low, he says the most dreadful things about leaving me to go and live in some horrid hostel for crippled servicemen.'

'He isn't a pet to be kept though, Topsy. It hurts a man's pride to be entirely dependent on others. They don't like to be cared for as charity cases by women who are neither kith nor kin to them.'

'No. No, I don't suppose they do.' There was a rare moment of silence as Topsy's tongue was still for once. She looked thoughtful, and a little sad. Bobby regarded her friend curiously as they walked.

No one could ever call Topsy selfish. In fact she was generous to a fault, always willing to help someone in need or do a favour for a friend. Yet Bobby knew that Topsy was always at the centre of Topsy's world, wherein everyone else was a mere player. Partly that was the fault of an overindulged childhood, and partly it was just Topsy. But now, watching Topsy watching Teddy, her eyes constantly drawn to him while they walked… it really seemed as if her friend had found a new idol to build her world around. Bobby was sure, if Teddy asked Topsy the question she knew he longed in his heart to ask, that despite every obstacle standing between them the answer would be yes.

After a moment, Topsy roused herself. 'But I'm chattering on about myself as always. What was it you wanted to talk to me about?'

Bobby flushed. She had no doubt that Topsy's generous nature would grant the huge favour she was about to ask, but it didn't make it any less humiliating that she was being forced to throw herself at her titled friend's feet.

'Well, Charlie told me… that is, I heard you were looking for a gamekeeper for the woods around the lodge,' she began hesitantly.

Topsy brightened. 'Oh yes, do you know of someone? I've had an advertisement on the board in the post office for weeks but not a single applicant yet. I suppose it's the same story as everywhere: not enough men left to go around. I really don't mind too much who I get, as long as they're trustworthy and come with good references. I had to dismiss the last man when I found out there was barely a trout left in the river after he'd sold them all to some local racketeer.'

Bobby's blush deepened at the reference to poaching. She had a strong suspicion that the racketeer in question was her dad's friend Pete Dixon.

'Well, he doesn't actually come with any references except from me, but he is capable and trustworthy,' Bobby said, sincerely hoping this would prove to be true. 'This is embarrassing for me, but I need to ask you for the hugest favour.'

'Of course, darling,' Topsy said, looking puzzled. 'There's no need to be embarrassed. You know you can ask me for anything and I'll help if I can.'

Bobby smiled at her. 'I know you will. Still, this is a big thing. I wouldn't ask if I weren't desperate. It's... it's my dad. I need to find him a job.'

Topsy blinked. 'All right. Well, if he can do the work then I'd be happy to take him on. Does he have much gamekeeping experience?'

'Very little. He's done some work trapping animals – pests and vermin and such,' Bobby added hurriedly. 'But he's a mill man really. I moved him out here when I came back to work for *The Tyke* so I could keep house for him, but he's really struggled to find a job.'

'I see,' Topsy said slowly. She looked a little worried, her desire to help a friend clearly doing battle with what even Bobby had to admit was everyday common sense. She was hardly offering a boon in presenting her friend with a fifty-one-year-old gamekeeper who had no experience of the work.

'He can do the job,' Bobby said, a pleading note entering her voice. 'He's strong, and fit for his age. He loves the outdoors, and of course he won't be called up. You wouldn't regret it.' Her cheeks grew hot. 'And... he needs to work, Topsy. He was in the war – the last war, in the trenches. It affected him terribly, what he saw there. If he isn't working he dwells on things, and when he dwells on things he... he becomes depressed. If I have to beg for this for him, I will.' She swallowed a sob. 'I honestly didn't know what else to do or I'd never have dreamed of asking for such a big favour.'

'Oh, Birdy. I'm sorry, I had no idea,' Topsy said, squeezing her arm. She glanced at Teddy. 'Isn't it awful what war can do to a man?'

'It's evil,' Bobby agreed fervently.

'Of course if he needs it so badly then the job is his. I'm sure he'll make a fine gamekeeper, if he works as hard as I know you do on your little magazine. If he has even a tenth of his daughter's brains and energy, he'll be the best keeper I've ever hired.'

'Oh, thank you!' Bobby stopped walking to give her friend a hug. 'You don't know how much that means to me. I'll persuade him to send you a letter of application.'

'And I'll pretend this conversation never happened when I offer him the job. He's proud, I suppose, the way working men so often are.'

'He is; very much so. Thanks, Topsy – you're a good friend. And if I can do anything at all to pay you back...'

'Well, you can do one thing.'

'What?'

Topsy grinned at her. 'You can agree to be my Cinderella.'

Chapter 8

Bobby was lighting the fire when her father emerged from his bedroom the next day.

She had had a late shift at the ARP shelter the evening before, and when she'd arrived home her dad had already been in bed. The bottle of green spirits he'd bought from Pete had again been on the table, however, with an empty glass beside it. Since her dad had bought it himself, Bobby hadn't thought it a good idea to lock it away with the spirits she got for him from Don Sykes. She was always cautious of doing anything that might humiliate him, which of everything was most likely to send him spiralling back towards the state he had been in when he had tried to take his own life in the winter. Clearly he had been drinking, since the level in the bottle had gone down, but at least he hadn't had so much that he was unable to put himself to bed.

'Good morning.' Bobby glanced up at him, noticing his puffy features and red-rimmed eyes.

'Aye, morning,' he said wearily, throwing himself into his armchair.

There was the sound of the letterbox being opened, and a couple of envelopes popped through on to the mat. Bobby went to pick them up.

'Owt for me?' her dad asked.

'Why, were you expecting something?'

'Couple of jobs I wrote about. Thought I might hear today.'

She glanced at the envelopes and shook her head. 'No, sorry. Both for me.'

He sighed. 'Thought as much. Who from? Your sister?'

Bobby examined the envelopes. One bore the RAF censor's stamp and the other had a Bradford postmark, with Don's familiar writing on the front.

'One from Don, one from Charlie,' she said.

'You going to open them then?'

Since neither envelope looked particularly well-stuffed, Bobby thought she would have time to read them before work. She tore open Don's first.

'Any Bradford news I should know about?' her dad asked.

'Not much. Joan's due date is in mid-December so Don is in rather a panic getting everything ready for the baby. He thanks me for the layette set I sent. I made it in mustard yellow, so it would do for a boy or girl. He asks after you, and—' She stopped, frowning. 'Oh. He says he's letting Tony Scott go from the paper.'

'Good, about time he did. I wonder that loafer managed to hold on to an honest job as long as he did.'

'Yes, but Don was attached to Tony in his own way. He must have done something pretty bad to make Don sack him.'

'Does he say what?'

'He just says he's fed up with his laziness and wants to hire someone who'll pull their weight. I'm sure there must be more to it than that though.'

She didn't mention to her dad Don's other suggestion, which was that now would be a good time to consider returning to the *Bradford Courier*. He often mentioned that he'd always have a job for her if she wanted it, but Bobby had no intention of leaving *The Tyke*.

'Knowing Scott, he'll have been messing about with Don's wife,' her dad muttered. He'd always had a low opinion of her old friend on the paper, although he was fond of Don.

Bobby laughed. 'She's seven months pregnant, Dad. Besides, Don and Joan are devoted to each other.'

'Aye, well. He'll have done summat to deserve it, mark my words, and I'd bet money it involved some lass. Owt else to tell us?'

She scanned the rest of the letter. 'Just bits and pieces about life at the *Courier* and the scrapes that new cub, Freddie, has been getting himself into. Nothing to interest you.'

Bobby wondered whether to save Charlie's letter until she was alone, but there didn't seem much point. Anything he was willing for his barrack officer to read couldn't be too intimate. His letters were often short and taciturn these days. Bobby tried not to take it personally, aware that self-consciousness about the third pair of eyes he knew would be reading every word was what prevented Charlie from being too flowery in his expressions of affection. She tore it open.

'Charlie doesn't have much news either,' she told her father. 'ENSA are putting on a Christmas concert party at Skipton Town Hall for local servicemen and the cadets have all been given leave to go. Civilians are allowed to attend too if they're accompanying a man in uniform. He wants to know if I can go with him.'

'Will you?'

'Of course. I don't want to miss an opportunity to see him when he so rarely gets leave, and I'd like to see him amongst the other men. It's good they're being given some entertainment for Christmas. From what Charlie told me when I saw him last, it sounds as though the CO there has them living like medieval hermits. It must have a terrible effect on morale.'

'That all he's got to say?'

Bobby skimmed the rest of the letter, disappointed. 'It's the only bit of real news. The rest is just about meals and the wireless and such. He never writes much nowadays, although when he was at his old billet he'd write pages and pages about the adventures he was having with the other lads. I don't think he's very happy at Ryland Moor.'

'Well, he's not much training left to do.'

'I know.' She shivered, feeling the chill suddenly. 'I'm not looking forward to what comes after that though.'

Bobby slipped the letters into her dressing gown pocket and went back to crouch by the fire.

She had been glad not to see a letter with her dad's name on it in the post today. She hadn't forgotten that John Cartwright was due to write about his engagement to Lilian, and she still needed to break her sister's news to their parent. But this morning, she had a more pressing conversation planned – one that required a certain amount of delicacy.

'Any plans for today?' she asked casually as she stacked the coke and firelighters.

'Not minded to stir outside with the sky glowering,' her dad said. 'Looks like a storm coming on. Sure I'll find summat to do wi' missen.'

'All right.' Bobby nodded to a piece of paper she had left on the table. 'That's for you. It was advertised on the board in the post office.'

'What is it? A job?' he asked, snatching it up.

'Yes. I thought you'd be interested so I copied the details into my notebook.'

That was a fib, of course – she had got the details straight from the horse's mouth while she was visiting Sumner House – but Bobby thought it best to distance herself from Topsy while drawing her dad's attention to the gamekeeper position. It was important to his pride that when he got it, he believed he'd been selected entirely on his own merit.

Her dad scanned the pencilled message and snorted. 'Gamekeeper?'

'For the woods around that old hunting lodge where Piotr and Jolka live with their little lad. The land belongs to Lady Sumner-Walsh. You've been down there, haven't you?'

'Aye. Been down wi' Pete in t' summer. That's his patch.'

'Well, don't you think it could suit you?' Bobby said, trying not to sound too eager. She avoided meeting his eyes as she continued to build the fire. 'You'd be outdoors all day, doing healthy work, and it's a decent salary too. You know a lot about game, don't you?'

He laughed. 'About killing it, not about keeping it.'

'Still, look at what's involved. Trapping vermin – I suppose you know how to do that all right. Looking after the habitat. I mean, that's just gardening really. You always loved making things grow in that little allotment you had when Mam was alive.'

'A Bradford vegetable plot isn't five hundred acre of trout streams and rabbit warrens, lass. Her ladyship wouldn't look at me twice when she could have her pick of born-and-bred Dalesmen to tend the land.'

'There aren't many born-and-bred Dalesmen left around here now the war's had the pick of them. Those that are still here are already working on the farms, if they're young and strong. I think Topsy might consider giving you a trial, at least.'

'You reckon so, do you?'

'Of course, why not? You'd be good at it, Dad.'

'Huh. Position's been filled already, most likely. It's not for me, our Bobby.'

'It can't hurt to write a letter of application. You could draft it today and after work I can bring my typewriter home and type it out for you. I'll be going to the post office tomorrow anyhow so it's no problem for me to drop it in the postbox.' She glanced at his empty glass from the night before, which was still on the table. 'At the very least, it'll be something to keep you occupied while the weather's bad.'

'Nay, it's not for me,' he repeated. Still, he had picked up the piece of paper and was reading it again with something like interest kindling in his eyes.

'It could be for you,' Bobby said. 'You know, there's an old saying about poachers making the best gamekeepers.'

'I never heard it.'

'Nor had I until recently, but there is, all the same. That proves it must be a known fact, doesn't it?'

'Sayings are just sayings, Bobby. They aren't going to convince your nob friend I'm right for the job.'

'At least think about it, Dad. For me, eh?' The fire was sparking into life now, and Bobby stood up. 'I'd better get ready for work.'

When Bobby and her father went over to Moorside the following morning, Jessie was once again missing from the table, although everyone else was there – even Reg, who often ate before the rest of the family in his eagerness to start the working day. The little evacuee's empty chair was becoming a familiar sight in the mornings. This was the third day in a row that she had been missing when Bobby arrived for breakfast.

'Let me guess,' she said to Mary. 'The henhouse?'

Mary rolled her eyes. 'Aye, singing away. She's got a regular choir going on in there with the girls clucking along to "Hey Little Hen".'

'I'll fetch her. I might just start going straight there if this is going to become a regular habit.'

Bobby went out to the garden and poked her head through the henhouse door. Jessie was in there, jotting the number of eggs she'd collected down in her notebook. She started, as if caught doing something she shouldn't be.

'Bobby,' she said. 'You scared me.'

'Sorry, Jess, but you're late for breakfast again and Mary's fretting. You really ought to get up a little earlier if you must sing to the hens before school.'

'I'm sorry,' the girl said, looking downcast. 'Is Mary cross?'

'She's not cross, but she does want to make sure you're properly fed before you go to school. Have you collected up all the eggs?'

'Yes, there ain't no more today.'

'How many did you find?'

'One.'

'Only one?'

Jessie nodded. 'Henrietta laid it. The other three ain't laid today but Hetty did yesterday.'

'I think Mary may need to find an alternative to the omelette she was hoping to make us for tea then.' Bobby smiled. 'Still, your singing seems to be working on Henrietta.'

'So she won't get cooked for Christmas?' Jessie asked hopefully.

'Well, I can't promise that. To be honest, all the hens have been laying so badly lately that Mary might decide she can spare any one of them – or all of them. We could get more eggs going back on the ration.'

Jessie's face fell. 'Oh.'

'I'm sorry, sweetheart,' Bobby said gently. 'It's kind of you to try to save them, but people do need to eat as well. With a war on, we're lucky to have a chicken for Christmas. There'll be plenty of folk this year sitting down to nothing more than a chop or two, or even a corned beef fritter.'

'I'd rather eat corned beef fritters than my hens,' Jessie said gloomily, reaching out to stroke Henrietta's plump, feathery body.

'I know, my love, but it isn't our decision to make. The hens belong to Reg and Mary so it's really up to them. Come on inside and have your breakfast, eh?'

–

'How did yesterday go?' Reg asked as soon as Bobby had taken her customary seat at her desk. 'Get some good quotes from them wounded airmen, did you?'

Bobby flushed slightly. It hadn't really been her fault that she'd found herself swigging madeira at a party for newly betrothed waterfowl when she was supposed to be working, but nevertheless she felt guilty about it. Still, she had eventually persuaded Topsy to escort her to the airmen's hospital at Sumner House, where the matron had reluctantly allowed her to question a few of the men whose convalescence had progressed far enough for them to be active in village life. She had got quotes from Teddy, Ernie and Jolka before leaving the party too, so it had been a successful trip out.

All of the airmen Bobby had spoken to had been full of warm praise for the beauty of the Dales and the kindness of the local people, but she did feel there was something missing. She could tell there was a divide, still, between the village natives and the newcomers who now lived in their midst.

She hadn't quite been able to put her finger on why at the time. It wasn't that the villagers were cold to these new residents; in fact, just the opposite was true. Mary had been right when she had said that patriotism was in fashion in Silverdale at the moment – ever since the plane had come down on Bowside that summer, people had become quite fervent about supporting the war effort. The airmen at the hospital who were well enough to mingle had found themselves invited to Beetle drives, Rummy drives, Whist drives, chapel jumble sales, dances in the church hall and any number of other village events. Everyone was polite and considerate to these men who had been wounded in the service of their country. Yet Bobby could tell, despite the warmth with which they spoke of this place, that they still felt like outsiders.

She had spent last night in bed trying to puzzle it out. Bobby, too, had been an outsider here once, but it hadn't taken long for Silverdale to feel like home. And yet she hadn't been shown half the consideration that the villagers now displayed to their wartime guests.

Eventually she came to the conclusion that this was exactly the problem. The men were treated like guests; like they didn't really belong here. Not only that but they were homesick – for their own towns and counties, and for the families, wives and sweethearts they had left behind. Topsy had been absolutely right when she had observed that morale was low at the hospital as the Christmas season approached. Silverdale may be beautiful and its residents kind and welcoming, but when a man's heart was with his wife and children far away, how could it ever feel like home?

Bobby had thought at first that Topsy's pantomime idea was just another of her mad schemes, which with any luck she'd have grown bored of within the week, but after talking to the men she was starting to think it could be just what was needed to bring the village natives and their wartime guests closer together. Working side by side on something jolly for the children would be worth any number of formal cups of tea at Women's Institute bazaars. Not that Bobby wasn't still rather terrified at the scale of the undertaking, but since a promise to help had been reluctantly extracted from her in exchange for the huge favour Topsy had offered to do her father, she was determined to give of her best.

'I got some quotes that I think I can use,' she said in answer to Reg's question. 'I was thinking though – when were you planning on running the article?'

'Not sure I'll be running it at all till I've seen it. What were you thinking?'

'I was thinking… well, when I spoke to the men I realised I wasn't going to get quite the story I was hoping for.'

'Oh?' Reg looked up from the book he was using to make notes for an article.

'Yes. I wanted to write a piece about how the war is bringing people the opportunity to find friends they wouldn't have met otherwise, and learn about ways of life different to their own. But the men at the hospital, even the ones who've been to dances and things down in the village, still seem sort of… detached. They miss the lives they left behind.'

'Course they do. Were you expecting them to tell you any different?'

'Well no, but… I was hoping they'd feel a little more like a part of this place, even if they do miss their families. I think with Christmas not far away, that makes it even harder for them. But Topsy's had this idea that I hope might help them cope better with being far away from home for the festive season, especially if they have young children.'

He grunted. 'Her ladyship's had an idea, has she? She'll have moved on to summat else by next week.'

'But I won't. I offered to help, and there are some others she's roped in as well.'

'What is this idea then?'

'She wants to put on a pantomime at Sumner House, for the evacuees and the village children. Get the men there involved with organising it.'

'Hm. Sounds like a big job.'

'I suppose it is, but I do think it's a good idea,' Bobby said. 'I could write about it in my article, couldn't I? You could run it in the festive number next year. It'll be all about how organising the show brings the villagers and their wartime guests closer together – or at least, I hope it will.'

'Might not be a war on next year,' Reg said absently as he jotted something down. 'I bloody well hope not.'

'You mean you don't want me to write it?'

Reg sighed. 'Aye, go ahead then. You might as well now you've had an afternoon off collecting quotes for it.'

Bobby beamed at him. 'Thanks, Reg. It'll be good, I promise.' She glanced down at her desk. 'Oh. Have we run out of envelopes?'

For as long as she had worked at *The Tyke*, Bobby's mornings had been spent filling envelopes with back numbers of the magazine. These were then sent out to names and addresses gleaned from the telephone directory in the hope they might choose to invest in a four-shilling annual postal order for a subscription. Reg always left a stack of envelopes and magazines on her desk next to the directory at the start of the working day.

'You can lay off that work for a bit,' Reg said. 'Not much point wasting postage on it now. We can barely manage to fill the subscriptions we've got with this damned paper ration. Happen we might have a bit more of the stuff if the government stopped wasting it all on bloody propaganda leaflets, but anyhow, got summat else for you to make a start on. New section I'm bringing into the magazine next February that you're to take charge of.'

Bobby sat up straighter. Her own section! That sounded promising.

'What is it?' she asked. 'Is it my idea for a regular "Yorkshire in Literature" page?'

'No, although that might do well for another time. I'm starting a women's section. All the papers and mags have got summat for housewives now there's a war on, and since they're the ones who usually pay the subscription fee it don't do for us to neglect them. Besides, I can sell some advertisements off the back of it. Recipes, knitting patterns, how to make the most of your clothing coupons; that type of thing, but with a Yorkshire flavour. I'll leave it to you to decide what you think will work. I know I can trust your judgement.'

'Oh.'

Reg must have noticed the disappointment in her voice. He looked up from his work. 'Owt wrong, is there?'

'No, it's just… never mind. It doesn't matter.'

'Double-page spread each month and you'll have complete editorial control,' Reg said. 'Hire your own freelance writers, do whatever you want. Your name on it an' all. Damn sight better than filling envelopes, eh?'

'Yes.'

'You can have a new job title to go with it. Women's Editor, how does that sound? Impress your mate Don Sykes at the *Courier*, I bet.'

'It will.' She smiled weakly. 'Thanks, Reg. I'll… give it my best.'

Chapter 9

'Reg wants to start a new section in the mag for women readers,' Bobby told Mary glumly in the kitchen later.

Bobby had offered to help her friend make the Christmas cake after work today. Around two months before Christmas was the ideal time, Mary had told her. This would give it time to mature and mellow, ready for the big day. She had scheduled today, the 22nd of October, to bake it and Bobby was rather looking forward to being involved. She hadn't helped to bake a Christmas cake for a long time – not since her mother was alive.

All the ingredients were laid out on the table. Not as abundant and luxurious as they would have been before the war – walnuts were to take the place of almonds, extra sultanas were to be used in place of glacé cherries, a bowlful of grated carrot had been prepared to bulk out the fruit, and margarine had to bolster the butter. Still, with her usual economy Mary had managed to save enough from their ration to produce a cake that would be as moist and rich as the season deserved.

With the sweet, spicy scent of cinnamon and cloves mingling in the air, the kitchen had a truly festive flavour that afternoon. Bobby, who had never been one to get into the Christmas spirit much, nevertheless felt something stir within her in response to smells that evoked memories of childhood.

'Do I take it you're not happy about this women's page then?' Mary said. 'I thought you'd be all for it when Reg told me he was bringing it in. Your own little bit of the magazine to do as you like with.'

'Huh. As long as what I like is patterns for Fair Isle vests and tips on how to brighten up the inside of your blackouts.'

'You can make a start beating together the fat and sugar while I dredge the flour.' Mary placed a bowl and wooden spoon in front of her. 'It needs to be good and creamy.'

'You'll have to give me the recipe. I can put it in the new women's section.' Bobby sighed as she weighed out the butter, margarine and sugar according to the directions in Mary's heavily annotated Be-Ro cookbook. 'I know Reg is trying to be kind in letting me have my own bit. He knows I get frustrated doing dull office work when what I want to do is write. It's just... I don't want to become simply "the woman reporter". Do you know what I mean?'

'I'm not sure as I do. You are a woman reporter.'

'I know I am, but I don't want to be just that. Male reporters aren't assigned only to stories appropriate to their sex, are they? They get to write about whatever they like, so long as it's newsworthy.' She started creaming the fat and sugar together somewhat violently with her spoon. 'When I was with the *Courier* as a typist, one of the male journalists, Tony, would get me to write some of his copy for him. Only it was never the really good stories; the ones he referred to as "juicy". It was WI bazaars and things like that. Women's-interest stuff that he thought was beneath him. And when I got my job here with Reg...'

'...you thought that would be the end of all that,' Mary finished for her.

'Yes. Not that I think there's anything wrong with patterns and recipes. But if you're a woman reporter, once your name gets attached to the cosy domestic pieces then that's all you're seen as good for.'

'Reg will still let you write other things. He doesn't have much choice, with an entire magazine to fill.'

'Perhaps. But what if I have to move on from *The Tyke* one day? I hope I don't, but you never know what the future might hold. I don't want to have a portfolio of nothing but recipes to show prospective employers.' Bobby jabbed savagely at her butter in an attempt to soften it up. 'People before things, Reg is always telling me. That's what engaging writing is all about – what *The Tyke* is all about. And here he is giving me pages of nothing but things to write about.'

'You'll be married soon enough,' Mary said, taking up some dripping to grease the cake tin with. 'Then you won't need to worry about it.'

'I won't give up on my career, married or not. Not unless I'm forced to.' Bobby stopped creaming for a moment to give her arm a rest. 'Besides, it isn't only that. It's something Reg said when he offered it to me.'

'What did he say?'

'That he trusts my judgement. He trusts my judgement as a reporter for this new section – enough to give me complete control – but I still have to fight him tooth and nail for every article I pitch for the mag. I've spent a year trying to impress him with my work and the only thing he trusts my judgement on is bloody knitting patterns. Sorry for swearing.'

Mary finished greasing the tin and wiped her hands on her apron. 'Well, if that's the way you feel about it then you ought to speak to Reg. I'm sure he wouldn't want you to be unhappy in your work.'

Bobby sighed. 'It would sound so ungrateful. He's very generous to offer it to me, and I don't know if I could ever make him understand why I don't want to do it.'

Two curly ginger heads peered around the door. A hairy black-and-white rocket shot out from under them and positioned itself hopefully at Mary's feet.

Mary laughed. 'Oh, no. No dogs in the kitchen while we're baking. Girls, you'll have to take Ace upstairs until we're finished.'

'Please, Mary, may we just have some currants to eat until it's time for supper?' Florrie said, making her eyes wide and appealing.

'I've no currants to spare, I'm afraid. Christmas baking is going to be hard enough this year without you pair of gannets gobbling up everything in sight.' Mary lowered her voice. 'But if you don't tell Reg, I'll let you lick the bowl and spoon when we're done.'

'Thank you, Mary,' they chanted dutifully.

Jessie eyed the large brown mixing bowl hopefully. 'Are you nearly done now?'

'No we are not, we've just started. Now clear out, both of you, and take this trouble-causing puppy with you. I'll call you down when we're ready.'

Soothed by the promise of cake mixture later, the evacuees disappeared. Bobby heard them a moment later thundering upstairs to their attic bedroom with Ace at their heels.

'Poor souls, they get so little that's sweet these days,' Mary said as she began dredging the flour. 'You hardly see spice in the village shop now, and I've been hoarding sugar, fruit and peel like a miser to make cakes and puddings. Still, they'll be grateful for it on Christmas Day.'

'I hope we can still give them a good Christmas in spite of the shortages,' Bobby said. 'They're going to miss their dad terribly.'

Mary sighed. 'They are. Both wrote letters to Father Christmas asking for the same thing. The war to be over, and Daddy to come home. Although being children, there were also requests for a new dolly for Jessie and a toy sword for Florrie. She's become quite a little tomboy since she got to be playmates with that Louis Butcher in her class.'

'I wish I could take them to Bradford to see the Santa Claus at Busby's, the big department store there,' Bobby said. 'It's always such a magical part of the season for my two nieces.'

'How do you and your family celebrate Christmas, Bobby?'

'Nowadays we don't do much. We exchange simple gifts, and decorate a small tree. It's really for the children's benefit that we observe it at all − I mean my brother Raymond's little girls, Susie and Rose. Christmas doesn't seem the same as it did when I was young.'

'Why do you say that?'

'It's never been the same since... since my mam wasn't here to share it with us any more,' Bobby said, not looking up from her mixing. 'She was the one who made it feel like Christmas for us all, even when times were hard. Since then, it's always felt like there was something missing. An empty seat at the table.'

Mary didn't say anything, but she reached out to press Bobby's shoulder with her floury hand. Bobby knew she understood. She and Reg had lost their little girl, Nancy, just a few days before what would have been the child's third Christmas.

'But this year we'll make it fresh again, won't we?' Mary said after a moment's silence, summoning a smile. 'You'll be spending it with your new family here at Moorside. The man you love will be home on leave, not to mention the two motherless little girls with a father far away who'll be needing the magic of Christmastide more than ever. It's always been rather a bittersweet time for Reg and me, but now, with the prospect of bairns to share it with, I must admit I'm right looking forward to it.'

Bobby smiled too. 'It does feel different to be spending it here in the countryside with you and Charlie and the children. I'm looking forward to it too.'

'And of course there'll be Topsy's pantomime,' Mary said. Bobby had filled her in on their friend's latest scheme over breakfast. 'The girls will love that. All the village children will. I don't think we've had a pantomime in Silverdale since before the last war.'

'Do you and Reg decorate a tree at Christmas?'

'Aye, with glass baubles and fairy lights, and I go out gathering greenery to trim the place up with. I've set the girls to making paper chains out of flower paste and old newspaper. We'll need to save some to wrap the gifts as well, now they've banned the sale of wrapping paper. It would be a shame for the bairns not to have that thrill of surprise when they open their presents.'

'I do miss the jolly wrapping we used to have, with little robins and sprigs of holly printed on,' Bobby said wistfully. 'It's going to seem so dark and colourless this year. No wrapping, no big lighted trees in the town squares or fairy lights in the streets, no church bells on Christmas morning and only newspaper to make our decorations.'

'We can bring our own colour,' Mary said firmly. 'Nature has always been generous in that respect. They can't ration holly, can they?'

'Have you thought what gifts you might give the bairns? I went into the toy shop in Settle the last time I was there but there was so little, and all of it poor quality and expensive. Eight and six for a little raggedy teddy bear!'

'Eight and six! You might have got three for that before the war.'

'I think it will need to be handmade presents this year. I pulled out all the old jumpers I could spare and I've been knitting like mad during my ARP shifts, making toys and dolls' clothes for the girls and my nieces.'

Mary smiled. 'Oh, the girls' faces are going to light up on Christmas Day, don't you worry. Leave off your mixing a moment and check round the door to make sure they haven't crept down, then I've summat to show you.'

Bobby did as she was asked.

'They're still upstairs,' she said. 'What is it, Mary?'

'Come into the pantry and you'll see.'

Bobby followed her into the walk-in larder, wondering what the big secret might be. Mary pushed a few things aside. At the back, behind a box of dog biscuits and some sacks of potatoes, was something hidden away. It was large and not quite square, covered by a bedsheet.

Mary twitched this away to reveal the most beautiful dolls' house Bobby had ever seen – the sort she must have dreamed of when she had been a child herself. It had been lovingly carved and painted, with black and white Tudor gabling, bay windows and painted ivy around the door. For a doll-sized person, it would be every bit as luxurious as Sumner House.

'Oh, Mary!' Bobby crouched to look more closely. 'This is beautiful, just beautiful. There was nothing even half so nice in the Settle toy shop. However did you and Reg afford it?'

'We didn't. Charlie sent it.'

'Charlie? Where would he get the money to buy something like this?'

'He made it,' Mary said fondly. 'He always was good with his hands. Seems he's been spending every night in his barracks carving and painting it to give to the girls at Christmas. All the furniture inside too. He must have worked at it for months. He's really got a good heart, Bobby.'

'Charlie made it. My Charlie,' Bobby murmured. 'I had no idea he could... I don't know what to say. Whenever I think I know that man, he surprises me with something new.'

For some reason, she found herself welling up. She dashed the tears away before Mary noticed.

'Reg has been sneaking down to the woodshed to whittle and paint some little dolls to go in it, and I'm sewing tiny outfits for them to wear,' Mary said. 'There are some girl dolls for Jessie and some soldier boys for Florrie, since she's military-mad at the moment. I can't wait to see their faces. I don't think any wealthy child in a big house will have such a fine present this Christmas; not even the princesses themselves.'

'They'll hardly be able to believe it.' Bobby stood up to give her friend a hug. 'Here. This is for you and Reg, who I'm sure will be happy to have you pass on his share. Charlie's I'll keep to give with a kiss the next time I see him. You're all so kind, making sure those little girls have a magical Christmas after the awful things that have happened to them.'

'Of course as his foster mother I'm rather biased, but I'd say you've got a good man there, Bobby.' Mary arched an eyebrow as Bobby released her from the hug. 'If I were you, I'd want to make certain of him as soon as I could. It isn't too late for ye two to arrange a Christmas wedding while Charlie's home on leave.'

Bobby smiled. 'You're still determined to trim up that trousseau for me, aren't you?'

'Well, I've stacks of doilies and net curtain in the linen cupboard doing nothing. Shame to let them go to waste.'

'Except they're not going to go to waste. There'll be gowns galore to trim soon, Mary, and I intend to put you in charge of all of them.'

Mary stared at her. 'Mercy, you're not telling me you and Charlie have finally set a date for the wedding?'

'No,' Bobby said, laughing. 'I'm telling you I want you to be the wardrobe mistress for our Christmas pantomime.'

Chapter 10

As autumn marched towards winter and the trees started to grow bare, Christmas preparations began in earnest – and so did the plans for Topsy's pantomime, which was to take place on the afternoon of Christmas Day at the hospital. Despite her friends' predictions that Topsy's initial enthusiasm would soon wane, she remained excited about her new pet project. Bobby, however, was learning that organising a play in wartime – even a small amateur production – came with problems of its own.

Their greatest enemy was the much-maligned clothing ration. How theatre impresarios managed to clothe entire professional pantomimes, with a cast of seventy or eighty all requiring multiple costume changes, Bobby had no idea. Not to mention that clothing, shoes and material were all so expensive now. Even if you could get the coupons, it was likely to cost a small fortune.

And of course Topsy would insist on *Cinderella* as the Silverdale pantomime, 'because isn't it everyone's favourite, really?'. The boys involved had argued for something more adventurous – Ernie would have had *Ali Baba*, and Archie, who had been eager to take a role now his mother had decreed they would be staying for Christmas, made a strong case for *Sinbad* – but as usual, Topsy had her way. *Cinderella* seemed to have more clothing requirements than any other fairy tale they might have picked – not one but two dames in the Ugly Sisters, and two principal boys in Prince Charming and his valet Dandini. Then there was the transformation scene before the ball, when Cinders' rags were magically changed into a beautiful gown by her Fairy Godmother… it made Bobby's head spin to think of how much material was going to be needed. With only five weeks to go until the performance, the situation was growing quite desperate.

Everyone had been very generous, once an appeal had been put out to the wider Silverdale population. Mary had happily given up the contents of her linen cupboard. Others had contributed old curtains and bedsheets; butter muslin; blackout material; even in one case a yard of parachute silk. Those with coupons to spare had pooled them for the production, and Topsy, generous as ever, had contributed badly needed funds from her coffers to buy what was needed. But with a cast now numbering twenty, they were still struggling to clothe everyone.

Backcloths were another problem. At first they had thought to paint the scenery on to large sheets of paper, but, as Reg was so fond of complaining, paper too was rationed, and what could be had was thin and of poor quality. They couldn't paint directly on to the walls of Sumner House, of course, and any bedsheets donated were to be cut up for costumes. Bobby turned the problem around in her head as she strode over the fells to her friend Andy Jessop's farmhouse one Sunday morning, but no obvious solution presented itself.

Pantomimes were supposed to be lavish affairs: a colourful, tinsel-strewn escape from the drab everyday world into a place of fairy-tale enchantment. This Christmas, as war raged and shortages bit, that mattered more than ever. Even an amateur production such as theirs needed to be able to transport its audience far away from war and worry to a world of magic. How they were supposed to do that with seventy clothing coupons, two old net curtains and a single thin roll of paper for a backdrop was anybody's guess.

At least the man shortage hadn't affected them too badly. Bobby had read in the newspapers that some productions were struggling dreadfully thanks to the call-up, with a number being forced to cast female dames. However, while the Silverdale pantomime's chorus numbers might be a little lacking in the lower registers, they had managed to fill all the traditionally male parts with actual men. Ernie King was to be Buttons, and had impressed Bobby with his comic abilities. His Canadian comrade-in-arms Sandy had stepped into the breach to play Ugly Sister Clotilda opposite Archie Sumner's Lavinia. The other Canadian airman, Chip, had been recruited too, and cast as one of the Broker's Men alongside one of the convalescent patients from the hospital. Where the young Canadians went, so, too, did the village girls, several of whom had now volunteered for the cast and chorus. There was even a part for Teddy, who was to be playing Cinderella's father Baron Hardup at Topsy's insistence. Being involved in an active role had improved his mood greatly, although his brow often lowered when Ernie or Archie were present.

The children from the village school were to be involved as well, with their choir singing a song called 'The Fairy Dance' at the finale. Florence, who had joined the choir just last month, was beside herself with excitement and badgering Mary perpetually about what she was to wear.

Bobby had to admit that in spite of the challenges presented by wartime shortages and the large amount of time this new project was taking up – every minute she didn't spend at work or on duty at the ARP hut these days was filled with rehearsing, sewing costumes or painting props – she was rather enjoying herself. For so long, whenever she closed her eyes to go to sleep she had found herself worrying. About her brothers, about Charlie, about her father, and above all about the outcome of the war. When she did sleep, her dreams were too often haunted by the horror of that night she had climbed Great Bowside to rescue the Polish airmen, and seen the smoking body of their comrade in the plane. Now when she closed her eyes she saw enchanted woods and fairy-tale castles, and puzzled happily over how she could make these visions real for the Parry girls and other children in the village.

She loved the camaraderie of it too. Bobby had lived in Silverdale for over a year now, and she did feel like she belonged to the place. She had friends here, and was greeted warmly whenever she visited the village. Still, she had never been part of a gang before. Now, she really felt like she belonged to something – that she had a little group of like-minded friends in Topsy, Teddy, Jolka, Archie, Ernie and the others involved. Theirs was a friendship group that spanned countries, continents and social classes: a reminder that at the end of the day, people were just people and it was always possible to find things in common despite their differences. The idea brought her comfort.

When Bobby had told Reg she believed working on the pantomime would help the newcomers to the village feel less like outsiders, she hadn't felt she needed to include herself in that. Now she realised that she needed this as much as any of them.

Bobby liked both Ernie and Archie, now she knew them better. She had worried when she met him that Archie might intend something with his attentions to her, but now she had seen him with the other women involved in the show, she realised it was in his upbringing to be attentive and chivalrous to ladies – all except Topsy, who he teased as mercilessly as any brother could have done.

Like his cousin, Archie had nothing of the snob in his nature and worked happily side by side with people from backgrounds very different than his own. He had become a great friend of Sandy, the Canadian airman who was to play the other Ugly Sister, and his willingness to laugh at himself had made him popular with the men in the hospital. Bobby had still to meet his terrifying-sounding mother, who according to Topsy was quite disgusted at the idea of her son and niece being involved in something as vulgar as a pantomime, but it was a relief to find Archie had inherited none of her toffee-nosedness.

Ernie, by contrast, wasn't chivalrous to Bobby at all but joked and teased in a way that reminded her of Charlie in the old days, before he had gone off to war and seemed to become so very serious. Ernie flirted a little with Topsy but never with her, which Bobby was glad of. It meant they could be friends without anyone gossiping, now they had the pantomime to share. She had always appreciated the friendship of men just as much as that of women, but friendship with the other sex too often brought problems – and when you were engaged, those counted for double. Ernie didn't feel like too much of a threat though. She loved talking with him of life in his home country, which sounded a beautiful place: full of mountains, lakes and exotic wild animals like bears and elk.

Bobby realised that, for the first time in a long time, she was actually rather content. She missed Charlie, of course, and the war was a constant worry, but in other respects life had taken a happy turn over the past few weeks. Fortune seemed to be smiling on her. She had the pantomime to focus on, a new group of friends whose company she enjoyed and the jollity of a family Christmas to look forward to. Her father, after some arm-twisting, had eventually been persuaded to apply for Topsy's gamekeeper job and for the past fortnight had been gainfully employed once again, which had greatly improved his mood. The letter from John Cartwright announcing his engagement to Lil, which Bobby had worried would cause her dad some anxiety, had been written in such terms as to win over even the sternest patriarch. Her dad was naturally wary when it came to men who wanted to court his daughters, but the young naval lieutenant had spoken so eloquently of his great respect for his fiancée's father and his affection for Lilian herself that her father was now almost as enthusiastic about the wedding as the prospective bride and groom must be.

Bobby cursed as she slipped in a patch of mud, grasping on to a nearby bilberry bush to stop her landing on her bottom.

It was increasingly difficult to get up to Newby Top Farm to see her elderly friend Andy Jessop and his wife Ginny, although she tried to do so as often as she could. There was so little daylight, and the fells, which had started to feel like old friends when she had spent her summer days exploring their lush greenery and hidden fruits, were hostile and forbidding now the cold weather had arrived.

It wasn't truly winter yet but already they had had a heavy fall of snow, a dusting of which still remained to give an alpine appearance to the undulating landscape spreading out before her. There had been rain, wind and hail in abundance too.

This was the first time Bobby had been able to visit Andy in over a month thanks to the weather. The walk was far from pleasant, with peat bogs and slippery limestone all determined to make her come a cropper before she reached her destination. Her trousers were splattered with mud up to the knees. It reminded her of the very first time she had made this journey, when she was still a green new country reporter and Reg had sent her to interview Andy about his memories of Dales Christmases in times gone by.

Bobby was very glad to arrive at the farmhouse and be ushered into the warm parlour by Andy's granddaughter Mabs, who bustled away to brew a pot of tea for them. A peat fire was roaring in the hearth, which Andy and his wife Ginny sat either side of in their rocking chairs with Andy's elderly dog Shep between them. Andy was smoking his pipe contentedly while Ginny read to him from a newspaper: one of the national dailies.

'Who is it, our lass?' Andy asked his wife on hearing Bobby come in. His eyesight had been growing worse these past six months, although for a man of eighty-two he was generally in good health. He squinted at Bobby in the dim glow of the fire, trying to make her out.

'It's young Miss Bancroft,' Ginny said, beaming genially. 'Here, love, sit yoursen down. You'll bide for a cup o' tea?'

'That would be lovely.' Bobby did as she was told, pulling up a chair. 'Sorry it's been so long since I visited.

The weather's been stinking, and it feels like it's only light for a few hours each day. It seems like ages since I was able to get up and see you both.'

'Aye, we've sore missed seeing thee.' Andy put on his spectacles so he could make her out better. 'White ovver still, like?'

'There's snow on the tops but it's walkable,' Bobby said, feeling rather proud that she had finally learned to decipher the many Dales words and phrases used to describe weather conditions.

'Bring us our paper, did tha?'

'Of course.' Bobby took the latest number of *The Tyke* from her bag and handed it to Ginny. Andy had never learned to read, so he relied on his wife to be his eyes.

'Ahh,' Andy said, sounding satisfied. 'That'll be better nor t' big paper, Gin. Nowt but war, war, war, and all on it bad news. I'm right sick o' bad news, I don't mind telling thee, Miss Bancroft.'

Bobby nodded sympathetically. 'I know just how you feel. What were you reading about, Mrs Jessop?'

'Bad news for farmers is what,' Ginny said soberly. 'Says here there's a new bill being discussed in Parliament that'll scrap the Reserved Occupations Schedule. Lord knows who'll run this place if they take t' lads. There's even talk of conscripting women to war work if they aren't married. If our Mabs has to go, I don't know how me and her mam will manage the house and cooking between us. I'm too old to do much these days, though I've always kept an active body.'

'I've been worrying about it myself,' Bobby said. 'I want to do my part for the war effort, of course, but I'd hate to leave *The Tyke*.'

'Waste of that brain o' thine to be put to making munitions or the like,' Andy said. 'But happen they'll think better on it. Says in t' paper some politician is worried about it damaging birth rate if they send all our young lasses off to war.'

'Or helping it,' Ginny muttered darkly. 'I wouldn't like to send any young female kin of mine off to barracks wi' all them soldiers.'

'Well then, Miss Bancroft, what news?' Andy asked, sitting up straighter as he prepared to enjoy a much-missed gossip. 'Long time sin I was able to get down to t' village, and young 'uns don't tell us stories tha does. The Jessops are farmers, not writers. Their news is nowt but tups and yows.'

'Tell us of yoursen first,' Ginny said. 'Is your father keeping well?'

'Yes, he's started a new job just recently,' Bobby said. 'Lady Sumner-Walsh has made him the gamekeeper for the woods on the edge of her estate.'

'Hard job for t' winter, that,' Andy observed. 'How does he find it?'

'He's cold and tired at the end of the day but I do believe he loves it,' Bobby said, smiling. 'My dad's not a Dalesman by birth but being outdoors comes naturally to him, all the same. So does the work. He's been sleeping like a baby since he took it up, and of course the extra money comes in handy.'

'Right glad to hear it. What else? Rest o' t' family well?'

'As far as I know. My sister is engaged to be married to a young naval officer. They're aiming to tie the knot in March, or earlier if they can.'

'Thy father happy wi' it? He likes the young man?'

'They haven't met yet but Dad's given his blessing. Lilian's fiancé wrote him a very eloquent letter asking for permission to wed her, and of course that put him straight into my dad's good books. He appreciates any old-fashioned mark of respect from young men aiming to court his daughters.'

Mabs came in with the tea tray and a little plate of arrowroot biscuits, which old Shep cast a hopeful eye over from his position by the fire. She started setting them out on a little table.

'Do send our congratulations,' Ginny said. 'Is there owt new happening in the village?'

'Everyone's bustling about getting ready for the festive season,' Bobby said. 'The church Sunday School have been rehearsing a Nativity play, the ladies of the WVS are haranguing everyone about donating Christmas comforts for the troops and there's a pantomime being organised for the children and injured airmen at the hospital. It's to be *Cinderella*.'

'Oh aye? Whose idea were that then?' Andy asked.

'Lady Sumner-Walsh's. She's working ever so hard to bring it about. A lot of people are, including me.'

'I heard about that,' Mabs Jessop said as she handed Bobby a cup of tea. 'Laura Bailey told me she were to be Fairy Godmother.'

'That's right,' Bobby said. 'A few of the girls in the village are going to be involved.'

'Who's Cinderella then?'

'Um, I am,' Bobby said, blushing. 'I'd rather have done something backstage but Topsy – that is, Lady Sumner-Walsh insisted. Since she's paying for everything, we have to go along with what she wants really.'

'Them Canadians doing it, are they?' Mabs asked in a suspiciously casual tone as she handed a cup of tea to her step-grandmother.

Bobby smiled. 'They are. Ernie is to be Buttons, Sandy an Ugly Sister and Chip a Broker's Man. It sounds a little strange in their accents but they're all very funny. Actually, it's a very international pantomime. Jolka Zielinski, who is the wife of one of the Polish airmen, is playing Prince Charming, and another Polish airman is Baron Hardup.'

'Not the young man who was so badly hurt in that dreadful crash?' Ginny asked with interest.

'Yes: Teddy Nowak, the pilot. He and Topsy have rewritten the part so his wheelchair is accounted for. It's improved his mood a lot being involved.'

'Happen I might be in it if you're still short o' folk,' Mabs said nonchalantly. 'I seen a pantomime once. It had a cat in it – I mean, not a real cat. It were a girl dressed as a cat. I never laughed so much.'

'If you're to be in it, who's to help me get this house ready for Christmas, I should like to know?' Ginny said sharply. 'You spend too much of your time chasing lads, Mabs Jessop. Don't think I don't know what's on your mind. I've heard all about these young foreigners bewitching our girls.'

'Why should I not be in it if Laura is? I can sing and dance fair. I took a prize for dancing at school,' Mabs added, somewhat proudly. 'Laura never took no prizes for it. What's more I've got better legs than what she's got, and I think if she's to be fairy then I ought to be summat too.'

'Ah, let the bairn have her fun, Gin,' Andy said to his wife. 'She'll spend time enough doing chores when she's grown and wed. Besides, I can remember when tha were as keen as any a bonny young lass round here to have a dance and a song. Sounds like half the village is ganging to be in this pantomime. Not right for our Mabs to be stuck up here missing out on t' Christmas festivities while others gad.'

'We'd certainly be happy to have you involved, Mabs,' Bobby said. 'We only have a small chorus, and Maimie would be very grateful for someone to help her with the choreography. It sounds as though you'll be the most accomplished dancer.'

'Can I then?' Mabs asked her grandparents eagerly. 'I'll not shirk my jobs here, promise.'

'Aye, well,' Ginny said, softening. 'If Miss Bancroft is there to keep you honest and your mind off lads in uniform, happen you might play at dressing up wi' t' other girls. But mind you don't neglect your duties at home, Mabs.'

'I won't, Ginny.' Mabs went to give her step-grandmother a kiss, and Ginny, mollified, patted her hand.

'Well, you're not a bad lass. Back to Mam, then, and get Sunday dinner on.'

'Saw a pantomime missen once,' Andy observed thoughtfully as Mabs went back to the kitchen. 'Christmas were nowt but another day to me as a bairn, as tha knows, Miss Bancroft, but there were one year when chapel Sunday School took us to see a play out Skipton way as a treat. A charity paid for us poor childer to go. Don't remember t' story, but there were a harlequin and a fairy queen, and a demon in a cape who appeared out o' nowhere in a cloud of smoke. For a lad of eight year who'd never seen so much as a magic lantern show afore, it were like real magic. Afterwards they give us a toy whistle each and an orange to take home. A whole orange apiece! I'd never had such riches.' His eyes sparkled with the memory. 'Is that what tha's planning, Miss Bancroft?'

'Yes, it will be something like that,' Bobby said, sipping her tea. 'We aren't charging for tickets, so everyone who wants to come can do so. We hope it will cheer the evacuee children who are forced to spend Christmas away from their parents, and the wounded men in the hospital who'll be missing their own bairns. Everything's so awful at the moment, a little magic feels like exactly what people need.'

'Aye, I'd say it is at that.'

'We had them in the village when my bairns were small,' Ginny said, her eyes far away. 'Oh, how they shouted! It were their favourite part of Christmas. I don't know why they were ever stopped. I suppose the war put an end to them.'

'And now it's taken another war to bring them back,' Bobby said, smiling. 'It isn't easy though. We need to find clothes for twenty people – or twenty-one, if your Mabs is going to be joining us. Most of the principals will need at least one costume change for the ball. But clothes and material cost so much now, and it's almost impossible to get enough coupons to cover it even with everyone pitching in. I can't think what we're going to do about the scenery either. The only paper we can get is too thin to paint on, and there's barely enough of that.'

'Oh! I might have the very thing to help you,' Ginny said, pushing herself to her feet. 'Now you finish your tea, Miss Bancroft, and I'll be back in no time. Summat I need to fetch.'

Bobby had just drained her cup, grateful for the warmth of the hot liquid as it settled in her belly, when

Ginny reappeared with a roll of something grey under her arm.

'Canvas panels from an old tent. I found them in Andy's attic when I were clearing it out,' she said as she laid the roll down at Bobby's feet. 'I wouldn't be surprised if they'd been up there sin his mother were alive. I'm afraid they're filthy wi' dust but if there's nowt better then you're welcome to have them. I was going to put them out for salvage.'

Bobby bent down to examine the material. She rubbed away some of the greasy dust that gave it its grey appearance, discovering that underneath the muck, the thick canvas was a yellowing cream in colour. It was stiff and rather ancient-looking, too inflexible for costumes, but it would be good enough to paint scenery on to.

'You really don't mind if I take all this, Mrs Jessop?' she asked.

'You're very welcome to it, my love, if it'll make those poor bairns far away from home smile this Christmas. Please, have it with our blessing.'

Chapter 11

The canvas Ginny had given her was rather heavy, and Bobby made slow progress downhill with it under her arm. She was due to meet Topsy and the others at Sumner House for the principals' costume fittings, and she couldn't wait to surprise them with her unexpected contribution.

She had been planning to cycle from Silverdale to the stately home – her bike was waiting for her against the wall of the post office, where she always left it – but there was no way of securing her treasure to the old machine. Instead she waited outside the Golden Hart, knowing that old Bert the coalman would be along shortly with his wagon and elderly arthritic horse. When Bert arrived, she paid him the shilling fee for a lift, threw her bicycle and the canvas in the back of the wagon and climbed up.

Bert's horse went at a speed only marginally faster than Bobby's walking pace, but nevertheless, the coalman dropped her off at the top of the Sumner House drive half an hour later. Bobby left her bicycle leaning against a tree and made her way to the house. When she reached it she dumped her pile of canvas outside the door, not wanting the dust and soot with which it was currently afflicted to compromise the cleanliness of the ward. Her own clothes were bad enough.

The matron, once so wary of civilian outsiders, was all smiles as she opened the door to Bobby in answer to a pull on the bell rope. She approved very much of Topsy's pantomime scheme, despite the disruption it was causing to the hospital's routine, and was always glad to grant access to any of those involved.

'I do think it's wonderful, what all of you are doing,' she told Bobby warmly as she guided her to the dormitory in the big hall where the pantomime preparations were taking place. 'Those boys have been so brave, and it just broke my heart to see them downcast. Now the ward rings with laughter. I'm sure it's true when they say it's the best medicine.'

There was indeed laughter coming from the ward. When Bobby was shown in, she discovered the hilarity was being caused by Archie and Sandy in their hideous Ugly Sister costumes and wigs. They were performing a comic song for the men in the beds, who heckled them good-naturedly. Ernie was up a ladder, fixing up a spotlight, but he had stopped to smoke a cigarette and watch the entertainment below. Topsy, Mary, Piotr and Jolka were there too, with little Tommy holding on to his father's hand. Jolka was in her new principal boy costume, her long legs showing to perfection in the short tunic and tights. Her husband couldn't take his eyes off her, and some of the patients were slyly stealing glances her way as well.

'Birdy, you're here at last.' Topsy claimed her and dragged her to the little group of fledgling impresarios. 'Oh, and your clothes are filthy! Where have you been? We've been waiting for you this last hour.'

'I had something to bring. I'll tell you in a moment when the boys have finished messing about.' Bobby laughed as Archie pretended to trip over and Sandy kicked him in the rump. 'They really work well together, don't they?'

'You look like my old woman after she's had one over the eight, Archie,' a man with a cockney accent called from his bed while Archie staggered to his feet again.

'Where do you think I got these clothes?' Archie called back, and everyone laughed.

'Well, Archibald, shall we dance?' Sandy asked him with a formal bow.

'Only if I can lead.'

They launched into another routine, waltzing, deadpan, along the aisle between the beds.

Bobby looked around the room as the two men played the fool, feeling rather proud of what they had achieved so far. It was true that they had no scenery, and as yet only a small handful of the costumes that would be needed, but they had done a lot in the three weeks they had been working. The men from the hospital had been keen to get involved, and there was a job for everyone, even those unable to leave their beds. Nearly all of the patients had helped to make and paint props, or toys that would be given as gifts to the children – many of those in bed currently had some small item by them that they were working on. A large piece of wood had been cut and painted to look like a pumpkin and was drying against a wall. Once dry, the other side would be painted as lavishly as wartime shortages would allow to become Cinderella's coach.

There had been another row of beds at the front of the room when they had begun, but since these were presently unoccupied, the matron had given her permission for them to be dismantled and stored until after

Christmas. In their place a stage area had been demarcated, with medical screens set up either side for the 'wings'. A pair of drop curtains had been constructed from blackout material, decorated with tinfoil stars to give the impression of a night sky, which one of the more technically minded hospital patients had hooked up to a rope and pulley. Their little pantomime was unlikely to give Francis Laidler any sleepless nights, everything done on the hoof with what scraps they could muster, but the effect was impressive nevertheless.

'Well, Birdy, what is this big surprise that's made you late?' Topsy asked when the two men had finished their dance.

'A solution to our backcloth problem, I hope,' Bobby said. 'Ginny Jessop donated a roll of canvas from an old tent. It's rather antique and very dirty, but I think it ought to scrub up well enough. I left it at the front door so I wasn't filling the place with dust.'

Topsy clapped her hands. 'Oh, wonderful! I'll take it back to the cottage so Maimie and I can get to work cleaning it up. You are clever, Birdy.'

Bobby laughed. 'I didn't do anything except bemoan the lot of the wartime pantomime producer. Mind you, I did have a heck of a time getting it down the hill.' She turned to Mary. 'The Sisters' costumes look spectacular. I mean, they look horrendous, but in a spectacular way, which of course is the whole point. Well done, Mary.'

'Your friend is talented in many ways, Bobby,' Jolka observed. 'Mary, you must show Bobby and the rest what you have done for us.'

Mary blushed. 'Oh, it isn't anything very impressive. Nothing like what Jolka could have made, but she insisted I ought to do it.'

'May we see?' Topsy asked.

Mary took a card folder from her handbag and removed a sheet of paper from it. She handed it to Topsy.

'It's a poster,' she said a little shyly. 'I thought we could put them in the shops around the village.'

'But Mary, this is excellent!' Topsy said. 'I didn't know you had art skills as well.'

Bobby took the paper from Topsy to examine it. It bore the name of the pantomime in old-fashioned illuminated lettering, along with the venue, time and date of the performance. Vivid line drawings of Cinderella in her ballgown, the glass slipper and pumpkin coach brought the story to life.

'Did you really draw this, Mary?' she said.

'Yes. Reg is going to take it to the printer in Settle and have him mimeograph some copies for us. I'm sorry it isn't better.'

'It is far better than anything I could have produced,' Jolka said. 'Never do I paint figures, because my figures never come out right. I could not make the magic you have made here, Mary.'

Jolka was a much sought-after landscape painter, whose work sold for large sums. Mary flushed with pleasure at the compliment from a professional artist.

'It's nothing, really,' she said. 'I must leave and get back to the bairns soon, before the house is turned upside down. Bobby, it's you I was waiting for. I want you to try on your ballroom costume so I can see where it will need adjusting.'

'Oh. Has it been made? I didn't think we had enough material.'

'Yes, I scraped together just enough from some curtain net Ida Wilcox donated. Go into the little room and try it on – there's a mirror in there. I'll watch the door to make sure no man walks in on you.'

Bobby took the bundle of white material Mary pushed into her arms and went into the little study adjoining the ward. It had previously been used for storing bedframes and screens, but had now been repurposed as a dressing room for the pantomime cast.

She shook out the frock Mary had sewn for her. It was white, constructed of an assortment of material oddments. The shift was of cheap butter muslin, sewn double to give it the necessary thickness. There was an overskirt and train of net, trimmed with little white roses Mary had crocheted.

It didn't look like much draped across her arm, but when Bobby had divested herself of her mud-stained slacks and woollen pullover to put it on… it was beautiful. The gauzy curtain net floated as she twirled in front of the mirror. Mary had found a small amount of satin from somewhere for the bodice – or perhaps it was parachute silk – and it clung flatteringly to Bobby's curves, the neck-line showing just the smallest amount of bust. Somehow, her friend had managed to take the cobbled-together scraps of second-hand material and make something fit for a princess. Or for a bride…

There was a knock on the door.

'Are you going to come out so we can see you?' Mary called. 'It's no use being coy now you're an actress, young Bobby.'

Smiling, Bobby emerged.

'Don't think I don't know what you're up to, trying to tempt me,' she whispered. 'You and your trousseaux.'

'Oh, sweetheart.' Mary held her back to look at her, then turned her around. 'You look just beautiful. I wish our Charlie were here to see you.'

Ernie, who had come down from his ladder, gave a low whistle. 'Nice job, Mrs A. Now that's a real Cinderella transformation. You know, Slacks, you almost look like a girl.'

Bobby laughed. 'Ernie, you say the sweetest things.'

'Worst things about this war, if you ask me: women in uniform and women in pants. Give me a girl in ribbons and satin gowns any day.'

Archie, who was still in his polka-dot Ugly Sister dress, winked at him. 'I'm all yours, darling.'

'I always did say you'd make a better fairy than a dame, pal,' Ernie said, and Archie laughed.

'You ever going to join us for a crack at the Boche, Archie?' the cockney airman who'd heckled him before asked. 'We can use every man.'

'Just waiting for His Majesty to give me the word my services are required, Jack,' Archie said. 'Raring to go as soon as I'm wanted.'

Bobby frowned. Hadn't Topsy said Archie had been invalided out of the RAF due to some problem with his blood? Why wouldn't he tell the other men that?

Archie turned his attention back to Bobby. 'You do look smashing, darling. Ready for the altar, eh? If your young man ever leaves you in the lurch, you need only say the word.'

'Oh, stop teasing me, Arch,' Bobby said. 'Mary, may I change back now?'

'Let me have a good look at you first.' Mary cast her needlewoman's eye over the dress, turning Bobby around to see it from all angles. 'Hmm. A little tight around the bust, and too loose around the waist. All right, take it off again while I go see to Jolka. I'll have it adjusted for next time.'

Bobby, feeling embarrassed at having so many male eyes casting appreciative looks over her figure and décolletage, was glad to get back into her mud-splattered walking clothes. When she emerged from the changing room, she found Archie waiting outside. He was still in his dame dress but his large orange wig was now tucked under his arm.

'Sorry for lurking about while you were in your scanties, old girl,' he said. 'I bagged the next go at the changing room. Ernie thinks I'm becoming a bit too fond of the dress.'

'Well, it's all yours,' Bobby said. Archie made to pass her, but she put a hand on his arm. 'Archie. Is that true, what you told the others? Are you still waiting for your call-up?'

'That's right. I seem to be bottom of the list.'

'Only… sorry, I know it isn't my business, but Topsy did say you joined the Volunteer Reserve after Munich and the RAF invalided you out last year for medical reasons.'

'Told you that, did she?' He lowered his voice. 'Look here, Bobby, I wish you wouldn't say anything in front of those fellows. Only it's rather embarrassing, you know, to be hoofed out like that because you don't pass muster. They'll send me up something rotten about it.'

'Of course. Not if it's a secret. I'm sorry, I ought not to have mentioned it.' She paused, but she couldn't stop herself asking. 'I hope it isn't anything very dreadful. The thing that's wrong with you.'

Archie smiled, looking away. 'Nothing worse than being left-handed.'

'They don't invalid you out for that, do they? Topsy said you had a blood disease or something.'

He laughed softly. 'Yes, that's about the size of it. Something in my blood.'

'What did you mean, then, about being left-handed?'

'Oh, just my little joke. Perhaps I'll explain it to you one day.' He examined her face keenly. 'You know, Bobby, I almost think I might. You've got the right sort of eyes.'

Bobby blinked. 'So you're all right? You're not terribly ill or anything?'

'If I was, would you cry at my graveside?'

'I've become rather fond of you in the last few weeks, if that's what you mean. Strictly in a friendly fashion, I should add,' she said, waggling her engagement ring at him.

Archie smiled. 'I'm all right. Thanks for caring though. You promise you won't say anything to the boys?'

'I told you I wouldn't.'

He clapped her on the shoulder as he passed her to go into the changing room. 'You know, I could tell you were a decent sort the moment I met you. Thanks, Bobby, you're a trump.'

He disappeared and Bobby walked away, feeling puzzled. She wasn't sure what Archie considered so shameful in having been invalided out of the RAF. Plenty of men failed their medicals, or had to leave the forces due to injury or illness, and if Archie had been courageous enough to join up before conscription then surely his new friends wouldn't rib him for it. But if he wanted her discretion, he was welcome to it.

She approached Piotr, who, she noted, was now out of hospital blues and back in his regular RAF uniform. He was watching Jolka proudly while Mary examined her costume a little distance away, taking measurements and jotting them down. Their son Tommy, meanwhile, was being entertained by one of the patients, who had created a puppet from one of his bedsocks and was performing a ventriloquist act for the little boy. Tommy giggled as the sock puppet snake pretended to bite his nose.

'See how all eyes turn to my wife,' Piotr said to Bobby. 'She is very beautiful, is she not?'

'As beautiful as she is talented,' Bobby said with a smile. 'Don't you mind, Piotr?'

'What should I mind?'

'Well, that so many of the men here are looking at her legs.'

'Why should I mind this? It is a compliment to her beauty. It is right they should pay her compliments.'

'Some husbands might feel jealous. They wouldn't like their wives showing off their bodies to other men in that fashion.'

'Such husbands do not trust their wives to be faithful, perhaps. It has never occurred to me to feel that way.'

'You know, Piotr, I never knew a couple quite like you and Jolka,' Bobby said. 'It always does me good to see you together.'

'But sadly we will not be together for much longer,' Piotr said soberly. He gestured to his uniform. 'You see, I am considered fit to resume my duties at last. Next week I will return to barracks to complete my training. I will be glad to rejoin the fight, but I will miss my wife and boy.'

'They'll miss you. We all will.' Bobby turned to him. 'You will write to us, won't you?'

'Of course. I shall write to you especially, my saviour on the mountain, and you may share all my news with Tadeusz and Topsy at the cottage. I hope to find him there with her still when I return.'

'How do you mean?'

'You know very well, I think.'

Bobby smiled. 'Perhaps I do. Teddy seems determined to disappoint all of us who would play Cupid for him though.'

'God will find a way, if something is meant to be. And I believe this is meant to be.'

'Piotr, will you do something for me?' Bobby asked.

'If it is in my power.'

'When you get back to your camp… will you keep an eye on Charlie for me? He's been so serious and sad lately, in his letters and when I saw him last. I can't help worrying something is wrong.'

'Hmm.' Piotr pursed his lips. 'He spoke to you of this man Hunt, I suppose.'

'The CO,' Bobby said, her brow knitting. 'He did, but he wouldn't tell me much. I don't think he wants me to worry. I'm sure something there is putting him under stress though.'

'Well, I will see what I can learn. But I may not be able to write much of it – at least not openly. Every letter sent out will be read first by Hunt or one of his spies.'

'I understand that, but I'll feel better for knowing he has a friend there. Thank you.'

Piotr turned to look at her. 'You are blooming today, Bobby, despite your worry for the young man. So often lately when you have been to visit Jolka and I, you have seemed wan and tired. You are happy?'

Bobby looked around the room: at Ernie, Sandy and Archie, now back in his regular clothes, as they joked and laughed together; at Mary, Topsy and Jolka, deep in conversation about costumes and posters; at little Tommy, being petted and spoiled by the men in the beds who missed their own children far away; at the makeshift stage with its starlight curtains, and the dusky orange of their painted pumpkin.

'For the first time in a while… yes, I think I am happy,' she said. 'This, planning the pantomime – it's brought something into my life other than worry about the war. I thought when it all started that I was doing it for the children in the village, and the men here. But I needed it as much as any of them, I think. I suppose these days, we all need a little magic to believe in.'

Chapter 12

Two weeks later, Bobby was beginning her morning routine as she always did: lighting the fire with numb fingers while she waited for her father to rise. It was now the 3rd of December, and the weather had taken a decidedly wintry turn. There were two inches of fresh snow outside this morning – not to mention inside, where the wind had blown back the draught excluder to deposit some soft, loose powder on the doormat.

The weather couldn't stop intrepid Gil Capstick, the sub-postmaster, from going about his work, however. Three envelopes dropped through the letterbox just as Bobby was applying a match to one of the firelighters. She went to pick them up, scanning the envelopes eagerly in the hope of finding something from Charlie. It had been over a week since she had heard from him last, and as dry as his letters tended to be these days, they at least helped Bobby feel a little closer to her absent sweetheart.

Her stomach leapt when she saw that one of the envelopes bore the familiar RAF censor's stamp. A quick glance at the service number and rank scrawled on the back, however, showed it wasn't from Charlie. Disappointed, Bobby tore it open.

It was from Piotr, who had now returned to his station. She skimmed through his reports of drilling, gun range practice and navigation training to see if he had sent any news of Charlie. Sure enough, the fourth paragraph of the letter contained the information she had been hoping for, although it was of necessity rather cryptic.

> *Of the young friend of whom you wished me to make enquiries, I send the good news that he is in fine health. You must not fear he does not find friends here, Bobby – he is well liked by both men and officers. He has one close friend in particular: a shy, quiet young man of rather tender years named Bram. You must ask him of this friend when you see him in person. I will say no more for now, but you may trust in me.*

After that, the letter moved on to more everyday concerns. Presumably by smuggling the news about Charlie between more mundane passages and keeping it suitably vague, Piotr hoped to avoid drawing the attention of his CO, this Squadron Leader Hunt, and his spies.

Bobby read his words again, puzzling over them. What did it mean? Piotr seemed anxious she should know about this friend, Bram, although Charlie had never mentioned a Bram in his letters. It wasn't a name she had encountered before, and she wasn't sure whether it might be a Christian name or surname. She wondered if the man was perhaps Polish, like Piotr, and why her friend was so keen for her to know about the connection to Charlie. It was all rather mysterious, but since she and Charlie couldn't communicate freely by letter, she supposed it would be some time before she was able to learn more.

Her father appeared from his bedroom as she was tucking the letter away. He was already dressed in his outdoor wear, ready for another day of work.

'I heard t' post,' he said as he sat down. 'Owt from your sister about the wedding?'

Bobby looked at the other two envelopes. 'No, nothing from Lil. There's one from our friend Don and the other feels like it might be a Christmas card.'

'What's Don got to say then?'

She tore open Don's letter and smiled as she read it. 'Oh, how lovely.'

'What?'

'The baby's arrived – a little boy. Joan went into labour on Tuesday night. A little earlier than expected but mother and baby are none the worse for that. Don was worried to death about the birth, with all the trouble they had conceiving and Joan's age, but it sounds like it was all straightforward. Five pounds eleven ounces.'

'I'm right glad to hear it,' her dad said, although he blushed slightly at hearing the details of the birth. 'Have they picked a name for the little lad?'

She skimmed the letter. 'Yes, they're calling him – oh! He's to be named Robert, after me – and after you too, I suppose. Isn't that wonderful? And what's more, we're both asked to be godparents.'

Her dad swelled proudly.

'Godparents, eh? That's a devil of a responsibility,' he said. 'Reckon you're up to it, our Bobby?'

'I don't know. It's a scary prospect. I'd like to think I can do right by him.'

'Surprised they're asking me.'

Bobby smiled. 'I don't see why you should be. You and Don seemed to become bosom pals pretty quickly after I moved out here. Every time I had a letter from him, he mentioned another drinking session with you in one of the locals. I was constantly berating him for leading you astray.'

'Huh,' he said with a small smile. 'I'm sure his missus thinks it was other way around.'

Her dad tried to look unconcerned, but Bobby could tell he was touched by the gesture. He had always thought a lot of Don, who, she knew, reminded him of the brother he had lost in the last war. A friendship had sprung up between the two when she had asked Don to keep an eye on her father after she had left him to take a job out here in the Dales. Although Don's visits to her dad had been a favour to her at first, a genuine regard had grown up between them during that time. This proof of his friend's liking and respect for him clearly meant more to her dad than he felt comfortable expressing.

'Joan must be so happy,' Bobby said. 'Don said she'd always wanted one of each.' She scanned down the letter. 'Sal's been worrying about her mam, Don says, but she's thrilled to have a new baby brother. The christening is at St John's Church in Great Horton in ten days' time. The parents were keen to have it before Christmas. Will you come?'

'Can hardly say no if I'm to be godfather, can I? Tell him I'd be honoured.' Her dad nodded to the other envelope. 'Who's the card from?'

Bobby opened it and pulled a face. 'Ugh. It isn't a Christmas card, it's a party invitation from Topsy. I was hoping I wouldn't have to go.'

'Having a Christmas do, is she?'

'Yes – well, sort of. She's holding a fundraising event at Woodside Nook for all her wealthy friends in a couple of weeks to raise money for our pantomime. We want to give all the children who come a tea after, and a little toy to take home. She says in her note that she'd like all of the pantomime organisers to show their faces – best bibs and tuckers required.'

'Will you go then?'

'I suppose I shall have to. Usually I try to think of an excuse when she invites me to these fancy things, but if it's for the pantomime I ought to be there.' Bobby put the card away. 'How was work yesterday?'

Her dad sat up a little straighter, always enthusiastic when it came to discussing his new job. 'Aye, not bad. Flushed out a nest of rats that had been causing trouble for waterfowl on t' lake. They won't be giving her ladyship any more worry.' He nodded to the pantry. 'Present for you and Mary in there too. Brought us home a brace of rabbits for supper.'

Bobby frowned. 'Dad...'

'Oh, don't give me that look. They were a gift, all right? We're having to cull some before their breeding season in February.' He laughed. 'Pete must be slacking if there's conies to spare round here.'

'Topsy gave them to you?'

'Aye. Never had much time for toffs but she's not a bad sort, your friend. Don't look down her nose at you like most on 'em do. That aunt of hers looks at me like she's wiped me off her shoe.'

'I didn't realise you'd met her.'

'She come down wanting to organise summat for Boxing Day. Called me "Bancroft" like she were saying a dirty word. It's always "Mr Bancroft" from t' young lady. That's true class, that is.'

'What's Mrs Sumner organising for Boxing Day?'

'A hunting party for her and some pals. Tradition, apparently.' He sniffed. 'Don't much fancy a bunch of upper-crust types playing horsey around my place, looking down on us common folk. Still, it's the job.'

'Well, thank Topsy from me for the rabbits if you see her today. I'll take them over to Mary when I go for breakfast.'

Bobby went to the pantry to take a look at them. They looked a little stringy and lean, as she supposed winter rabbits would tend to be, but meat for supper would be a rare treat. As glad as she was when her father had given up poaching with Pete, the whole family had missed the meals of rabbit, trout and pheasant they had occasionally enjoyed in the summer.

Bobby was about to go back to her room to get ready for work when she paused. Her eyes were drawn to the bottle of green liquor her father had bought from Pete Dixon. As far as she knew, he hadn't touched the stuff since going to work for Topsy. She smiled when she saw that the level in the bottle hadn't changed.

–

The side door at Moorside was usually unlocked by Mary in the mornings so Bobby and her father could join the Athertons for breakfast whenever they were ready, but when Bobby had traipsed through the snow to the farmhouse with the rabbits over her shoulder, she was surprised to find it still locked. She knocked, and a moment later it was opened by Florence. The little girl was in her school clothes, a funereal expression on her face.

'Why do you look like that, Florrie?' Bobby asked, alarmed. 'Did something bad happen?'

Florrie glanced behind her to make sure no one was listening.

'It's Jessie,' she said in a low voice. 'She's in disgrace.'

'In disgrace? Whatever for?'

'Telling stories. Mary sent her to our room without breakfast and she ain't half giving her a telling off, Bobby. I never seen her so cross before. She hardly ever shouts.'

The child sounded scared, and Bobby crouched to bring herself level.

'I'm sure Mary's just flustered from getting everything ready for Christmas,' she said soothingly. 'I know Jessie doesn't lie.'

'She has been telling lies though, for ages and ages. Mary found it out this morning when she weren't on time for breakfast again.' Florrie blinked frightened eyes at her. 'You don't think her and Reg will send us away, do you?'

'I know they wouldn't.' Bobby's gaze drifted towards the stairs. The sound of raised voices was coming from the attic. 'I'd better go see what's going on. Don't worry, Florrie. We'll soon smooth things over again, I'm sure. Now take this brace of rabbits to hang in the larder and finish your breakfast.'

After handing over the rabbits, Bobby made her way upstairs to the attic. Jessie was sitting on a little chair, brow knit into a scowl and cheeks wet with recent tears, while Mary stood over her with her arms folded. Reg was there too, leaning on his stick and looking worried.

'Well?' Mary demanded of Jessie. 'What do you have to say for yourself?'

'Nothing,' the girl said petulantly. 'I ain't sorry. I didn't do anything wrong. It's you who's doing the wrong thing, not me.'

'This is my home, young lady, and while you're in it you abide by my rules. I don't appreciate being tricked and lied to under my own roof.'

'Go easy on the lass, Mary,' Reg said. 'She's nobbut a bairn.'

'A bairn old enough to know better. I've a good mind to write to your father of you, Jessica Parry.'

'Mary, what's going on?' Bobby asked. Jessie was generally a well-behaved child: meek, polite and hard-working. Certainly she had never shown any tendency to be either stubborn or deceitful, yet here she was with her arms folded defiantly while she refused to apologise for telling a deliberate lie.

'Perhaps you ought to ask madam here,' Mary said, indicating Jessie.

'What did you do, Jessie?'

The child sniffed and wiped her nose on her sleeve. 'Nowt.'

Reg's lips twitched at hearing her lapse into the local vernacular, but he managed to keep a straight face.

'You must have done something or Mary wouldn't be cross,' Bobby said.

'She's been lying to me about those ruddy hens for weeks now,' Mary said. 'Every day I ask her to tally up how many eggs there are and which hen they're from. She's been keeping them on rotation to stop me finding out Henrietta still isn't laying.'

'That ain't as wrong as killing Henrietta to eat,' Jessie said, jutting her chin out stubbornly. 'Killing's loads worse than lying – God says. It's a Commandment and everything.'

'There are no Commandments about hens. There is, however, one about lying. Now are you going to say sorry and come down to breakfast?' Mary demanded. 'If not, you may stay up here and think about what you've done until it's time to go to school. And you needn't think you'll be going with your friends to the Sunday School Christmas treat this weekend either.'

Jessie's lip wobbled, but she stayed firm. 'I shan't say sorry. I did it to save Henrietta and that ain't a wrong thing, so… so there.'

'Then you may stay here. I've no patience with you today, young lady.' Mary left and marched back downstairs.

'Well you've done it now, haven't you?' Reg said to the little girl, trying and failing to look stern. It was clear he was sympathetic, although he felt he ought to back up his wife.

'I never meant to make Mary cross,' she whispered. 'I just didn't want Henrietta to get killed, and I don't think I should have to say sorry when I tried to do something good. I am sorry Mary's upset but I ain't sorry for trying to save Henrietta.'

Reg sighed. 'Happen she'll have calmed down by the time you're back from school. But one way or another, Jess, one of the hens is going on the Christmas table. I'm sorry but that's life in the country. If you're going to stay with us here, you'll have to learn to cope with how things are.'

The wobbling lip wobbled a little more, and Jessie burst into tears.

'Come on now, none of that. Stiff upper lip, eh?' Reg said, looking embarrassed by the girl's tears.

Bobby crouched down to give her a hug, and Jessie buried her wet face in Bobby's shoulder.

'Will we be sent away, Bobby?' Jessie whispered. 'Florrie said Mary might send us away for making her cross.'

'No one's going to send you away.' She glanced up at Reg. 'Are they?'

'Certainly not,' Reg said firmly. 'This is your home.'

Jessie sniffed. 'But Mary never shouted at us before.'

'Well, you never lied to her before,' Bobby said. 'You really ought to say sorry, Jess. I know you wanted to help Henrietta, but you must understand why that would hurt Mary's feelings after she's been so kind to you. You know, she loves you both very much.'

'Does she?'

'Of course she does. Don't you know where the new hat and mittens she gave you in the autumn came from?'

'Mary knitted 'em for us.'

'Not only that. She pulled something of her own apart to get enough wool for them, like every new thing you have. Not because she didn't want or need it, but because she cares more about you and your sister being warm than she does about herself.'

Jessie was silent for a moment while she thought about this.

'Mary says the cold makes her fingers and legs hurt,' she said after a while.

'That's right. It makes her rheumatism worse.'

'She lets them hurt so's me and Florrie can be warm?'

'That's how love can look sometimes. Like hats and gloves,' Bobby said with a small smile. 'You see why her feelings are hurt, don't you?'

'Yes, I… I think so.'

'You know, I bet if you said you were sorry for making her sad and gave her a great big hug, then everything would go back to how it was.'

'Then would I be allowed to go to the treat this weekend?' Jessie asked hopefully.

'I'm sure you would.'

'And Henrietta wouldn't be killed?'

'I'm sorry, my love, but I don't think there's any way around that.' Bobby stood up. 'I'll tell you what. Just give me a few minutes to talk to Mary, then you come down with Reg and do as I said. You can be friends again before school.'

'All right.'

Bobby went downstairs to find Mary in the kitchen, angrily scrubbing a pot at the sink. Florrie was nibbling her breakfast toast in silence, looking scared. Even Ace, under the table hoping for scraps, looked nervous.

'Florrie, you may take your toast into the parlour to finish,' Bobby said. 'I need to speak with Mary alone.'

Looking relieved to be given leave to escape the oppressive atmosphere of Mary's bad mood, Florrie hurried away to the other room with Ace.

'I suppose you're here to take the child's part, are you?' Mary muttered. 'You're as soft as Reg, Bobby.'

'I'm here to take your part, and ask what the matter is,' Bobby said gently. 'Is your rheumatism bothering you?'

'Haven't I every right to be aggrieved?' she demanded. 'I'll not be dictated to in my own home. The hen's to be killed for Christmas and that's that. It's for the bairns' sake at the end of the day. What do they understand of rationing and shortages? I honestly think Jessie would have us all starve for her soft-heartedness.'

Bobby looked around the kitchen. Every shelf seemed to be filled now with jars of preserves, jams and pickles that Mary had made for Christmas. A cupboard in the parlour was filled with toys and clothes she had knitted to give as gifts, and piles of paper chains she had helped the girls to make were waiting to be put up. On top of that, of course, she had been busy making costumes for their twenty-one-strong pantomime cast. It was no wonder Mary was feeling the strain.

'Here. Sit down.' Bobby guided Mary to the dining table. The fire of her anger seemed to have died out now, and she sagged as Bobby pushed her into the chair.

'You've been working too hard,' Bobby said.

'And it's made me a cross, irritable old woman.' Mary gave her a small smile. 'Happen you're right. Still, the child needs to learn that what Reg and I say goes in this house. She can't make up rules to suit herself. I never would have believed she could be so wilful. Refusing to apologise like that.'

'She's really very upset at having hurt your feelings, even if she isn't sorry for trying to save the hen.'

'She's an artful little madam.' Mary sighed. 'No she isn't, that's not fair. She's a good child. But I was hurt when I found she hadn't been truthful with me. Perhaps I was too hard on her.'

'You've tired yourself out making gifts and food and trying to get the pantomime off the ground, Mary.'

'I just want to be sure they have a good Christmas. They've lost so much.' Mary rubbed her forehead. 'It's the first time I've given bairns Christmas, really. We lost Nancy before she was old enough to understand what it was all about.' She smiled. 'Oh, but she loved the tree though. Stared at it, mesmerised, for what felt like hours, reaching out sometimes to touch one of the glass baubles gently with her fingertips. You'd never have believed a babby that age could be so gentle, Bobby.'

'That's a beautiful memory,' Bobby said softly.

'That's the look I want to see in Florrie and Jessie's eyes on Christmas morning. I want it to be perfect for them, in spite of the war.'

'But it isn't trees or pantomimes or presents that will give the girls a perfect Christmas. It's being with their new family here, and having the kind, jolly Mary they love. You know, they're both terribly afraid you're going to send them away.'

Mary blinked. 'Send them away! What could have put such a ridiculous notion into their heads?'

'I suppose they feel that if you're angry with them, you won't want them here any more.'

'Nonsense. This is their home now.'

Bobby smiled. 'That's what Reg said too.'

There was a faint little knock at the door, and Jessie's tear-stained face appeared around it.

'Mary, please may I say sorry now?' she said meekly. 'I did want to save Henrietta. I don't think that was a wrong thing. But I never meant to make you cross and not like me any more, so I'm really, really sorry I did that. And I want to make friends again please.'

'Not like you any more? Oh, you foolish girl.' Mary stood up. 'I love you very much, as I would have thought you knew by now. No matter how much of an old crosspatch I am, I want you to remember that. And I want you and your sister to know that Moorside will always be your home, as long as Reg and I are alive to welcome you into it. Now come here to me.'

She stretched out her arms and Jessie ran into them, burying her face in Mary's apron. Bobby saw her friend blink back a tear as she bent to kiss the curly crown.

'I'm sorry I shouted,' Mary said softly. 'But we must have no more tall stories in future, Jessie, and no more fuss over Henrietta. You are to be truthful with me always from now on. All right?'

'I promise I'll be good. I'm sorry, Mary.'

Chapter 13

By Sunday afternoon, when Bobby was due to meet Topsy and the others for their next pantomime rehearsal, not only peace but a generous measure of festive jollity had been established at Moorside.

Mary had given the girls leave to start decorating the house for Christmas after church that morning. While it was still only the 7th of December, rather earlier than the Athertons usually put up their decorations, Florence and Jessie had now made so many paper chains that Mary laughingly said if they didn't start putting them up now, they would never have them all in place by Christmas Day.

Bobby had offered to help while her father was doing some out-of-hours trap-setting to deal with a family of troublesome stoats on Topsy's estate. She soon found herself getting into the Christmas spirit while she worked. When she had put up their few decorations in the family home on Southampton Street, it had felt like just another chore. Now, seeing it through the eyes of the children – the excitement sparkling in their eyes as they strung up the weedy newspaper chains of which they were so proud and hung blobs of cotton-wool snow in the windows – Bobby felt almost giddy, as she had at Christmastime when her mother was alive. She remembered how she, Mam and Lilian had sung Christmas songs together while they made the house gay and colourful, and led Florence and Jessie in some of her favourite carols as they worked.

Mary, meanwhile, had ventured out into the woods to collect ivy, holly, mistletoe, pine cones and other decorations with which Nature was generous enough to furnish them. The greenery was strewn over every bare surface and decorated with scarlet bows. Even Reg, who had watched disapprovingly for the first hour while muttering about 'foolishness and frivolity on the Sabbath', had eventually been infected by the Christmas gaiety of the two Parry girls and gone with Bobby to dig up the little pine in the garden that was to serve as their Christmas tree. It had been replanted in a pot in the parlour, and Bobby was sure she actually heard Reg whistling as he hung glass baubles and strands of coloured tinsel over the branches.

Jessie was given the honour of placing the Christmas angel on top of the tree, which she did with great solemnity while standing on a chair. By the time they all sat down to a well-earned Sunday dinner of roast rabbit – Rob was still reaping the benefits of Topsy's cull – Moorside Farm was alive with verdant green foliage and bright red holly berries. There was a fresh, clean smell of pine needles in the air that seemed to belong to the season.

'May Florrie and I come with you to the pantomime practice, Bobby?' Jessie asked when Bobby had excused herself and stood to leave.

'You may not. Then it wouldn't be a surprise on Christmas Day, would it?'

'Aww.' Florrie put out her lip. 'But we want to see you wearing your Cinderella gown for the ball. Mary said you looked like a lady from a story book.'

'Miss Havisham, I should think,' Bobby said, laughing.

Mary tutted. 'Pay her no mind, girls. She looked ever so bonny – like Maid Marian in that Errol Flynn picture we saw the last time Reg and I took you into Settle.'

'Really?' Jessie looked Bobby up and down with a sceptical expression that suggested a dress would indeed need to be magical to transform her into Olivia de Havilland. '*Please* may we come and see you in the Maid Marian dress, Bobby?'

'I'm not wearing it today,' Bobby said. 'It isn't a dress rehearsal. You'll see it on Christmas Day with the other children, and enjoy it all the more for the anticipation. Christmas Day surprises are the best kind of surprise.'

'You're getting into bad habits with our Charlie gone, you know, Bobby,' Mary said, her unimpressed gaze following Jessie's to Bobby's customary weekend costume of thick beige trousers and woollen jumper. 'Other than the costume fitting, I can't recall the last time I saw you in a skirt or frock in your free time.'

Bobby glanced down at her trousers. 'I suppose I have been wearing my walking things a lot recently. It's the only costume that keeps me dry and warm in this weather, plus it saves on stockings. Besides, I don't want any of my good clothes to be spoiled when I know I shan't be able to get anything new to replace them until May. I contributed all my coupons to the pantomime.'

'Still, it doesn't do to lose sight of what makes you feminine just because your young man isn't here to appreciate it. You could pass for one of the Land Girls dressed like that.'

Bobby experienced a pang at the mention of Charlie. It felt like a long time since she had last had a letter from him. His letters had been becoming less regular for the past six weeks, in fact. She hoped nothing was wrong between the two of them. When he had been with her last, on the bandstand in Settle, they had felt as close as ever. Once he was back at his barracks and she had only infrequent dry letters to give her any clue as to whether or not she was still in his heart, though, it was easy to feel he might be drifting away from her. Could he have started to cool towards her? She wished she could see him, even if just for a moment, and find comfort and reassurance in his arms.

She summoned a smile for Mary, however. 'Perhaps I should make more of an effort when I'm going to be in company. Ernie King, that Canadian officer, is always ribbing me about the fact he hardly sees me in anything other than trousers.' Bobby rubbed at a patch of mud on her beige breeches, so ground in now as to be stubborn enough to resist the most vigorous wash. 'I could put a skirt on for today, I suppose. The ground's frozen hard so it isn't muddy out. I'll change before I go.'

'Where is the rehearsal to be? The hospital?'

'No, we don't want to keep causing disruption there. We're having it in the library at Woodside Nook instead: that strange little building of Topsy's on the edge of the woods. She says it's a bigger space than her cottage for rehearsing. I'm meeting Jolka at the lodge so we can walk there together.'

–

Once Bobby had changed into a skirt and jacket suitable for the winter weather, she set out to meet Jolka. The former hunting lodge her friend occupied was in an attractive wooded clearing, close to a small lake. Topsy's other property, Woodside Nook, was about a mile distant on the same dirt track.

It was the sort of weather Bobby loved out here in the countryside, as long as she was wrapped up warm enough to enjoy it: freezing, but with blue skies and bright sunshine. Shafts of sunlight sparkled in the hoarfrost which hung from the trees and hedges, making the woodland look almost enchanted. A brisk walk soon got Bobby's blood flowing and put some colour in her cheeks, and she felt quite invigorated when she arrived at the lodge.

Jolka answered the door with Tommy in her arms, her glossy black hair shining in the dazzling winter sunlight.

'Bobby.' She smiled warmly. 'How well you look. The winter air must agree with you.'

'I rather think it does, when it's free of gales and rain. Shall we go?'

Tommy was fussing to be out of his mother's arms. Jolka put him down to walk between them, holding one chubby hand each. He looked a little sullen, but soon cheered up in the fresh air. His mother and Bobby occasionally swung him between them as they walked, and he squealed with appreciation.

'He has been in a fit of pique all day because I will not go out to fetch his father home,' Jolka told Bobby. 'He will not believe it is out of my power to simply click my fingers and make Piotrek appear.'

'You miss him enormously now he's gone, I suppose.'

'I do, but I have my work to occupy my thoughts. He would not be happy being too long away from the fight to free our homeland, so we are both in the right places even if not those places that would make us happiest.' She scowled. 'I would wish him to be elsewhere, however. That squadron leader... I do not trust his judgement. He ought to have been removed from his position for making so poor a decision as having his men fly in thick fog.'

'I wonder why nothing is done about him. Charlie dislikes him enormously. I suspect he's very harsh with the men. It sounds as though he allows them no freedom at all.'

'The old school tie, Piotrek tells me, is the phrase the English use when fools like this Hunt are given power by old friends in high places,' Jolka said darkly. 'Favours and nepotism are no way to conduct a war.'

Tommy was pulling on their hands now, making impatient sounds as if anxious to get free so he could run ahead. Jolka smiled, nodding to a hunched figure in the distance.

'Here is the reason he would escape,' she said. 'Your father, I believe. He and Tomasz are great friends. Your father puts him on his shoulders so he may see where the birds and squirrels sleep in the winter.'

Bobby smiled. 'Does he?'

Tommy broke away and ran off to his friend. Bobby saw her dad stand up from whatever he had been doing to greet the little boy, and a demand was quickly made which had evidently been made many times before. Tommy was swung up on to Rob's shoulders, and when Bobby and Jolka reached them he was cantering about with the giggling toddler holding tight to his cloth cap. Bobby didn't know when she'd seen her dad looking so free from care.

'Afternoon, young ladies,' he said jovially, lowering Tommy to the ground again. 'You're off to your play, are you?'

'That's right,' Bobby said. 'Mary says to go over to Moorside when you get home and she'll heat up your dinner for you. Did you deal with the stoats?'

'Putting some traps down now. Hopefully they'll be filled by the time I get to work tomorrow.'

'Is this the trap you will use, Mr Bancroft?' Jolka asked, nodding to a contraption at his feet. It looked rather broken up to Bobby, and too small for a stoat.

Her dad scowled. 'Not one of mine, that, no. That's for hare.'

'Who does it belong to?'

'Someone as ought to know better. Someone I'd have hoped for better from.'

'Pete,' Bobby said quietly. 'He's still working this patch?'

'Aye.'

'Have you told Topsy?'

'I haven't, nor will I. I won't bear tales on an old mate to her ladyship, even if he is a slippery beggar. He'll find more of his traps smashed up than he's used to though.'

'I don't see why you shouldn't speak to Topsy about him. You don't owe Pete anything. I thought he'd at least do you the kindness of moving on to a new patch, for friendship's sake. There's plenty of other land round here.'

'Aye, well, I won't. You mind your business, our Bobby, and I'll mind mine. I'll see you back at home.' He strode off to continue his work.

'Your father is enjoying his new position,' Jolka observed as they started walking again.

'Hmm?' Bobby, lost in thought, roused herself. 'Oh. Yes, very much.'

'Who is this Pete?'

'A friend of my dad's – or a former friend. He's a poacher and all-round ne'er-do-well, but my dad's got certain principles. I hope it isn't going to cause him any problems. He loves this job, and for a born townie he seems to have a good feel for it too.'

'Yes, Topsy has been singing his praises to me. She appreciates a man who works hard and is honest. You have done both her and your father a service in recommending him to the position, Bobby.' Jolka instinctively scooped up Tommy, observing that the boy was growing tired and his steps had become stumbling. 'And you. Do you enjoy your work at the magazine as before?'

'Yes.' Bobby paused. 'Yes, I do, but… there is something on my mind. I'd like to talk it over with you. You don't see these things the way other women I know do.'

Jolka laughed. 'This is a compliment, I hope. You may share your worries if you believe that I can help.'

'My editor, Reg, has set me working on items for a new section. A part of the magazine just for women. You know: dress patterns, child nutrition, good housekeeping advice; all that type of thing. I'm to take charge of it entirely, and have a new job title of Women's Editor.'

'And you are aggrieved by this. I would feel the same.'

'I knew you'd understand,' Bobby said with a grateful smile. 'I don't object to working on pieces for a domestic section, but once it's my name on it… even with the new job title, it feels like a step back. Like I'm suddenly a woman first and a reporter second. I suppose it's something of an impossible dream to expect that a woman doing a man's job will ever be seen as equal by them, but it seems very hard that we should be confined to the kitchen at work as well as at home.'

'These limitations are placed on women by men not because of what women can and cannot do, but because of what men would wish us to believe we cannot do. They fear a world where women break free of domestic confinement and claim an equal place. Society has made us too ready to accept that we are incapable, and so the men have everything their own way.'

'Do you think so?'

'It is very clear to me. There is little good about war, but at least it shows us how different life can be for women when we are no longer so confined. In war we learn what we are really capable of. You would not have your job if there was no war, I think?'

'No. Reg only hired me because there was no man or boy left who would work for the salary.'

'When men see women doing work they had persuaded them they were unfit for, and see them doing it as well as they could themselves, they become afraid and push against the change. Even when it is of necessity that women do such work, because a war has come, men do not wish them to forget what they perceive to be a woman's true place and nature.' She nodded to Bobby's skirt. 'As here. The Canadian does not like women to wear trousers. They are practical and comfortable, but they make less distinction between the sexes and so they are to be feared. And you, who are so used to putting the needs of men before your own even without thinking, change how you dress to please him. Am I not right?'

Bobby was silent while she considered this. It had been Mary who had made her feel guilty for not making herself tidy and feminine before being in company, but Jolka was right: Ernie's teasing and his nickname for her, Slacks, had been on her mind too.

This was why she had wanted to speak to her friend about her worries. While some found the confident, self-assured young Pole abrasive – even masculine – in her manner, Bobby appreciated her straight talk and unique perspective on the challenges women faced. Jolka was a wife and a mother, yet she still made her way in the world as an independent woman, committed to her career, with a husband who treated her as a friend and equal. Bobby admired Jolka enormously for having the courage to challenge her place in society, and hoped she could be brave enough to do the same.

'I suppose that is part of what made me abandon my usual walking clothes today,' Bobby admitted.

'The Canadian officer teases you, but there is a serious consideration behind his teasing. He wishes women to look and behave as he feels they ought to, not as they would like to, and reminds them that they make themselves unappealing to men when they do not do so. And your employer, he does the same thing when he gives you women's work to do instead of the work he hired you for.'

'Reg is rather traditional but I don't believe that's what he was thinking. He does respect me, in his way. I'm sure he believes he's doing me a favour by giving me my own section.'

'In his conscious mind, perhaps. But in his unconscious mind, he thinks to himself that a woman, no matter how talented, should not occupy a man's place. And if she must do so, she should be made to do so in a way he deems appropriate to her sex. You have spoken to him of your feelings?'

'Not yet. I don't know how to bring it up. He is my boss, after all, and it would sound so ungrateful.' Bobby turned to look at her friend, striding purposefully forward with her dozing child against her hip like a Valkyrie marching into battle. 'What would you do, Jolka?'

'If I were me my choices would be different to yours, because I have money of my own and so am free to make my way as I wish. If I were you, with little money and an ageing father who depended on me…' Jolka paused. 'The situation is difficult. I would wish to keep my position, but I would not wish to compromise on what I felt to be right. And yet it is so hard to make men see how constrained is the world women must occupy. Nevertheless, I believe I would make an attempt to change my employer's mind. Do you think that he would dismiss you for questioning this new section?'

'Not dismiss me, but he would be disappointed in me. Give me less writing to do, perhaps, so I'd become not much more than a glorified typist.'

'Then you must decide whether it is worth the risk, I suppose. But I know this: the war has changed things for women, at work and in the home. Men will push for the old order to be re-established when it ends. Women like you and I, Bobby, must fight to make sure that it is not.'

'Yes,' Bobby said, regarding her friend with admiration. 'You're right. I hope I can be strong enough.'

'Men will tell us that to be a woman is weakness. This is untrue. To exist as a woman in this world made for men – in this lies our strength. Do not forget.' Jolka shifted Tommy to her other side and nodded to a house in the distance. 'Here is our destination. Let us join our friends.'

Chapter 14

Woodside Nook, which would have been home to a porter and his family under previous generations of Sumners and Sumner-Walshes, was an odd hexagonal building on the edge of the woods between Silverdale and Sumner House. Despite the cosy-sounding name, it was a sizeable dwelling: ideal for rehearsing. Topsy had told Bobby the place had been rather neglected when the war began, but once the big house, lodge and cottage were all occupied, she had spruced it up so it could be pressed into service for guests.

Bobby thought the stone building was quite charming with its unusual shape and church-like arched windows, although no doubt not up to the usual standards of Topsy's snooty aunt. Since she disapproved of the pantomime, Aunt Constance had presumably made herself scarce for the afternoon. That suited Bobby, who was in no hurry to be introduced to her.

There was no answer when she pulled the bell rope. Possibly since the house had been so long neglected, it was no longer hooked up to a bell. However, the front door swung open when Bobby tried the knob. She and Jolka wandered inside to a panelled hallway, with a staircase leading to a second floor.

'Tommy is fast asleep,' Jolka said. 'Topsy has said to me that her guests do not mind if I claim an unoccupied bedroom for him to rest. Bobby, you will tell the others where I have gone.'

Jolka strode off towards the stairs with Tommy in her arms, leaving Bobby to wonder which of the handful of doors would lead to her fellow cast members.

One of the doors was ajar, she noticed as she made her way down the corridor. There was the hum of low voices from within. She peeped inside, but this didn't look like the room they were to rehearse in, being only a small study.

The blackout curtains were drawn; no lights were on. Nevertheless, she could hear a man's voice speaking. Bobby blinked as her eyes adjusted to the thin daylight that seeped in from behind the curtains.

'Won't you, darling?' the voice was saying softly. 'You'd be doing me the most terrific favour if you'd only say yes. I promise I'd never make you sorry for it.'

'Arch, do stop being such an ass. You know we could never suit in a thousand years.'

That was Topsy's voice. Topsy and Archie, sitting alone together in the gloom. Archie was leaning forward with Topsy's hands grasped in his, sounding gentler and more earnest than Bobby had ever heard him. Topsy sounded different too. Her tone wasn't light and teasing today as it usually was with her cousin. She seemed rather sad.

'Why shouldn't we suit?' Archie said. 'We've always had jolly times together. I'd do everything I was supposed to – love, honour and cherish and all that rot. I could keep my townhouse down in London, and we'd have Mother's money someday to keep a roof on the ancestral pile up here. I know how you love the place. As for Father's old ruin in Derbyshire, we can sell that for rubble for all I care about it.'

'We could never be happy.'

'Of course we could, if we weren't living in each other's pockets. I'd never stop you doing just as you like. And I'm dashed fond of you, Tops; always have been.'

'I wish I could, Archie,' Topsy said, and there was a tenderness in her voice that Bobby had only ever heard her use when speaking to Teddy. 'You know I'd do anything for you – almost anything. If you'd asked me after Edward died... but I'm sorry, I can't. Not now.'

He smiled sadly. 'It's that foreign pilot, isn't it?'

'Teddy.' Topsy seemed to rouse herself. 'I must go to him. I'm sure he frets when I'm not there.'

'So it's happened at last,' Archie said quietly. 'You really ought to tell him, you know, old thing.'

Topsy didn't answer. Bobby, who had been listening as if spellbound, withdrew silently without making her presence known.

She thought over what she had seen as she continued along the corridor. She felt slightly guilty at having listened to so much of what had evidently been a private and rather intimate conversation, but mostly she just felt puzzled.

Had she witnessed a proposal? That had certainly been what it had sounded like, if a somewhat odd one. Yet Topsy had told her that Archie was just as opposed to the idea of them making a match as she was. He'd certainly sounded eager for marriage just now.

There was so much that Bobby didn't understand. Who was the Edward that Topsy had mentioned? A boyfriend who had died – perhaps killed in the war? Topsy had never spoken of any strong attachment to Bobby.

And then it had sounded as though Archie wanted Topsy to declare her feelings for Teddy, even though he had proposed to her himself only moments earlier. That had been odd too. Disappointed lovers standing nobly aside in favour of a preferred rival was certainly something that happened often in books, and probably at least sometimes in real life, but surely rarely with such dizzying speed.

It didn't make any sense. Archie couldn't be in love with Topsy. He had never shown a sign of seeing her in any other light than as a sort of surrogate sister.

Bobby tried to put the scene out of her mind when she heard merry voices coming from behind one of the doors. She pushed it open, and sure enough found her fellow cast members behind it, preparing for the rehearsal.

The room was a sort of combined library and parlour, of a good size now the furniture had been moved to the sides. Like Moorside, it had been trimmed for Christmas with greenery collected from the woods outside. The fashion this Christmas was to dip woodland evergreen in a solution of Epsom salts to give it the appearance of being frosted, which added a magical sparkle to the holly that adorned every picture and shelf. There was a piano and plenty of floor space, so it was ideal for rehearsals.

Chip, Sandy and Ernie were all there, along with Laura Bailey, who would be playing the Fairy Godmother, and Mabs Jessop, who had been cast as Baroness Hardup. Some others from the village and hospital who were to play principal roles were present too, as was Mrs Hobbes, their choreographer, and Teddy in his role as Baron Hardup. Bobby was pleased to see that while he seemed somewhat thoughtful, Teddy looked significantly less depressed than last time she had seen him.

'Hey, Slacks.' Ernie cast an approving glance at her skirt and silk stockings. 'So you did have legs under those pants. Pretty good ones too. I was starting to wonder.'

Bobby tried not to look too flattered, remembering her conversation with Jolka. Her friend was right: it was difficult to persuade yourself not to care what men thought of you when you'd grown up being taught that ensuring their pleasure and comfort was to be your primary duty in life. But Ernie intended it as a compliment, and in the absence of Charlie, it was nice to be reminded that she still had some charm for the opposite sex. She treated him to a smile.

'Jolka is just coming,' she said. 'Tommy fell asleep on the walk here so she's going to put him to bed upstairs while we rehearse.'

'Did you perhaps see Topsy on your way inside?' Teddy asked.

'Er, no,' Bobby lied. 'Didn't she come with you?'

'Yes. She went out to speak some words to Archie about repairs to this house, I believe.'

'Oh. Well, I'm sure they'll be back soon.'

'Shall we start without them?' Sandy asked.

There was no need, however, as Topsy and Archie came in at the moment. Jolka followed closely behind them, having divested herself of her sleepy child.

Bobby watched Topsy for any sign of strong emotion, but the tender sadness that had been present when she was alone with Archie had disappeared now. She was all smiles – her usual bouncy, jolly self – as she immediately went to Teddy and rested a proprietorial hand on his shoulder. Teddy smiled up at her, evidently pleased at this mark of regard. Archie, meanwhile, was no less jovial and friendly than usual as he went to shake hands with his friends the Canadian airmen. Bobby could half fancy she had dreamed that strange proposal in the study, seeing the pair so apparently unaffected.

'Well, shall we get on?' Topsy said, adopting the commanding director voice that always made Bobby want to smile. It felt a little like being bossed about by a canary when Topsy took charge. 'Maimie is going to go through some of the dance routines with us first of all, then I should like to concentrate on the scenes with the Sisters, Buttons and the Broker's Men, since our Canadian friends will be in the air for our next two rehearsals. Let's begin with "Lambeth Walk".'

The cast members obediently took their positions for the song and dance that were to open the pantomime.

Bobby had found she enjoyed being on stage a lot more than she might have imagined, relishing the experience of putting workaday Bobby Bancroft aside for a few hours while she became the Cinderella of fairy tale. That feeling didn't extend to dancing on stage, however. She could hold a tune, remember lines and had found to her surprise that her acting wasn't at all bad, but when it came to the dance routines Mrs Hobbes had planned for them, Bobby seemed to have two left feet.

It felt much harder than dancing with Charlie. They didn't often take part in the more energetic numbers, preferring instead to wait for the slower tunes that would allow them to sway around the floor in each other's arms. There was no skill to that sort of dancing. All it took was being in love.

This type of coordinated group dance, however, was another kettle of fish, Bobby thought as she enviously watched Mabs Jessop kicking up her heels in front of her and tried to copy the steps for 'Lambeth Walk'. The girl had a natural talent, being both flexible and light on her feet. All Bobby could do with her feet was trip over them.

Ernie King, who was performing his Lambeth Walk perfectly beside her, shook his head.

'Should've led with your left foot,' he said. 'Now you're backwards to the rest of us, Slacks.'

'How am I supposed to remember left from right when I'm busy trying to stop my knees banging into each other?' Bobby responded crossly. 'It's all very well for you. I told Topsy I couldn't be on stage.'

'Of course you can, you're good at it. Most of it. You need practice is all.'

'We only have two and a half weeks left, Ernie.'

Mrs Hobbes clapped her hands for silence, and the airman from the hospital who had offered to play piano for them stopped.

'Well you're in a nice muddle, aren't you?' she said, putting her hands on her hips. 'Lieutenant Sanderson, it isn't a race and there's no prize for finishing first. Try to keep pace with the others. Miss Bailey, a little more fluid in your movements – you're rather too stiff. And Bobby, you're leading with the wrong foot and your hands are here, there and everywhere. All of you, watch Miss Jessop this time. She's doing it perfectly.'

Mabs preened a little, shooting a smug look at her old schoolmate and long-time rival Laura Bailey.

'All right, from the top,' Mrs Hobbes said, nodding to the man at the piano.

'Here. Let me help you,' Ernie said to Bobby as the pianist played the introductory bars.

Before she was aware of what was happening, Ernie was standing behind her and had taken her hands in his. Bobby stiffened, uncomfortable at his proximity. She could feel his hot breath on the back of her neck.

'What are you doing, Ernie?'

He laughed. 'Oh, don't worry, I'm not going to molest you. You're really not my type, Slacks. Just follow my movements, OK?'

Bobby relaxed a little and allowed Ernie to guide the movement of her arms as they went back into the dance. It did help. After enough repetition, her limbs started to remember the dance of their own accord.

'Thanks,' she said when the music stopped. 'I think I've got it now. Mostly.'

'Happy to help.' He gave her a chummy nod as he took his place beside her again. Bobby, reassured that his intentions had been pure, smiled back. Friendships with men could feel like navigating a minefield sometimes.

Afterwards, when the dancing practice had ended and people were getting into groups ready to rehearse their scenes, Bobby glanced at Topsy. It seemed her friend was currently navigating a man-filled minefield of her own. Bobby hadn't realised Topsy's romantic life had become so complicated. She was still standing close to Teddy, seeming reluctant to leave his side after her encounter with Archie.

'I hope to God that lassie of mine makes the right choice,' a voice at Bobby's elbow observed quietly.

She turned to find that Mrs Hobbes was at her side, watching the pair darkly.

'I suppose you mean she ought to marry Archie,' Bobby said. 'I know it's what her father wanted for her.'

'I mean no such thing. I've no wish to see the family curse handed down to another generation.'

'Family curse?'

'I hoped Topsy would escape it, at least. She was always strong.' Mrs Hobbes cast a worried look at Archie, who was running through his lines with Sandy a little distance away. 'Still, she's fond of the boy. They were very close as bairns. She might throw her life away for his sake yet.'

'Do you mean... is that what Topsy was talking about when she mentioned something in Archie's blood? Is it a hereditary thing you're worried about being passed down?' Bobby had heard of such things in upper-class families where marriages between cousins were common.

'Nothing to do with that. I've been with that family long enough to know all their little secrets; the gossip and the whispers; every skeleton in every cupboard. The curse of the Sumners, Bobby, has always been duty. And the curse of this world we live in is being unable to see past what's different.'

Bobby frowned, puzzling over the words. There seemed to be some mystery at work, and it concerned Topsy, Teddy and Archie.

It was strange. She could understand Ernie as a potential rival for Teddy, but Archie didn't seem to fit the bill at all as the third in any love triangle. Yes, he and Topsy were close in their way, but Bobby was convinced it was the closeness of siblings, not lovers. But when she had heard Archie speaking to Topsy earlier, it hadn't sounded as though duty had been behind his proposal. There'd been an earnestness and need in his tone that went beyond simply what he felt he owed to his family, or a wish to please his mother. Archie really wanted to marry Topsy; Bobby was sure of it.

'I don't understand all this, Mrs Hobbes,' she said. 'I overheard Archie say something today that I could swear... and yet he can't be in love with her, can he?'

'Well, that isn't for me to say. I'm speaking out of turn, I suppose. I forget sometimes that I'm only the help, not the girl's mother.' Her dark look lifted, and she smiled as she nodded to something green and white hanging above Topsy and Teddy. 'Shall we tell them, do you think?'

They were too late, however. Ernie had also spotted the mistletoe over the pair's heads.

'I hope you don't think you're getting away with ignoring an old custom just because you can't get up to claim it, buddy,' he called out. 'You'll bring the panto-mime bad luck.'

There was a shout of 'Go on, Teddy!' and some chivvying cheers from the other men present.

Teddy glanced upwards, noticed the mistletoe hanging from the ceiling, then looked at Topsy. There was an expression in his good eye that Bobby hadn't seen there before: soft, eager and enquiring. Another thing she had never seen before was Topsy blushing, but her cheeks certainly coloured now.

'May I, Topsy?' Teddy asked her quietly.

Topsy's blush deepened. 'I suppose you ought to, if it's for the good of the pantomime.'

Teddy took her hand and pulled her towards him, and she stooped to plant a soft kiss on the still undeclared suitor's mouth.

It wasn't a long kiss, but it felt as though it lingered nonetheless. Topsy drew her lips away rather reluctantly, it seemed to Bobby. Teddy still kept hold of her hand, as if unwilling to relinquish her touch.

It felt like there was a long silence, with all eyes on the young lovers who had eyes only for one another. The kiss had changed something between them, and everyone in the room seemed to sense it. The atmosphere was broken, however, by a raucous cheer for Teddy from the Canadians. The young Pole smiled a little bashfully, pleased at this mark of male camaraderie. Topsy seemed confused now she was reminded of the presence of others, and unsure where to look.

'Well,' Mrs Hobbes whispered to Bobby. 'There was something that ought to have happened before now, wouldn't you say?'

Chapter 15

'We must get on,' Topsy said, covering for her confusion by retreating into the practical. 'Let's do the first scene with Cinderella, Buttons and the Sisters in the kitchen, then we'll move on to the Sisters getting ready for the ball with Buttons. To finish we can do the Baron tricking the Broker's Men.'

Bobby got into position in front of the large bookcase that was serving as the backcloth for today. She loved the scenes that included her, Archie, Sandy and Ernie. Archie and Sandy were so funny together as the Ugly Sisters that it was all she could do to stop herself bursting into laughter, and she had some humorous lines herself too. In the pantomimes she had been to see, the principal girl often had little to do but swoon and be rescued by the hero. The Cinderella that Mrs Hobbes had created had a little wit about her, however, and formed an effective double act with Ernie's Buttons in their scenes together.

Today, though, Bobby found herself distracted from the scene by the sight of Teddy and Topsy in earnest conversation together. Was her friend getting her second proposal of the day? It was none of her business, but the journalist in her was naturally curious. She couldn't help wondering what the future held for the two of them.

'Oh, Lavvy my darling, we shall be single forever,' Sandy wailed, in character as Ugly Sister Clot.

'I do wish we could find a husband,' Archie said. He looked at Bobby expectantly.

'Slacks, it's your line,' Ernie mumbled under his breath when she didn't respond.

'Hmm? Oh.' Bobby pulled her gaze away from Topsy and Teddy. 'Sorry. If I were you, girls, I'd try to find one each.'

'Personally, I should love one for the week and another for Sunday best,' Sandy said. This was the cue for a comic song by the Sisters, and the pianist struck up the opening notes.

'Thanks,' Bobby muttered to Ernie as Archie and Sandy performed their song-and-dance routine.

'No problem.' He nodded to Topsy. 'Lucky for you, our director's too distracted by her boyfriend to notice you dropping lines.'

Bobby wasn't in the next scene that was to be rehearsed. Observing that Topsy was discussing something with Mrs Hobbes, she went to speak to a now solitary Teddy.

'You look thoughtful,' she said in a low voice, crouching beside him. 'I thought you'd be walking on air after what happened under the mistletoe. Aren't you?'

'I am happy. And yet, I am sad.'

'Why are you sad?'

'Because the doctors say I am to be discharged in five days' time. Civilian life is beckoning once more, Bobby. Only, civilian life will be very different for me now than it once was.' He smiled wanly. 'So valuable I was to them, once. I was a student of aeronautical engineering when I joined your RAF, with my private pilot's licence gained in Poland. They opened their arms to me like a lover. Almost before I could blink, I was an officer. Now, this same RAF throws me away with the rubbish.'

Bobby frowned. 'You're not saying… you can't still be planning to leave?'

'I must.'

'But she loves you! You must know that. We all saw the way she kissed you.'

'Yes.' Teddy sighed. 'Yes. I believe she does love me, although I once thought it impossible. Such a thing I never could have dreamed of. But still I must go.'

'Why? If you asked her to marry you, I'm certain she would say yes.'

'Perhaps she might, and then be tied forever to a man who can do nothing for her. Who cannot give her a child, or earn money to provide for her – who cannot even take her in his arms and dance with her. A man who cannot do these things is not a man at all. It is not the life I would have her live.'

'Shouldn't that be her decision as well as yours? Topsy has ideas about how she wishes to live her life too, I should imagine.'

'She is but a girl. The romantic notions she cherishes now will not prepare her for life as the wife of a helpless thing.'

'She's no younger than you are. She isn't a child to have her mind made up for her, Teddy.'

Teddy didn't say anything. His eyes had fixed on Archie, who was waltzing with Ernie in character as Lavvy the Ugly Sister in the scene where they got ready for the ball.

'Perhaps in my jealousy, I was unfair on this young cousin of hers,' he said at last. 'He is a kind man, and he makes Topsy smile. See, she laughs as she watches him. It would give her family much joy if the marriage were to take place, and bring her wealth and property too. I know he wishes to marry her – for her own sake, not simply to please his mother. All of this I have observed. The match would be a good one from all sides.'

'I don't think he—' Bobby stopped herself, recalling the scene she had witnessed that morning. 'At least, I don't believe Topsy wishes to marry him. She's in love with you, Teddy.'

'Please, do not try to persuade me differently. It will be a comfort when I am gone to know she is with someone who makes her smile as she now smiles. Topsy will be happy, and I will be content to remember that once, in spite of what I now am, I was loved. I am satisfied with my lot, Bobby.'

Bobby sighed. 'I know I can't possibly understand how it feels to be in the position you are. Perhaps I'm rather fond of making things too simple. Still, I do wish you would reconsider. You could be so happy. Make Topsy so happy.'

'But I will not reconsider. After Christmas, when our pantomime is over, I must go.' The scene with the Sisters was ending now. 'And here, it is my turn to perform. I would please ask you to save my tired arms and push me to the bookcase.'

Realising her protestations were useless, Bobby took the handles of his chair to wheel him over.

'Please, my friend, do not grieve for me,' Teddy said, looking up at her. He looked wistful, but also oddly serene. 'I find that I am strangely resigned to my fate. In real life, as much as we may wish it, not every story can have the ending of a fairy tale.'

The next scene was the last they were to rehearse. It was now well into the evening, and the cast were beginning to flag. Bobby, exhausted as much by the emotions the day had brought as the exertions of performing, had claimed a seat for herself on a settee in a quiet corner by the door while Teddy performed his scene with the Broker's Men. The sensitive, thoughtful young man was rather funnier than Bobby might have expected him to be by his nature, summoning a gormless expression as he tricked the two bailiffs out of the rent money he had just given them. The slightly formal, stilted English he used as a non-native speaker of the language created a deadpan delivery that seemed to make the humorous lines even more comical.

She was laughing at his performance, watching him befuddle Chip as he counted out coins, when she noticed a woman enter the room. This person was middle-aged, tall and willowy, with a handsome, delicate Grecian profile, elegantly dressed in an old-fashioned style.

Archie, who had been talking to Sandy and Ernie, frowned when he saw her. He made his excuses to the others and approached her by the door.

'Mother. I thought you were going to be out all day.'

So this was the Aunt Constance whom Bobby had heard so much about. She regarded the woman with interest. Constance Sumner was genteel and striking in her looks, with Archie's grey eyes and flaxen hair, but there was a sneer about the lips that she didn't share with her son.

'I suppose I may be allowed to enjoy supper in my own residence, since it will soon be eight o'clock,' she told him stiffly. 'Well, Archie?'

Reluctantly, Archie pecked her cheek.

'You won't be joining me, I suppose,' she said, glancing around the room with disapproval.

'My friends are here. I arranged for a cold supper to be prepared.'

His mother's gaze drifted to the scene in progress in front of the bookcase. 'So this is how you waste your time with these low friends of yours, is it?'

Bobby wondered if Constance Sumner believed being of a lesser class also made people deaf. Certainly she seemed to be making no effort to lower her voice, which carried easily to Bobby over the other sounds in the room.

'Mother, please,' Archie said in a low voice. 'You promised you wouldn't make a scene. This is Topsy's place, you know, and she's entitled to have her friends rehearse here if she wishes.'

'The only reason I agreed to let you be involved in this nonsense at all is in the hope it might bring you and Honoria together.' She curled her lip at Ernie and Sandy, talking together a little way from them. 'Instead I find you consorting with louche foreigners and servicemen. I ought never to have allowed you to be on the stage.'

'I am of age, you know, Mother. Besides, I hardly think a village pantomime in a hospital ward really counts as being "on the stage". It isn't the Palladium. You and Father used to send me every year to the pantomime as a child, didn't you?'

'A professional production is another matter. A real actor knows what he is and keeps to his own kind – a lesson you might do well to learn, my boy.'

'These people are my kind,' Archie said quietly.

His mother continued as if she hadn't heard him. 'These sorts of amateur affairs, on the other hand, result in all kinds of degenerate behaviour by what ought to be industrious, respectable working people. Men in female clothing, and women half naked on stage! One worries they'll develop a taste for such perversions, and where does that leave us? The war is bad enough for encouraging loose morals and debauchery in the lower orders.'

'Mother, I promise I won't have a single loose moral or debauched habit by the time we finish the pantomime that I didn't have already,' Archie said solemnly, putting his hand on his heart.

'Don't be frivolous, Archie.'

Constance turned to watch the scene in progress. Jim, the airman playing the second Broker's Man opposite Chip, had realised he'd been cheated out of his rent money and was squaring up to Teddy's Baron for a fight.

'I would have satisfaction, sir,' he was saying. 'Stand up and face me.'

'He can't stand up, you fool,' Chip said. 'He's legless.'

'How dare you!' Teddy said. 'I am as sober as a judge.'

Mabs, who was on stage as the Baroness, jumped forward as if Teddy had pinched her bottom.

'My husband may be legless, but he certainly isn't 'armless,' she said, with an arch glance to the audience.

There was a ripple of appreciative laughter from those watching. This section had been added at Teddy's request, who wanted his injuries not to be ignored but made into a part of the story. He had written the new lines himself, with Topsy's help, and they always got a good laugh. Aunt Constance, however, was certainly not laughing.

'And this is the sort of bawdy barrack-room humour you feel is suitable for a children's entertainment, do you?' she said to Archie. 'Jokes about sex and drinking?'

'It isn't only for the children. It's for their parents and guardians, and the men in the hospital. Pantomimes are always a little ribald, it's part of the tradition.'

'I wonder you can stomach having *that* on stage, at any rate.' She nodded to Teddy. 'I can hardly bear to look at him.'

Archie scowled. 'Because of his skin grafts, I presume you mean.'

'It's grotesque. He'll frighten the children, looking like something from a circus. You'll have them running out in tears.'

'I don't believe he'll frighten anyone. And you might remember, Mother, that he gained those burns in service of this country. Teddy Nowak is a brave man, and entitled to carry his wounds as a badge of honour. Would you say these things if it had been me who had come home crippled and burned?'

'I'm sure you would never have been so careless.'

Archie laughed. '*Careless?* Do you think carelessness is what causes men to be injured or killed in wars?'

'Don't take that tone with me, young man. Now are you coming to supper? It seems high time these friends of yours went home to me.'

'I am not. I told you, Osborne is going to bring me a supper of cheese and cold meats. I'll see you tomorrow at breakfast.'

'Well, if you won't be reasoned with.' She presented her cheek to him again, and after scowling at it for a second, he gave it a grudging peck.

Once his mother had left the room, Archie walked wearily towards the settee. He gave Bobby an embarrassed smile when he spotted her there, tucked into a corner with her feet beneath her.

'You heard all of that, I suppose,' he said.

'I did. Sorry, I ought to have moved away.'

'It's all right. I'm glad you heard.' He took a seat beside her. 'Listening to my mother speak, you might think Haw-Haw has a point about the poisonous nature of the British upper classes.'

'Why do you stand it?' Bobby asked. 'I'd have cut ties long ago if my dad talked about my friends in that way.'

'The governor left all his money and property to her when he shuffled off this mortal coil four years ago. Didn't trust my grubby mittens on them, I expect. The town-house I live at in London, the crumbling country seat in Derbyshire – it all belongs to Mother. She doles out a measly monthly allowance to me and thinks I have to come like a lapdog when she whistles.' He flopped back in his seat. 'The pathetic thing is, she's right. I need the money.'

'It's funny. I always thought people with titles were rich,' Bobby said, half to herself.

'Not when the title doesn't come with property attached. I'd sell the damn thing for a fiver if I could. I never wanted it in the first place. Mother's been ten times worse since it came our way.'

'Can't you work?'

He rubbed his head. 'I haven't had a job since the RAF booted me out. No one seems to want me: title, Oxford degree and all. Can't even get a junior civil service position.'

'Really? I thought employers were crying out for young men.'

'Not this young man,' he muttered. 'It's a funny thing, Bobby, getting invalided out when people can't see anything physically wrong with you. Makes them wary –

as if you must be a shirker or a coward. So as long as I've got bills to pay, I have to come when Mother calls, like a good boy.'

Bobby wondered if this was behind his keenness to marry Topsy. His cousin had money and property of her own, which would presumably be at his disposal if they were wed. His mother might find it in her heart to be generous if her only son finally gave in to her dearest wish and married. But in that case, why had he seemed to urge Topsy to declare her feelings to Teddy?

Bobby almost opened her mouth to ask, but she stopped herself, embarrassed to admit she had eavesdropped on such an intimate conversation.

'I suppose she'll make me sorry tomorrow for my little rebellion over supper,' Archie said. 'Well, I shall appease her somehow. Not tonight though.' He looked at Teddy and the others, who were finishing their scene, and patted Bobby's thigh in a friendly fashion. 'You won't rush off after this, will you, old thing? I don't want to be stranded here alone with Mother and the servants. Topsy, Teddy and the Canadian chaps have said they'll keep me company for supper and a snifter or two. We'll gorge ourselves on minted mutton, put the wireless on and dance until dawn, eh?'

'I don't think I can stay quite until dawn,' Bobby said, smiling. 'But I'd be very glad to stay for a drink with you, Archie.'

The planned convivial evening took an unexpected turn, however, when the rehearsal had ended and Archie turned on the wireless set. There was no music on the Forces Programme, but a newsreader was making an announcement that brought an instant stop to the merry voices filling the room. There was a moment's silence while they all absorbed the momentous news.

'I don't believe it,' Ernie murmured.

Bobby could hardly believe it either, but she supposed it was true. There had been a large-scale attack on an American naval base in Hawaii that day. Japan had entered the war.

Chapter 16

The news of the attack on Pearl Harbor marked the beginning of an eventful few days in the course of the war: days that brought Britain a powerful new enemy, and a powerful new ally. In the wake of the attack on the naval base, both America and Britain declared war on Japan. Germany then came to the support of their Axis partner to declare war on America, and Roosevelt announced to the world that what many on the Allied side had anticipated and hoped for had now occurred. His hand had been forced, and America had joined the war.

'Late again,' Bobby's dad grunted as he read the news of America's declaration of war in the paper that Friday. 'They'll be sending a load of 'em over here, I suppose. Still, it'll put an end to things quick enough. Six months at worst, I reckon.'

'That was what you said when the Soviets came in,' Bobby remarked, picking their post up from the doormat. 'Yet here we are, still fighting.'

'Aye, well, this is different. The Yanks have got brass and men to help us turn the tide. We need them, sad to say it.' He folded up his paper. 'Hitler must be a madman to declare war on the United States when he'd no need. No sense in it at all.'

'He is a madman. A power-hungry little madman. Everyone knows that, don't they?'

'Aye, all right, but I never thought he were stupid wi' it. He's thrown t' war away this time, no mistake about it.' Her dad nodded to the single envelope in her hand. 'What's your post then?'

Bobby examined the envelope. She felt her heart jump at seeing the RAF stamp, and Charlie's service number written on the back. It was nearly a fortnight since she had heard from him last.

She was starting to feel so far away from him. No talks, no touch, and only the barest sliver of a glimpse into his life away from her when he wrote – when he remembered to write. If she hadn't had the pantomime to focus on, she'd have been fretting herself silly.

As usual, it wasn't a long letter – one side of a single sheet of paper – but just the sight of her fiancé's hand-writing made her feel closer to him.

'It's from Charlie,' she told her dad.

'Any news?'

Bobby read through the letter. It began more warmly than Charlie's letters often had of late, and with a little of his old humour, which reassured her somewhat. However, as she read on, she soon had other things to worry about.

> *Dearest Bobby,*
>
> *Sorry to leave you waiting so long for a letter from me. If you haven't decided I must have left you for a pretty WAAF and run away with some handsome swain in revenge, then you might be interested to hear some news I had this morning that has rather knocked me for six. I suppose we must call it good news, although my head is fairly spinning from it.*
>
> *It seems I'm to be moved on. Now the Americans are in with us, Bomber Command wants*

every man possible in the air to make a push that could end this thing decisively. All aircrew cadets with more than one hundred and fifty flying hours are to be entered for their final tests now, including me. If I pass, which none of the instructors seem in any doubt that I will, I'll receive my wings right away. After, I'll be transferred to an operational training unit to prepare me for front line duties, which is to be no more than four weeks, and so it seems I could be locking horns with the enemy as early as February.

I hope this won't give you too many sleepless nights, dear. I wish we could have some decent time together talk it over in depth, but I'm afraid that apart from the concert this weekend, all our leave has been cancelled for the foreseeable future.

It's going to be a cold Christmas for me this year, eating my dinner around the mess table away from you and the family, but since it's for a noble cause then I suppose I must bear it as best I can. Please explain to the girls for me. I had wanted to be there when they opened the dolls' house I made them, but orders are orders and it isn't to be helped – I'm sure our little Corporal Florence will understand, at least. And I do have some good news that I hope will make you smile as well. My days as an erk – that's what we call the aircraftmen, you know – are numbered. They tell me I'm to be promoted from AC1 to Pilot Officer when I get my wings. That ought to make Reggie happy.

My biggest concern isn't for my own safety, but in leaving behind the friends I have made here. I shouldn't be sorry to leave except for them.

As I said, our outing to the Christmas concert party goes ahead on Saturday as planned. I do hope you can still come. These could be the only hours we'll be able to spend together for some time. Save me a kiss for when I see you, darling.

All my best love,

Charlie

–

'Oh my God,' Bobby whispered. She sank into a chair.

Her dad frowned. 'What is it? Bad news?'

'Yes. Yes. Bad news.'

'Tell me the worst then.'

'All leave at their base has been cancelled. Charlie can't come home for Christmas after all.' She swallowed. 'And… he's to get his wings early. He says Bomber Command want every man who can fly in the air. They think now we have the Americans fighting with us, we could end the war quickly through one big push.'

'That don't sound like bad news to me. Not if it'll mean an earlier end to the war. Shame not to see the lad for Christmas, but duty comes first.'

'I know, and I am glad he won't be in the power of that nasty little squadron leader any more. It's just so frightening to think of him in the skies over occupied Europe, getting shot at and… and all that. I thought I had until at least April before I really needed to worry about him.'

'Happen he won't need to be up there long, if Bomber Command are right. Could be all over by spring.'

'What if they're not right? We've the Japanese to fight as well now, and Finland and Hungary. Even with the

Americans on our side, the Axis have got a lot of power. And they've got Europe. They're not going to just lie down and let us take it back.'

'No sense in "what ifs". We'll have to see what comes, that's all.' Her dad stood up and went to rest a hand on her shoulder. 'Try not to worry, eh, lass?' he said gently. 'Happen it'll all work out for the best. The Yanks are in, and it don't look like Jerry's going to take Moscow after all now – that's summat. I know you'll miss the boy but it's a brighter Christmas than last year, isn't it?'

'Yes, that's true.' But Bobby couldn't banish the unsettled feeling in her belly.

She looked again at Charlie's letter. It seemed strange that he mentioned friends he had made when he had so rarely talked about the other men in his barracks in his previous letters. Yet it sounded from this one that he had formed some close friendships after all. Piotr had mentioned a young man he'd grown close to – Bram. Perhaps that was who Charlie meant when he said he would miss his new pals. Bobby hoped she might have the chance to be introduced to the man when she attended the Christmas concert, and to have some private talk with Charlie about the myriad things that were on her mind.

–

The next day after work, Bobby attired herself in her best blue crepe dress – now rather short after she had hemmed and rehemmed the fraying skirt, but it was serviceable yet. She went to social events too infrequently to justify wasting money and coupons on a replacement – not that she had any coupons spare after donating all she had left to the pantomime.

Her stomach hopped as she prepared to make the journey to Skipton. She was to meet Jolka there, who of course had been invited to tonight's Christmas concert party by Piotr. Topsy and Mrs Hobbes were to babysit little Tommy for the evening so his parents could spend some time together. Perhaps Piotr, too, would be preparing to join the fight imminently.

It felt like so long since Bobby had seen her fiancé, although it had been less than eight weeks ago that they had cuddled on the bandstand in Settle. Bobby knew she ought to be grateful, when some women were away from their loved ones for months or even years thanks to the war – perhaps she would soon be in the same boat herself. But so much had happened in the last eight weeks, and there were a thousand things she wanted to discuss that couldn't go in a letter. In person, she hoped, she could tell Charlie all her thoughts and feelings.

Being a civilian, Bobby had never been to an ENSA concert before. The organisation that provided entertainment for the troops was often the subject of mockery – Every Night Something Awful, servicemen would joke the initials stood for – but they broadcast some good ENSA shows on the wireless sometimes, with big stars like Arthur Askey and Vera Lynn performing. She was curious to know what this one would be like, and if there would be the opportunity to spend a decent amount of time alone with Charlie.

Would there be dancing? She hoped so. After eight weeks without her lover's touch, all Bobby wanted tonight was to be in his arms as much as she possibly could so she might feel close to him again. Perhaps she would also get to meet his friend Bram.

And *he* might well be there, she supposed – Hunt, the hated squadron leader. A man with blood on his hands, whose reckless orders had caused the crash on the mountainside that summer and resulted in four unnecessary deaths without Jerry ever needing to get his hands dirty. A man who had left Teddy Nowak half blind and maimed for life, unable to be with the woman who loved him. Yes, Bobby would be very interested to see Hunt.

Reg drove Bobby to the bus stop at the Black Bull in the little pony and trap Charlie had bought before leaving for the RAF, and from there she got the bus into Skipton. Jolka, who had travelled into town earlier that day in order to visit an art shop that stocked some of her work, met her at the bus stop. Their escorts were to meet them by the war memorial outside the church so they could go to the town hall together.

'You are excited to see your young man, I suppose,' Jolka said as they walked.

'Very much so.'

In fact, Bobby's insides felt as though they were jumping all over the place. That wasn't only from excitement. It was nerves too.

Would Charlie be changed, in his feelings for her or in himself? Would he take her in his arms and kiss her? Could his passion for her have started to cool, and that was the reason his letters had become so infrequent? His last had been more affectionate than he was wont to be in writing, but he had given no reason for the long gaps between letters. She hoped sincerely that all was still well between them.

'I shall be glad to see Piotrek also,' Jolka said. 'It is less than a fortnight he has been away, but I confess I have missed him very much. The house feels so empty and quiet without him.'

'I wonder what the concert will be like. I've never been to an ENSA entertainment before.'

'No, nor I.'

'I hope we aren't expected to sit in silence all the while. I do want to talk to Charlie, and meet some of the men from his barracks.' Bobby flushed a little. 'I wouldn't mind a kiss and a cuddle before I go home either. Now Charlie's Christmas leave has been cancelled, I don't know when we'll have a chance to be with each other again.'

'Yes, I was thinking this too. I care more for my husband's company than whatever entertainment may be planned tonight.' Jolka broke into a warm smile at the sight of two uniformed figures enjoying a smoke together by the war memorial. 'But here are our brave heroes waiting for us.'

Piotr beamed when he spotted his wife. He crushed his cigarette underfoot and held out his arms to her.

'*Moje myszko*,' he said in a low voice. 'Come to me.'

His wife practically threw herself into his arms, surprising Bobby, who – while she knew her Polish friends were a devoted couple – wasn't used to seeing Jolka abandon her usual control and self-possession. Yet she fairly giggled now as Piotr lifted her and spun her around, pressing his lips to hers.

Charlie, on the other hand, looked oddly shy as he put out his cigarette. He took off his forage cap and started twisting it in his hands, as he often did when he was nervous. Bobby, too, felt shy, as if they were new sweethearts on their first date. She smiled bashfully at him.

'Hello,' she said.

'Hello.'

Charlie rubbed his neck, his eyes darting sideways to the warm, effusive greeting of their two friends before they came back to Bobby.

Jolka had regained her composure now Piotr had returned her to the ground. She looked at Bobby and Charlie, registering their awkwardness, and tapped her husband on the arm.

'Piotrek, come,' she commanded. 'Let us leave our friends to embrace in private. Not everyone is as careless of an audience as we two old married people.'

'Whatever you wish, my love.' He nodded to them. 'Bobby, it is good to see you again. I hope we will talk more later, at the concert.'

'Yes. Um, goodbye. I mean goodbye for the present.'

When they had gone, Bobby looked at Charlie, who was still twisting his cap in his hands. As the last time she had seen him, he looked tired and careworn.

'Are you well, Charlie?' she asked.

'I've nothing to complain of. A little fagged from training. Are you?'

'To the best of my knowledge.'

'Good. Good. And your father?'

'Very well. He's enjoying his new job.'

'I thought he would.'

'You and Piotr seem to be good friends now.'

'Yes. He's an easy man to like.'

There was a minute's uncomfortable silence. Then Charlie started to laugh. Bobby, relieved to hear that familiar, comforting sound, laughed too.

'Well this is foolish,' Charlie said. 'What's the matter with us, Bobby? Have we grown to be strangers since I've been gone?'

Bobby wished she could answer that question with everything that was in her heart. There was a distance between them these days that he clearly felt as well as her. A physical distance, yes, but a distance, too, in their lives and experiences. They no longer shared a home, a community, mutual friends, a daily routine. They occupied completely different worlds.

She could never be a part of Charlie's world now he had gone to war: that almost exclusively male domain, where the bonds of comradeship between men and men were valued as much or more as the bonds of love between men and women. And things were happening in her world too; things Charlie had only the vaguest idea about. Things like the pantomime, her sister's engagement, Jessie's distress over her pet hen; things she felt almost embarrassed to refer to, they seemed so trivial in comparison to the life-or-death events occurring in Charlie's life, but that mattered enormously to her. She loved him. She felt she would always love him. But still there was this distance that had arisen, and Bobby wasn't sure what would close it – except for the end of the war.

What made it so different for Piotr and Jolka? There was no shyness when they met again after a period away from one another; no embarrassment or awkwardness. No matter how far apart they might be, they would always come together just as they had tonight, as close and warm as ever they had been – as if they could read each other's hearts. Was it because they were married? Was it the child they had made together? If she and Charlie were husband and wife, would that same unbreakable bond exist for them?

Bobby didn't attempt to answer Charlie's question. Instead she asked, 'Why haven't you been writing regularly, love?'

Charlie sighed. 'I'm sorry. Are you cross with me?'

'Not cross. Worried.'

'There's so much I've wanted to tell you, Bobby, but it's hard when I feel I can't write freely. I know you must be disappointed with every letter you get. You know, in my head I write you these long, long letters full of everything I'm thinking and feeling. Every night I lie there composing them to myself, and imagining what I'd tell you if you were with me. But I can't actually write them – not when Jackson, the barrack officer, is going to read them. All I can send are the dry, picked bones.'

'I shouldn't mind him seeing, if it meant I was able to feel it was really you writing. It's a little embarrassing to think of him reading it but I suppose officers are very businesslike about censoring letters between lovers. They must have to do so many.'

'It isn't that,' Charlie muttered. 'It would taint it for me. Jackson's an unpleasant little rodent – lives in Hunt's pocket, and I'm certain he shares our letters with the man. I hate to think of his poisonous mouth laughing at how we feel about each other with his friends in the officers' mess.'

Bobby looked at the ground. 'How do we feel about each other, Charlie?'

He frowned. 'What does that mean?'

'Only you seemed so distant and formal just now, when you greeted me. You haven't kissed me – you haven't even touched me. I've barely had two letters from you this last month.' She swallowed a sob. 'I don't think I realised how far apart we seem to have grown until just now.'

'Is that what you think?' He approached her now, and took her in his arms. 'I'm sorry. I didn't mean to be distant. I'm not sure what I meant to be. I've had so much on my mind, I wasn't thinking clearly.'

She nestled into his arms, absorbing his scent. 'So do you… you still…'

'There's only one thing good and pure left in this world for me, Bobby, and that's how I feel about you,' he said earnestly. 'I know it's hard while we have to be apart. I know it'll get even harder before it gets easier. But I love you, and nothing can change that, I swear.'

Bobby gave a damp laugh. 'I was worried you'd started to forget me.'

'I think about you every day. Every hour. Every minute.' He punctuated his words with soft kisses on her lips. 'Now do you feel better?'

'A little.'

'And you haven't forgotten me either? There isn't some handsome chap desperate to sweep you off your feet now I've gone?'

'No one could be as handsome as the man I love,' she said, giving him another kiss. 'I wish you would write regularly though, Charlie, even if you have nothing of substance you feel you can tell me. Just seeing your writing on the page makes me feel closer to you. Reminds me you were thinking about me.'

'Then I will. I'll write twice a week with all my dull news of life at camp. Three times a week. I swear I'll never visit the NAAFI without immediately writing to tell you how many cigarettes I smoked and what I had to eat and drink.'

Bobby laughed. 'That's better. Now you sound like you. I've missed your daft jokes.'

'By the time I send you home tonight, you'll be thoroughly convinced that my feelings for you haven't cooled in the slightest. Just the opposite, in fact, as I intend to prove right now.'

He pulled her to him for a deep kiss, and Bobby felt her doubts and worries evaporate as she pressed her body against his. Everything would be all right, this kiss seemed to say. She was loved and desired, still, by the man she loved and desired. And while the future was uncertain, and Charlie soon to leave her to head out into mortal danger, in his arms she always found the comfort she needed.

'I do wish you were coming home for Christmas,' she whispered when they broke apart. 'It won't be the same without you. You ought to be there to see the girls' faces when they unwrap your dolls' house.'

'I wish I could. You must write and tell me about it.'

'Did it take you long to make?'

'A few months. I started it at my last place and brought it with me when I transferred. I was glad to have a project to keep me occupied at night, since Hunt isn't keen on letting us out to play. Some of the other boys took a great interest in it too, and contributed paint and supplies. Bram made some of the furniture.'

'It's incredible, Charlie. I never knew you were so good with your hands.'

'Only useful thing my father ever taught me,' he said quietly. 'It felt like an appropriate gift, since the poor kids have got no home of their own any more.' He gave her a squeeze. 'We'd better join the rest, before Hunt notices I'm missing and has me shot for desertion. I wouldn't put it past him either.'

'He's going tonight then?'

'Of course he is. He wouldn't trust us out of his sight for a whole evening. We might get ideas and start enjoying ourselves. Come on, beautiful.'

'Wait a moment.' Bobby put a hand on his arm. 'I wish you'd tell me. What it is that's on your mind.'

'What makes you think anything is?'

'I can see it in your face. Last time I saw you, you looked like you hadn't been sleeping properly. You look even worse tonight. Is something wrong at the camp?'

Charlie sighed. 'Never mind that now.'

'Charlie, please. If you want me to feel like you're still mine, like you're not drifting away, you need to share the things that are on your mind with me. There's something wrong; something other than the war. If you can't say what it is in a letter then say it now.'

'There'll be time for that later, when I walk you back to your bus stop.'

Bobby hesitated, examining his features in the dim, blackout-approved pinprick of light cast by a nearby streetlamp. There were circles under his eyes, and his handsome face, so dear to her, was haggard and pale.

'Will you promise?' she said. 'Promise to tell me, before I go home.'

'I promise. Just not now. You'll understand better afterwards.' He squeezed her hand. 'Let's go, and I'll introduce you to some of the chaps.'

Chapter 17

It wasn't a long walk from the war memorial to the town hall – in fact it was just across the road – but they decided to take a circuitous route along Sheep Street and back up, too content in each other's company to want to rush to be with others. With Charlie's arm around her shoulders, looking proud as they passed fellow servicemen meeting civilian sweethearts of their own, Bobby felt she could relax again. It was all right. Nothing had changed. The distance between them was no more than skin deep, and Charlie loved her as much as ever he had.

And yet at the same time everything had changed, because now he was really going to war. Of course Bobby had always known he would have to, but there had still been a tiny, lingering spark of hope inside her – a hope that something would happen to keep him safe. That the war would end before it was necessary for him to fly, or something else benign would occur to keep him out of the fight. Now she realised that wasn't going to happen, and her best hope for her lover's safety was a speedy end to the war now the Americans had joined them as an ally.

'Hey, Slacks. You look good tonight.'

She blinked at the figure who had hailed her. As her eyes adjusted, she recognised Ernie King lurking outside the town hall.

'Ernie. Hello,' she said. 'I didn't expect to see you here. Are you heading to the ENSA concert too?'

'That was the plan. The other guys are inside already with a couple of girls. They were supposed to set me up with a date too but she hasn't turned up, so looks like I'll be going stag this evening.' He nodded to Charlie. 'I'd ask you for a dance later, but I'm guessing this is your feller.'

Bobby smiled. 'It is. This is Charlie – I mean, Aircraftman Charles Atherton, if we're doing formal introductions. Charlie, this is Flying Officer Ernest King of the RCAF.'

'No need to salute.' Ernie grasped Charlie's hand for a vigorous shake. 'Swell girl you've got there, pal. Terrible dancer, mind you. Shocking at the Lambeth Walk.'

Bobby laughed. Charlie, however, looked a little uncertain how to react.

'She is a swell girl,' he said. 'How do you know her?'

'Oh, we're old friends. I'm the personal servant of her ugly sisters.'

Charlie looked puzzled for a moment, then he smiled. 'Oh, of course. You're from the pantomime.'

'Sure am. Buttons, at your service. I guess your girl here wrote you of it, did she?'

'She told me a little. Sorry, but we ought to get inside before my CO marks me absent without leave.'

'Yeah, I'll join you in a while. I'd better give my date a few more minutes before I give up on her.'

'Well, nice to meet you. Um, sir.'

'Do you have to call him "sir" when he's in a foreign service?' Bobby asked as they went inside.

'I… don't know. I expect so, since he has a King's Commission.' Charlie looked a little dazed by the encounter. 'He's not like I pictured him when you wrote to me about the pantomime.'

'How did you picture him?'

'I thought he'd be older. And uglier. Wizened and hideous is how I like to imagine any men you might be getting chummy with while I'm away.'

Bobby smiled. 'You're jealous.'

'A little. Is that so unreasonable?'

They reached the hall where the entertainment was to take place and Charlie gave their tickets to the ATS girl on the door. After they'd put their coats in the cloakroom, he offered Bobby his arm and escorted her into the hall.

Bobby had been worried it might be a sit-down affair, and they would have to spend their evening in silence while confined to a row of chairs. However, she was relieved to find only a few people seated at the tables around the edge of the room. Most were on their feet, dancing to a jolly eight-piece band in slightly tatty evening wear who were playing on stage. They weren't the most precise of musicians but they played with energy and enthusiasm, which was all their audience really cared about.

'You know you don't need to be jealous of me, Charlie,' she said, raising her voice over the music. 'Ernie's a friend, that's all.'

'Mmm. A young, handsome, very male friend, with the film-star accent that sends women weak at the knees. I did notice.'

'So did all the girls in the village. Mabs Jessop is half silly over him. Don't worry, he's getting far too much female attention to take any notice of me in my mud-splattered trousers.'

'He was giving your legs a good look just then.'

'Probably the novelty of seeing them. I nearly always wear slacks to rehearsals – hence the nickname.'

'He's an officer as well,' Charlie went on. 'If he likes, he can probably just order me to hand you over.'

She smiled, and stood on tiptoes to kiss his cheek. 'You know, I rather like you being jealous over me. Ever since I've known you, you've had girls chasing you. I'm sure I'm owed a little revenge.'

'Cruel, heartless woman.'

'I'm sorry. Forgive me?'

'Dance with me and I'll think about it.'

The band struck up a new tune, 'How Deep is the Night'. Laughing, Bobby let Charlie sweep her into his arms and on to the dance floor. It almost felt like everything was back to normal, now Charlie was teasing and flirting as of old. She could half imagine they were back in the dance hall in Settle where they had spent some of their happiest courting days. Charlie held her tight as they danced, and she pushed down her worries about the future and the war so she could enjoy being in his arms once again.

'Still my girl, Bobby Bancroft?' he whispered.

'Always.' She met his eyes. 'You're not really jealous of Ernie King, are you?'

'Perhaps I am. I can't help it.'

'You don't need to be. Ernie doesn't think about me like that, and I certainly don't think of him like that.'

'Why wouldn't he think about you like that? You're beautiful, Bobby. The man isn't blind.'

'You're very sweet.' She gave him a quick kiss. 'But if Ernie has his eye on anyone, it's Topsy. I mean, naturally it's Topsy – me he just teases.'

'I remember when you believed the same of me. Entirely mistakenly, as it turned out.'

'This isn't the same. Honestly, you don't need to worry about Ernie having anything romantic in mind. Not where I'm concerned.'

He sighed, holding her closer. 'It isn't only that. It's that the two of you are sharing something. All of you back in Silverdale, not just you and King. You've got your pantomime and these new friends, and I can't be any part of it.'

'It's the same for me, thinking of your life in barracks with these men I've never met.'

He smiled a little sadly. 'It's hard, isn't it? Being apart.'

'But we'll get through.'

'I wish I could say you were really mine though. Forever mine.' His voice was soft as his breath whispered against her cheek. 'I know I said I wouldn't ask again, but since I'm going to war soon I'd like to give it one last shot. Would you think about it, Bobby? Before I go.'

Bobby was silent. She just pressed against him, her face against his neck, feeling the familiar prickle of a tear. Piotr and Jolka were dancing not far away, and Jolka waved to her as they spun by.

It was tempting. Too tempting. To be able to say they really belonged to each other. To be together, as man and wife, before Charlie went off to war. The Cinderella dress Mary had made for her, so clearly designed for the altar, could be pressed into service again for their wedding day. And when Charlie came home on leave, it would be a wife's loving arms he came home to...

There were so many worries, still. The future, the war, children, her job. But Bobby wasn't thinking about her worries at that moment, intoxicated by the music, the dancing, and Charlie's body against hers. All she was thinking about was him.

'I'll think about it,' she found herself whispering.

'Before I have to go?'

'Yes, Charlie.'

'That was all I wanted to hear.' He pressed a kiss to her lips.

Charlie pointed out some of his comrades as they spun around the room.

'That's our drill sergeant – Alfie McLeod, a Scot,' he said. 'Randy so-and-so. He's got eight children so far, and no sign of wanting to call it a day. I'm sure his wife must have fallen to her knees to praise God the day he enlisted. There's Dan Gardener with his girl. Keen amateur boxer, sings in the unit choir. And Dennis Jansen, a Dutchman. Oldest cadet on the base at thirty. The lads call him Grandad.'

'Are there a lot of foreigners at your barracks?'

'Only Piotr, Dennis and Bram since the all-Polish crew were lost.'

'Is *he* here?'

Charlie nodded. 'Sitting at the back looking like he's sucking a lemon, with the specs and the big red face.'

He spun Bobby around so she could see. She recognised Hunt at once from Charlie's description. He was a tall, spare man with a ruddy complexion, clipped moustache and hollow cheeks, watching his men enjoying themselves with his eyes narrowed. Beside him sat a sallow-faced man with a weak chin and ferret-like eyes.

'Who's that with him?' Bobby asked.

'Flying Officer Jackson, our barrack officer. Crawler of the first water. He's Hunt's favourite stooge.'

'They look an unpleasant pair.'

'Peas in a pod. I don't think Hunt would have let us come tonight if it had been up to him, but then he'd have had to explain to his superiors why a Christmas concert put on especially for local servicemen had been so ill-attended by his cadets,' Charlie said. 'He doesn't approve of dancing. Or women. Or foreigners. To be honest, he doesn't approve of much.'

'Is he really harsh with you all?'

'Huh. Not with all of us.' Charlie scowled in the direction of his commanding officer. 'You know how there's always that one teacher at any school? The one who delights in torturing the small and the weak?'

'My games mistress,' Bobby murmured. 'She was a monster. The headmistress at the evacuees' school in Sumner House reminded me of her, but she didn't beat the children. Miss Malone relished doling out physical punishment with the back of her hand to the children she took a dislike to.'

'It was my Latin master for me. His weapons of choice were the cane and the ruler. Hunt's just the same sort.'

Bobby blinked. 'He doesn't beat the men, surely?'

'He doesn't need to, he's the CO. He's got other ways of making them suffer in the name of military discipline.' His expression softened, and he gave her a kiss. 'But I'd better not talk of that where people can hear. We can discuss it later. Besides, I want to enjoy having you close to me without thinking about Hunt.'

'Do you get on well with the other cadets? You rarely mention them in your letters.'

'Most of them. There are some bad apples though.'

'Piotr said you'd become good friends with this man Bram. I thought he must be another Pole with a name like that. I'd like to meet him.'

'Bram isn't a Pole,' Charlie said quietly. 'He isn't a man either.'

Bobby frowned. If her fiancé's new friend wasn't a man, what was he? A carrier pigeon?

'I mean he's barely a man,' Charlie said, noticing her puzzled expression. 'He's not long turned eighteen, poor kid. He was assigned the bunk below mine when he arrived two months ago and I sort of took him under my wing – more like a big brother than a pal really.'

'Is he here?'

'He is. I'll introduce you after this tune. I promised him he'd get to meet you tonight.'

Chapter 18

When the dance ended, Charlie took Bobby's hand and led her to a young man sitting by himself, watching the couples twirl around the floor with a slightly awestruck expression on his face.

Charlie was right: the boy did look very young – even younger than his eighteen years. He was small and slight, and rather wan in his complexion. Bobby was a little surprised he had passed his medical. He didn't look strong enough for military life.

'On your feet, airman,' Charlie said jovially when they reached him, clapping the boy on the back.

Bram smiled shyly as he got to his feet. 'You're not an officer yet, Charlie.'

'Well, it's good to get some practice in.' He nodded to Bobby. 'This young lady spotted you from across the room and demanded to be introduced. Mind you're not too charming, Bram. I've got enough competition for her favours.'

Bram smiled a little uncertainly and held out his hand to Bobby. Then he snatched it back, as if suddenly remembering himself, and took off his cap before presenting the hand again.

Bobby smiled too as she shook it. 'It's very nice to meet you.'

'Um, hullo,' the boy said. 'You're Charlie's fiancée, aren't you? He keeps a photo of you in a frame by our bunks.'

Bram had a strange accent. It was almost English – almost. However, there was a hint of something slightly foreign underpinning it that Bobby couldn't place.

'That's right,' she said. 'Bobby Bancroft.'

'Soon to be Bobby Atherton, if I have my way,' Charlie said, giving her waist a squeeze. 'Bobby, this is my good pal Aircraftman Abraham Liebner. Bram to his friends. He's going to ask you to dance in a moment.'

Bram looked at Charlie with horror. 'Oh, no. I couldn't do that.'

'Why not? You ought to be practising for our wedding day, you know. I'm planning to ask pretty girls enough to dance with all my single friends. Bobby can teach you how to do it.'

'I'd love to dance with you, Bram,' Bobby said. 'As long as it isn't the Lambeth Walk, which I learned recently I'm shockingly bad at.'

'No, really. I'd be ever so awkward, and step on your feet and all sorts. Besides, the CO wouldn't like it.' He glanced at Hunt, who was glaring at him, and hastily put his forage cap back on. 'You'd better dance with Charlie.'

Charlie glanced at Hunt too. 'Perhaps you're right. We don't want to make trouble for ourselves. Come and join us after the dancing though. I think there's a comedian of some sort on after the band finish playing.'

It was a merry evening, although the entertainment was a mixed bag. After the band stopped there was a rather good comic revue that Bobby watched with interest, hoping to pick up some tips for her performance as Cinderella in two weeks' time. A man of middling talent then regaled them with bird impersonations, followed by a passable crooner.

Once the live entertainment had ended, gramophone records were played and there was more dancing. Charlie introduced her to the friends he had made, who seemed a cheery bunch, and she enjoyed catching up with Piotr when he could tear himself out of his wife's arms for five minutes. By the time the evening was coming to an end, she felt reassured that Charlie's life at the barracks wasn't as awful as she'd been imagining in spite of the ruthless CO. Certainly he had made some good friends there, and seemed to be well-liked. She noticed how his gaze often drifted to young Bram, however, and his brow furrowed with worry whenever he looked at the boy.

When it drew close to the time her last bus was due, Bobby prised herself somewhat reluctantly out of Charlie's arms.

'I ought to remind Jolka it's nearly time for us to leave,' she said. 'Will you walk back with us? There's only half an hour.'

'Let's go for a walk by ourselves and you can arrange to meet Jolka at your stop. I'm sure she'd appreciate as much time alone with her husband as she can fit in. Besides, I promised to have a talk with you.'

'You did. I haven't forgotten.'

Once they had arranged things with Jolka, they reclaimed their coats from the cloakroom and Bobby slipped her arm through Charlie's. He led her across the road to cobbled Sheep Street, where there was at least a little light, and they took a seat on a bench. Charlie looked pensive now they were alone.

'It's that boy Bram, isn't it?' Bobby said softly. 'That's what's been worrying you. Is he sickly?'

'Not in his body. In his mind…' He sighed. 'I'm so afraid, Bobby, about what's going to happen to that kid when they move me on. He's not strong enough to fight on alone.'

'To fight what?'

He took her hand and pressed it tightly in his. 'You noticed the trace of accent?'

'Yes. What is it? You said he wasn't Polish.'

'No. He's German – at least, he was born in Germany, although he's really as much English as German. His mother is British-born, and he's a naturalised British citizen now. His family are Jewish refugees. They fled here in '33 when Bram was a little lad of ten, after the Nazis came to power.'

'That must have been frightening for him.'

'I suppose it was, but at least it got them out of Hitler's clutches.' He shook his head darkly. 'And then they come here, where you might think people would show a bit of compassion for their plight. They had to leave Germany because Hitler doesn't believe Jews can be true Germans, and now Bram's father is locked up every night as an enemy alien because the British can't see him as anything but a German. The family's had a hell of a time of it, Bobby.'

'Were they interned?'

'No, but Bram's father lost his job after Munich. He was a teacher at a boys' school and the parents complained they didn't want a German teaching their children. He's struggled to find another job, so the family have been on their uppers ever since. It's ridiculous when Hitler's just as much their enemy as ours. Every time Bram's mother goes out to post a letter or use a public telephone, people look at her like she must be handing over military secrets to the Führer.' He scowled. 'And then there's Hunt.'

'You said he doesn't like foreigners.'

'Can't stand them. I've always felt it was no coincidence that it was a Polish crew who were flying in the fog the night the plane came down. Whenever there's anything dirty or unpleasant to be done in our barracks, the barrack officer makes sure it's Bram who's picked to do it – acting on Hunt's wishes, of course.'

'Because he's a German?'

'Because he's a Jew,' Charlie muttered darkly. 'Hunt hates them even more than he hates foreigners. Stops the lad worshipping his own way and makes him attend Christian services with the rest of us. Destroyed the book of Jewish scripture he had with his kit. Calls him offensive names, belittles him in front of the other men, puts him into isolation for the slightest thing. Pushes him to the limit of his health and sanity with physical activities Hunt knows the kid isn't strong enough for.'

'The poor boy,' Bobby said with feeling.

'Bram joined up because he wanted to fight back against what the Nazis were doing to his people in Germany.' Charlie gave a bleak laugh. 'He was so proud to get into the RAF. Do you know how rare that is: for a German to be training as aircrew? Enemy alien refugees who join up nearly always get shunted into the Pioneer Corps with the old men. Bram's one of the few – I suppose because he's a naturalised citizen. Then he finds the same fanatical prejudice in his commanding officer that he and his parents fled from eight years ago.'

'Isn't there something you can do to help him?'

He rubbed his temples. 'I do what I can. Some of the other men went gunning for Bram when he arrived as well. He was different, and he was young, which made him vulnerable. A few of us were able to see them off right enough, but Hunt's our CO. We help where we can but we can't openly disobey his orders.'

'This is why you never mentioned Bram in your letters?'

'That's right. Everyone knows Jackson is nothing more than a tool and a spy for Hunt, and if he found out we'd been trying to protect the boy, he'd make his life not worth living. You saw how afraid Bram was to dance with you tonight, because he knows Hunt will give him hell if he has the presumption to touch a Christian girl. He's terrified of the man. Honestly, he's so close to snapping, I can tell.'

'Snapping in what way? You don't mean he'd desert?'

'He might do something drastic, at any rate,' Charlie murmured. 'He's started to get a look in his eye that reminds me of your father. He screams in the night, sometimes – and then gets put on a fizzer by Jackson for disturbing the barracks. Between them, him and Hunt have given the boy combat fatigue without him ever having to go near a battlefield.'

'You mean you think Bram might… hurt himself?'

'Perhaps, if Hunt doesn't let up. And when me and the other lads who've been trying to look out for him get packed off, there'll be no one to come to his aid. It'll be his only way out.' Charlie looked fierce. 'That bastard'll end up killing him by proxy and never have to answer for it until Judgement Day, just like that Polish aircrew he as good as murdered. I wish I could punch his face, just once.'

'But… there must be something you can do, Charlie,' Bobby said, feeling helpless in the face of his helplessness.

'Is there no one you could speak to? None of the instructors or... or anyone?'

'No one I could be certain wasn't one of Hunt's cronies. He rules the place like a tinpot dictator.'

'You could report him to his superiors in writing, couldn't you? Write to Group Command? Surely he'd be removed if they knew he was driving a young cadet in his care almost to insanity with harsh treatment.'

'How could I write to them? Jackson reads everything that goes in or out of our barracks, and he'd go straight to Hunt with anything of that nature. If I make the pair of them angry, it's Bram who bears the brunt of it, not me. Hunt doesn't dare to be too harsh with the British cadets, but he knows no one asks questions when foreigners are badly treated.'

'I could write to them for you. I could write to Bomber Command; go straight to the top.'

'And tell them what?' Charlie rubbed his head. 'A second-hand account from a civilian, with no solid evidence, about a German being mistreated. They don't care about Germans being mistreated. Most likely it'd be Bram who'd find himself in the glasshouse, not Hunt, and me there with him for telling you about it.'

'They might investigate.'

'They wouldn't find anything. Hunt's careful. Besides, these are the same people who put him in charge in the first place. Hunt's got friends in high places – he's from that class that always has friends in high places.'

'Could Topsy help? She's got friends in high places too. Her father has old school chums in all sorts of influential positions.'

'Not as influential as Hunt's. His cousin's in the cabinet, Bobby.'

Bobby was silent for a moment, thinking.

'When I found out how that headmistress at the evacuees' school was mistreating the children, I wrote about it for the *Courier* and she was dismissed,' she said.

'This isn't the same. It's the military. You'd never get accusations like that past the censor to print them.'

'But he can't just be allowed to get away with it! He's already got innocent men's blood on his hands. He's going to have a lot more by the end of the war, if he isn't removed from a position where he's in charge of vulnerable young recruits.'

'I know. I wish I knew what to do for the best,' Charlie said. 'Perhaps when I'm moved on, I can speak to the new CO about it. But like I said, Hunt's careful. If he was taken to task, no doubt he'd just say it was a matter of discipline: toughening the kid up for military life. His officer friends with the same old school tie would shrug and dismiss it, and Hunt would make Bram's life even more of a living hell than it was before. The best I can hope for is that Bram stays mentally strong enough to stick out the training until he's moved on.'

'What if you could get some solid evidence that Hunt's singling out one recruit for mistreatment? They'd have to do something then, wouldn't they? Relieve him of his command?'

'I suppose so. But what evidence can I get? It's my word against his, at the end of the day.'

'The other men witnessed it too. They'd back you up.'

'Some of them. The ones who aren't prejudiced. There'd be plenty more who'd take Hunt's side, either because Bram's a German or because he's a Jew.' He stared at his hands. 'Too many of these Jew-baiters about. Makes you wonder, doesn't it? If it could have happened here. If it could have been Mosley instead of Hitler, and we'd be the ones rounding up our own people and sending them to forced labour camps while good men stand by and do nothing.'

'That's a horrible thought.'

'Isn't it?' He sighed. 'We're running out of time, darling. Here, let me hold you. It could be a long time until the next time.'

Bobby snuggled against him, and he bent to kiss the top of her head.

'I'm sorry I've not written as often as I should,' he said. 'It has been on my mind, the situation with Bram. That doesn't mean my feelings for you have changed. You're still in my thoughts, every day.'

'I know that now. I'm sorry. I suppose all my ramblings about pantomimes and engagements have seemed very foolish when you're grappling with these big, weighty things.'

'They haven't at all. I like to be reminded that there's still joy in the world, and know the children will have a happy Christmas in spite of the war. You must send your sister my congratulations too.'

'I wish I could help you, Charlie. I hate to think of Hunt mentally torturing that poor boy and just being allowed to get away with it.'

'I wish you could too, but I really don't know what's to be done. I don't want to make things any worse for Bram. If I take action somehow, I need to be damn sure it's going to result in Hunt's removal.' He squeezed her tight. 'It's been lovely to see you tonight though. I almost felt like my old self for a while, having you in my arms while we danced. Being with you makes the war feel far away, Bobby.'

'I wish it could stay that way.'

'So do I. But it can't.'

'When will I see you again?'

'I don't know. I hope it won't be too long.' He tilted her face up to his. 'Sweetheart, you won't forget, will you? What you promised to think about?'

'I won't forget. I love you, Charlie.'

For the last time in what might be a long time, Charlie took her in his arms and kissed her.

Chapter 19

The next day was Sunday – the day set for the christening of little Robert Sykes, Bobby's new godson and namesake. She rose early to dress herself in her smartest skirt and blouse, then knocked on her dad's bedroom door to make sure he was awake.

It felt like a long time since she had seen her friend Don, the proud father, and she was looking forward to it very much. Hopefully there would be time to catch up on each other's news when they adjourned to the pub after the ceremony for the traditional wetting of the baby's head.

Bobby pondered Charlie's problem as she and her father travelled to Bradford. It had been on her mind all night, which had contained very little sleep once she had returned home from the concert. The idea that this Squadron Leader Hunt, already responsible for the deaths of four men and the life-altering injury of a fifth, should be allowed to get away with torturing a physically weak young man to the point of ill health was abhorrent to her. Every maternal instinct she had cried out against it. Surely if there was a God in heaven who believed in justice and fair play, He would see that Hunt got the comeuppance he deserved.

But waiting for the Lord to move in His famously mysterious ways could take a long time, and Bram needed help now. If something wasn't done about Hunt before Charlie and the friends who had been looking out for the boy were moved on, who knew what the consequences could be? If the man felt no remorse for the four deaths he had caused in the summer, he was unlikely to lose much sleep over one more. Yet Bobby couldn't light on a solution that she could be certain would end Hunt's reign of terror at the training centre once and for all. Charlie was right: if she took any action, she needed to know it would guarantee Hunt's removal – otherwise he would take out his anger on Bram.

There had to be something she could do though, even if Charlie, trapped at his camp with Hunt, was unable to do anything. She had friends with some power and influence, didn't she? Topsy for one, and Archie for another. Perhaps they could help. Or there was Ernie King. He was a flyer too, and an officer, even if he was in a foreign service. Possibly he could intercede, and speak to someone higher up who could take it further. Or there were the men at the hospital, all RAF, many with commissions…

It would be risky though, discussing the situation with others. She wasn't supposed to know anything about it as a civilian, probably – Charlie could get into trouble for sharing it with her. And her fiancé was right about another thing: there was a lot of prejudice around. You never knew who might be harbouring anti-Jewish sentiment they had never openly expressed. As for anti-German sentiment, these days that was considered positively patriotic. None of her friends held such views, she hoped, but if they spoke to others… things could be made worse instead of better, and it would be her fault. Charlie had said Bram was teetering on a knife-edge, mentally. It wasn't worth taking a risk that might send him toppling over.

Her mind kept coming back to Miss Newbould, the headmistress of the evacuees' school that for a short period had been established at Sumner House. Don's daughter Sal had been posted there, and when Bobby had gone to visit her, she'd discovered the child cowering in fear because another girl was making her life hell. The only response to this by the headmistress was to tell the sickly little girl to 'toughen up' and take extra Games. When the school governors had refused to take action, Bobby had written an investigative piece for the *Bradford Courier* that had led first to the removal of the headmistress, and ultimately the closure of the school when a number of parents had chosen to withdraw their children.

Words had power. They could comfort and console. They could inform and persuade. When used by someone who knew how to manipulate them, they could stir people up into a fire of righteous anger that could bring down civilisations. That was why this war was different from all those that had gone before: because now nearly everyone had a wireless in their living room, and the powers that be were able to weaponise words as well as firearms. Well, wasn't she a reporter? Couldn't she make her words count for something just as well as Dr Goebbels?

It was a case of where to direct those words though. An RAF training centre wasn't an evacuee school. The military kept a closed shop, and anything that might affect wartime morale or cause embarrassment to Bomber Command would likely be hushed up by the Ministry of Information – she knew that from her days working on the *Courier*, when any stories of military significance had been heavily censored by the office in Leeds responsible for signing off their copy before publication. It was of no use writing a story exposing Hunt's treatment of his young recruits when no newspaper would be allowed to print it, and given that Bobby's only evidence was Charlie's word, it would be a libel risk too.

'You're quiet this morning,' her dad observed as they got off the train at Forster Square Station in Bradford and started walking to the nearest tram stop. 'I hope that Charlie Atherton didn't get you tiddly when you were out on the town last night.'

'Hmm?' Bobby roused herself. 'Oh. No. Sorry, Dad, I've just got something on my mind.'

'Owt you want to share with your old man? Happen I can help.'

'I'm not sure anyone can help with this. I probably oughtn't to discuss it either, since it's a military matter. Charlie shared it with me last night but I don't think he was supposed to. He needed to get it off his chest.'

Her dad frowned. 'Summat bad, is it?'

'It's not good,' Bobby admitted. 'Something at his camp that's making him unhappy. But never mind that today. We've got an important job to do.'

'Aye. I've never been a godfather before. Hope I can make a good job of it.'

Bobby smiled at him. He was in a jovial mood today, his cheeks ruddy and healthy from outdoor work, and looking smart in his best suit. It was nice to see him happy.

'Don thinks a lot of you, you know,' she said.

'I think a lot of him.' He turned his face away. 'Saved my life, that man.'

It wasn't like her father to make any reference to the events of the previous January, when his mental state had been at its lowest following the loss of his job at Butterfield's Mill. Bobby vividly remembered the phone call for her at Moorside, when Don had broken the news that her father had been hospitalised, and the nightmare journey that followed as she hurried to Bradford hoping she would find him still alive when she arrived. Don had indeed saved her father's life that night. If he hadn't gone over to check on her dad, as Bobby had asked him to do occasionally in her absence, it would have been too late to pump his stomach clean of the substances he had taken to try to end his life.

This was the first time she had ever heard her father acknowledge what had occurred that night. His attempted suicide, like his flashbacks to the last war and his problems with drink, wasn't something he found easy to talk about. His usual practice was to act as though no such thing had ever happened. It felt healthy that he was able to accept what had taken place at last. Not wanting to embarrass him, Bobby didn't say anything in response, but she took his hand briefly and gave it a squeeze.

When they arrived at St John's, the church was already half full. Don came forward to greet them. Usually a typical gruff, taciturn Yorkshireman, her friend looked practically vivacious today. He was beaming from ear to ear, his chest almost bursting out of his shirt with pride. He shook Rob's hand vigorously, then submitted to a hug from Bobby.

'Congratulations, Don,' she said. 'I'm so happy for you both.'

'Aye, well done, lad,' her dad said, clapping him on the back. He glanced at the baby by the font, swaddled up in a christening blanket and cradled in his mother's arms. 'Our godson looks a proper little corker, I must say. We're fair capped to be asked.'

'You'll have a pint and a cigar with the proud father at the pub after the service, I hope, Rob,' Don said. 'Well, a cigarette anyhow. I couldn't get any cigars.'

'Couldn't keep me away.'

'Come and have a proper look at the little one before we start.' Don took them both by the shoulders to guide them to his wife. 'You've never seen a bairn like him. Legs long as your arm. He'll be playing centre forward for Park Avenue before he's out of napkins, mark my words.'

'Here are our two godparents,' Joan said with a smile when they reached her. 'Bobby, come and hold your namesake.'

She placed the baby into Bobby's arms. Robert looked wonderingly up at her as Bobby looked wonderingly down at him. She drew one fingertip over his little face, shining and rosy, and found herself blinking back a tear.

'Joan, he's perfect,' she whispered. 'Well done. You too, Don.'

'I don't see what he did that's so wonderful.' Joan beamed at the baby, whose hands had emerged from his blanket to explore this strange new human holding him. 'He does have his father's ears though, poor soul. We could pick up the Home Service on them.'

'And his mother's right hook,' Don said with a laugh as he arrested one flailing baby fist. His voice softened as he stroked the tiny fingers. 'Robert Donald Sykes. Our little miracle. Born in the midst of war, to a mam and dad who never thought they could be so blessed again. If mankind can give him one christening present, I hope it's a world at peace to grow up in.'

'Amen,' Rob murmured.

Chapter 20

After the ceremony, the christening party spilled out of the church and into the Bull's Head to wet the baby's head – although the baby himself wasn't in attendance, going home with his mother and sister for a rest after the excitement of the day. Don proudly distributed cigarettes to the men present in lieu of cigars, and as was traditional, the consumption of much beer began.

Most of the women had gone home after the ceremony, leaving their menfolk to celebrate Don's virility at the pub. Thinking it was best to leave the men to it for a bit, Bobby bought herself a half of brown ale and claimed a quiet corner by herself. She never minded being left alone at events like this. Perhaps it was her journalist's curiosity, but she found it enjoyable to just sit and observe people.

It did her good to see her dad enjoying himself with the other men. He was a social being by nature, although in his lowest spirits he was prone to shutting himself off from his acquaintances. Spending time with others, outside the world in his head, was good for him. Bobby would always be grateful to Don for befriending him when she had left home to work out in the Dales. He'd been a good friend to her in a lot of ways since they had first met while working on the *Courier*, and a mentor to her as a reporter too.

Don was the guest of honour at the gathering, of course, and as time went on, Bobby started to worry there would be no opportunity for her to speak with him quietly before she and her father were due to travel home again. However, when he had done his duty as host, he came to take a seat by her.

'Thought I'd forgotten you, did you?' he said.

'I don't mind. You've got a lot of people wanting your attention today.'

'What did you think of him then?'

She smiled. 'He's a real bobby dazzler, Don. You must send me a photograph so I can bore everyone to tears back in Silverdale showing off my beautiful baby godson.'

Don looked a little bashful, but he beamed with pride. 'Aye, he got his mother's looks, lucky sod. Our Sal thinks he's the best thing since sliced bread. She always wanted a little brother.' He nudged her. 'Happen you're feeling broody now, are you?'

'I'd be lying if I said I wasn't a little, when I held him and he was pummelling me with his tiny fists.'

'He's the makings of a boxer in him all right,' Don said with a smile. 'Still waiting to hear when we'll be in church for you and your young man, Bobby. Hope Joanie'll have time to give the suit a press.'

'It won't be for a little while yet. At least… I'm not sure. I'll let you know.' She smiled at him. 'It's like old times, this. We should call up Tony and Freddie to come join us for a game of darts.'

Don scowled. 'Don't talk to me about that pair of loafers. Honestly, the only reason the boy's not in the dole queue with Scott is his age. Hope he don't make me regret it.'

'Oh. Yes.' She rubbed her forehead. 'I forgot you let Tony go. Too much on my mind. It's a shame. I know he was lazy and workshy and a general pain in the neck, but the *Courier* won't seem like the *Courier* without Tony Scott. He was fun to have around, at any rate.'

'Aye, well, he should've thought about that before he started using his position on the paper to lead innocent lasses astray.'

Bobby frowned. 'That's why you let him go?'

'That and the fact he never does any bloody work.'

'How was he using his position on the paper to lead innocent lasses astray?'

Don supped his pint of beer. 'It was Freddie I caught at it. Sent him out to cover a talent show at a church hall in Shipley. I knew one of the girls singing in it a bit – young friend of Joanie's from the WVS knitting circle. She told Joanie that some cheeky cub from her husband's paper had told her he could get her name in the press – maybe even a photo.'

'In exchange for her getting pally with him, I suppose,' Bobby said, pursing her lips.

'That's it: seduction by column inches. I hauled the kid into Clarky's office for an earful and he told me he picked up the trick from Tony. If Tony wants a girl to take out, apparently he just tells her he can get her a mention in the paper, or offers to suppress some story about her or her family. Dirty little beggar. Well, I gave the kid another chance seeing as he's nobbut seventeen, but Tony's more than old enough to know better and he's had his nine lives many times over already. When he's exploiting his position to prey on girls, that's beyond the pale.'

'Oh Lord,' Bobby muttered. 'I think I know what started it.'

He frowned. 'You do?'

'Yes. He tried it on with my sister. Told Lil he'd pull a negative story about someone she was fond of in exchange for a date. He obviously thought it worked well enough to add it to his little book of tricks.'

Don shook his head. 'Morals of a tomcat, that man. I can't deny I couldn't help liking him in spite of my better judgement, and God knows where I'm going to dig up another journalist in this ghost town, but this time enough was enough. Won't be too many more years that our Sal will be at the mercy of men like him. It's not on.' He glanced at her. 'What's all this you've got on your mind then? Wedding worries?'

'Oh. No. Well, yes, but not only that.' She lowered her voice. 'You'll be discreet if I tell you?'

'Why, is it a military secret or something?'

'Not exactly but it's… delicate. Something Charlie told me about when we went to an ENSA show together last night.'

Don started filling his pipe with the Tom Long tobacco he always smoked. 'Well?'

'There's this CO, Squadron Leader Hunt. He mistreats some of the men – one man in particular. Nothing that would be likely to raise eyebrows among top brass, Charlie says. It's all within the rules. But this boy he's singled out is quite weak and small; only eighteen. Hunt gives him physical activities to do that the lad isn't capable of and punishes him excessively for any perceived wrongdoing. Charlie says it's akin to mental torture, and his friend is close to snapping from it.'

Don frowned as he lit his pipe. 'Same training centre, is it? The one the plane that crashed came from?'

'Yes, and it was Hunt who gave the order the Polish crew were to fly in bad weather.'

'Why this boy in particular?'

'He's a German Jew. His family came here as refugees eight years ago.'

'Hmm. Doesn't go a bundle on foreigners, eh?'

'Or Jews. Charlie says he won't let this boy, Bram, worship freely and calls him offensive names.'

'Make my blood boil, men like that. They're no better than the ones we're fighting.'

'I know,' Bobby murmured. 'But it's not uncommon for people to be prejudiced in that way, is it? If Charlie tried to expose this CO to his superiors, or if I tried on his behalf, they might hold the same views as Hunt on the quiet. Any attempt like that... if it fails, it's Bram who'll suffer.'

'Aye, that is a worry. What's he going to do then, this young man of yourn?'

'I don't think there's anything he can do. His barrack officer censors all the other ranks' letters, and he's the CO's right-hand man – anything like that he'd be bound to pass on.' She swallowed down the last of her beer. 'I wish I could do something.'

'Well, do something then. Even working on that glorified parish magazine of Reg Atherton's, you're still a reporter. You got that evil headmistress sacked, don't forget.'

'Yes, but this isn't like when I wrote the piece about Sal's school. Even if I had any more solid evidence against Hunt than Charlie's word, which I haven't, no paper is going to be allowed to print anything critical of a senior RAF officer with a cousin in the cabinet.'

'Cousin in the cabinet, has he?'

'So Charlie says. I don't see how being a reporter is any help to me in this case.'

'Hmm.' Don was silent for a moment. 'What would your lady journalist do – the one from the last war you were always such a fan of? Disguised herself as a soldier and served at the front.'

'Dorothy Lawrence?' Bobby blinked. 'I don't know. Dress up as a WAAF and bluff her way into the camp or something. But I can't do that. Even if I did, I'm not sure what good it could do. I've got a man on the inside already, and he's as powerless as I am.'

'Here. Have some of this, I've had enough,' Don said, pouring some of his beer into her glass. 'Joanie'll wring my neck if I go home too well-oiled.'

'Thanks,' Bobby said with a smile. 'Any advice then?'

He took his pipe from his mouth. 'You're not thinking of it in the right light, Bobby.'

'How do you mean?'

'Well, what's a journalist? I mean, what's the job all about?'

'Words. Information. Creating clean, engaging copy that people want to read.'

He shook his head. 'That's only half of it. Where do you start with a story?'

'I'm not sure what you're getting at, Don.'

'What's Reg got you working on now? Owt?'

'Apart from this damned women's page he wants to bring in… a piece about the village's wartime guests and how they're fitting in. Why?'

'Right. And what was the first thing you did when you started work on this story? You didn't just sit down and write it, did you?'

'Well, no. I went out to interview some of the newcomers to the village to find out how they felt about the place – the airmen at the hospital, evacuees and others.

Then I used those interviews to decide what angle I ought to pursue.'

'Exactly. Research. Don't matter how engaging your copy is if you haven't got the research behind it.' He finished his remaining beer. 'This Hunt wasn't always CO for a training centre, was he? He had a life and career before the war.'

'I suppose so. What of it?'

'If I were you, I'd find out as much as you can about the man. His military career, his family, where he served and who with, what military honours he's been awarded, if he's ever published anything, what groups he's been a member of – anything you can.'

'How will that help?'

'You'll pardon my language, but if a man's a bastard now, he was probably a bastard most of his life. That's something that would tend to leave a trail. Take that Bingham chap, for example.'

'Who?'

'School Tie Bingham, the press were calling him. Lieutenant-colonel; CO of an army training centre. Wrote a letter to *The Times* giving his view that officers should only be drawn from the upper classes. Naturally there was uproar, and Bingham was relieved of his command.'

Bobby stared at him for a moment as she finally caught up with what her friend was suggesting.

'You mean if Hunt had ever said something publicly...'

'Aye, now you're getting it. Man doesn't like Jews. If he'd said owt in praise of the Fascists before we went to war, it might've been overlooked. Dig it out now and he'll be hauled over the coals for it, I reckon, regardless of how sympathetic his superiors might be on the quiet. Anything in his past could give you a clue. You know where to look. You bloody should; I trained you.'

'I do,' Bobby said slowly. 'Thanks, Don. I don't know if I'll find anything, but I'll feel better for trying to help.'

—

It was late in the day when they arrived home to Cow House Cottage. Bobby had been pondering Don's words all the way back. He was right – there was more to being a journalist than writing. Ferreting out information, reading the meaning hidden between the lines; that was all part of it. She had those skills – Don had taught them to her. If she could use them to help Bram and Charlie, and get Hunt removed before he ruined any more young lives, she would.

'It's not quite bedtime but I'm pretty tired out after today,' she said to her dad. 'Shall we make it an early night?'

'Aye, I'm ready to hit the hay. Exhausting work, being a godfather.'

'You get into bed. I'll bring you some Horlicks to help you drop off.'

They were interrupted, however, by an urgent knock at the door.

Bobby frowned. 'Who's calling at this time?'

'Happen it's Mary with some news from t' farmhouse.'

Bobby was surprised to discover on answering the door, however, that their visitor wasn't Mary but Topsy. Bobby took one look at her friend and pulled her inside.

Topsy wasn't at all her usual neat, tidy self. Her stockings were caked in mud almost to the knee, as if she had been wading through a bog in them. Her face was white as paper, and her eyes red with salty tears.

'Topsy, what on earth has happened?' Bobby said. 'You look a fright. Did you walk here in the dark?'

'I didn't know where else to try. I've been to all our friends but no one knows where he is. Not Jolka or Maimie or anyone. Please tell me you know, Birdy, or I'm sure I shall go out of my mind.'

'What? Who is it you're looking for?'

'It's Teddy.' She swallowed a sob. 'He's gone.'

Chapter 21

'Gone?' Bobby shook her head. 'He can't just be gone. How could he go? He can't walk.'

'He is gone. I left him alone at the cottage, only for an hour while I went out to fetch something for him, and when I came back he wasn't there.'

'Mrs Hobbes has taken him somewhere then. Up to the hospital, perhaps.'

'She was in the village. I met her there. There wasn't anyone with him.' Bobby had never seen her friend look so frightened. 'Someone must have taken him, Birdy. I'm so afraid he's hurt or... that he won't come back to me. Or that he can't.'

Of course there was no early night for Bobby that evening. She immediately put her shoes back on so she could help Topsy search for their missing friend.

'Is there anywhere you haven't tried already? Anywhere Teddy might have been taken to by someone he knows?' she asked as she pulled on her coat.

'There's Woodside Nook. You don't think he could have gone there with Archie, do you? They get along together well enough but I wouldn't call them bosom friends.'

'If you haven't tried there already, it would be worth checking,' Bobby said. 'I don't expect they have a telephone, do they?'

'No.'

'Then we'll have to go on foot.'

Bobby went to fetch the torch that she used when she needed to journey anywhere in the dark, made her apologies to her father and the two women set off, walking at a brisk pace.

Rules about the use of electric torches in the blackout were strict. Apertures could be no more than an inch in diameter, the light must be dimmed using a circle of newspaper, and it must be pointed downwards at all times. The dim, narrow beam was some help but not much, and Bobby cursed under her breath as she stumbled over another rock in her path.

'Through the woods is the quickest route, but we daren't risk it in the dark,' she said. 'My dad has stoat traps all over the place that could do us an injury. We'll have to take the road to Sumner House and go through the park, where there's a surfaced path.'

'Yes, that's sensible.' Topsy smiled wanly at her. 'I'm glad you're here, Birdy. You're so calm and clever whenever there's an emergency happening. I was half frantic with worry when I came home and found my boy was gone.'

'Tell me what happened,' Bobby said, keeping her eyes fixed on the ground in the weak torchlight as they made their way up the rocky track from Moorside Farm. 'He can't just have disappeared of his own accord.'

'I'd bicycled into the village to see if I could buy a seed cake from the bakery. Teddy had been quiet all day, although he didn't seem sad, but I thought that a little tea between the two of us and a slice of cake would put a smile on his face. Maimie had gone out too. You know how she always visits the pub with Norman after her lunch. I met her there and we rode together back to the cottage. When we arrived home, Teddy wasn't there.'

'Had he taken anything with him?'

'His civilian clothes were all gone, and his ration book, gas mask and small suitcase. He left his hospital uniform behind.'

'Then he must have intended to go, if he was packed and ready,' Bobby murmured. 'Anything else?'

Topsy choked a little. 'He... he left the gifts I gave him on his birthday.'

'What gifts were they?'

'Some books, and a valuable watch of my father's that I wanted him to have. They were all left behind.'

'How far can he wheel himself in his chair?'

'Short distances, that's all. It tires him to go too far. Besides, I'm certain he couldn't have left the house by himself. He'd never have got over the doorstep.'

'I don't understand,' Bobby said. 'It sounds like he must have planned to leave, but he couldn't have gone anywhere without help. I don't suppose he arranged with the matron to go back to the hospital and stay there until his discharge?'

'He's had his discharge.'

'Has he?'

'Yes, the doctor in charge of his case signed him off yesterday. He wanted to send him to a recuperation centre somewhere miles away where he can stay until a hostel place can be found, but of course I said there was no need of that and he could stay at the cottage as long as he needed to. Forever if he liked.'

Bobby stumbled on a stray rock that had found its way into the road, and took hold of Topsy's arm to steady herself. Topsy, who seemed to find the touch comforting, threaded her arm through Bobby's.

'You don't think he's gone for good, do you?' she asked, her eyes wide in the drab light of the torch.

'I'm sure he isn't,' Bobby said soothingly, but nevertheless she felt a bleak foreboding.

'I'll just… I'll just die if he's really gone,' Topsy said vehemently. 'What could have made him run away like that? He must know that I—' She stopped, flushing.

'He knows.' Bobby glanced at her friend, who was wearing only a thin cotton dress and damp, mud-splattered stockings. 'Here. Take my coat.'

'Shan't you be cold?'

'Not as cold as you must be in that dress. I've got a thick jumper on. Take it.'

Topsy consented to take the coat and snuggled into it gratefully.

'I know he wanted to leave as soon as he was well enough, but why so suddenly?' Bobby muttered, half to herself. 'He told me he at least planned to stay until after the pantomime. Did anything happen this weekend, Topsy?'

'Not at all – at least, nothing bad. Actually we had rather a jolly time. Teddy and I visited Archie at Woodside yesterday to help decorate before my Christmas party next week. Teddy was in the best spirits I'd seen him in for a long time. Archie and I were teasing each other as usual, and Teddy was smiling at the two of us being silly and singing Christmas songs while we put up paper streamers and refreshed the greenery. I never would have left him alone today if he'd seemed in low spirits, but he was so smiling and happy…' She trailed off. 'I was only gone for an hour, Birdy.'

'Have you told him how you feel about him?' Bobby asked gently.

Topsy gave a wan smile. 'Does everybody know about it?'

'Everybody with eyes. We saw how you kissed him under the mistletoe that day.'

'Perhaps it's old-fashioned but I've always felt it ought to be the gentleman who speaks first. But he must know. I'm sure I show him a thousand times a day that I...' She hesitated, looking suddenly shy. '...that I love him. I thought he might feel the same, but perhaps... perhaps I was deceiving myself after all.'

'I don't believe so. Still, it's not for me to speak on his behalf. When we find him, he can tell you himself.'

They had reached the grounds of Sumner House now, and were following the narrow path that led through the park, past the cottage and eventually down to Woodside Nook on the edge of the woods. Topsy blinked as they drew closer to her cottage.

'I see someone,' she said. 'Outside the door.'

Bobby squinted, directing her torch beam up a little as she tried to make out the shadowy figures. 'Two people. One in the doorway – I expect that's Mrs Hobbes – talking to one on the doorstep.'

Topsy clutched her arm. 'Do you suppose that's him?'

'It can't be. He's standing.'

'Oh. Yes.'

'It might be someone with news of him though.'

'You don't think anything could have happened to him?' Topsy breathed. 'That he could be hurt or something? If he tried to leave on his own and fell out of his chair... oh, Birdy!'

'I'm sure everything's all right. Let's go and find out what's happening.'

The two women approached the cottage. As they drew closer, Bobby realised the figure on the doorstep was a man in uniform, talking to Maimie Hobbes in the darkened doorway. She soon recognised a Canadian accent.

'It's Ernie King, I think,' she said to Topsy.

'Ernie? What can he want at this time?'

Bobby could make out the conversation now.

'It doesn't matter how urgent it may be, Mr King. As I've told you, I'm afraid she isn't at home,' Mrs Hobbes was saying rather impatiently. 'I'll be sure to tell her you called.'

'I have a note for her. Would you be able to pass it on?'

'I'd as soon not play at postmistress for young ladies and gentlemen, thank you. You'd do better to come back another day.'

'No need,' Bobby called. 'Here's Topsy. I presume that's who you're looking for, Ernie.'

She wondered what was in the note Ernie had brought to give to her friend. If it was a proposal or a love letter, he'd picked a terrible time to deliver it.

Topsy paid no attention to Ernie as they reached the cottage. Her focus was all on Mrs Hobbes.

'Has there been any news?' she demanded at once. 'Has he come home?'

Mrs Hobbes shook her head sorrowfully. 'I'm afraid not, lassie. Come inside out of the cold, the three of you, then we can put the lights on.'

They all went inside. Mrs Hobbes closed the door and flicked on the electric light.

'Sorry about all this,' Bobby said to Ernie, who she felt was owed some explanation for the object of his affection's frantic state. 'Topsy's rather distressed. Teddy seems to have disappeared.'

'I know,' Ernie said quietly.

Topsy frowned. 'You know? How can you possibly know?'

'Here. You'd better read the note I brought.'

Topsy gave him a puzzled glance as she took the piece of paper and unfolded it. Her eyes were wide and wet as she began to read it, but after a short time her brow furrowed. When she had finished, she looked up at Ernie with a very different look in her eyes. A look of pure, hot rage.

'Now, Topsy,' he said in a warning tone. 'Don't look like that. It's no more than Teddy asked me to do.'

'You… you *beast*!' Before Bobby had had time to register what was going on, her friend had flown at the man and was pounding her little white fists against his chest. The letter from Teddy fluttered to the floor. 'I hate you! Do you hear? I'll hate you until the end of the world for this, Ernie King. I hate you more than… than Hitler and Mussolini and all of them!'

'Hey. Come on, kid.' He arrested the hands beating on his uniform and held them gently but firmly in his own. 'The man's got his pride. You get that, don't you?'

The fight seemed to go out of Topsy now she was forced to be still. She sagged against Ernie's chest, looking defeated and utterly, utterly broken.

'You took him away from me,' she gasped. 'You took him away, and now he'll never… never be…'

'I didn't take him anywhere except where he wanted to go.'

'You wanted him out of the way, didn't you? Wanted to take his place with me. I should have listened when people tried to warn me about you.'

'You're hysterical. Here.' Ernie guided her to Mrs Hobbes, who glowered at him as she wrapped her charge in a hug. 'The old lady will look after you. I'd better scoot, since it's clear you can't stand the sight of me right now. Slacks, I guess you're in need of an escort back home.'

'Er, yes,' Bobby said, rather dazed. 'Topsy, I'll come over tomorrow after work. Don't you worry. We'll soon find him and bring him home.' Her friend, who was sobbing in Mrs Hobbes's arms, was too distraught to respond.

'Can't find a man who doesn't want to be found,' Ernie murmured, dipping down to scoop up the dropped letter. He tucked it into the breast pocket of his uniform.

–

They walked in silence for a while. Ernie's brow had lowered, as if he was deep in thought. Bobby was still trying to process what had happened.

'Afraid of the dark, Bobby?' Ernie murmured when they had gone some little distance into the gloom, not looking at her.

'I don't think I knew what darkness really was before this war. Are you?'

He laughed bleakly. 'Yeah, the long kind. Still, there's worse things than death. Teddy Nowak knows that.'

This wasn't a mood Bobby had known him in before. The Ernie King of their pantomime rehearsals was full of jokes. Now, however, his expression was solemn and thoughtful.

239

'What happened back there?' she asked.

'Nothing I couldn't have predicted.' Ernie sighed. 'Poor kid. I knew she'd take it hard, but that was bad. A girl's never hit me before. I feel a total heel.'

'You helped Teddy to leave?'

'Yeah.'

'Why?'

He shrugged. 'Because he asked me to.'

Bobby shook her head, frowning. 'Why would he ask you?'

'Weird, right?' he said, smiling. 'I could tell he never liked me much. I didn't take it personally. If I were him and he were me, I guess I wouldn't like me much either. I suppose that's why he asked me and not one of the other fellers.'

'Why?'

'Because he thought I'd be glad to get him out of the way. Topsy thinks the same. I mean I've got my shot now, right? The rich, beautiful lady of the manor has a heart and hand unencumbered, ready for the fortune-hunting colonial upstart to sweep in and claim them. I've heard my share of village gossip, Bobby.' He glanced at her, hugging herself as she tried not to shiver. 'Didn't stop to put a coat on?'

'I gave mine to Topsy. She was only wearing a thin dress.'

'Very gentlemanly of you. Seems only right I repay the favour on her behalf, in that case. I sure owe her a few.' He took off his coat and held it out to her.

'I'm fine. You keep it.'

'I've already taken a pounding from one woman tonight for unchivalrous behaviour. The least you can do is let me start making it up to your sex.'

She hesitated. 'Charlie might not like it.'

'Jealous type, is he?'

'No, but... I wouldn't like him to think there was anything in it.'

'I'd say he might not like his girl freezing to death while her escort stays toastie warm either. Go on, take it. It's a coat, not an engagement ring.'

Too tired now to argue, Bobby accepted the voluminous Air Force greatcoat and put it on. It was heavy and comforting; still warm from the heat of Ernie's body.

'So was that why you helped Teddy?' she asked. 'To clear the way for you and Topsy? I suppose you knew how they felt about each other. Everyone else seems to.'

'You think that little of me, do you?'

'Well, if not that then why?'

Ernie was silent, scowling, as they walked on.

'Had a pal once,' he said after a bit. 'Trained together. One day I got word his Welly had caught fire coming in to land. Rest of the crew bought the farm, but Harry made it. Except making it for Harry was worse than joining the rest of them in the Great Beyond. Burns all over his face and body. Made him look like a living corpse. I went to visit him at this specialist hospital they sent him to down in London.'

'I'm sorry,' Bobby said quietly. 'What happened?'

'We talked. Almost made me sick to see him but I tried my best not to look away. Harry told me that the worst of it wasn't the pain, or the sight of his own reflection – he'd been a good-looking boy, before. The worst thing, he said, was the *pity*. The pity, and the well-meaning lies that came from pity. And to know that for the rest of his life, however long or short that was likely to be, he'd have to be cared for like a babe in arms by charitable strangers who pitied him. Told me he could take anything but that.'

'Where is he now?'

'Gone,' Ernie murmured. 'Didn't make it out of the hospital.'

'What went wrong?'

'Oh, he came through all the surgery OK. It was his mind couldn't stand it. Didn't want a single more day of the pity of strangers, so he took matters into his own hands.'

'Suicide?'

'Yeah, and died a hero all the same – just as much as if he'd died with his crew.' Ernie sounded angry. 'Harry had a God-given damn *right* to make that choice. It's a cruel thing to force a man into a life he can't stand. Harry knew one way to live and when he couldn't live that way any more, he chose not to live at all. In his situation, I'd have made the same decision.' He glanced at her. 'I expect that sounds pretty yellow to a civilian. You think I'm a coward now, right?'

'I do not.'

'Dames never get it. They believe in all that love and heroism stuff the movies dole out. Can't cope when the world gets messy.'

'You're wrong,' Bobby said quietly. 'Women know well enough what a messy world can look like. Women who have to be mothers and wives; daughters; nurses. Don't underestimate us because the only women you meet are at dance halls.'

He turned to look at her. 'Hmm. Maybe you do get it.'

'Would you ever do what Teddy did? Leave someone you loved for what you believed was the greater good?'

Bobby wasn't sure why she asked him that. She couldn't tell whether Ernie was a serious suitor for her friend's affections or not, now. He was hard to read when he wasn't joking around. If he was intending to court Topsy then he had done himself no favours today, even if he had managed to clear a rival out of his way. She had genuinely looked like she hated his guts when she had flown at him.

'Dunno if I could be that noble for a woman's sake,' Ernie said. 'Whoever she was, she'd have to be a hell of a girl.' He paused under the thin needle of light from the lamp opposite the Black Bull pub. 'Here. You might as well read this.' He handed her Teddy's letter from his pocket.

'Oh, no. I couldn't read a private letter he wrote for Topsy.'

'He didn't. This was to all of us. I just figured she was the one who needed to see it first.'

Curiously, Bobby unfolded the piece of paper.

My dear friends in Silverdale,

I believe some of you may be sorry to read this and learn that I am gone. Others may be relieved, perhaps, to be spared the sight of me in future, although they are too kind to say so. This is the choice I have made, however, and I hope that those who are truly my friends will understand why.

I am grateful to Ernie King for his help in getting to my new place of residence. I will be staying at an RAF recuperation centre until a Salvation Army hostel place becomes available to me, and then... I do not know what will happen to me then. I hope there are charitable people willing to keep me alive long enough to return someday to Warsaw, so that I may see my mother and father once more before I die. After that, I believe I could welcome the end of my life with equanimity, knowing that all those on earth I care for are safe.

I will miss you all dearly. I send particular goodbyes to my dear friend Miss Bancroft, who has been so kind and understanding to me always, and to my brother-in-arms Piotr Zielinski, who saved my life on the mountain. Bobby, I beg you will not grieve for me. I am content, and you must attempt to be so also.

Finally, to my nurse and my dearest, my very dearest, Topsy. I believe you must be aware, my darling, of the feelings for you that I have long tried and failed to bury. If you care for me, as I dare to hope you may do a little, then I would ask you for only one favour. Be happy, and be in love, and fill every day with the joy and life you were so kind for a little while as to let me share. There is nothing greater in my life than the love I have felt for you. I will be happy and contented in my new lodgings if I can only believe you have happiness and contentment also. There are many men in your life who would make you a fine husband, and would be a good father to the beautiful children I know you will someday have. All my love, sweetest girl, and bless you a thousand times over.

I leave no address at which you may contact me. Please do not search for me. This is what I have chosen. If you would think of me sometimes and raise a glass to your old friend, that is all the remembrance I would expect.

Topsy, I am very sorry about the pantomime but I felt I must leave as soon as possible, for your own sake. Jack at the hospital can now walk with the aid of a stick and would make a fine Baron Hardup in my place.

My dearest love to all,
Tadeusz Nowak (Teddy)

'Poor Topsy,' Bobby whispered when she had read it. 'She must be heartbroken. Surely we could find him for her, Ernie. We could speak to the doctors at the hospital or... I don't know. There must be a way.'

'I know where he is,' Ernie said quietly. 'I won't be sharing the address with anyone – gave him my word as a gentleman. Besides, seems to me the man's made his wishes clear. We ought to respect them, if that's what he's chosen.'

'I suppose you're right. It's just so tragic. I'm sure they could have made each other happy, despite all the obstacles. They loved each other so.' She glanced at him as they started walking again. 'Why did you help him? You knew Topsy would hate you for it.'

'Because I get it. Guess he sensed that somehow.' He sighed. 'I can kid around with everyone except myself, Bobby. There's a good chance that one of these days, before this war ends, they'll send me on a sortie I won't come back from. But if there's one thing I dread more than the last goodbye, it's being cheated of death like Harry – like Teddy. I hope if it ever came to it, that there'd be someone who understood enough to help me do what needed to be done.'

Chapter 22

There followed several days of frantic, almost hysterical behaviour from Topsy as she tried to track down her lost love. She kept on at Ernie King mercilessly to reveal Teddy's location, but he wouldn't put aside his promise and refused to speak another word on the subject. Nor would any amount of pleading and cajoling with the doctor who had been in charge of Teddy's care at the hospital vouchsafe her the information she wanted. For perhaps the first time in her life, Topsy found that all her money, her rank and her powerful connections counted for nothing. Her lover had been clear in his wishes. Comradeship mattered more than all her pleas, and although Ernie was clearly moved by her distress, he wouldn't betray Teddy's trust.

'I really think he might not be coming back,' she said to Bobby five days later as they took tea together at the cottage. 'I was so sure he would, once he started to miss me.'

Bobby lowered her gaze. 'I'm sorry, Topsy. I think you're right.'

Topsy reached for the teapot to pour Bobby a fresh cup. It would have made Bobby smile, in other circumstances. When she had met Topsy the woman had barely known how to boil a kettle, so accustomed was she to being waited upon, yet today she had quietly prepared tea and sandwiches for the two of them with a deft hand. Caring for Teddy over these past six months had changed a lot about Topsy. It had made her self-sufficient in a way nothing else could have done.

'When he was in low spirits, he would sometimes say he wished he had died on the mountain with the others,' Topsy said in a tremulous voice. 'Now it almost feels as though he had. That he was killed in the war before he was ever part of my life, and having him with me for that little time was just a sad, beautiful dream.'

'Oh, sweetheart.' Bobby reached for her friend's hand and pressed it in hers.

'I wish he had at least said goodbye. If he'd given me a chance to make him understand... did he really think I took care of him only out of duty or pity? I might have worn a nurse's uniform but I did it all for love, Birdy. Even that first day, when Charlie brought him to the hospital half dead and I helped to save his life, I think I did it for love. Before he ever spoke a word to me.' She choked on a sob. 'Do you think he knew that?'

'I don't know. Perhaps not. But even if he did, it would have taken a lot to persuade Teddy that your best future lay with him.'

The wireless was on in the background, the newsreader droning on about the new National Service Act that had just been passed. Topsy cast it a listless look, then reached over to turn it off.

'I wish there was something I could do for you, Topsy,' Bobby said with a sigh. 'I hate seeing you this way.'

Topsy looked up at her, something like hope kindling momentarily in her eyes. 'You're a journalist. That means you have to know how to find things, don't you? How to find people. You're always at that library in Skipton finding things out.'

Bobby had indeed been spending some of her free time at the library in Skipton over the past few days. There they kept an archive of old newspapers, and she was following Don's advice to discover what she could about Hunt. So far it had been to no avail, however. The man was as clean as a whistle.

'I don't think I could find out where he is, if that's what you were thinking,' Bobby said. 'The household register isn't available to press. Besides... I'm sorry, Topsy, but I really think Ernie's right. If Teddy wants to be left alone then we ought to respect that. I hope he changes his mind, and I wish he would at least write so we know he's all right, but we can't force him to come back home.'

'Then he's really lost to me,' Topsy said quietly. 'Oh, Birdy...'

The tears that never seemed to be far away started to fall, and Bobby pulled her friend into a hug.

'I wish I could say it will all turn out all right in the end, but honestly, Topsy, I don't know,' she whispered.

Topsy drew back and wiped her eyes. 'I can't see how it could. He's gone from my life – as surely as if he had died on the mountain. I don't know how women who lose the men they love in wars can get out of bed the next day. I'm not sure if I shall tomorrow.'

'Please don't say that.' Bobby put down her teacup. 'Topsy, may I ask you something rather personal?'

'If you wish,' Topsy said vaguely. Her damp eyes drifted to the window and the soft snow falling outside. 'Nothing really matters much any more.'

'Who was Edward?'

She blinked. 'Edward?'

'Yes. I once heard you talking to Archie about someone called Edward who had died.' She flushed. 'I'm sorry, I ought not to have listened. I never meant to. It sounded like he was someone you cared for once, and that's why you and Archie had never become engaged. I wondered if he was a sweetheart who had died in the war.'

'A sweetheart?' She laughed softly. 'Yes, I suppose he was.'

'Does Archie wish to marry you?'

'I don't know that he wishes to, but he would if I'd agree to it. He's certainly proposed plenty of times in his silly Archie way.'

'I thought he wasn't keen on the idea of you two making a match.'

'No.' Topsy roused herself. 'It's rather awkward, to be honest. I'd prefer not to discuss it. Not that I like having secrets from you, Birdy, but it's really my cousin's affair.'

'Right,' Bobby said, puzzled. 'You don't intend to marry him, do you?'

'I almost think I might as well, now,' she said quietly. 'It doesn't matter what I do now, if Teddy is really gone forever.'

–

Pantomime rehearsals continued with greater frequency as they drew close to the performance. Every night that Bobby wasn't on duty at the ARP shelter she spent rehearsing, either at the hospital or Woodside Nook.

Rehearsals felt rather joyless after Teddy's departure, however. Topsy appeared listless and bored, as if she was sleepwalking, and she was so cold to Ernie King that Bobby wondered why he didn't drop out of the show entirely. Jack from the hospital was recruited as Baron Hardup, but he was very wooden and struggled to learn his lines. If it hadn't been for Archie keeping everyone's spirits up with his usual jokes and jollity, Bobby would have been tempted to give up on the whole affair.

'How was our friend at yesterday's rehearsal?' Mary asked one Saturday afternoon as they made mincemeat together at Moorside. It was now less than a week until Christmas, and Mary more or less lived in her kitchen in a flurry of flour and elbows. A Yorkshirewoman's elbows were truly a force to be reckoned with, Bobby reflected as she chopped dates for the mincemeat, watching them whir about. God help the Germans if they ever did invade, and found themselves face to face with a Yorkshire house-wife and her elbows.

'No better,' Bobby said with a sigh. 'Poor Topsy, it's awful to see. She's always been so bright and full of life. It feels like all the colour's drained out of her now Teddy is gone.'

'It's a shame,' Mary said as she began grating an apple. 'I understand why the young man never declared himself, but still – watch that kettle please, will you, Bobby? – still, I'd have been fighting furious if my Reg had decided to resign himself to the single life when the doctors told him he'd always be lame in one leg. He'd have had a clout round the lug if he'd tried telling me he was leaving me for my own good.'

'But Reg has some independence. Teddy has almost none. It's hard to say how you or I might feel in his situation.'

'True. The poor boy though. It's a tragedy to see him close himself off to happiness like that.'

There was a knock on the door and young Florence appeared.

'May I help with what you're making, Mary?' she asked. The girls had worked out by now that their best bet for getting an early taste of the goodies being prepared for Christmas was by offering their assistance in the kitchen.

'Aye, you can knead the dough for the Yule cake and start working in the currants if you've nowt better to do,' Mary said. 'I've a job for your sister as well. Where is she?'

'In the henhouse.'

Mary rolled her eyes at Bobby. 'Always that lass is in the henhouse. I thought we were done with this nonsense about Henrietta.'

'Jess hasn't been telling fibs about the eggs again, has she?'

'No, but she still spends every minute she can singing to the hens. Still hoping she can spare Henrietta before Reg wrings her neck on Christmas Eve, as if she can lay twenty eggs tomorrow and she'll be saved.' Mary sighed. 'Soft-hearted little thing. But it has to be done.'

'Are you going to the library before your party, Bobby?' Florence asked.

Tonight was the night of Topsy's Christmas party: an evening of dancing and cards for some of her wealthy friends in order to raise funds for the tea they were putting on after the pantomime. There was to be no cost for pantomime tickets, so that no child in the village would be excluded from the entertainment regardless of their circumstances.

'Yes, as soon as I've finished helping Mary I'm going to take the bus to Skipton,' Bobby said. 'I won't be late back though.'

'May Jessie and I help you get ready for the party?'

Bobby smiled. 'You may, and make my hair nice for me. You do it better than I ever can.'

Florence clapped her hands. 'Hooray! I wish we could come too. Mary, when will I be old enough for grown-up parties?'

'There'll be plenty of time for growing up, Florrie. No need to be in a rush about it. The day will soon come when you'll be very glad to turn the clock in the other direction.' Mary turned to Bobby. 'What are you looking for in your old papers at that library anyhow?'

'Oh, nothing important,' Bobby said. 'It's just a little research project I'm working on.'

—

After she had finished helping Mary, Bobby walked to the stop by the Black Bull to wait for the Skipton bus. Snow fell lightly while she waited, hugging herself. The fluffy flakes floated towards the ground, landing on her eyelids and the tip of her nose, which made her sneeze.

It was very cold, but the patchwork of the fells looked beautiful blanketed with snow. With the Christmas-card scenery spreading out around her as far as the eye could see and the scent of nutmeg and cherry brandy from the mincemeat she had helped to make still in her nostrils, Bobby felt like it was really Christmas at last.

Yet the season felt bittersweet, now. So many people who ought to have been there to share it were going to be missing. Friends and loved ones serving in the military – her brothers and sister, Piotr, Captain Parry – would have a bleak Christmas in their barracks far from their families, although at least Lilian would have her Lieutenant Cartwright nearby to console her. Charlie, likewise, would be confined to barracks, his planned leave cancelled as he prepared to join the fight.

And then there was poor Teddy. What sort of Christmas would he have this year, under the care of strangers to whom he was no more than another ex-serviceman who had been chewed up and spat out by war? She wished they could all be together on Christmas Day, even if it would be the last time until the war ended.

After she alighted from the bus in Skipton, Bobby walked down Sheep Street to the library. Her gaze drifted to the war memorial where she had met Charlie the night of the ENSA concert, and she thought about how it had felt to be in his arms that night.

He had been as good as his word – Bobby had had no fewer than two letters from him in the eight days that had elapsed since the concert party. There was little in them other than mundane news of barrack life, but still, they made her smile. As long as she knew he was thinking of her – that he still cared for her – she could bear anything.

She only wished she could do something to alleviate his worries about his friend Bram. An easy mind would be a better Christmas present than the scarf she had knitted for him. But so far, Bobby's search for information on Hunt had been a dead end. She had always known it was a long shot, but still, it was disappointing. The hardest thing was knowing where to look.

She had begun with the military records of the period during which she supposed Hunt would have been active. Bobby had guessed his age at around sixty, which had turned out to be close to correct. Hugo Hunt, she discovered, had had an unremarkable but unblemished career in the armed forces, transferring from the army to the Royal Flying Corps in the last war when he was in his early thirties and proceeding to work his way slowly but surely through the ranks. He was from a minorly titled family, his older brother a baronet somewhere in Derbyshire. That was where the Hunt family hailed from, but although Bobby had found out all she could about their history and connections, there was nothing to tie Hunt to anything untoward that she could use as concrete evidence of his prejudices.

She wasn't sure what she had been hoping to find, really. Don's advice had created a glimmer of hope, but short of being a vocal and active member of the British Union of Fascists, Bobby couldn't imagine what was likely to give Hunt away. And if he had been a member of any groups considered subversive or friendly to the Nazis, it would be ridiculous to think she could uncover that when the government must surely have thoroughly vetted the man before he was given a command. He'd have been interned with the rest of them if he was a known fascist, or absconded to Germany before war was declared as William Joyce had done.

Don's other suggestion – that the letters pages of the newspapers might furnish evidence of Hunt's prejudices – had sounded optimistic at the time, but she was looking for a needle in a haystack there. Hunt had been alive a long time, and there were a lot of both national and regional papers he could have communicated with. Nor would he necessarily have been as considerate as this School Tie Bingham chap had and written to them under his real name. Most people used a nom de plume when they wrote to the press, even if they were ordinary nobodies off the street like her. A senior RAF officer would be even more likely to exercise caution.

Still, Bobby asked to be shown to the archive of news-papers when she arrived at the library, and took out a sheaf of old copies of *The Times* from the early 1930s. When she thought about Charlie's worried, fretful expression, and the haunted look in the eyes of that young boy... no, she wasn't ready to give up yet.

It was two hours later when the elderly librarian approached her.

'Are you nearly done, Miss Bancroft?' he asked. 'I was about to lock up, but I can leave the key if you're staying a spell. We close at four on a Saturday.'

Bobby had a special arrangement with the librarian to access the newspaper archive out of hours when she needed to do so, since she was press. She felt a little guilty about using this privilege for her current purposes, since it was personal rather than work-related, but it was the only way she could find enough hours in the day.

She folded up the newspaper she had been trawling through. She hadn't intended to stay so long, with a party to get ready for this evening.

'No, I'm done. Thank you,' she said.

'Find what you were looking for?'

'No. Not yet.' Her brow knit with determination. 'But I'm not going to give up.'

Chapter 23

It was a little after 7 p.m. and pitch dark when Bobby picked her way precariously along the little path that led from Sumner House to Woodside Nook, once more in the blue crepe dress that was now her only serviceable party frock. Reg had dropped her off at the bottom of the drive in the trap, but Boxer couldn't take her any further than that and she was compelled to go the last mile on foot by the light of her little blackout torch.

She soon bumped into a fellow party-goer, however. Archie was coming up the path where it branched off to Topsy's cottage. He hailed her when he realised who it was stumbling along in the dark, and when he reached her immediately offered his arm.

'Thank you,' Bobby said, taking it with a smile.

She was always a little wary of accepting Ernie King as an escort. Not that she worried he would try to take advantage in the blackout as some men might, but she remembered how Charlie had been jealous of their friendship that night at the concert. That was fair enough – she wouldn't much relish the idea that Charlie was offering his arm and his company to pretty girls alone in the dark while she was far away. Archie felt different, though. He felt safe, somehow.

'I thought you'd have been at the party already,' she said to him. 'You are sort of the host. What were you doing at the cottage?'

'I came to fetch Tops so I could escort her in,' Archie said. 'Mother was keen for us to arrive together. Typical the girl would have trotted off somewhere and left me to turn up alone. I'm glad I found a woman to go in with, at any rate. I've got a reputation to uphold.'

'Where's she gone?'

'Who knows? Perhaps she's there already, hobnobbing with Mother, the poor unfortunate creature. I've just got back from a trip to Derbyshire.'

'Your mother's going then?' Bobby said, trying not to make a face.

He sighed. 'Sadly, yes. She isn't keen on the pantomime but she likes the idea of a Christmas party with "the right sort of people" in the midst of this uncivilised land. That's Mother.'

Bobby had fallen silent, however. Archie gave her a nudge.

'Anything wrong, old girl?' he said. 'You look as solemn as Topsy has since the foreign chappie disappeared. I've barely been able to get a word out of her this past week.'

'Hmm?' Bobby roused herself. 'Sorry. Did you say Derbyshire?'

'That's right, Mother sent me on an errand. Went to see the help at our crumbling family pile there to make sure they had everything ready for when she goes home at New Year. Pray God, I'll be given leave to go back to London then.'

'Derbyshire,' Bobby murmured. 'That's where he comes from.'

'Eh? Who?'

'Archie, do you know a family called Hunt? I under-stand they're local squires somewhere in that part of the world. There's a baronetcy.'

'You must mean the Egerton Cross lot,' Archie said breezily, as if this was naturally common knowledge. 'Sir Henry, isn't it? I was at school with his grandson – different house, mind you. His eldest daughter is a great friend of Mother's.'

Of course Archie would know the family. The upper classes all knew each other, didn't they? It seemed that way to Bobby, at any rate.

'It's the younger brother I'm interested in,' she said. 'Hugo. He's a squadron leader with the RAF.'

He laughed. 'Oh Lor, is old Hugo still around? The bard of Egerton Cross? I'd forgotten about him.'

'Yes, he's my fiancé's commanding officer at RAF Ryland Moor.' She frowned as his words registered. 'Why do you call him that?'

'Oh, Hugo was a notorious local joke round our way for a time. He started writing the most atrocious war poetry during the last bit of unpleasantness. Fancied himself another Rupert Brooke, I'm sure.'

Bobby blinked. 'Hunt wrote poetry?'

'Yes, all laboured rhymes and frantic death-or-glory stuff about the indomitable English spirit.' Archie laughed again. 'I can just imagine him torturing the poor recruits with his verses every night at lights out. Won't old Jefferies howl when I tell him?'

'Who?'

'Oh, he's Mother's aged retainer over in Derbyshire – the butler, you know. He thought Hugo was a riot when he used to give recitals at Mother's card parties back when I was a boy. Used to keep a straight face while he was on duty, but we did guffaw about it together after we'd escaped. He was rather attached to me – more than Mother and Father ever were, at any rate.'

Bobby was silent while she absorbed this. Whatever she might have expected Archie to tell her about Hunt, it hadn't been that. The man had hardly looked like he had the soul of a poet when she'd seen him at the concert.

'What do you know about Hunt's politics?' she asked Archie.

'Tory, of course. Cousin Cyril's responsible for something or other in the war cabinet. Why do you ask?'

'I just wondered if he had any sort of, um, remarkable views.'

'Only about the quality of his versifying, I should think,' Archie said, laughing. 'Used to send reams of it to the press, presumably with a bribe so they'd print it. Even published a little volume about ten years ago – at his own expense, of course. The family bought it out of pity, then it drifted into obscurity where no doubt it belonged.'

'Funny I've never heard of him. I read a lot of newspapers.'

'A little before your time, I should think. Besides, he didn't publish under his own name. I suppose the other flyer chappies would have laughed him into next week if they knew he was the author. Used a nom de plume, some Latin horror… Principatus, that was it. Of course, all the local families knew it was him.'

Bobby frowned. 'Principatus?'

'Yes. Don't ask me what it means. I slept through most of my Latin grammar.' He glanced at her. 'Why so interested, old thing? Is Hugo giving your young man a hard time? If he is, I could ask Mother to have words with the niece. Mind you, that might do more harm than good, you know.'

'No,' Bobby said vaguely. 'Not exactly. I just wondered if you knew the family.'

She was trying to remember something – something she had seen in one of the hundreds of newspapers she had trawled through this week. That name, Principatus, was ringing all kinds of bells, but she couldn't for the life of her put her finger on why.

–

They arrived to find the party had already started, in the same spacious parlour-library they used for their rehearsals.

Topsy's parties had a reputation for being jolly affairs and she had well-to-do friends who would come from miles around to attend them. The room was suitably crowded in consequence. Most of the women were in ballgowns, and the men present who weren't in uniform wore dinner suits and black bow ties. Bobby felt rather underdressed in her too short and slightly faded old frock, but it was all she had.

An area had been cleared for dancing, a small swing band hired for the evening, and tables set up for games of cards, dominoes and other opportunities for low-stakes gambling. A man dressed as Father Christmas was wobbling in merry fashion around the room with a bucket, exhorting those present to give generously towards the planned Christmas entertainment for the village children.

But as jolly as it was, the guests seemed a little sedate. Bobby was surprised there weren't more couples dancing.

Perhaps the evidently solemn spirits of the hostess, who was sitting alone watching the dancing with a blank expression in her eyes, were the reason for the slightly subdued merriment.

'Poor Topsy,' Bobby whispered to Archie as he escorted her into the room. 'Do you think she'll always be so?'

'She usually bounces back quickly when life gets dismal. Still, this feels different. I haven't seen her this bad before.' He glanced at his mother. Aunt Constance was holding court among a handful of upper-crust sorts near the piano, which was serving tonight as the drinks table. 'Mother's frightfully bucked the boyfriend is out of the way, of course. Teddy leaving plays right into her hands.'

Bobby raised an eyebrow at him. 'And you? Are you bucked too?'

'Well, I wouldn't say that. It works in my favour in one sense, but I do hate seeing the dear girl so depressed. I'd grown to rather like the chap myself.' He looked at her. 'She told you all about it, did she?'

'Not exactly. I overheard a little, and she told me the rest. She said you'd proposed a few times.'

'That's true.' He was silent for a moment, looking at Topsy. 'For rather selfish reasons, perhaps, but I'd do my best to make her happy.'

'Do you love her?'

Archie laughed. 'Love her? Rather, old thing. Everyone does love Topsy, you know.'

'You know what I mean.'

'Yes. I suppose I do.'

Archie fell into a reverie, his gaze fixed on Topsy. Bobby made a movement to reclaim his attention.

'Was Topsy this way after Edward died?' she asked.

He turned to her sharply. 'Edward?'

'The boyfriend who was killed in the war.' She looked up at him, surprised at the change in his manner. 'That is what happened, isn't it?'

'Yes. He died all right.'

'How?'

He smiled slightly. 'You ask a lot of questions, don't you?'

She shrugged. 'I'm a journalist.'

'Edward was another flyer. Fighter pilot. Shot down by a Jerry plane in the Battle of Britain. One of the many of the Few who never came back.'

'And now she's lost Teddy too. Poor Topsy,' Bobby said with feeling. 'I ought to go to her. Will you come? You can always make her smile.'

He groaned. 'Hang on a tick; here comes Mother. I shall have to introduce you. Try not to mind her, will you?'

Archie fixed on a false smile as his mother joined them. She ignored Bobby entirely, focusing her attention on her son.

'Where on earth have you been, Archie?' she demanded. 'Your cousin has been sitting alone this quarter of an hour. I thought you were going to escort her in.'

'She must have decided she'd prefer to escort herself. It's all right, I found another young lady who needed my arm on the way.' He nodded to Bobby. 'Mother, this is Miss Roberta Bancroft. She's a very dear friend of Topsy's – and of mine too, now.'

For Archie's sake, Bobby endeavoured to smile. 'It's a pleasure to meet you, Mrs Sumner.'

Aunt Constance curled her lip. 'Bancroft. Like the gamekeeper.'

'That's right. He's my father.'

Constance examined her as if she were some species of poisonous slug, then proceeded to ignore her as she turned her attention back to her son. 'Archie, you must come along with me. I want to introduce you to some of *our* people – I believe you and Roderick may have had the same housemaster at Durnford. Then I think the least you could do is engage your cousin for a dance or two.'

'I'm so sorry,' Archie murmured to Bobby as his mother walked away, clearly expecting him to trot after her like a good little dog. 'Keep Topsy company for me and I'll join the two of you as soon as she lets me out of her clutches. Don't forget to save me a dance later, will you, darling?'

'I won't.'

Bobby was preparing to join Topsy when Ernie King appeared at her side. He pressed a glass of something warm into her hand.

'Here. I thought you might need this after your brush with the Witch of the West,' he said, gesturing to the retreating Aunt Constance.

'What is it?' Bobby asked.

'Mulled punch of some kind. Got a decent kick to it considering the lack of supplies these days. It ought to warm you up, at any rate.'

Bobby sniffed the steaming drink. It smelled of apples, cinnamon and cloves. She swallowed some down, feeling it making its way through her body to the numb extremities.

'Thanks, Ernie,' she said. 'Listen, would you do something for me?'

'For a lady, anything,' he said, pressing a fist to his heart. Bobby smiled, glad to find him back to his usual foolish self after the sombre conversation they had had the night Teddy left.

'Will you ask Topsy to dance? I hate seeing her sitting all alone, looking so sad and different to normal.'

He followed her gaze to Topsy. 'I would, if I thought there was any chance of her saying yes.'

'Has she still not forgiven you?'

'Not sure she ever will. Not unless I tell her where her boyfriend's hidden himself away, and I swore to him I'd never do that.' He smiled and clinked his glass against hers. 'Blew my shot with her pretty well, didn't I?'

'You don't seem too cut up about it.'

'Plenty more pretty girls about. Their blood doesn't need to be blue to satisfy my tastes. I'm not a fortune-hunter, Bobby, whatever the gossips have been whispering.' He glanced down at her dress. 'I'll give you a dance if you like.'

She laughed. 'How very generous of you.'

'Well? How about it, Slacks?'

Bobby hesitated. 'No, I... it's kind of you to ask but Topsy should have some company. Besides, my fiancé wouldn't like it.'

'That old excuse,' he said, rolling his eyes. 'You're saving a dance for Archie, aren't you? I heard him ask you.'

'That's... not the same.'

'Come on. You can't sit out the whole night like an old maid just because your fiancé wants to keep you pure and chaste until after the duration.'

'Maybe in a little while.' She turned away. 'I'm going to see if Topsy needs anything.'

She went to claim a glass of whatever the spiced drink Ernie had given her was from one of the waitresses circulating with trays of the stuff before approaching Topsy.

'I brought you this,' she said, pressing it into her friend's hands.

'What?' Topsy looked at the drink as if she couldn't understand how it had got there. 'Oh. Thank you, darling.'

'Are you all right, Topsy?'

'I suppose so.' She summoned a weak smile that didn't extend to her eyes. 'It's a nice party, isn't it? It looks like everyone's having fun.'

'All except one person,' Bobby said softly. 'Don't you want to talk to your friends? I suppose they came to see you as much as to go to a party.'

'I shall put on my happy face and go make small talk in a moment. It takes more effort than usual tonight, that's all.' She cast a listless look at the untasted drink in her hands and put it down on a table at her side. 'Where do you suppose he is at this moment, Birdy?'

'At a Christmas party of his own, perhaps, with the other men at his lodgings.'

'No. I don't think he would care for that, unless they were people he knew well. He wasn't the social being I was.' Topsy winced. 'Isn't, not wasn't. I must stop speaking of him as if he were dead. It's probably the most awful luck.'

'Where do you think he is?'

'Alone, probably, in a sad little bed with nothing and nobody to amuse him. It makes me cry whenever I think of it. My poor boy.' Topsy smiled wanly. 'In the evenings, do you know what his favourite thing to do was?'

'Tell me.'

'He liked to have me read to him. Charles Dickens – he loved Dickens, especially *Pickwick*. How he laughed! Sometimes Maimie would read and I'd make a fool of myself by acting out the characters for him, like a play. Those were our happiest times.'

Bobby took her hand. 'He'd hate to think of you grieving for him this way, Topsy. You know he said in his letter that he'd be happy if he only knew you were happy.'

'And isn't that like a man's selfishness?' she said with a tremulous smile. 'As if I could change my emotions at a command from him, while never knowing where he is or if he's well. He says he can only be happy if he knows me to be happy, and never thinks that the reverse might be equally true.'

'He didn't know, I think, how strong were your feelings for him. You're so fond towards everyone, perhaps he thought your love was only a passing fancy.'

Topsy hid her face for a moment.

'Oh, if only I'd told him!' she said in an anguished voice. 'And now I'll never see him again, because of his sheer, stubborn, pig-headed man-ness! Ernie is just as bad. I could strangle the pair of them for treating me so: like a child who can't possibly know her own mind.'

Bobby knew there was no answer to this. She rubbed her friend's back while Topsy struggled to get her emotions under control, leaning forward to shield her from the rest of the room before anyone came over to ask awkward questions about her distressed state.

'But this won't do,' Topsy said at last, a forced calm creeping into her voice. She took out a handkerchief to dab her eyes. 'It's terribly unpatriotic of me, I suppose: weeping for my own selfish sake when I've thrown a party for the good of others. If there's one thing my class is supposed to be good at, it's hiding how we really feel.' She fixed her face into a smile. 'There. Lady Sumner-Walsh is ready to ride into battle, at the head of her troops like Blanche of Castile. Be proud of me, Birdy.'

Bobby smiled. 'I am proud of you.'

Archie approached at that moment, looking flustered.

'Oh Lord, please won't one of you girls dance with me?' he pleaded. 'Mother's threatening to introduce me to an ornithologist. I don't know what an ornithologist does but I've no doubt he'll be just as tedious as the last three chaps she forced me to meet.'

Bobby nudged Topsy. 'Go on. Archie can put a real smile on your face, I'm sure.'

'Yes, come on, Tops,' Archie said. 'It might persuade Mother to leave me alone for a while, at any rate. If she sees me doing my filial duty by standing up with you, I might actually be allowed to enjoy some of this party.'

Topsy hesitated. 'Will you be all right on your own, Birdy?'

'I'll be fine. There's Ernie and Chip and Mabs, and loads of people I know from the pantomime. You try to enjoy yourself. It is nearly Christmas, you know.' Bobby lowered her voice. 'And he'd want you to.'

'Yes. I suppose he would.'

Bobby watched them dance. It was a slow song, a waltz of some kind, and her friends performed it well. It was a pleasure to watch them twirl one another around the room among the other four couples on the floor. She could see that they were talking as they danced, but whatever they were saying, it didn't seem to be cheering Topsy up much. She still looked solemn, and Archie's expression had grown rather earnest as well.

Bobby wasn't left too long alone with her thoughts, however. A man soon approached, slightly wobbly, as if he had had too much to drink. He was in army uniform, wearing the insignia of the Royal Engineers – a captain according to his pips, and probably a good ten or fifteen years older than she was. Since she didn't recognise him from the pantomime, Bobby assumed he must be a personal friend of Topsy's.

'You look like you need a partner, dear,' he said, holding out his hand as if he was doing her a great favour by offering.

'Oh. No,' Bobby said, rather alarmed at the idea of dancing with a man she didn't know. 'I prefer to watch, really.'

'Come on. Not married, are you?'

'I'm engaged,' she said rather coldly, irritated at the man's inability to accept a simple no.

'He here?'

'No. He's training with the RAF.'

'Then it's not really any of his business what you get up to. Least you could do, after I've been chivalrous enough to ask you. Wouldn't want to be ungrateful, would you?'

Bobby was casting frantic looks in the direction of Ernie King in the hope he'd take the hint and come to her rescue. He was some distance away talking with Sandy and Mabs Jessop, who was clearly having the time of her life seeing how the other half lived. He failed to see Bobby's look of entreaty, however, and when all her excuses were dismissed, she had no choice but to dance with the charmless captain.

She soon discovered that dancing wasn't the only area of his life where the captain, who didn't bother to introduce himself, wouldn't take no for an answer. His hands had a mind of their own, wandering all over the place. Bobby had to keep all her wits about her so she could repeatedly guide them back to an appropriate position around her waist. She could see Topsy and Archie, sitting down now and talking in what looked a very intimate way, but every time her eyes drifted in their direction, the Royal Engineers captain took advantage of her distraction to slide his right hand to her bottom. It was like dancing with an octopus.

'One more, eh?' the man said jovially when the tune they'd been dancing to came to an end.

'Er, no. I need to… powder my nose. I'll be back in a little while.'

Chapter 24

Bobby took her time in seeking out the lavatory, hoping that by the time she rejoined the party, Captain Octopus would have grown bored of waiting for her and found some other poor woman to annoy.

When she re-entered the room, she was surprised to find the music had stopped and a hush had fallen over the assembly. Archie was standing at the front where the band were set up. She sidled over to Ernie and the other Canadians.

'What's happening?' she whispered.

'Archie asked for silence,' Ernie said. 'Looks like he's going to make an announcement.'

Bobby felt a cold sensation grip her. 'An announcement?'

'Thank you, everyone,' Archie said when all were silent. 'I won't keep you too long from your festive merriment. I just wanted to announce that what you believed to be a Christmas party tonight has now taken on the mantle of a rather different sort of celebration. I'm very proud to inform you all that my dear cousin and friend Lady Sumner-Walsh has just now done me the honour of agreeing to become my wife. After years of cajoling, begging and pleading… yes, that's right, I've finally given in and said I'll have her. Topsy, do you want to come and join me?'

Bobby clapped a hand to her mouth. 'Oh my God!'

There were murmurings of surprise in the room, which quickly became a cheer as people absorbed what was happening. Aunt Constance looked like her horse had come in at a hundred to one. She beamed proudly, and a little smugly, at the newly engaged couple as Topsy went to join her cousin. It was clear she took credit for the whole affair.

I almost think I might as well, now. Bobby remembered Topsy's words about marrying Archie when she had seen her last, mourning Teddy's departure. Was that it? Had she decided that since she couldn't have the man she really loved, she might as well settle for Archie? Or had she just run out of the willpower and energy required to keep refusing him? Bobby couldn't believe there was any love in the case; not the real, romantic sort. And yet Topsy did look almost happy as she joined Archie by the band. Or not happy exactly, but... satisfied. Accepting of her lot, just as Teddy had said he was. Topsy smiled as Archie planted a kiss on her cheek, and everyone in the room applauded.

'Thank you all,' she said to the party-goers. 'Well, I couldn't keep turning him down forever, could I?'

There was a chorus of laughter from her friends, who, it seemed, were well aware of Archie's matrimonial intentions towards his cousin. Bobby didn't laugh, however.

'When's the wedding, Topsy?' one person called out.

'Oh, we're both far too impatient for long engagements,' Topsy said gaily. 'As soon as possible in the new year, I intend to furnish Sumner House with a master again.'

Archie laughed. 'Steady on, old girl. I'm thrilled you're so keen, but let's do the thing properly, eh?'

'To hell with properly.' Topsy's eyes sparkled with a manic gleam, as if she might be capable of any impulsive action at that moment. 'I almost wish we'd invited a priest so we could settle the matter right away. But if we must wait, I want it to be no later than February.' She beamed at everyone. 'Of course you're all invited. Then we'll really have a party.'

'Won't we just?' Archie said, smiling as he slipped his arm around her waist.

She turned to Archie. 'And now I must have a dance from my future husband. What shall it be, Arch?'

'Oh, "In the Mood", of course. A taste of things to come, I hope. Strike it up, chaps.'

The band started to play and Topsy led Archie on to the floor.

'Well,' Sandy said, blinking. 'I didn't see that coming.'

'Jealous, Ernie?' Chip asked his comrade with a grin.

Ernie looked rather windswept. 'Don't know about that but you could knock me down with a feather. Could've sworn it was the other guy she wanted.'

'I don't understand,' Bobby murmured.

Chip shrugged. 'Archie's got money coming to him when the old lady goes, I guess. It's what their families want, and she's fond of him. I guess the title makes a difference to you Brits. Love's a nice idea but there're plenty of other things that count towards a marriage.'

'I know, but Topsy never cared about those things before. And yet... she looks so happy.'

'All women want a husband, don't they?' Sandy observed. 'Archie's a nice-looking boy. It's a good match for both of them.'

'I've heard about this type of thing happening,' Chip said. 'Nurses who believe they're in love with their patients – happened all the time in the last war. I liked the man but what was Teddy, really? A foreigner and a cripple, no money or rank, his face all disfigured like that. Topsy's a real lady. Now he's gone, I suppose she's come to her senses again.'

'Yes.' Bobby stared at Topsy and Archie as they capered to 'In The Mood', laughing and carefree, with none of the earnestness she had noted in their earlier interaction. 'Perhaps.'

-

The party felt so false and unreal after that; everybody in celebratory mood as they drank to the future health and happiness of the newly betrothed couple. Bobby couldn't feel happy for them, or believe Topsy's rather frenzied gaiety to be genuine.

She would have liked some conversation with her friend to see if she could discover how she was really feeling – why she had suddenly decided to accept Archie when she was in love with another man – but Topsy was surrounded by well-wishers claiming her attention. When they finally left her alone then Aunt Constance took her aside, presumably to discuss the wedding arrangements.

Bobby would have quietly left the party at that point if she could, but Ernie demanded the dance she had half promised him earlier before she was allowed to leave, and then the man she had nicknamed Captain Octopus oiled up for another turn.

'I'm afraid I really can't dance another step,' she said to him after another battle with his frantically wandering hands. 'I've got the most terrible headache. I probably ought to go home.'

'Nonsense,' the man slurred. 'Party's just getting started. Can't go home before midnight. Bad luck or whatnot.'

Bobby was starting to wonder if she actually had transformed into Cinderella. But if this man was her Prince Charming, then her Fairy Godmother had got something very badly wrong.

'I believe the young lady has promised the next dance to me,' a soft voice behind her said.

She smiled with relief. 'Archie.'

Captain Octopus looked put out. 'Don't see your name on her, pal.'

'He's right, I did promise him a dance,' Bobby said. 'Besides, it's only good manners to dance with the groom-to-be when he asks. Sorry.'

Archie took her hand and led her into the dance.

'I thought I ought to rescue you,' he said in a low voice. 'I know that chap. He's a frightful bore, and all my girlfriends tell me he isn't to be trusted on the dance floor. Did he bother you much?'

'I certainly had a difficult job keeping his hands where they were supposed to be.' She smiled uncertainly at him as he twirled her around the floor. 'Um, congratulations, by the way. I was waiting for a chance to speak to you, but you and Topsy have been rather monopolised since the announcement.'

'Thank you.'

'It was certainly a surprise. I had no idea I'd be coming to an engagement party this evening.'

'Yes, for me too. I thought I might as well take another crack at it, to show Mother I was being a good boy and taking my courting seriously. I nearly swooned when Tops actually said yes. I say, do you really have a headache?'

'No, but I am feeling a little fagged from fighting off your friend the captain. I wouldn't mind some fresh air.'

'Then let's fetch our coats and step outside for a moment. I could do with a break from all the merriment myself.'

He offered her his arm, then they sought out their coats in the untidy heap that had been piled up on an old chaise longue and went outside. Bobby breathed deeply, relishing the cool winter evening on her burning face.

'Do you want a cigarette?' Archie asked, offering her one from a packet.

'Thanks, I don't smoke.'

'Nor me. First trick I learned when I joined the RAF: always carry a pack of smokes and a light. It gives you a good excuse to talk to girls.'

Bobby turned to him, standing close to her in the darkness. 'What did you do in the RAF, Arch?'

'Fighter pilot – at least, that was the idea. I was Volunteer Reserve when war broke out so they called me up for active service pretty much right away. I sat twiddling my thumbs through most of the Phoney War, then when I finally got into the thick of things, I only got to fly two sorties before they grounded me for good.'

'Fighter pilot...' She paused, frowning. 'Like Topsy's boyfriend. Did you know him?'

'Yes, I knew Ned,' he said quietly. 'We were at Eton together. He was in Durnford House with me.'

'He's the old schoolfriend you joined up with? Topsy mentioned something about it.'

'That's right. Best friend I ever had.'

He looked sombre, and Bobby pressed his arm. 'I'm sorry. I hadn't realised you knew him well too. No wonder you seemed upset earlier when I mentioned him.'

Archie was silent, looking thoughtfully out into the darkness. Bobby wondered what to say. She wanted to ask about his engagement, and why he really wanted to marry Topsy if, as she suspected, there was no romantic love on either side, but it wasn't an easy subject to just drop into the conversation.

'Topsy sounds keen to hold the wedding as soon as possible,' she said instead.

He smiled slightly. 'That's Tops. Never wastes time when she's made up her mind to something. I suppose you know that.'

'It's funny. The day I met you, Topsy told me you were as against the two of you making a match as she was.'

'And yet here we are, about to be man and wife,' he said, laughing. 'I admit, if I had only my own inclinations to follow then I'd be happy never to marry at all. But if I must do it, it can really only be with Topsy.'

'Your mother must be pleased.'

'Oh, thrilled. She's already taken me aside and told me she might see her way clear to loosening the purse-strings now I'm a betrothed man. With a wife on my arm, I might even manage to find a job.'

'Does being married make a difference to employers?'

'For me it does.'

He turned to look at her. There was no light except that of the waxing crescent moon and a very dim glow that escaped through the blackout curtains, but she could tell he was scrutinising her face. He looked like he was trying to make up his mind about something.

'You're a good sort, I think,' he said at last.

'Um, thank you.'

'I felt when I met you that you were the type I could trust. Not too quick to make a judgement. Willing to consider things outside your own little world.'

'I hope I am.'

'I know what you're thinking, Bobby. Why is he marrying his cousin when he knows she loves another man? And why is she marrying him?'

'I am a little curious,' she admitted. 'You don't love her, I think. Not as a man ought to love a wife.'

'Well, I can't speak for the lady, but there are reasons a man might want a wife other than love. If Topsy agreed to be my wife, it would... let's say it would make it a lot easier for me to live my life the way I want to live it. It would open certain doors to me that are currently firmly closed. And it would allay Mother's suspicions too, which might persuade her to be a little more generous from a pecuniary point of view. I'm not an avaricious man but I do value independence, and independence is what marriage to Topsy could bring me.'

Bobby frowned. 'Suspicions? What suspicions does your mother have?'

He laughed softly. 'All right. Why not tell you? There's no going back now we've come this far, and I don't believe you'd be ungracious about it.' He seemed to be speaking as much to himself as to her.

'I don't understand, Arch.'

'Mother had suspicions... about Edward.'

'Topsy's sweetheart?'

He turned away from her. 'No. Not hers.'

Bobby frowned. Then she stared at him as realisation dawned.

'Oh,' was all she could manage to say.

'Do I revolt you now?' he asked quietly, still not looking at her.

'Of course I... I mean I've never... I'm sorry.'

'You know, I think I will have one of these.' Archie took out his packet of cigarettes, shook one out and lit it. He coughed a little as he drew on it, then took it from his mouth to look at it.

'Ned used to smoke this kind,' he said softly. 'I never can get used to them, but they taste like him.'

Bobby's head was still whirling from Archie's confession. She wasn't so green that she didn't know such things happened, of course. She had worked in the all-male environment of the *Courier* for a long time and heard the jokes bandied by her colleagues about 'nancy boys' and 'cream puffs', or dark mutterings that men needed to watch themselves in the company of this or that chap who was deemed too effeminate to be quite right. Probably she had laughed unthinkingly at the jokes along with the rest, and joined in her brothers' sniggers when the radio comedians made innuendo-laden references to men who preferred their own kind. But she had never really thought about it. What it must be like for those men to live with such feelings. Many people would no doubt feel revulsion at the idea, but when Bobby observed the pain of grief clearly written in Archie's features, all she instinctively felt was compassion.

'You loved him?' she said gently.

'He was everything. My life and my soul.' Archie lifted the cigarette to his nose and inhaled, as if the familiar scent of his lost lover could bring him back.

'I'm sorry. It must have been dreadfully painful for you.'

Archie looked wistful as he gazed into the distance; into his past.

'Funny thing, public school,' he said after a while. 'The masters lock you in there with a lot of other adolescents of your sex, stuff your head full of Ancient Greek texts that make boys being with boys sound almost nobler than the other type of love, turn a blind eye to the little romances they know all too well are going on behind study doors, then they shove you out into the world and expect you to find yourself a wife. I know plenty of old boys with a little woman and a brood of ruddy children at home who still enjoy something rather more Uranian on the side. Unfortunately for some of us, it isn't so easy to switch back and forth. Women just leave us cold – I mean in the sense of real passion. Can you understand that, Bobby?'

'I... don't know. I've never had to think about it before.' She was quiet for a moment, watching him. 'But I understand pain and loss, very well indeed. Do you still grieve terribly for him?'

'Every day,' he said quietly. 'And then there's the pain of never being able to share it with anyone. Tops is the only one outside my London set who knows, and the nanny, Maimie, who we were close to as children. It's almost a relief to tell someone else at last.'

'Topsy knows?'

'Of course. I wouldn't ask a woman to marry me under false pretences; I'm not a cad. She's known since we were children – before I did, probably. Tops has always been a complete brick about it.'

'I'm glad,' Bobby murmured. If her friend was really determined to do this thing, it was some comfort to know she was doing so with her eyes open.

'It's an odd thing,' Archie murmured. 'To grieve for someone you loved as other men love their wives, and at the same time have to laugh louder and longer than the other chaps whenever anyone makes a wheeze about fairies or pansies, hoping they'll never realise…' He sighed. 'It felt so pure, what Ned and I shared. I feel like I'm betraying him whenever I join in with those jokes, but to be exposed could cost me everything.'

'Is that the real reason you left the RAF? Topsy told me there was something in your blood.'

'Well, she's not lying. It's certainly part of me in a way I can't change.'

'No different than being left-handed,' Bobby said slowly, remembering an old conversation. 'Isn't that what you said to me once?'

'That's how I think of it. Neither a sin nor a disease; only a difference. Society and the law don't take that view, of course.' He took a meditative draw on his cigarette and coughed again. 'I suffered terribly, after Ned died. Used to wake up screaming from these nightmares where he had come back to life, but burned and broken as he had been when they fished his body from the drink. The other chaps were kind to me. They thought it was the grief of a comrade-in-arms, mourning as for a brother. I was plagued with guilt about what had happened to Ned; that it was him who bought it out there and not me. And then I was plagued with guilt about the pity I got from the men who didn't know what my real feelings were, and terrified they'd figure it out when I screamed his name in my sleep. Eventually I was so miserable that I took myself to the squadron quack and confessed it all. Threw myself on his mercy.'

'That was risky. He could have had you locked up, couldn't he?'

'He could have certified me mentally unbalanced and sent me for hormone treatment, or even had me court-martialled. That doesn't happen too often though. The armed forces don't want the embarrassment, or the publicity. Mostly chaps of an incurably invert persuasion like myself are quietly invalided out and sent back to civilian life so they can become someone else's problem.'

'And that's what happened to you.'

'Yes. The quack was sympathetic. Got me my discharge on health grounds and told me to find a like-minded chap to settle down with. Get a job and live quietly, out of the public eye.' Archie finished the cigarette and stamped it out under his foot. 'Problem is, civilian employers know what it means when someone's been invalided out of the forces on a flimsy pretext with nothing visibly wrong with them.'

'That's why you can't find work.'

'And why a wife would be greatly in my interest. Employers would be reassured that my tendencies were as ordained by God, as it were, and Mother would be happy I might produce the grandson and heir she craves with some true blue Sumner blood – although there I fear she's destined to be disappointed. In the worldly environs of London I could live my life among others like me without judgement, with a convenient wife back in Yorkshire to screen me from the law.'

'I do understand,' Bobby said. 'Still, it seems rather hard on Topsy. What does she gain from the arrangement?'

'I'd be a good husband. Observe all my conjugal duties except one. It might be a marriage of convenience but I do care for her, Bobby; very much. And with Mother leaving everything to us someday, Tops could be sure she'd have finances enough to look after that old house she loves.'

'A house is a cold substitute for a loving husband, Arch.'

He shrugged. 'I'd never stop her doing exactly as she wanted in that respect. If she likes Ernie King, or anyone else, she could take them as a lover with my wholehearted blessing. I wouldn't hang around her, getting in the way: I'd keep to my own set in London. And if a baby came of it, so much the better for us. I'd never tell.'

'Yes, but she loves Teddy. Ernie might agree to a bohemian arrangement like that, perhaps, but Teddy never would. He's not that sort.'

'I know.' He was silent for a moment. 'I admit I got what I wanted, but still, I am sorry in a sense that it had to end this way. I did think it was the best arrangement for the two of us when Tops was emotionally unattached though. There's too much alive about the girl to be trapped in the sort of conventional marriage where she'd be no more than "the little wife" of some brainless, boorish squire. That's the type her father's friends would push her towards, and I know a husband like that would stifle everything that was original and wonderful about her. I never would. With me, Tops could have the respectability that marriage with her own class would bring without any of the confinement. Get Mother and all those friends of her father's who pester her constantly about it off her back so she could do just exactly as she liked.'

'But she wouldn't have love, Archie. You were in love. You know how that sort of companionship feels – how much it matters to have it in your life.'

He sighed. 'Yes, that's the crux of the matter, isn't it? I do hate to see her little heart breaking into bits. I'd have stood aside for the man if he'd declared himself to her – if not exactly gladly then at least with the warm glow of knowing I'd done the right thing. But he's gone, isn't he?

He was clear about what he wanted. I believe Topsy's best future, now Teddy is out of the picture, is with me.'

Chapter 25

Bobby left the party shortly after Archie's confession. She couldn't get into the festive spirit after what she had learned. She would have liked to be able to speak privately with Topsy, but her friend seemed to have been spirited away somewhere by Aunt Constance. Not wishing to spend the rest of her evening doing battle with the wandering tentacles of Captain Octopus, Bobby had slipped out without saying goodbye to anyone and walked home alone.

She was glad to find when she got back to the cow house that her father had retired for the night. He sometimes stayed up late when she went out to social events, to make sure she arrived home safely, but she had no energy for conversation tonight.

She felt utterly exhausted, unsure what to think and feel after the events of the night. All she wanted was to crawl into bed.

Tomorrow was Sunday, and it was going to be far from a day of rest for her. After church she wanted to visit the library and see what she could find out about this nom de plume, Principatus, that Archie had told her Hunt used to publish his terrible poetry. Most importantly, she wanted to speak confidentially to Topsy, as soon as she could. She had to know what had really been in her friend's heart when she had said yes to Archie tonight, and if it wasn't too late to change her mind. She did feel for Archie's predicament and the grief he felt for this lost lover, Ned, but the idea of Topsy throwing her life away on a loveless marriage... no. There had to be another way.

Bobby stripped to her slip in her dark bedroom, took her girdle off under it and crawled into bed, too tired to get into her night things. She would wake up freezing in a few hours, no doubt, but now all she could think of was sleep: lots of it, and as soon as possible.

She found a surprise waiting for her in bed, however. There was already somebody in there.

Bobby squealed, and a hand shot out of the bedclothes to cover her mouth.

'It's me, you goose,' a woman's voice said. 'Don't scream the house down about it, for mercy's sake. Dad'll have a fit.'

'Bloody hell! Lil?'

Bobby jumped out of bed and fumbled for the light switch. She stared in amazement at her sister, who had shuffled into a sitting position in bed. Her Wren uniform had been folded and left over the back of the chair.

'Sorry for the scare,' Lilian said. 'I was planning to wait up for you. I got into bed to get warm, then I must have nodded off.'

'What on earth are you doing here? Why aren't you in Greenwich?' Bobby asked, wondering if she was so tired that she'd actually started hallucinating.

'I was able to get some unexpected home leave for Christmas. Aren't you pleased to see me?'

'Well of course I am. It's a surprise, that's all.' Bobby broke into a smile as her tired brain caught up with what was happening. 'Oh my goodness, I'm glad you're here. I've missed you to pieces. Here, give me a hug.'

She sat down on the bed so she could absorb her twin into an embrace.

'You ought to have asked if you could take your leave at New Year,' Bobby said. 'Then you could have stayed with us in Bradford and met this new girl of Jake's. The boys will be home from New Year's Eve until the 2nd.'

'I couldn't wait until then. I hope you'll have enough turkey for one more.'

'It'll be chicken, not turkey. But I wouldn't mention that over at Moorside if I were you. It's a bit of a sore subject.'

'Oh yes, you told me in your last letter,' Lilian said. 'Jessie's still upset?'

'Yes, still trying to save Henrietta from the noose by getting her to lay again.' Bobby drew back from the hug to smile at her. 'I'm so pleased you've come. I've got a thousand things to tell you that I couldn't put in a letter.' She frowned, noting something unusual in her sister's expression. 'But something's wrong.'

Lilian turned away. 'Don't be daft.'

'It is, I can tell. What is it, Lil?'

'Never mind about that. We've got a whole week to talk about it. But I do need to ask you for a favour while I'm staying – that's why I came. I had to beg for this leave, to be honest. There's a job I need you to help me with.'

Bobby regarded her curiously. 'What is it?'

'I'll tell you another day. I don't want to think about it just now. I want to snuggle under the covers and share secrets like we used to do as children, and pretend everything's back to how it was.' She sounded a little wistful.

'All right.' Bobby dug out her flannelette winter night-dress and threw it on over her slip, then turned out the light and got into bed again. 'Everything's OK though? The wedding plans are going well? I thought you and John would want to spend Christmas together.'

'He's got leave as well. He's visiting family in Scotland.'

'Things are OK between the two of you?'

'Never mind him. Tell me about everything here. Is Dad still enjoying his new job?'

'He is but Pete Dixon gives him some trouble, I think,' Bobby said. 'Dad breaks up Pete's traps but he refuses to tell Topsy what the man's up to on her land. Honour amongst thieves and all that. I hope it doesn't get him into any trouble.'

'Not drinking, is he?'

Bobby shook her head. 'He's barely touched a drop since he started working again – not the strong stuff anyhow. He sometimes has a beer or two with Reg in an evening, or at the pub, but the only time he has spirits is to chase away a nightmare.' She squeezed her sister's arm under the bedclothes. 'I am glad you're staying for Christmas. Now you can watch the pantomime and meet Jolka and Archie and Ernie and Teddy—' She stopped herself. 'Oh. No. Not Teddy.'

'Your Polish friend? Why not?'

Bobby sighed. 'He's gone, Lil. Just disappeared one day without leaving an address. Everything's in a big old mess at Topsy's cottage. She's so heartbroken over Teddy leaving that she's going to marry another man, one I know can't possibly make her happy, purely out of convenience. And once Topsy's made up her mind to something, however ill-advised, she won't listen to anyone who tries to persuade her otherwise. I don't know what anyone can do to fix it.'

'You mean you don't know what you can do to fix it,' Lilian said, tapping her sister's nose. 'I know you can't stop yourself sticking your oar in, trying to play Fairy Godmother for everyone.'

Bobby smiled. 'Well, I am a godmother now.'

'And it's clearly gone to your head,' Lilian said, laughing.

'Perhaps I am of a more Fairy Godmother than Cinderella inclination in real life. My success rate isn't very good so far though.'

'Why did Teddy leave? Doesn't he know Topsy loves him?'

'He knows. He thinks she can't possibly be happy with him.'

'Why?'

'Because he's crippled, and she'd have to care for him all his life. Because he can't give her a child.' Bobby frowned. 'And yet Archie said... I don't believe he and Topsy could have a family together either.'

'Archie being the other man?'

'That's right. He's her second half-cousin once removed or something.'

'Why don't you believe they could have a family?'

'There's some problem with Archie's blood that would make it impossible,' Bobby said, borrowing Topsy's own euphemism. 'She wouldn't have to care for him as she would Teddy but it would be a loveless marriage, childless and lonely – they're not planning to live together afterwards. Is tying herself to Archie really a better life for her than the one she could have with Teddy?'

'Maybe she could learn to love this Archie, in time,' Lilian said. 'As a husband, I mean.'

'I don't believe that could happen. They're too much like brother and sister. Besides, he... there was someone else he cared for, once; someone who died. It isn't something he's likely to get over.'

'Perhaps if Teddy knew she was planning to marry this man, he might realise she could have a better future with him.'

'Yes.' Bobby stared thoughtfully into the darkness. 'Perhaps so.'

–

It was nice to wake up without the usual chill nipping at her nose and toes the next morning, Bobby reflected as she reached to turn off her alarm clock. There wasn't much room with Lilian squeezed in next to her, but it was one way to keep warm.

'Are you coming to church with me and Dad?' Bobby asked as her sister yawned beside her.

'Do you go to church now?'

'Someone has to take the Parry girls to Sunday School. The Athertons are all Chapel. I usually try to drag Dad along, keep him godly.'

'I'd better not. I might burst into flames as soon as I set foot on holy ground.'

Bobby laughed. 'Been up to no good?'

Lilian shrugged. 'You know me.'

Her sister's tone was breezy and playful, but in the full light of day, Bobby could see that Lilian was pale, with purple semi-circles under her eyes.

'Something is wrong,' she said softly. 'What is it? Is it John?'

'Wait until Dad's gone,' Lilian said in a low voice. 'Then I'll tell you all about it. You're not going out today, are you?'

'For a little while. I need to go to the library in Skipton after church, and I'd like to call on Topsy on the way.'

'About her wedding plans?'

'Yes. If she's determined to do this I won't be able to talk her out of it, but I need her to look me in the eye and tell me this is what she really, truly wants. Otherwise it's going to prey on my mind forever.'

'Is the library open on Sundays?'

'No, but I've got an arrangement with the librarian to use it out of hours, being such a very important reporter as I am,' Bobby said loftily.

Lilian bowed. 'Your highness.'

'You're welcome to come along with me, and then you can tell me what's wrong on the way. I should probably talk to Topsy alone though.'

'I'd rather do it here, in private. It's not something I'd care to talk about in public. We can send Dad to the pub.'

'All right. I haven't got an ARP shift tonight, and there's no pantomime rehearsal until the dress on Tuesday. We can have a nice gossipy evening, just us.' She squeezed her sister's hand before getting up. 'Whatever it is, don't worry. Between us we can sort it out. We always do.'

'I really hope you're right,' Lilian said quietly.

–

Bobby had too much to do that day to eat Sunday dinner with the rest of the family. She told Mary to give Lilian her share, then packed up some jam sandwiches and set off on her bike to visit Topsy. However, she was destined to be disappointed. When she reached the cottage, she discovered only Mrs Hobbes at home.

'I'm afraid you've just missed her,' Mrs Hobbes said when she answered the door with Norman tucked under her arm. 'That termagant aunt of hers turned up and dragged her away. They're off looking at wedding dress material in Manchester, I understand.'

'You heard the news then,' Bobby said.

Mrs Hobbes put Norman down, and he waddled off into the house. 'Aye. I'd like to say I'm pleased for them both, but something in my waters tells me it's all going to end in tears.'

'I think so too.' Bobby lowered her voice. 'Archie told me. Why it could only ever be a marriage of convenience. He said you knew all about it.'

'I do. Topsy's father was the same sort.'

'You mean he…'

'That's right.' She sighed. 'Poor boys, both of them. I grew very close to William, her father, after his wife died. He'd tried all his life to push it down until it drove him half mad, and his unfortunate wife into the bargain. It made me realise that if the world could just open its mind a fraction to things that are different, it could save a lot of people from unnecessary misery. Who does it harm, after all? But people will always fear what they don't understand.'

'That was what you meant, wasn't it?' Bobby said quietly. 'When you said that duty was the curse of the Sumners.'

'I did. Generations of unsuitable marriages arranged for wealth or status or convenience, and even in these supposedly enlightened days, still the business goes on. William ought never to have married to make his wife and himself miserable, but of course it was expected he'd provide the house with a mistress and the family with an heir. Now the next generation are about to repeat the same mistake.'

'It seems so unfair.'

'I had hoped Topsy would be brave enough to resist. Archie I had no real hope of. He's a nice boy, but that mother of his has him wrapped around her little finger.' Mrs Hobbes shook her head. 'I wish Teddy had stayed. They were good for each other. I thought he might be the one to break the curse at last.'

'We must be able to talk her out of it, mustn't we?'

'Don't you believe it, dear. I was talking at her half the night when she came home, endeavouring to persuade her to change her mind. I say talking at her, because I'm sure not a word of it went in. She's as stubborn as a mule once she's set on something.' She looked across the park to the lake in the distance, her expression far away. 'I don't know how she can bring herself to say her vows, before God and all. I'm sure they'd stick in my throat.'

'I wish we could find out where Teddy is,' Bobby said. 'If he only knew... He left because he thought he was acting in her best interest. Because he wanted her to marry a man who could make her happy – give her a family. Now she's going to commit herself to an empty, loveless marriage, and he's the only person with any hope of convincing her not to go through with it.'

'Teddy's as stubborn in his own way as Topsy is. You'd think that pair were chalk and cheese, but living here with them both, I could see they were more alike than people realise. A thousand times a day I found myself wanting to bang their two silly heads together.' She smiled. 'But they suited each other. He softened her hard edges; taught her what no amount of my moralising could – to think more of others and less of herself. And I never saw that boy light up except when Topsy came into a room. It wouldn't have been an easy life, but they'd never find anyone to suit each of them better.'

'I wish I could have just five minutes' conversation with Teddy,' Bobby said fervently.

'Then you might try your luck with the Canadian lad. He's the only one can tell where the boy is, and he'll be more likely to respond to your charms than whatever are left of mine. Perhaps now he sees he's got no chance with Topsy himself, he'll give it up more willingly.'

'I suppose I could ask,' Bobby said doubtfully. 'I don't know though. He had a lot to say about comradeship and things the day Teddy disappeared. I don't think him helping Teddy really had anything much to do with Topsy. Still, I can try.'

Chapter 26

When she had caught the bus into Skipton, Bobby called at the home of the old librarian to collect the key to the building, which he was only too glad to loan her for an hour or two. She walked to the library and let herself in.

It always felt a little eerie being there alone, in the dismal gloom of the blackout shade, walled in by books new and old. Without the librarian and his intimate knowledge of the cataloguing system, it was also hard to know where to look for anything. However, Bobby searched the shelves until she found the one she was looking for: Poetry, M–R. For some reason, she felt the need to tiptoe.

They wouldn't necessarily have Hunt's book. Archie had said it was published at the man's own expense, sales being mostly to his relatives, and for all she knew they now had the only surviving copies. She was relying on Hunt's ego to have donated copies to public libraries, since he'd surely have wanted as many readers as possible for his supposed works of genius. Even then though, it didn't necessarily follow they would have one here. He may well have chosen to confine himself to Derbyshire.

She ran her finger along the spines. Parrish, Peacock, Pearse, Poe…

'Hallelujah!' she whispered as she made out the name Principatus, picked out in gold leaf on the spine of a book entitled *Poems of War and Glory*.

She took it down from the shelf. Clearly no expense had been spared in its printing and binding. Hunt had lavished gilt and glorious red leather on his one foray into publishing.

Bobby bore her prize to one of the little tables and began leafing through. The first poem was called 'Brotherhood'. As serious as her task today was, she quickly found herself smothering laughter. Constance Sumner's butler must have a will of iron, she decided, to have kept a straight face during Hunt's poetry recitals.

Side by side as we march to the end
I fight by my brother, my comrade, my friend
A legion of warriors: brave, strong and fair
Who go where only the lion would dare
Though we face certain carnage, there's never a frown
As the winds of Britannia blow up and blow down...

Half an hour later she closed the inappropriately luxurious book, disappointed. While the poetry could rival the legendary McGonagall in its dreadfulness, and Hunt would no doubt be a laughing stock among his men and fellow officers were it ever discovered he was the author, there was nothing in the poems to prove his prejudices. Yes, there were hints – a lot of references to what the author called 'true blue British stock': young men who were muscular, fair and Aryan-sounding – but nothing solid.

She was sure, though, that she had seen that name – Principatus – before Archie had mentioned it to her. It must have been in one of the newspapers she had trawled through in the last week. Had he written more than simply poetry under that name? Opinion pieces, perhaps, or letters?

What did it mean anyhow: Principatus? Bobby left the volume of poetry on the table and went to seek out a Latin dictionary in the reference section.

'Principatus,' she murmured as she read the entry out loud. 'Rule, leadership, supremacy. Huh.'

Supremacy. Well, that certainly fitted, but it wasn't exactly proof the man was a fascist sympathiser. Bobby replaced the Latin dictionary and went to the small side room where the newspaper archive was stored.

She wasn't sure where she had seen the name, but she had focused mostly on the larger national broadsheets in her research so far: *The Times* and *The Daily Telegraph*. She had been working backwards through the 1930s, but it definitely hadn't been in yesterday's stack. Perhaps the evening before... 1937 to 1938...

Bobby took out a pile of copies of *The Times* and started combing through the letters pages. It took over an hour of searching before she finally lit on what she was looking for.

There it was. That name, Principatus, under a letter to the editor from around the time of the Munich Crisis. And oh, what a letter it was! Her lip curled as she read.

IN PRAISE OF HITLER

Sir,

In response to the recent column from your international correspondent, I would challenge you to show me one instance in which Herr Hitler

has acted the humbug or hypocrite in his deal-
ings with Mr Chamberlain and other international
leaders. For myself, I thank God for the man,
for he has stood between his people and the three
greedy wolves that wait at the door of Europe: the
Communist, the Bolshevik, and most pernicious
of all, the usuring Jew. Of our own politicians,
only Redesdale and Mosley have proved they've
the stomach to…

And so it went on for several rambling paragraphs, praising
Hitler, the Nazis and Oswald Mosley's Blackshirts, but
always coming back to this bogeyman of the writer's own
creation: what he referred to as 'the pernicious, poisonous, poisoning Jew'.

'This is it,' Bobby murmured. 'I've got him.'

It had to be Hunt. There couldn't be two men
writing under the same Latin name and sharing the
same venomous views. She could even detect similarities
between the language used in the letter and the vocabulary
of his poetry. Bomber Command surely couldn't ignore
this. Hunt wouldn't dare to deny he was the author, when
there must be a dozen or more Derbyshire acquaintances
like Archie who could testify that he was Principatus.

She felt so elated, she almost wanted to laugh out loud.
But she didn't, forcing herself to be calm and methodical
as a good journalist ought to be. First of all, she carefully
copied out the letter and name three times, along with
the title and date of the newspaper and the page number
it could be found on. Then she turned to a fresh leaf of
her notepad and began a letter.

My dear sirs,

I think it my duty, as a concerned citizen, to bring to your attention the views of a squadron leader in a position of command…

–

'Well? What did she say?' Lilian asked when Bobby arrived back at Cow House Cottage. Lil was at the stove in Bobby's apron, stirring something in a pan.

'Who?'

'Topsy. You went to speak to her, didn't you? About this doomed marriage she's determined to enter into? I've never been so invested in the fate of people I've never met. It's better than the pictures.'

'Oh. No. She wasn't in.'

'Oh,' Lilian said, disappointed. 'Well, then did you find what you were looking for at the library? You've been gone forever.'

'Yes, in and amongst some of the worst war poetry I've ever read,' Bobby said with a grimace. 'Something about Britannia having wind, I think it was.'

'What are those?' Lilian asked, nodding to the three envelopes in her hand.

Bobby sank into a chair by the fire, put her envelopes on the table and stared at them.

'Letters,' she said. 'I'm going to take them out to post tomorrow morning, before work.'

'Who are they to?'

'See for yourself.'

Lilian came over to look. One envelope was to Bomber Command, with a Buckinghamshire address, and the second to the editor of *The Times*. The other only bore a name. Tadeusz Nowak.

'You haven't got an address on that one,' she pointed out.

'No.' Bobby roused herself. 'But I'm going to do my best to get one. I don't care if I have to get Ernie King out of bed practically in the middle of the night.'

'He knows where Teddy is?'

'Knows but won't say. I'm going to throw myself on his mercy. Beg on my knees if I have to. If Teddy doesn't reply to this then I'll know his feelings are unchanged in spite of Topsy's engagement. But he deserves to know what she's planning to do, and I'm just the interfering biddy to tell him about it. I just have to convince Ernie I'm right first.'

It wasn't going to be easy though. Writing the letter had been hard enough. She wanted Teddy to understand that love, the love of a man and wife, could never exist between Archie and Topsy. That there could never be children from the union, and, she was convinced, there could never be happiness either. All the same, she couldn't give away the secret Archie had trusted her enough to share with her. He'd be ostracised if people knew, or imprisoned – perhaps even committed to a mental hospital, where horrible attempts to 'cure' him might be inflicted. Convincing Ernie was going to be even harder. He had less reason to care.

'What about the one to Bomber Command?' Lilian asked. 'Why are you writing to them?'

'Oh, that's another story. I'm using my journalistic skills to help Charlie and the other cadets at his camp – one in particular.' Bobby looked rather proud as she regarded her letter. 'I've been like Sherlock Holmes this last week, Lil, hunting around for clues. This is the culmination of a lot of work. I only hope it does the trick.'

'What are you trying to do?'

'Get Charlie's awful CO relieved of his command.'

'Relieved of his command! That's rather ambitious, isn't it?'

'Perhaps, but someone needs to do it. He's a dangerous man to have power over young recruits. A bully and a Jew-baiter. Practically a fascist himself, I discovered today – at least, he was all for Hitler and Mosley before the war.'

Lilian wrinkled her nose. 'Really?'

'Yes, and he's a terrible poet to boot. I only hope this will be enough. There's no doubt it was him who wrote the letter I found today but if Bomber Command think it will be embarrassing to them for Hunt to be exposed, they might prefer to brush it under the carpet and cry "military secrets" at anyone who tries to follow it up. Hence the letter to *The Times*.'

'What does that one say?'

'It's an exact copy of the one I'm sending to Bomber Command. I told them I'd be sending a replica to the press – I suppose that is a little like blackmail, but honestly, this man Hunt needs to be stopped. I don't know if the editor could print anything about it that would get past the censors, but knowing it's been made partially public already might make Hunt's superiors less likely to try to cover it up.'

'That's some proper reporter work,' Lilian said, sounding impressed. 'You're just like Dorothy Lawrence, Bob.'

'Lil, that's the nicest thing you've ever said to me.' Bobby looked up at her. 'Where's Dad?'

'I gave him a bowl of soup and then sent him to the pub like we agreed.' She went back to the hob. 'And now you can have a bowl and get yourself warmed up. You must be starving.'

'Are you going to tell me this secret of yours?'

'Soup first, secrets after.'

Bobby obediently ate the potato and carrot soup her sister served her. Lilian had always been the better cook of the two, and it was rather nice to be waited on. When she had finished, Lilian handed her a cup of tea and sat down in their father's easy chair with one of her own.

'Well?' Bobby said. 'I suppose it's about John, is it?'

'Yes.' Lilian sighed. 'I don't know how I'm going to break it to Dad. The wedding's off, Bob.'

'Oh, Lil.' Bobby put down her tea and reached over to take her sister's hand. 'I am sorry. You sounded so happy in your letters. What on earth happened?'

'It was my fault. You mustn't blame him.' She was silent for a moment, thoughtfully twirling a strand of hair around her finger. 'And do you know, I didn't feel nearly as cut up about it as I would have expected. When he was gone, I started to think, did I love him really or was it only the idea of him I loved? John Cartwright felt like the perfect man – almost too much so. Like one day I'd scratch the surface, and discover no substance under that shiny uniform and soap-scrubbed face at all.'

'But what happened? What did you do to upset him?'

Lilian didn't answer. She blew on her tea, not meeting her sister's gaze.

'What do you do, when your Charlie has leave and he takes you out?' she asked after a while. 'Where do you go?'

'Well, he's very rarely granted a pass out. His awful CO sees to that. When he is we usually just go down to the bandstand in Settle. Why?'

'He doesn't... take you anywhere else?'

'To a dance, maybe. But these days, we see each other so infrequently that we prefer just to go somewhere quiet where we can be alone and have a kiss and a cuddle.'

'Just a cuddle?'

'Of course.' Bobby felt the familiar sensation settle on her, of something bad on the horizon. 'Lil, what's happened?'

Lilian put down her tea and swallowed a small sob. 'I've been the most terrible fool, Bobby.'

'You... you mean...' Her gaze drifted to her sister's stomach. 'No.'

'Yes.'

'I don't believe it.' Bobby's brow knit. 'That... bastard!'

'He really isn't. He's a wonderful man.'

'Wonderful man my foot!' Bobby stood up and started pacing the floor. 'We'll... we'll sue him for breach of promise, that's what we'll do – if we can stop Dad from killing the man first. To trick you into thinking he wanted to marry you, just so he could—'

'Bobby.' Lilian reached out to grab her arm. 'Stop. He didn't do anything.'

'Didn't do anything? It sounds like he did plenty to me, if you're in the family way. I hope they throw him out of the navy for... caddish behaviour. I hope they court-martial him and lock him up. I'll write another letter.'

'I mean, it wasn't him. He isn't the father.'

'What?' Bobby stared at her. 'Well then who the hell is?'

Lilian lowered her gaze, her cheeks burning. 'It's... it's Tony. Tony Scott.'

Bobby was speechless for a moment.

'Tony,' she whispered. 'But how... when...'

'You remember August. Those dates we went on so I could pay him back for getting Dad out of trouble. There were more, when I went home for a weekend's leave in September...' She closed her eyes. 'You must think I'm so weak.'

'You mean he... I'll bloody kill him!'

'Sit down, Bob, please.'

Bobby glared at the fire for a moment, as if she could see Tony's stupid grinning face in the flames. Then she consented to sit down again.

'He didn't take advantage, if that's what you're thinking. I was a willing participant, more or less.' Lilian sighed. 'I suppose he caught me at an unguarded moment. I'd been worried about Dad and the war, and he was being so kind to me. I still felt like I owed him for pulling that article about the black-market meat and saving Dad's hide. When we went out and he suggested we go to a hotel...' She looked away. 'You'd never have been so stupid, I know. Are you very disappointed in me?'

'Not disappointed. But I wish to God you'd told him to drop dead, Lil.'

'Everything was so bleak. We were losing the war, it looked like Russia was going to fall... I just thought, to hell with it all. We could die tomorrow. The Germans could invade at any time. It might be my only chance to find out what it would be like. Can you understand that?'

'I suppose so,' Bobby said quietly. Then, curious in spite of herself, she asked, 'What was it like?'

'I hardly remember. Brief. Hot. Disappointing.' Lilian swallowed a sob. 'What an idiot, to risk so much on something so empty and pointless.'

'Does Tony know?'

'Of course he doesn't.'

'And when you told John…'

'Well, what was he going to do? He said we'd break the engagement quietly, to spare me embarrassment. The shock and disappointment in his face were the worst part of the business.' She gave a damp laugh. 'Poor man, he always did believe I was something better than I was.'

'But… what are we going to do?' A feeling of helplessness settled on Bobby as her anger at Tony started to dissipate. 'You'll lose your position, you'll…' She put a hand to her head as the full reality of the situation hit her. 'A baby! It's really coming, Lil.'

'Not necessarily.' Lilian reached forward and took her sister's hands. 'Bobby, I need your help.'

'Anything I can do for you,' Bobby said earnestly, giving the hands a squeeze.

'I bought something. From one of those advertisements in the newspaper. You know, the ones for women's remedies.'

Bobby knew those advertisements. The sort that promised their pills would clear 'blockages' and cure 'irregularities'. Most women knew what they were really offering. A desperate solution for a girl who had got into trouble.

'Here, I'll show you,' Lil said.

She went to fetch a package from the case she had brought with her and tipped the contents out on to the table. There was a little box labelled 'Dr Woodstock's Famous Female Pills' and a booklet called *Advice to Married Women*.

Bobby gave them a worried look. 'Are those things safe?'

'I suppose so. Otherwise they wouldn't be allowed to advertise them, would they?'

'Do they work? Do you know anyone who's used them?'

'Well, no. It isn't the type of thing people talk about, is it? But they must do. The advertisement said they were prescribed by Harley Street doctors. I got the most expensive kind.'

'I don't like it, Lil.'

'What choice do I have?' She let out another sob. 'How could I have a baby? I haven't got a husband, or money. I haven't got a rich family who could take care of us both and protect us from the sort of people who'd whisper behind their hands about the illegitimate child and their mother who was no better than she ought to be.'

'I know, but… we don't know these are safe. It isn't legal, Lil. What if… what if they make you dreadfully ill or something? What if they don't work properly, and the baby is born deformed? I couldn't bear it if you were hurt.'

'What else can I do? Marry Tony?' She laughed damply at the idea. 'He'd be over the hills before I finished my sentence. Even if he agreed to it, he'd make a terrible husband. He's far too feckless and lazy to support a wife and child.'

'Well, I can't argue with that,' Bobby murmured. 'You know he lost his job at the *Courier*?'

'No, but it doesn't surprise me. I'd as soon try to support myself and risk all of people's viciousness than tie myself forever to Tony Scott.' She closed her eyes. 'Good God, but if I could only go back in time! That stupid, stupid girl I was.'

'But you can't.'

'No.' Lil picked up the pills. 'This is the best way, for me and the baby. It's no life to bring them into, with a world at war and a mother tarnished with shame. There'll be a proper time for babies.'

Bobby took the packet from her and looked at it. 'What will happen? After you take them?'

'There'll be cramps and bleeding, it says in the booklet, but the heaviest of it should be over in a few hours.'

'How far gone are you?'

'About three months, I suppose. It was September – late September. I should have noticed my monthlies had stopped but I was so caught up with John and... and everything. It was only when I started feeling sick and went to see the quack...' She sighed. 'Another fine mess, as they say.'

'Is it still safe after three months? Or are you supposed to take them right after?'

'It doesn't say. I suppose you can take them any time.'

'You hear things, Lil,' Bobby said in a low voice. 'I really wish you wouldn't. I'm afraid for you.'

'It'll be all right. This isn't some back-alley affair. The alternative would be far worse.' Lilian looked at her with pleading eyes. 'Please, Bobby. I need you.'

'I wish... God, I wish I'd never introduced you to Tony bloody Scott,' Bobby said in an anguished voice.

'Do you think it's OK?' Lilian whispered. 'Is it a terrible sin?'

'It feels like the women forced to choose it are more sinned against than sinning. I don't suppose those men who beg and push and plead and force, then walk away once they've got some poor girl into that condition, lose much sleep over it. Still, I wish there was another way.' She took a deep breath. 'But I love you, and you're my sister, and I'll do whatever you need me to do.'

The tears came then: first Lilian's, then Bobby's. For a few moments, they just held each other and wept.

'When shall we do it?' Lilian asked in a tremulous voice when she had recovered herself sufficiently to be able to speak.

'Thursday,' Bobby murmured. 'Dad's working longer hours that day, getting things ready for the Boxing Day hunt Topsy's aunt is organising, and Reg is letting me finish at twelve since it's Christmas Eve. I'll take care of you until everything's all right again.'

'Thank you. I knew I could rely on you, little sister.'

Chapter 27

Bobby had a fitful sleep that night. After a few hours of restless dreams, she awoke in the early hours of the morning and found herself unable to doze off again. Not wanting to disturb her sister, she eventually rose, lit a candle and went to build the fire in the parlour. It was 3 a.m., and she had an early call to make before work.

It would have been easy, so consumed was she by concern for her sister's predicament, to forget other pressing matters. Bobby was still determined, however, to do what she could for her other friends.

She could hear the rhythmic snoring of her father in his room, happily oblivious to his daughter's delicate condition. Bobby could imagine his reaction if he found out. He'd haul Tony Scott out into the streets of Bradford and have him pleading for his life before the day was out. And if Dad ever found out that he was to some extent responsible – that it had been to protect him that Lilian had first gone out with Tony... Bobby dreaded to think what effect that might have on his ever-precarious mental state.

He'd been right all along, of course, when he'd voiced his distrust of Tony and warned his daughters about keeping company with such a 'nowt'. Bobby had been blinded by Tony's more affable qualities, believing her friend to be flirtatious but essentially harmless to women, and now her sister had paid the price.

Poor Lilian. Bobby wished there was something she could do for her beyond the grisly task Lil had asked for help with. What a way to celebrate Christmas Eve that would be.

She wondered what she would do if she were in her sister's place. Lilian had always been more at risk from men: beautiful, curvy, fond of the company of admiring boyfriends and with a lust for life and fun that her quieter twin had never shared. Still, there would always be unscrupulous men pressing girls for what they wanted, and all it took was one weak moment to fall prey. As quick as others always were to condemn, any girl could be that girl given the right circumstances. Even her.

What would she do if it were her? Charlie wasn't Tony, of course. He would step up and do his duty, if he were responsible. But what if it wasn't Charlie? What if it was someone else – someone like Ernie King, for example? If Bobby found herself in the family way and the man responsible wasn't someone she could rely on, would she take the gruesome way out her sister had chosen? Could she? It made her feel nauseous just to think about it.

She wondered if Tony would offer to make an honest woman of Lil, if he knew of her condition. He wasn't entirely hopeless, perhaps. As flirtatious as he was, he'd often spoken of his desire for marriage with a suitable girl. He'd been engaged before – he'd even been in love, which for men was probably rarer. And then Bobby was certain he had a fondness for Lil, even if he wasn't madly in love with her. But what then? The child would have a father... and her sister would be trapped in a marriage with a man she couldn't depend on, feckless and unemployed with a reputation as a Lothario. Another lonely, loveless marriage, just like the one Topsy was proposing to enter into – only worse, because in this case there'd be a child in the middle of it.

Bobby's Cinderella ballgown was drying on the clothes horse by the fire, ready for the pantomime dress rehearsal the following day. She tried not to look at it in the flickering light of the candle. The bridal style only made her unhappy. It reminded her of the tragic end to the engagement her sister had been so ecstatically happy about, and the feigned happiness of Topsy and Archie as they prepared for their empty wedding. Weddings were supposed to be joyous events, but just thinking about them was enough to depress her at the moment.

Bobby laughed softly at herself as she stacked coke in the grate. Funny sort of Fairy Godmother she was. She certainly didn't seem to have bestowed many happy endings so far this Christmastime, for all her interfering.

But it wasn't too late. She still had a chance to help Bram and Charlie, and perhaps Teddy and Topsy too, if she could only persuade Ernie to do as she asked.

Once the fire was lit, she fetched some suitable clothes from her room and dressed herself quietly in its warm glow while the rest of the household slept. Then she took her three letters and ventured into the cold darkness of the winter dawn to seek out Ernie King.

–

The morning was damp and oppressive with mist as Bobby trudged into the village on her errand. It felt very early – she wasn't usually out and about at this time – but Dalesfolk were early risers and Silverdale was already bustling.

First of all, she stopped at the box outside the post office and dropped in two of her letters: the one to Bomber Command and the one to the editor of *The Times*. Then she walked to the home of Louisa and Wilfred Clough, where the three Canadian airmen had been billeted. All were now on Christmas leave, so unless they had had emergency orders summoning them to their base, they should be there.

Louisa blinked when she answered the door. 'Miss Bancroft. What's to do this time? There's noan another plane come down in t' fells?'

'No.' Bobby felt a little befuddled as she stood on the doorstep, clutching her last remaining letter. Her head had been filled with thoughts of her sister on the walk here, and she had forgotten to rehearse this part of the conversation. 'Um, I just… brought this letter.'

'Oh aye?' Louisa said, looking both puzzled and amused. 'Well, just drop it in t' box then. Or if it's a stamp tha's after, I'll be opening up at eight same as allus.'

Bobby rubbed her forehead. Louisa Clough was the postmistress, of course. She must think Bobby was having a funny turn, showing up on her doorstep first thing in the morning to bring Mrs Clough her post personally.

'No, I have a stamp already,' she said. 'What I need is… that is to say, may I please speak with Flying Officer King?'

Louisa blinked. 'Ernie? He's fast off, I should say. Lads are on leave this week.'

'I know, and I'm sorry to be knocking him up so early, but it is rather urgent. I can't really explain, but… look, could you wake him and tell him it's me?'

Louisa still looked confused, and far from willing to disturb her guests.

'Um, it's about the pantomime at the hospital on Christmas Day,' Bobby fabricated wildly.

'Ah. For t' pantomime, is it?' Louisa nodded knowingly, as if this made sense of the matter. 'Well, if it's urgent happen he won't mind me getting him up. I'll fetch him for thee.'

She disappeared, and a few moments later Ernie appeared. He had clearly just woken, his usually smart, styled hair rather tousled. He was wearing striped pyjamas and a navy-blue dressing gown.

'Bobby,' he mumbled sleepily. 'What's the matter? Mrs Clough seems to think the airmen's hospital must have burned down or something.'

'It isn't anything like that.' She glanced at his pyjamas. 'Sorry if I woke you. I know you're on leave. I just wondered… could I talk to you privately? Only for a moment.'

'Nowhere private in here. We're packed in like sardines.' He examined her face, taking in her worried expression. 'Give me ten minutes to put my uniform on and we'll go for a walk.'

Bobby smiled with relief. 'Thank you.'

Mrs Clough reappeared in the doorway while he was getting ready, her arms folded. She had clearly listened to every word they'd spoken.

'Thy Charlie well, like?' she asked, with a pointed look at the hump of Bobby's engagement ring under her gloves.

'Yes, thank you. His Christmas leave was cancelled though, so I won't have the chance to see him until the new year at least. I'll miss him on Christmas Day.'

'Mmm, I bet tha will,' the old lady said, her tone clearly conveying what she thought about mice who laiked while their cats were away.

Ernie reappeared shortly after, now in his uniform, greatcoat and Air Force cap.

'Breakfast in half an hour,' Mrs Clough told him sternly as he stepped outside to Bobby.

'Yes, Mother,' Ernie said with a grin. 'I won't be late, I promise.'

Louisa couldn't help smiling reluctantly back. Very few of the village women were completely immune to the Canadians' charm, no matter their age.

'We'll take a stroll up to that old stone bridge, shall we?' Ernie said to Bobby.

'Yes, all right.'

Bobby didn't speak until they had gone a little way from the heart of the village, where tradesmen and farmers were preparing for the business of the day.

'Well, Slacks, what's the secret?' Ernie asked as they approached the old packhorse bridge where she had so often sat with Charlie in their courting days. 'Something worth getting up for, I hope.'

Bobby turned to him. 'Ernie, look. I know you feel strongly about not sharing Teddy's address with anyone, but I really think you ought to reconsider. Things aren't the same now as they were when Teddy asked you to keep it secret.'

He scowled. 'Topsy sent you. Well, my answer's the same no matter who she sets on me. I made a promise to Teddy and I've no intention of breaking it for any female.'

'Nobody sent me and nobody knows I'm here. I had to do it, or I'd spend my whole life feeling guilty about standing by and doing nothing while people I cared about made the biggest mistake of their lives.' She looked up at him. 'You must know Topsy doesn't love Archie, any more than he loves her.'

Ernie lit a cigarette. While he smoked he leaned over the bridge to watch the beck, swollen after the recent snowfall, chattering on its way to join the River Wenning.

'Don't see why I should know that,' he said. 'Don't see why I should care. They're both of them over twenty-one.' He glanced at her. 'How do you know he doesn't love her? He hangs around her enough.'

'Because… I just do.' She paused, trying to word it carefully so she wasn't telling a deliberate untruth. 'Archie's affections are engaged elsewhere.'

'You know that, do you?'

She nodded. 'He told me – in confidence, so please don't spread it around. There was a sweetheart who died and he never got over it. He only wants to marry Topsy to please his mother, and because it makes sense financially. His feelings for her are strictly brotherly, he confided in me. And Topsy only wants to marry him… well, she doesn't want to marry him. Not really. She's doing her cousin a favour because now Teddy's gone, she thinks love and happiness are out of her reach.'

'You seem to know a lot about it.'

She shrugged. 'Like Archie said to me once, I ask a lot of questions. That means I get a lot of answers.'

'What skin is it off your nose if Topsy marries the illustrious Lord Sumner? Did you have an eye on Archie yourself? I saw the two of you sneaking out together at the party.'

She flushed. 'Don't be daft.'

'Girls like that sort of thing, don't they?' Ernie clutched his heart and sighed melodramatically. 'The lonely aristo-crat and the lost love he never got over. The heart reserved for only one woman… until that day he catches sight of poor lowly Cinderella across a crowded room and realises he can know love again. Perhaps they'll make it into a movie, after the two of you are married. I'm seeing Leslie Howard and Katharine Hepburn as you and Archie. I'll leave you to decide which way round it ought to be.'

'Can you stop being ridiculous?' Bobby said, frowning. 'This is serious, Ernie. Topsy's my friend. I don't want to see her trapped in an unhappy marriage because she's letting her broken heart make decisions for her instead of her brain.'

Ernie's expression changed, and he became serious. 'Teddy made his choice. Topsy made hers and Archie made his. I guess they're all old enough to know what they're doing. Why stick our necks out trying to persuade them differently?'

'Because Teddy wouldn't have made that decision if he'd known what Topsy would do – I'm convinced he wouldn't. You read that letter he wrote. He thought he was leaving her behind to find happiness with someone else. If he knew her marriage with Archie would be a sham, he might see she could have a better future with him after all.'

Ernie looked into her eyes, frowning. 'You really care about this.'

'Yes I do.'

'Why? It isn't your love affair.'

'Because it's all *wrong*,' she said, pressing her fingertips to her temples. 'It's going to make three people unhappy in the end, people I care about, and if I've got the power to fix it by sticking my big fat nose where it wasn't invited then that's what I'm going to do.'

Ernie shook his head, smiling. 'You're a funny sort of girl. Not sure I know another like you.'

'Never mind what sort of girl I am. Will you do me this favour or not?'

He paused for what felt like a long time, scrutinising her face. Bobby met his eyes with a determined expression.

'What is the favour?' he asked at last.

'I'm not going to ask you to give me the address, so you can do it without breaking your word to Teddy.' She produced her letter and held it out. 'Just send this to him. See, I already put a stamp on it – all you have to do is fill in the address and give it to Mrs Clough. It explains everything: what Topsy is planning to do and why I think it's a recipe for misery. If Teddy doesn't reply then I'll know his views are unchanged, but all the same, he deserves to know.'

'Here. Give it to me.' Ernie took the letter from her and stashed it in his coat.

Bobby watched him pocket it anxiously. 'Are you going to send it?'

'I'll think it over.' He glanced at her. 'Not as a favour to Topsy, or Teddy either, much as I like the guy. This is for you, Slacks.'

She frowned. 'For me? Why?'

'Because you interest me. I believe you don't give a hot damn what anyone thinks about you, least of all me. You stick your chin out and stand your ground like a man, and yet you care about people as only a woman can. You're a queer fish, Bobby Bancroft.' He smiled at her. 'That's a compliment, by the way. Come on, we'd better get back before old Mother Clough decides we're rolling around in the hay together and rushes off to telegraph your fiancé.'

'You won't forget though? You'll post it?'

'Like I said. For your sake, I'll think it over.'

Chapter 28

Lilian was so merry the next day as she helped the household at Moorside prepare for Christmas that Bobby could almost forget there was anything wrong. She played games with the Parry girls, helped Mary with the Christmas chores, cooed appreciatively over the presents Bobby had made for the children and the beautiful dolls' house Charlie had built, showed a solicitous care for their father, and in every way acted as though life was carrying on as normal. She even went along with Bobby to the pantomime dress rehearsal that evening, where she showed enthusiastic interest in all of her sister's new Silverdale friends, basked in the appreciative glances of the bedridden airmen and laughed in all the right places as the actors performed. Other than a touch of mild nausea in the morning, which thankfully went unnoticed by their father, there was nothing to give a clue as to her dreadful predicament.

But Bobby couldn't forget about it, even if her sister seemed to have. The next day, Christmas Eve, loomed large on her horizon and until then everything else felt unreal, like she was sleepwalking. That was the day they had set aside for Lilian to take the pills she had sent off for from the paper.

'You'd better watch out for yourself, Bobby,' Lilian said as they walked home arm in arm from the pantomime rehearsal. 'That handsome flying officer has his eye on you.'

'Ernie? You must be joking. Half the girls in the village are running after him.'

'But it's you he's struck on. He was watching you all night, whenever he thought you weren't looking at him. Trust me, we fallen women have an eye for these things.'

Bobby shook her head. 'How can you joke about it and act like everything's normal? Aren't you terribly worried about tomorrow? I've been in a blue funk all day.'

'I would be, if I let myself stop and think for too long,' Lilian said quietly. 'I have to pretend everything's all right until… until it isn't. I'll go mad otherwise.'

'You still think this is the best thing to do, Lil?'

'It's the only thing to do.'

–

Their dad went out to work early the next morning, reminding Bobby and Lilian that he would be working longer hours than usual emptying and taking up his vermin traps before the Boxing Day hunt.

'That's all right, we can amuse ourselves,' Lilian said brightly, giving him a kiss on the cheek. 'Go for a drink afterwards if you want, Dad. Bobby and I will leave something nice out for your supper and remind Santa not to forget you when he stops by.'

'Daft lass,' he said with a smile. 'It's nice to have you pair both here for Christmas. I'll sithee later.'

'I'll make something we can heat up for his supper this morning while you're at work,' Lilian said to Bobby when he'd gone. 'Then we don't need to worry about it if… well, if it takes longer than expected until I'm ready to be back on my feet.'

'Yes. All right.'

Before Lilian had come, Bobby had agreed to help Mary ice the Christmas cake and finish some other last-minute festive jobs that afternoon. Now, of course, she had something more urgent to attend to. After Reg had given her leave to stop work for the day, she called into the kitchen to make her apologies.

'Sorry, Mary, but I'm needed at the cow house this afternoon,' she said. 'My sister was feeling a little under the weather this morning – she might have a winter cold coming on, I think. I want to make some spiced parsnip soup for her, see if we can head it off at the pass. If she's feeling better later I'll pop back.'

'Aye, she looked a bit badly at breakfast,' Mary said. 'Barely touched her bacon and eggs. Never mind about coming back if you're needed at home. The girls have been begging me to let them help decorate the cake.' She smiled. 'I only hope there'll be enough fruit and paste left after that pair have had their fingers in it.' This year's cake was to be topped with a sweetened paste made of almond essence, pulped haricot beans and ground rice in lieu of the usual marzipan.

'Where are the girls?'

Mary laughed. 'Florrie's in the attic, arranging their stockings for the sixth or seventh time. She's terrified Father Christmas is going to miss them in the dark.'

'Poor chap. The blackout must be a terrible trial when it comes to delivering presents,' Bobby said with a smile. 'Is Jess with her?'

'No. I'm sure you can guess where she is.'

'Henhouse,' Bobby murmured. 'Still hoping for an eleventh-hour reprieve for Henrietta?'

'That's right, poor little chick. I suppose she thinks if Henrietta lays a dozen eggs this afternoon, Reg will spare her. I hope it's not going to put her in a mourngy mood on Christmas Day.'

Bobby returned to the cow house, where she found Lilian sitting on their bed with the box of pills clasped in her two hands.

'How is everyone at the farmhouse?' she asked, not looking up to make eye contact. 'Are the girls excited for tomorrow?'

'Florrie is. She's rearranging the stockings at the end of their bed to make sure they're as visible as possible for Santa. Jessie's in the henhouse saying a last goodbye to Henrietta, the poor soul.'

Lilian gave a weak smile. 'They're sweet little things, those two. Were we ever that way?'

'I was. You were a terror on Christmas Eve, bouncing about full of excitement. Mam used to say it was like having a kangaroo in the house.' Bobby sat down beside her and took her hand to give it a gentle squeeze. 'Are you ready, sweetheart?'

Lilian gulped back a sob. 'I think so.'

'Where will you do it?'

'I suppose I ought to go to the outhouse, in case there's heavy bleeding right away. I've got pads and the drawers on I wear for my monthlies, and I've covered our bed in towels. When the bleeding slows, I'll come back and lie down here until it's all over.' She turned worried eyes to Bobby. 'Where do you suppose he'll go, Bobby? Afterwards?'

'You mean John?'

'The baby. I don't know why, but I feel it's a he somehow.'

'I don't know, Lil.' Bobby put an arm around her sister, who rested her head on her shoulder. 'I'm only a journalist. That's a question for a vicar.'

'I suppose he has a soul,' Lilian murmured. 'Or perhaps not. Do babies have souls before they're born? They didn't teach us anything about it at Sunday School.'

'If he has a soul then it will go to heaven.'

'Even if he isn't baptised?'

'I'm certain of it.'

'A soul that never had a life to live,' Lilian said in a whisper. She let out a sob. 'I wonder, can he come back again when the time's right? Will I get another chance to be his mother?'

'That's too much like philosophy for me to answer.' Bobby's gaze drifted to the tablets in her sister's hand. 'The hypocrisy of it makes me angry though. The people who condemn women for it, women who have to make a hard choice because the world has given them no alternative, are the same ones happy to send men out to die in wars. Human life ought never to be that cheap.'

'I keep thinking, Bobby. About the man he could have grown up to be. My little boy. I'd have liked to have met him.' Lilian gave a weak smile. 'In five or six years he'd be waiting for Christmas Day just like those two little girls, hanging his stocking up ready for Santa. Bouncing like a kangaroo, the way his mam used to. He wouldn't understand what it meant to be illegitimate, or why he should be made to carry the shame of his mother's moment of foolish weakness.'

'You don't have to do this, Lil,' Bobby said softly. 'Not if you're having doubts. There are other ways. You could… you could move far away, perhaps. Tell people you're a widow. Young widows are common enough now. I'd support you every way I could. Send an allowance out of my wages to keep you both.'

Lilian gave a wet laugh. 'On twenty-five bob a week? You can barely keep yourself.'

'I'd find a way. Go back to the *Courier*, perhaps, where there are higher wages to be had. Don said he'd always have a job for me.'

'You don't want to be at the *Courier*; you want to be here. I know that. And what about after you're married and you've got a bairn of your own on the way? Who'd support us when you had to give up work?' Lilian wiped her eyes and stood up. 'No. I won't let anyone else suffer for my stupid mistake. It has to be this.'

Bobby followed her to the door. She held her sister's hand, unwilling to let her go.

'If you're not back in ten minutes, I'll come to check on you,' she said. 'Call out for me if you need me – I'll leave the front door open so I can hear you. I've written the number for the Smeltham doctor on a slip of paper if things get really bad. The phone in Charlie's surgery was disconnected when he left for the RAF but there's one at Moorside we can use in an emergency.'

'Thank you.' Lilian gave her hand a firm press before disappearing round the corner to the outhouse they shared with Moorside.

Bobby sat down, took off her wristwatch and laid it on the table in front of her, watching the second hand tick by.

Lilian seemed sure that the pills she had bought were safe. The booklet that came with them carried all sorts of testimonials from doctors and satisfied patients, testifying to their efficacy in clearing 'the most stubborn of block-ages'. If they worked as they should there would be a period of heavy bleeding, then it would settle down and be no different than Lilian's usual monthlies.

But testimonials were easy to forge. The law against wilfully terminating a pregnancy meant such medica-tions were by their nature unregulated, the language with which they were marketed couched in euphemism. And... you heard stories. Stories of women who had made themselves dreadfully ill seeking out illegal abor-tions. Women who... women who had died. Supposing Lilian's bleeding was heavier than the booklet said it would be? Supposing she bled and bled, and didn't stop? She could die, right there in the outhouse. Her twin sister, the person Bobby cared for most in the world...

Fifteen years ago, they had been two such little inno-cents as the Parry girls over the way, excited about what Santa would leave that night in their stockings. There had been no fear for the future, then. No knowledge of the trials they would one day face as they tried to navigate a woman's place in the world. How Bobby wished they could return to those days! To be safe under the care of their mother and father, with nothing to trouble their little minds beyond what would be for pudding that evening.

She slipped her hand into her pocket and pressed the paper on which she had written Dr Minchin's telephone number between her fingers. Pray God he wouldn't be needed today.

One minute... two... three... four... five. Still the door stood open, but Lilian didn't return, nor was there any call from the outhouse. Bobby's watch had just ticked past eight minutes when Mary came running over from Moorside, looking flustered and fretful.

'Oh. Bobby, thank goodness you're here,' she said, putting a hand to her forehead.

Lilian appeared behind her at that moment. She looked pale, and her eyes were red as if she had been crying, but Mary didn't seem to notice anything amiss as Lil passed her to go into the cottage.

'What's the matter, Mary?' Lilian asked.

'Have either of you girls seen Jessie? I can't find her anywhere. I thought perhaps she'd wandered over here to visit you.'

'She isn't here,' Bobby said, casting her sister a concerned look. 'She'll be in the henhouse, won't she?'

'I sent Florrie to fetch her from there, but she says there's no sign of the girl.'

Bobby frowned. 'That's odd.'

'Perhaps she was hiding to play a trick on her sister,' Lilian suggested, smiling. 'I used to catch Bobby out with my hiding places all the time.'

Mary looked relieved at this suggestion. 'Yes, happen that's it. I'll look now.'

'We'll come too,' Lilian said. 'I'd like to make sure she's all right, now she's got us all worried.'

Bobby took her sister's arm to hold her back as they started following Mary to the farmhouse.

'Should you be walking about?' she whispered. 'You ought to be lying down.'

'No need,' Lilian whispered back. 'I couldn't go through with it, Bob. I sat there for ages, thinking about it all, and… I just couldn't. I flushed the pills away.'

'Oh, thank God,' Bobby said with palpable relief, giving her arm a squeeze. 'I was so worried it would all go horribly wrong and I might lose you. But then what will you do about… you know?'

'I don't know yet. Let's just have Christmas, that's all. After Christmas I'll worry about it.'

The two women followed Mary into the garden, where she poked her head through the open door of the henhouse.

'Jess?' she called. There was no answer.

Mary withdrew her head, puzzled. 'There's no sign of the bairn.'

'Let me see.' Bobby bent down to take a look.

The henhouse was definitely empty of Jessie, but Bobby noticed something that Mary hadn't. Someone else was missing too.

Henrietta was gone.

Chapter 29

Within two hours, a full-scale manhunt was in operation in Silverdale. When Moorside and its environs had yielded no trace of either the missing evacuee or her pet, Bobby, Mary and Lilian had left Reg to tend to a distraught Florrie and headed into the village with Ace, hoping he might be able to sniff out his mistress.

They knocked at every cottage they passed to see if anyone had seen the little girl go by, but no one had any clues to give. A number of the younger adults came out to join the search party, however, including Chip and Sandy – Ernie, it seemed, was away from home that day. Topsy and Archie were also of the party, having bumped into Bobby frantically looking inside dustbins outside the village bakery while they took a stroll together. Ace had pulled her in that direction, but it turned out his interest was in cakes rather than children.

'Do you suppose she might be trying to get back to London?' Topsy asked when they had looked in the Golden Hart only to find another dead end. 'That's where the children came from, isn't it?'

'I shouldn't think she'd get very far: an eight-year-old girl travelling alone with a hen under her arm,' Lilian said.

'Hmm.' Bobby scanned the horizon, trying to decide on the most likely direction for Jessie to have gone in. 'She could have got as far as Skipton by bus, I should think. In farming communities, people wouldn't blink at a bairn travelling into the town on her own with an animal. But surely she'd never be allowed to board a train.'

'She only had ninepence,' Mary said in an anguished voice. 'Enough for the bus but once she got to town, she'd be stranded there. Oh Lord, what if someone took her? There are all sorts of... of people. Godless people who'd take advantage of a child on her own. You read such awful things in the newspapers.'

'She'll be hiding somewhere to give you a scare is all, Mrs A,' Sandy said soothingly. 'I guess kids do these things in Britain as well as Canada.'

'Nay, that sort of devilment's not in her nature. I know she wouldn't do this just to play a trick.'

'You go back home and leave it to us, Mary,' Topsy said. 'The cold must be causing you pain. We'll find the little girl and bring her back to you, just as safe as houses.'

'I can't sit at home while my doy lass is out there on her own.' Mary let out a sob. 'Oh, if anything's happened to her... her father will never forgive us if she's hurt. I'd never forgive myself. I shouldn't have let her out of my sight.'

While this conversation had been going on, Bobby had been applying her powers of deduction.

'Jess wants to save Henrietta,' she said quietly. 'I don't believe she's trying to run away — I think she's trying to help Henrietta run away. She'd take the hen somewhere she thought she could be safe. Somewhere she knows.'

Mary brightened slightly. 'Do you know where that might be, Bobby?'

'I do have an idea. The woodland around the lodge, where my father works. I've taken her and her sister there a dozen times for winter walks and to play Ducks and

Drakes on the lake. Dad shows them the nests of pheasants and other wildlife, and explains how he protects them from foxes and such. Perhaps she's planning to let Henrietta loose to live among the wild birds.'

'That sounds like one of the soft-hearted bairn's fancies,' Mary said with a small smile. 'I'm sure she believes the fairies will take care of her daft old hen.'

'It's worth investigating,' Chip said. 'No one's got any better ideas, and we've scoured the village already. Let's hurry to the woods and see if there's any sign of her.'

Bobby, who as usual in an affair of this kind had found herself naturally taking the lead, started to stride off at the head of the party with Ace. However, Topsy plucked her elbow.

'Birdy, it's going to get dark soon,' she whispered. 'There are all sorts of traps around the woods. Do you think the little girl can really have gone there?'

'It's the only idea I can think of. My father is there, taking up the traps before your aunt's hunt on Boxing Day. Hopefully most of them are up now, and if Jess runs into my dad, he'll make sure she's brought home safe. She's a clever girl and knows to keep to the paths, where no traps would have been set.'

'What if she wanders off the path to let the hen loose? What if she walks into a stoat trap and injures herself?' Topsy said, worry written all over her face. 'She could be lame for life.'

'We need to go as quickly as we can if we're to make sure that doesn't happen. Come on, Topsy.'

They hurried towards the woods, taking the dirt track that led to the hunting lodge where Jolka and Tommy lived. Some of the men peeled off to explore the woods around them. Ace pulled on his lead to get ahead, but

Bobby wasn't sure that meant anything other than the fact he was excited to be taken on an unscheduled walk. He didn't seem to be following a scent.

The sun was sinking now, and the woods felt rather eerie as long shadows were cast across their path. Poor Jessie must be scared to death as she wandered the woods alone. It was testament to the child's strength of feeling about the old hen she'd bonded with that she was willing to go to such lengths to save Henrietta's life.

Bobby tried to keep a brave face on, realising the others were looking to her for leadership, but she was finding it a real struggle not to give in to the panic inside. There were a lot of things that could hurt a little girl out alone after dark. It was going to be a very bleak Christmas at Moorside if Jessie wasn't found safe and sound before darkness fell.

There was no sign of her father as they explored, or of Jessie either, but Bobby did notice some strange markings on the sandy track.

'I think a vehicle of some kind might have been this way,' she said to Lilian, who was taking the lead with her. 'There are slim tyre marks in the sand where it's damp.'

'A vehicle? What could have got down this narrow track?'

'A small buggy, perhaps, or a pram — except pram wheels would be closer together so a buggy is more likely.' She lowered her voice so Mary wouldn't hear. 'Lil, you don't think someone's taken her?'

'If they had, it doesn't follow they had any nefarious purpose. It might be someone she knows, taking her back home. She could be there now with Reg and Florrie, waiting for us.'

'But no one in the village drives a one-man buggy like that.'

'There are some footprints where it's soft too.' Lilian bent to examine them while Ace sniffed them at her side. 'Too many to tell when they were made or by who. They could be Dad's or anyone's. They're all smudged together.'

'Ace seems interested in them. Mind you, that might just mean he smells Dad.'

The sun was setting now. Skeletal trees were silhouetted against a sky on fire. Bobby squinted through the fading light to the hunting lodge in the distance.

'Jolka might be able to help us,' she said. 'Let's call there and find out if she's seen anything.'

She cast a worried glance at the lake nearby as they walked on. It had frozen over in the cold weather, but a man-sized hole had been made in the ice a little way from the bank. Perhaps that was Pete Dixon, making a hole for an illicit fishing rod. Or perhaps… if Jessie had wandered out on to the ice, it didn't bear thinking about.

–

When they reached the lodge, Bobby knocked at the door. Jolka answered a moment later. She smiled with relief when she saw who it was.

'Oh, thank the heavens,' she said, ignoring Ace going mad around her feet. 'Then your father has reached you.'

'My father? No.'

'He did not see you at Moorside?'

'We haven't come from Moorside – not directly. We came from the village.'

Mary pushed anxiously through the group to the front.

'Have you seen her, Jolka? Did our Jessie come this way?'

'Yes, she is here, safe and sound.'

'Oh, thank goodness. Thank goodness!' Mary burst into tears of sheer relief, and Topsy went to put an arm around her.

'Come inside out of the cold, all of you,' Jolka said, standing aside for them to enter.

There must have been half a dozen or more of them, excluding Ace, but they all managed to squeeze in to Jolka's small hallway.

'The little girl is in the parlour with Tommy and her pet,' Jolka said in a low voice. 'I know she must have given you much worry, Mary, but I beg you will not be too angry with her. She was most distressed when she was brought here. Bobby, I summoned your father from where he was working in the woods to escort her back home again, but she would not go until she had a promise from Mary and Reg that the bird would not be hurt. Your father has gone to fetch some of you here, along with the promise.'

'Thank God,' Bobby said, feeling some of the tension leave her body. 'That means Reg and Florrie will know she's safe by now. Florrie was distraught when she realised her sister was missing.'

'Of course the bird won't be hurt,' Mary said, wiping her eyes. 'As long as Jessie's safe, I'll promise her anything. May I see her?'

'She is by the fireside with the friends who brought her here from the woods, where they said she wandered alone like a little girl in a fairy tale.' Jolka smiled at Topsy. 'You too will find a friend in there, Topsy.'

Topsy blinked. 'I will?'

'Yes, I believe Father Christmas has spirited him here for you. You will please go in first with Mary.'

Looking puzzled, Topsy followed Mary and they pushed open the door of the parlour. Bobby followed close behind with Ace, who, ineffectual bloodhound that he was, finally seemed to have sensed his mistress's presence and was pulling at his lead to get to her.

A cosy sight met their eyes. Jessie was sitting on the carpet in front of a lighted Christmas tree with her hen in her lap, looking not much the worse for her ordeal apart from a tear in her coat and a little pallor in her cheeks. Tommy was beside her, gently stroking Henrietta's feathers under supervision from the older child. And beside her on her other side… was Teddy. He was in the middle of telling the children a story – something about a fairy princess whose wings had been stolen. He fell silent, however, when the door opened and he caught sight of Topsy.

So that was what had made the tyre marks Bobby had seen. Not a buggy or pram but a wheelchair…

Ernie King was there too. He looked rather tired, but he was smiling, standing by the doorway watching the cosy scene. Bobby found herself next to him.

'Hey, Slacks,' he murmured. 'Brought you a Christmas present. I hope it's what you wanted.'

Bobby was too dazed to answer. She watched as Mary ran forward and bent to gather Jessie in her arms, earning a disapproving cluck from Henrietta as she hopped off the girl's lap.

'Oh, you silly, naughty, wonderful girl,' Mary gasped. 'Do you know how much danger you were in today? I don't know whether I ought to spank you or hug you. Except I can't help but hug you, despite you taking ten years from my life this afternoon.'

'I'm sorry, Mary,' Jessie whispered. 'I only done it for Henrietta, to save her from being killed. I was going to let her out in the woods to live with the birds there. I thought I could get home before you knew where I'd gone, only I couldn't find my way and I was frightened then. I thought maybe a wolf would come, like in Red Riding Hood, because I'd gone off the path.'

'It's all right now,' Mary said soothingly, drawing the child closer. 'You're safe again, and neither Henrietta nor the other hens will be harmed. You have my word. I ought never to have insisted on it when I could see how upset it was making you.' She drew back. 'How did you find your way here?'

She beamed at Teddy. 'Lieutenant Teddy and his friend found me. They was in the woods too, and they heard me crying and come to find me, then they brung me here to sit by the fire. I was cold as ice, but I'm warm again now.'

'Then we owe both men a debt,' Mary said quietly, looking from Teddy to Ernie. 'Thank you, from the bottom of my heart.'

'Will Father Christmas still come, Mary?' Jessie asked. 'Will Reg tell him I was bad?'

'You weren't bad on purpose, my love, but you must never, never do so again. And yes, Father Christmas will still come. But first we need to get you home – and Henrietta too. I'm sure she misses her friends in the henhouse.'

'All right. But oh, may we hear the end of the story Lieutenant Teddy was telling? It's called "The Princess of the Brazen Mountain". I ain't never heard it before. It's not in my big book of nursery tales.'

'That is because it is a Polish tale,' Teddy said quietly. He wasn't looking at Jessie but at Topsy, his eyes filled with tenderness and unspoken longing. Topsy, too, was staring at him as if mesmerised.

Mary glanced at Teddy and smiled. 'There'll be time for that another day, Jess. I think our Lieutenant Teddy may have other matters to attend to.'

Topsy approached him and dropped to her knees to bring them level.

'Are you really here?' she whispered.

'I am.'

'To stay? To stay forever?'

'If you would have me forever,' he said softly.

'It's all I've ever wanted.'

Jolka cleared her throat. 'We might leave our two friends alone for a little time, I think. Let the rest of us go through to the dining room, and I will prepare hot drinks to warm everyone after your afternoon's labour. I do not have enough tea and cocoa for all who might like some, but there is chicory essence to fill the deficiency.'

'I can help there,' Ernie said, picking up a bag at his feet and slinging it over his shoulder. 'I brought a ration pack along when I went to fetch Teddy. There's some tea and cocoa in it that I'm happy to contribute.'

Everyone filed out, Jessie taking charge of a now quite frantic Ace while Mary scooped up Henrietta. But Bobby hung around until the last moment, watching Topsy and Teddy. They were oblivious to everyone else now, lost in themselves. They held each other's hands and gazed at one another, as if they had never seen anything quite so wondrous.

Archie, too, hung back.

'Topsy.'

Topsy tore herself from Teddy's gaze to look at him.

'We've got a wedding arranged for next month,' he said in a low voice.

'I think…' She looked at Teddy, who smiled encouragingly at her. 'I'm sorry, Arch. I do care for you, ever so much. But…'

'…you're going to have to break our engagement,' he finished for her. 'I know that. You're not understanding me, Tops. I mean the thing's all booked and paid for, at your insistence. January 31st. The church, the reception, the dress…'

'I'll make sure you get your money back.'

'I don't want my money back. I loaned it from Mother anyhow.' He approached and rested a hand on her shoulder. 'What I mean is, I'm sure they can work with one bridegroom as well as another. Don't you think so?'

Topsy looked up at him. 'Oh Arch, do you mean it?'

'Never meant anything more in my life, old thing.'

He laughed as she jumped up and threw her arms around his neck. Teddy grasped his hand and shook it vigorously behind her back.

'I'm sorry, Arch,' Topsy whispered. 'I'll do anything I can for you, but this is one thing I have to keep for myself.'

'Nothing to apologise for, Tops. It was too big a favour to expect.'

'Will your mother give you a terribly hard time about it?'

'Oh, blow Mother. It's about time I stood up to her. Leave her to me; I'll settle it one way or another.'

'Won't she cut off your allowance?'

'I'll muddle along somehow.' He smiled. 'Don't forget I'm a star of pantomime now. Perhaps I might audition for ENSA. I think I should rather suit the theatrical life.'

He nodded an affable goodbye to them both and approached Bobby, who had been watching by the door. 'Well, my dear, I'm a single man again. That being the case, perhaps you'll allow me to hand you in to the dining room?'

She smiled, taking the proffered arm. 'With pleasure.'

'Bobby,' Teddy called before they left the room. She turned to him.

'Thank you, for the letter you wrote to me,' he said quietly. 'A thousand times, thank you.'

—

There was quite a little party happening in the dining room. Henrietta had been taken to a quiet room where she could rest her old feathers, and the two children were squealing madly as they chased Ace around the floor. Jolka had turned on the wireless, from whence Christmas carols rang out. Ernie smiled at Bobby as she entered with Archie, who relinquished her arm so he could go to greet his friends Sandy and Chip.

'Here you go,' Ernie said, passing her a steaming mug. 'I saved you some of this. Canadian cocoa. Better than the stuff you Brits get.'

'Thanks.' She took it from him and nursed it in numb hands. 'Tell me what happened, Ernie. I'm dying to know. I take it you sent Teddy my letter?'

'I did better than that. I delivered the thing personally.'

She blinked at him. 'You really did that?'

'Yeah. Thought about what you said and came to the conclusion I was being a selfish son of a gun about the business, washing my hands of it like that. It is the season of peace and goodwill to all men, even if there's precious little of those things going around out there in the world. I thought I could at least contribute a little goodwill of my own.'

'So you...'

'Travelled over this morning, early, to give him the letter in the hope it wasn't too late for a Christmas reunion.' Ernie smiled. 'I don't know what you said in that thing, Slacks, but it did the trick. As soon as he'd read it, he was asking me to help him pack his case. Seemed to think if he didn't hurry, Topsy might have married the other guy by this afternoon.'

'Where did you find Jessie?'

'I was pushing Teddy to Woodside Nook. He wanted to speak to Archie, man to man, before he saw Topsy again. And what should we discover but a little girl crying her eyes out in the forest with a chicken under her arm? Poor mite was just about turning blue so we brought her straight here to get warm.'

'Oh, Ernie.' Bobby stood on tiptoes to kiss his cheek. 'I know you don't need to hear this when no doubt you've got dozens of women telling you every day, but you're wonderful. Thank you.'

He rubbed his cheek where she'd kissed him. 'Shucks.'

'Well. It is Christmas.'

'Not worried about the jealous fiancé?'

'I think this counts as a special occasion,' she said, smiling. 'I'll make sure to tell him I don't make a habit of it when I confess all my sins.'

Topsy came in at that moment, wheeling Teddy. She was blushing all over her face, and smiling with more genuine joy than Bobby had seen her do since her lover had left. Teddy, too, looked serene and content as he regarded the roomful of people with an expression of bonhomie.

'Teddy and I have a little announcement to make.' Topsy reached over his chair so she could grasp his hand. 'I don't suppose I need actually announce it though, since you must surely already have guessed.'

'You certainly don't,' Archie said, smiling. 'But I think we owe it three cheers all the same.'

He led the room in three cheers for the newly betrothed couple, and Topsy beamed at them all. Some of the group looked a little puzzled at the turn of events as the jilted fiancé led the cheers for the announcement of the new one. However, most of those present knew or had guessed enough to realise this was how things were meant to be and joined in enthusiastically.

'Birdy, may I have a word in the hall?' Topsy said to Bobby.

'Of course.'

Topsy took her arm and guided her out of the dining room. As soon as they were alone, she threw her arms around her.

'Thank you,' she whispered. 'I ought to be terribly cross with you for interfering, but I'm so very happy you did. Now I have my pilot back and he's ten times more my pilot than ever he was, because he's really mine to keep at last. I shall never, ever be cross with you again. Today I don't feel I can be cross with anyone ever again. You're wonderful, Birdy.'

'I just said something very similar to Ernie King for his part in the business,' Bobby said, smiling. 'Every happiness, my love. You know, Piotr once told me that he felt you and Teddy were destined by God to be together. I believe he was right.'

'Oh, what a heavenly thing it is to have friends who won't mind their own business,' Topsy said, laughing as she wiped away a tear. 'And now you must be our maid of honour for making the match, and Maimie shall be matron. We may even manage to make a page boy out of Norman, if he isn't too old a married man himself now for such childish affairs.'

Bobby laughed. 'And Henrietta and Jemima for brides-maids, I suppose. Come on, let's go back in. We ought to take Jessie home. I don't think her sister will be able to relax until she sees that she's safe, or Reg either for that matter.'

'Well, I'm glad everything worked out for the best in the end,' Mary was saying when they joined the others again. 'Lord knows what I'm going to give the family tomorrow though. Seven mouths to feed and not a chop or a cutlet in the house. I've no meat in the pantry but bacon.'

Jessie looked worried. 'You promised though, Mary. About Henrietta.'

Mary smiled and stroked her hair. 'Don't worry, Jess. A promise is a promise. Henrietta is safe, and you mustn't get any more ideas into your head about running off. I don't think I could survive another scare like today's.'

'Oh! But I can help with that,' Topsy said, beaming at Mary. 'It was supposed to be the most terrific surprise, but I think I may tell you now. I'm sending round a pair of ducks to Moorside this evening, all plucked and trussed ready for the oven.'

Mary stared at her. 'A pair! Topsy, that's far too generous. I couldn't accept two whole ducks without giving you something for them.'

'I thought you'd say that, but these aren't really for you,' Topsy told her. 'They're a gift for Mr Bancroft – his Christmas box. I thought they'd be better than money now meat is so hard to get, and he's more than earned them since he came to work for me. I had a pair brought from the lake and fattened up for your table. I'm sorry, if I'd known you were struggling so for a bird on Christmas Day I'd have told you sooner. Like I said, I wanted it to be a surprise.'

'Well, in that case you've saved my bacon,' Mary said, going forward to press Topsy's two hands. 'In a very real sense, since that was all we were going to have to eat tomorrow. Thank you, dear, and every joy in the world to you and your young man.' She looked at Jessie and smiled. 'Now I think we had better be going home. After all, Miss Jessica Parry, it isn't very long until we can expect Father Christmas to be making his rounds.'

Chapter 30

There was a tearful reunion between the Parry sisters when the search party took Jessie back to Moorside. They had met Rob on the way, heading to the village to seek them out, and the inhabitants of Moorside Farm and Cow House Cottage had all returned to spend the evening at the farmhouse. There Henrietta was reinstated in the henhouse amid friendly pecks from her sister hens, while Jessie was enthroned on an armchair in the parlour to hold court.

'Did you see any wild animals when you were lost in the woods, Jess?' Florence asked, wide-eyed.

Jessie nodded solemnly. 'I saw a great big fox with big huge teeth. Bigger'n Mr Dixon's Alsatian, even. He wanted to eat Henrietta, but I put her under my coat and shooed him until he ran away.'

'Blimey!'

Bobby raised her eyebrows at Lilian beside her, smiling. Jessie's adventures had been growing in scope and magnitude every time she told of them. What had originally been rabbits and geese had now become foxes and badgers. Bobby supposed it was only a matter of time until a lion, bear or wolf became one of Jessie's assailants – perhaps even a dinosaur.

The doorbell rang and Mary stood up. 'Praise the Lord! That must be Topsy's ducks.'

She went to answer it, and a moment later the soft strains of 'Silent Night' being played on an accordion drifted into the house.

'It's carollers,' Mary called to them. 'Come and listen, everyone.'

All of those present – Bobby, Lilian, Reg, Rob and the two little girls – stood up to go into the hall. On the doorstep were a troupe of carol singers with soot-blackened faces and top hats on their heads, carrying a small blackout torch in lieu of the usual lantern on a stick. One played an old accordion while another held out the traditional wassail bowl, decorated with holly and ribbons. Mary was holding a brace of ducks that one of the carollers had presumably handed to her.

It was a beautiful scene. Soft snow began to fall as the men and boys sang their final carol, 'In the Field With Their Flocks Abiding'. A little lad who was with them took the solo. His young voice, piercing and sweet, rang out in the sharp air.

After the singing, one of the men stepped forward, cleared his throat and in a sonorous baritone recited that stirring poem 'Christmas Bells' by Mr Longfellow. In spite of the sooty face, Bobby recognised the man as a lay preacher from the village chapel, known for his impressive oratory.

'Thanks to you all, and a happy Christmas,' Reg said when they were done, shaking each man and boy heartily by the hand. 'I've sixpence here for each of you. Mary will fill your bowl with some mulled ale in the kitchen.'

'Aye, and we've some Yule cake too,' Mary said. 'Come on through, all of ye, and get yourselves warm by the fire before you move on.'

The rest of the evening passed pleasantly around the hearth at Moorside. The two desks that usually took up much of the space in the parlour had been transported to the cellar temporarily, and there was plenty of room for all.

After the traditional Christmas Eve supper of spicy buttered Yule cake served with a slice of cheese, each person chose the spot around the roaring fire that they liked best. Mary and Reg sat companionably together on the settee with their two old wolfhounds, Barney and Winnie, at their feet. Beside each dog was a child, sitting on a large cushion. Mary occasionally reached out to rest one hand on Jessie's curly head, the scare of her recent loss not quite banished yet.

Bobby sat on an old milking stool so that her sister could have one of the armchairs. Her father was in the other, doing his best to amuse a boisterous Ace who refused to accept that it was time to settle for the night. Everyone had a glass of something warming. Bobby nursed her steaming mug of gingery mulled ale, served with a head of 'lamb's wool' — a pulp of baked apples floated on top.

It was the only night of the year, Bobby was sure, when Florrie and Jessie begged to go to bed early instead of begging to stay up late. They had barely finished their supper before they began asking whether it was time yet to retire.

'Not now, or you'll be awake at cock-crow tomorrow,' Reg said, smiling. 'It isn't six yet.'

'What did you do at home with your father when you spent Christmas Eve together?' Mary asked the children.

'I'm sure he'd like to hear of us observing your family traditions.'

Jessie frowned. 'I don't remember. It was ages ago that Daddy was at home for Christmas. Before the war started.'

'I remember,' her older sister said, rather self-important with this weighty knowledge. 'We'd sing carols and play Consequences or Snakes and Ladders, and then Dad would tell us a ghost story. But not a really scary one so we'd have bad dreams though.'

Lilian looked at her father. 'You used to tell us all a ghost story on Christmas Eve, Dad. Do you remember? When Mam was alive you did it every year.'

'Aye.' Rob smiled slightly. 'Long time ago, lass.'

'It doesn't seem so long ago to me,' Bobby said. 'I'm sure you remember some of them still, don't you?'

'I could dust one off, for old time's sake.' He took a sip of his beer. 'Mind you, I'll need a hat.'

Lilian laughed. 'Oh gosh, the hat. I'd forgotten the hat.'

'Our dad used to have a special hat for telling Christmas ghost stories,' Bobby told the others. 'A battered top hat he had got from somewhere. He'd turn out all the lights and shine a candle under his chin to make it even more ghostly. He looked like Jacob Marley.'

'I think we can furnish Rob with a hat, if it's a part of your tradition.' Mary got to her feet. 'Florrie found an old top hat of Reg's father's in the attic chest last week, as it happens. I was going to take it for the Baron to wear in the pantomime tomorrow.'

She went out to fetch it, and presented it to Rob. He placed it solemnly on his head.

'And now you must turn out the lights and have a candle as Bobby says, Mr Bancroft,' Florrie told him, giggling.

Bobby lit a candle and handed it to her father while Mary turned out the lights; all except the fairy lights that twinkled on the Christmas tree.

'Now prepare yourselves for a tale of terror,' Rob said when the scene was set, deepening his voice dramatically as he drew out the last word. He launched into his story.

It made Bobby smile to hear him. When they were settled around the farmhouse hearth like this, an odd little patchwork family, her dad could be as she remembered him from her childhood – before grief and drinking had taken so much of him away from them. He had had his demons then, too, but when her mother was alive, those demons had rarely intruded into the happiness of the family home.

The story he chose was one she remembered from when they were children: his own version of an MR James tale about a cursed whistle and a ghost made of bed linen, softened for an audience of little ones. Florence and Jessie listened wide-eyed, relishing the thrilling shiver that passed down their spines with each surprise appearance of the ghost. Occasionally they would let out a little squeal of delighted terror.

Bobby glanced at Lilian. She was smiling too as she watched their dad tell the tale, her eyes rather dewy.

'What are you thinking?' Bobby whispered to her.

'Nothing important, really. I was just wondering what our family Christmases may look like five years hence.'

Bobby had been wondering this too. Would there be another child in the family group – Lilian's child? Would he, too, sit rapt while his grandfather sent shivers down his spine by candlelight in an old top hat? Or would the baby be given away, to grow up among strangers who could give him a better, more respectable life than his poor shamed mother would ever be able to provide?

After the story, they followed Florrie's suggestion and played a game of Consequences, which was the perfect antidote to the spooky tale they had just heard. Everyone, not only the children, was in fits of laughter as they read out the nonsensical stories they had created between them.

'Ooh. This one is about you and Uncle Charlie, Bobby,' Florrie said gleefully as she unfolded the paper.

'Oh Lord, must it be?' Bobby said with a groan.

Jessie giggled. 'Read it, Florrie.'

'Bobby met Charlie at the beauty parlour,' Florrie read. 'He said, "If I'd a face like yours, I should give it back again." She said, "Would you like treacle or jam on your parsnips?" He ate twenty yellow plums all at once. She kicked him in the pants. The consequence was that they both put out to sea on Christmas morning.'

Bobby laughed. 'Well I don't much care for this Bobby and Charlie. They seem like terribly ill-mannered creatures. I'm sure their families were very glad to be free of their tricks when they went to sea.'

Jessie yawned. 'I wish Uncle Charlie could be here tomorrow to have Christmas with us. Then I could give him the picture I drew for him.'

Florrie giggled. 'And you could kick him in the pants like in the story, Bobby.'

Mary smiled at her. 'I'm sure Bobby would prefer to give your Uncle Charlie a kiss than a kick when she sees him.'

'Eurgh,' Jessie said, sticking out her tongue.

Florrie added a yawn to the one her sister had just let out, and Mary tapped her on the shoulder.

'All right, I think if it's yawns all over the place then it must be time for bed,' she said.

Jessie jumped to her feet. 'Hooray!'

Mary rolled her eyes at the other adults. 'If only every night were like this.'

'And remember you must be fast asleep when St Nick comes around,' Reg warned the children. 'He can tell when you're pretending.'

Florrie's eyes widened. 'But what if we can't get to sleep?'

'Well, happen you'll find it easier than you think,' Reg said with a smile. 'Off you go then. You can stop in the kitchen with Mary and put out a mince pie and glass of beer for the old man when he gets here.'

Jessie rubbed her eyes. 'And we must leave a carrot or turnip too, for the reindeer.'

'Aye, mustn't forget them.'

The two girls dutifully kissed everyone goodnight, then Mary shepherded them out of the room and up to bed.

After they were gone, Lilian smothered a yawn.

'I don't think I'm going to be far behind the girls,' she said. 'It's been a tiring day, what with missing bairns and absconding hens. I doubt I can last until midnight communion on the wireless.'

Rob smiled at Reg. 'Late night for you though, St Nick. I remember my stint well: me and Nell sitting by the fire trying not to drop off while we waited for t' little ones to settle.'

'Oh, the girls will be fast off in no time after the day they've had,' Reg said, leaning back in his chair as he started stuffing his pipe. 'I'll be surprised if Jessie makes it up the stairs without Mary needing to carry her.'

'What will Santa be bringing for their stockings?' Bobby asked.

'He couldn't get any oranges. War shortages have hit the North Pole too,' Reg told her solemnly. 'But they've an apple and a stick of liquorice each to satisfy a sweet tooth. A little bar of coloured soap, new hankies, a toy soldier for Florrie, a peg doll for Jessie – oh, and a half-crown piece each, of course. Mary says they can open their proper presents after church. All but that dolls' house our Charlie made for them.'

'Why's that?'

Reg shrugged. 'Lot of excitement for them tomorrow; makes sense to spread it out a bit. Mary wants to save it as a surprise for Christmas night, after the pantomime.'

Bobby put a hand to her forehead. 'Oh my word, the pantomime. I've been so thrang with things to worry about today that I'd forgotten I have to be on stage tomorrow.'

'You'll do a grand job, our Bobby.' Her dad got to his feet. 'I reckon we all ought to get to bed. Busy day tomorrow.'

'And we have to be asleep when Santa comes, remember, or we'll get nothing either,' Lilian said with a laugh.

–

While Bobby got into her night things and their father visited the outhouse, Lilian heated some milk for them to take to bed. When Bobby emerged from the bedroom in her nightgown, she found the milk simmering on the hob while her sister hung three of their dad's long winter socks over the fireplace.

Bobby smiled, shaking her head. 'Lilian Bancroft.'

'Well. We want to get into the spirit of things over here too, don't we?'

'Dad's not going to be happy you pinched his socks.'

'He can have them back in the morning.' She went back to the hob to stir the milk. Bobby joined her.

'We've barely had a chance to talk all day,' she said in a low voice. 'About… you-know-what.'

'Perhaps that's for the best.'

'Do you know what you're going to do yet?'

Lilian put down her wooden spoon and rubbed her head. 'I thought about adoption. I could go away; stay at a maternity home for unmarried mothers until the baby could go to his new parents. When I came back, no one would need to be any the wiser. Tony might put up the funds, if I told him what he'd done.'

'Or he might not,' Bobby muttered. 'Don't forget he's out of work.'

'The thing is, I don't know if that's what I want. It's what I should want, I know. The least bad option for both of us. But it feels like once I've met him – the baby, I mean – I won't want to let him go again.' She smiled sadly. 'Dad was in his element tonight, wasn't he? When he was telling his story I could almost believe Florrie and Jessie were me and you, made little girls again.'

'He'd be a wonderful grandfather to the little lad, once he'd come to terms with your situation.'

'Hmm. And thrashed Tony Scott to within an inch of his life, probably.' She sighed. 'He's going to be so disappointed in me.'

Bobby squeezed her arm. 'Do you mean it, Lil? About keeping the baby?'

'I haven't decided yet. It would be a hard life for us,' Lilian murmured, lowering her voice as they heard the privy being flushed outside. 'It's all very well getting damp-eyed about family on Christmas Eve, but every day isn't Christmas. There are challenges to be faced. Prejudice and shame and poverty. It doesn't seem fair to bring a child into a life like that.'

'What will you do?'

'I don't know. But I do know that as soon as Christmas is over, I need to speak to Tony.'

Chapter 31

'Bobby! Wake up!'

Bobby was rudely pulled from slumber by her sister, who was shaking her arm excitedly.

'Huh,' she mumbled sleepily. 'Lil. What is it?'

'It's Christmas, you dolt! Get up and see what's to be seen.'

Bobby sat up, yawning. Her sister was already up and dressed, standing over her with sparkling eyes. She never had quite outgrown her kangaroo tendencies. The curtains had been flung open, and the room was filled with the exciting white dazzle that meant snow.

'We officially have a white Christmas here in the Dales,' Lilian announced importantly. 'A good four inches overnight. The girls are already up and outside. I saw them making a snowman in the garden when I went to the outhouse, and there's the most incredible smell coming from Mary's kitchen. Get up and stop wasting the best day of the year.'

'All right, Mam,' Bobby said with a smile as she swung her legs out of bed and pushed her feet into her slippers. 'Is Dad up?'

'Not yet, but he will be in a minute when I shout "Happy Christmas" in his ear.'

'You're a menace, Lilian Bancroft.'

Bobby followed her sister out of the room, and laughed when she observed the three stockings over the fire. Each was filled with an exciting collection of lumps and bumps, just as they would have been on Christmas morning when they were children.

'Who filled them?' she asked.

Lilian rolled her eyes. 'Santa Claus, of course.'

'You mean Dad.'

'All right, if you must ruin the magic. I suppose he filled ours, yes. I did his before I came to bed last night.'

'You daft old thing.' Bobby gave her a squeeze. 'I wonder what's in them.'

'You must come look at the snow before you start exploring stockings.'

Lilian practically skipped to the front door, Bobby following.

'Oh my goodness!' Bobby said when she looked out.

Everything was white, as far as the eye could see, and more fresh flakes were falling. The giants that loomed high above the village were clothed now in the purest white. Bobby felt as though she had woken in the North Pole, and Moorside must be Father Christmas's cottage. From outside the farmhouse she could hear the merry cries of the two evacuees as they rolled up snow for a snowman.

'Isn't it wonderful?' Lilian breathed. 'Every Christmas ought to be a white Christmas.'

'It's very pretty,' Bobby agreed. 'And very cold. I hope it won't stop people getting to the pantomime.'

'I'm sure the people in this part of the world are used to being out and about in this weather.' Lilian let out a contented sigh as she breathed air sharp with snow. 'You know I've never been one for the countryside, but sitting with the family at Moorside last night, and the way everything looks this morning, I think I could almost learn to love it here as much as you do.'

Bobby smiled. 'I knew we'd win you over eventually.'

'What's all this? Why're we letting the heat out?' a voice grunted. Bobby turned to see that her dad had emerged from his bedroom.

'It's a real white Christmas, Dad,' Lilian said gleefully. 'I can't remember the last time we had one, can you?'

'Best we ever got in Bradford was a grey Christmas, once the muck and soot had got into it.' He smiled. 'Looks like Ginger picked t' right present for his bairns anyhow.'

'What is it Captain Parry's sent them?' Bobby asked. 'Mary never mentioned it.'

'You'll have to wait and see. Reg asked me to hide it in the gamekeeper's hut until Christmas Eve, where there were no chance of nosy parkers finding it.' He nodded to the filled socks over the fireplace. 'Not going to see what Old Man Christmas brought for you then?'

Lilian clapped her hands. 'Oh yes, may we?'

'Can I just remind you that you're twenty-four years old?' Bobby said, laughing.

'Aye, go on,' their dad said placidly. 'Then we can all go over for breakfast.'

'You always used to make us wait until after Christmas dinner when we were bairns,' Bobby observed to her dad as Lilian handed her a stocking.

'Aye, well. Happen I'm going soft in my old age.'

They spent a pleasant quarter of an hour rifling through the old socks. Bobby almost felt like a little girl again. It was a long time since she had felt any real excitement on Christmas morning. This year she had expected to feel it only by proxy, on behalf of the little evacuees, but the half-forgotten sensation of pleasurable anticipation as she reached into a stuffed stocking with her sister beside her brought back the Christmases of her childhood so strongly that she could almost smell the pine needles of their little tree. It had been a happy thought of Lilian's, hanging up the socks.

The presents they had got for one another were as befitted wartime austerity – modest and practical, mostly home-made or second-hand, but very much appreciated in these days when treats for oneself were rare. There was a little bottle of almond oil for Bobby from her sister – this, Lilian told her, was what many of the Wrens were now using to moisten their skin in the absence of hard-to-get cold cream. A slim volume of poetry was the gift from her father – penned by Tennyson and not, thankfully, by Principatus, Bobby noted with a wry smile. Jake had sent the girls a bar of soap each – a much-valued luxury these days – and a small packet of Wills's Whiffs cigars for their father, who liked a smoke after Christmas dinner. Raymond and Sarah had sent a portion of their tea ration for Rob, and lavender pillows made by the children for Bobby and Lilian. Rob had a knitted scarf from Bobby and matching gloves from Lilian, the yarn for which had been gleaned from an old pullover Lilian had pulled out and divided with her sister.

'Thank you both,' Bobby said when they had fully divested the stockings of their treasures, getting up to give them each a kiss. 'I feel quite spoilt with my almond oil and the soap from Jake. I can't remember the last time I had soap that wasn't economy coal.'

'I expected to get a Christmas present from the lad sometime in mid-February, when he realised he'd forgotten to post it,' Lilian observed. 'That new girl of his must be putting him in order.'

'About time someone did,' their father said with a smile.

'We ought to get dressed and go over to Moorside, where it's warm,' Bobby said. 'There's no point wasting coke on a fire when we shall be out all day.'

Lilian smiled. 'Yes, and the little girls will be desperate to go to church so they can come home and open their presents.'

Bobby washed herself with her new scented soap and dressed in her smartest clothes, ready for the Christmas service at St Peter's, then they went over to Moorside to join the rest of the family.

'Happy Christmas one and all,' Mary said when they joined her in the kitchen, beaming at them. 'The bairns are out back with Reg, dressing up that snowman of theirn. Bobby, can you fetch them all in for breakfast? We've frumenty and treacle for everyone. Some real cream in it too.'

Bobby had never had frumenty before, but apparently it was a Dales tradition to eat it on Christmas Day. She discovered when it was served that it was a thick, creamy porridge of crushed wheat, cooked slowly in the oven. It was flavoured with cinnamon, nutmeg and currants, with a dollop of treacle stirred through to sweeten it.

'This a custom, is it?' Rob observed as he scraped his bowl clean with relish.

'It is,' Mary said. 'Always eaten on Christmas morning in days of yore. When I was a bairn, we'd a tradition that we all ate from the same bowl. The two eldest must eat first, then the next two eldest, then two at a time right down to the babby.' She smiled. 'But as we only have wartime portions, I think for Jessie's sake we had better

355

have a bowl each. Eat up, everyone. There's hot coffee to follow.'

The porridge certainly warmed and lined the stomach, making Bobby feel as though even the snow outside couldn't get into her bones today. After breakfast, she and the others pulled on their sturdiest boots in order to make their way to the village for church. She, Lilian and her father took charge of the two little girls as they headed for St Peter's, while Reg and Mary separated from them to attend the Methodist service at the chapel. Silverdale looked quite Dickensian that morning, with a blanket of snow covering the little terraced houses, the old wishing well and the bridge over the beck.

Snow continued to fall while they were at church. Bobby occasionally cast it a worried glance through the stained glass. Would it deter people from coming to Sumner House for the pantomime? It was a good three-mile walk from the centre of the village when the long driveway through the park was taken into account. It would be very unfair, after they'd all worked so hard, if the children couldn't have their Christmas entertainment after all.

In spite of the snow, the girls fairly raced ahead on the way home. Bobby could hardly keep up with them. Of course, they remembered well Mary's promise that after church they could open the little pile of newspaper-wrapped presents waiting for them under the tree.

Sure enough, they ran into the kitchen as soon as they arrived home. Mary was bending to put the pair of ducks Topsy had given to them – now stuffed, basted and lined with fatty slices of bacon – into the oven.

'May we open presents now please, Mary?' Jessie panted.

Mary laughed, wiping her hands on her apron. 'Let me put some tea on to brew so everyone can get warmed up then yes, you may open them. Happen when you've playthings to amuse you, you might leave off your mithering so I can finish dinner.'

Once Mary had furnished everyone with a very welcome cup of tea and a hot mince pie, all went into the parlour and drew up a chair by the fire while Reg, as the man of the house, took charge of distributing the presents.

'Bobby, one for you from Mary,' he said, handing her a parcel. 'Rob, from me and Mary, and another one for you from the girls. Lilian, here's one for you from me, Mary and the girls.'

'I'm sorry, it's a rather last-minute gift,' Mary said with an apologetic smile for Lilian. 'We didn't know we'd be having both Bancroft twins here for Christmas.'

'It's very kind of you. I wasn't expecting anything.' She opened it to find some pale pink rosewater, in a pretty glass bottle in which rose petals floated like a fall of snow. 'It's wonderful – thank you all. Now I shall smell like a real lady when we go to the mansion for the pantomime.'

'Jess and me made it when the roses grew here in summer,' Florrie said, puffing herself up. 'Mary helped a little but mostly we made it all ourselves. There's a bottle for Bobby too, so you can smell the same. We thought twins probably like to smell the same.'

Lilian smiled. 'That's very thoughtful, Florrie.'

The children had second-hand storybooks from Rob and a rag doll each from Bobby – each doll with two sets of knitted clothes that could be changed as they liked. Lilian had brought them both a little bar of chocolate from Greenwich, which was rare enough these days to cause round eyes when they opened it. From Mary they had Fair Isle vests, marching soldiers in bearskin hats forming the pattern on Florrie's and gingerbread men all in a row on Jessie's. From Reg they received handmade toys: a wooden whistle for Jessie and a bow and arrow for Florrie. Jessie was thrilled with her whistle, which she immediately began training Ace to respond to. This led to a quick ban from Mary, who decreed that whistles and bows and arrows were to be outdoor toys only.

'I don't think there can be two luckier children in all of England today,' Bobby observed, watching them among their pile of treasures. 'And a pantomime to go to this afternoon too, with a tea to follow. You'd hardly know there was a war on at all.'

Florrie turned to her sister solemnly. 'I bet we are the luckiest children in England, you know, Jess. Louis in my class has got a bow and arrow too. It's the next best thing to an airgun, he says.'

Jessie was cradling her new rag doll with maternal tenderness. 'I like my new Alice even better than Jane, who was in our old house when it got bombed.'

'It's the most loveliest Christmas we've ever had,' Florrie announced. 'I mean, if Dad and Uncle Charlie were here it would be,' she added, looking rather guilty for her perceived act of treachery.

Jessie beamed around the adults. 'Thank you for our presents. We think they're… they're… they're *wizard*.'

She said this with such earnestness that it was clear no higher praise could be summoned. Bobby smothered a laugh.

'You're welcome, my loves,' Mary said. 'We're glad you like them, even though the war means we couldn't get you many things that are new.'

Florrie's face had fallen, however.

'Jess, there's nothing from Dad,' she said. 'He didn't send us any presents this year. He always did before.'

Jessie's face fell too. 'Do you think he forgot about us while he was away in the war?'

'He certainly didn't,' Reg said. 'That's the best present of all, which is why it was saved for last. Rob, would you do the honours?'

'It'll be my pleasure.' Rob stood up and left the room.

'Ooh! I wonder what it is,' Florrie said. 'Do you know, Bobby?'

'I wouldn't tell if I did,' Bobby said. 'That would ruin the surprise. But no, nobody knows except Reg and my dad. It's been kept the most secret of secrets until today.'

Florrie turned to her sister with shining eyes. 'Gosh!'

There was a gasp from the children when Rob came back into the room, carrying under his arm a sturdy wooden sledge with a red ribbon tied to it.

'I reckon your dad must've sent snow an' all,' he said to the girls as he put it down in front of them. 'That was bonny luck for you, it coming today.'

Florrie stared at the sledge. 'Is it really for us?'

'That's right.'

'It's beautiful,' Jessie whispered. 'Mary, may you take us out to play with it please?'

'I may not,' Mary said firmly. 'Bobby, Lilian and I have got a hundred and one things to do in the kitchen to get the dinner ready, and then we've to get Florrie into her fairy dress and you in your best party clothes ready for the pantomime. Ask one of the men to take you.'

'Aye, Rob and I can take you out,' Reg said. 'I know the best spot for sledging, up Coppermine Hill. Used to take our Charlie there when he were nobbut a lad.'

'Uncle Charlie didn't forget you either,' Bobby told the girls. 'You're to have your present from him later, after the pantomime.' But the children were too entranced by the new sledge to hear her.

'Now upstairs and put all your warmest things on before you go out, and take a change of socks too,' Mary said, clapping her hands at them. 'At least three layers each and winter coats before you set foot outside. I'll not have anyone catching their death of cold. You must take turns nicely with the sledge as well – no quarrelling. There mustn't be any cross words between us on the Lord's day.'

'Yes, Mary,' the girls chorused dutifully.

They ran out to get into their winter things. Then Jessie ran back in, gave Mary an impulsive hug and ran off again.

'That's what I wanted to see today,' Mary said with a smile. 'Happy, glowing faces. Now you men make sure you wrap up warm too, and Reg, if you feel the cold in your leg then you'd better leave Rob to mind them and come home to warm it by the fire. I've no wish to call the doctor away from his Christmas dinner today. Bobby and Lilian, you can join me in the kitchen.'

'Hang on.' Reg handed Bobby a hard rectangular parcel. 'Still one present left, for Bobby. This is from me. Can't beat what I gave you last year, I'm afraid, but might come in handy.'

'My press card,' Bobby said, smiling. 'I'll never forget opening the envelope you gave me on Christmas morning and feeling like a proper reporter for the first time.'

'Open this one then.'

She did so. Inside was a book, *Rules for Compositors and Readers* by Horace Hart.

'Not new, I'm afraid,' Reg said, looking embarrassed. 'It's the copy I used to work from at the *Mercury*. Thought you could use it now you've got "editor" in your job title – no editor should be without a copy. Any question of style, you'll find the answer in there.'

'Thank you. That was thoughtful of you.'

'Not much, I know, but you'll get some use out of it. Served me well, that little book.'

He reached for his stick to get to his feet, and Bobby looked at him. 'Reg, may I have a word with you quickly before you go out? In private?'

He looked surprised. 'If you like. Nowhere much private round here today, mind.'

'We'll go in the garden. I want to see the girls' snowman anyhow.'

She left the others and went out into the garden through the back door, Reg limping after her.

The snowman made her smile. He was a rather wartime snowman. Lacking spare currants for his mouth, the girls had instead used one of Reg's pipe cleaners bent into the shape of a smile. His eyes were cold ash from the fire, his nose a wedge of turnip, and he puffed happily on Reg's pipe. Round his neck was an old scarf of Charlie's, and he wore on his head the top hat Bobby's father had donned the evening before to tell them a ghost story.

'He's a handsome chap, isn't he?' she said to Reg.

'Aye, a very fine fellow. I've named him Charles. He's about as likely to do a hard day's work as my brother ever was.'

Bobby glanced again at the book she was holding.

'Reg, look,' she began. 'I'm really so grateful to you for everything you've done for me. I know you never wanted me for this job, but you gave me a chance, got me my press card, my first bylines; taught me how to be a better writer and to always focus on people before things. I owe you so much, and I don't want you to think I'm not sensible of that because I am – very much so. I've tried to always work hard for you, and give you my best.'

He frowned. 'What's all this talk? You're not fixing to give notice, are you? Bloody funny day to do it if you are, lass.'

'I don't want to give notice. I love my job, and my life here in Silverdale. That's exactly why…' She took a deep breath. 'Why I wanted to talk to you. It's about the women's page.'

'What about it? I thought it were shaping up nicely. You've done a good job.'

'Thanks. I've tried to do my best work on it, like I always do. But… please, I wish you'd take back the new job title you gave me. I don't want to be the women's editor. If we're to have a section for housewives, I'm happy to work on it but I don't want to only work on it, and I don't want my byline to appear with it – as women's editor or anything else.'

Reg blinked. 'Am I hearing you right? Roberta Bancroft, begging me *not* to give her a byline?'

'I know you probably think I've gone strange in the head,' Bobby said, flushing in spite of the chill. 'Yes, I've always dreamed of writing under my own byline, and even more so of having the word "editor" in my title one day. But not like this. When I get that word in my title – if I ever do – I want to have earned it, Reg. I don't want it to be by default, because I am the sex I am. I want it to be because I've gained your admiration and respect as a writer.'

'Who says you've not gained that?'

Bobby looked up to meet his eye. 'Well, have I?'

'Aye, I'd say you have.' Reg went to Charles the snowman and reclaimed his pipe, slipping it into his pocket for a smoke later. 'Probably ought to have told you more often, but you know me: I'm a Yorkshireman. Don't go in much for a lot of soft talk. That said, you've been a right good little worker, and you can write a fair treat too. More important than that, you've got pluck – more than I'd have expected to find in a female.'

Bobby smiled at him. 'Thank you.'

'So there you go,' he said, patting her shoulder. 'You've no need to worry you haven't earned the new title, if that's all you're concerned about. If I didn't think you'd make a good job of it, I wouldn't offer.'

'It isn't only that.' She sighed. 'It's hard to explain, but… I don't suppose you'd much relish the job title Men's Editor, would you?'

'No such thing, lass.'

'I know there's no such thing. That's exactly what I mean. Male reporters write about whatever they want. When they're appointed editors and correspondents, it's of something specific like politics or rural affairs, because those are the areas they've proven themselves in. But the only area women reporters are expected to specialise in is being women – and once you're tied to that, it's all you're ever seen as good for. Do you understand?'

Reg was frowning. 'Suppose there's some truth in that. Never thought about it.'

'Because you're a man and you've never had to. But I have.'

'Aye, well, I won't press the new title on you if it makes you unhappy. And we can keep your name off the women's page if that's what you'd prefer. Long as it gets done, I'm not bothered who it's credited to. Don't want you miserable in your work.'

She smiled. 'Thank you, that's a weight off my mind. I was so worried I wouldn't be able to make you understand. That you'd think me ungrateful.'

He hobbled past her to go back into the house. On the way, he nodded to the book in her hand.

'Hold on to that,' he said. 'Happen you'll find yourself with "editor" in your title again one of these days.'

Chapter 32

The girls spent a happy morning sledging with the two men while the womenfolk retreated to the kitchen to prepare the dinner. A few hours' activity in the cold gave the children a good appetite, with both declaring themselves ravenous when they arrived home. It was to be a somewhat earlier Christmas dinner than usual, owing to the pantomime performance at 3 p.m.

'Well, Mary, I must say you've done yourself proud,' Bobby said as the three women surveyed the groaning kitchen table.

It was quite a feast even by peacetime standards, making the frugal meals they had been having for the past six weeks as Mary attempted to conserve their precious rations finally seem worth it. A special ration of dried fruit, sugar and suet had been issued for the festive season, and with the ingenuity of a housewife who knew her work well, Mary had made the most of every little bit extra.

There were potatoes prepared in every way possible – roasted, boiled and mashed, swimming with fresh farmhouse butter carefully saved from their allocation. A thick, rich gravy in a silver boat filled the air with an appetising aroma. There was mashed turnip and carrot, boiled leeks and cabbage, parsnips roasted in honey, faggots wrapped in bacon, sweet buttered chestnuts they had gathered back in the autumn, fresh bread sliced to the thickness of door-stops, and – thanks to the contributions of their feathered friends in the henhouse – a Yorkshire pudding apiece standing a good four inches high. There was a bottle of Ida Wilcox's home-made rhubarb wine to share, and a jug of beer from the Hart for the men. Christmas crackers were scarce thanks to the paper restrictions, but they had still gleaned enough for one to a pair. And in the centre of it all steamed the ducks Topsy had provided: glossy, glorious and golden-brown, fragrant with the herbs, apple and breadcrumbs with which they had been stuffed.

'Then you put the Bremen station on and the Germans try to persuade us that we're starving,' Lilian observed. 'Well done, Mary.'

Mary looked proud. 'Aye, it's a spread and no mistake. Not a thing on our table we aren't entitled to either – nowt black market in this house. I'll be eternally grateful to young Topsy for sending those birds to us. And we've a little pudding for afterwards out of the extra suet, and a custard jelly for the bairns, and mince pies, cake, pickles and stewed fruit enough to see us through to New Year's Day. Anything left over I'll package up to take over to Sumner House. We ought to share what we have on today of all days, and I'm sure there'll be hungry bairns enough to do the sweet things justice after the pantomime.'

'I feel like we've enough here to feed the five thousand,' Bobby said with a laugh. 'Mary, you ought to draw a picture of it and send it to Hitler.'

'No time for that.' Mary raised her voice. 'Dinner is served, everyone. Come and get it, while it's hot.'

The meal wasn't quite enough to feed the five thousand, but it was enough to feed two hungry children and five appreciative adults who couldn't remember the last time they'd enjoyed such a fine meal.

When she'd finished, Jessie looked regretfully at her empty bowl, then at the remaining custard jelly.

'You may have a second helping if you want it, Jess,' Mary said. 'There's enough.'

'My brain wants a second helping, but my tummy says if it has any more it might pop open.'

Mary smiled. 'Then you had better not. We don't want you throwing up during the pantomime. There's a tea afterwards, don't forget.'

'Ooh, it's the pantomime today!' Florrie said, clapping her hands. 'May I put my fairy dress on now, Mary?'

'Wait a moment for your food to settle. Don't be jumping about straight after eating.' She glanced at Bobby. 'But you can leave the table whenever you're ready, Bobby. You'll need to get to the house before we do to put your costume on.'

'Yes, I had better go soon,' Bobby said. 'It could take me a little while to walk there in the snow. I had been hoping to take Boxer, but he couldn't get through this.'

The nerves had started to affect Bobby now. She had avoided drinking too much of the rhubarb wine with her dinner, knowing she would soon have to perform, but the small glass she had drunk had done little to help her burgeoning stage fright.

She stood up. 'I'll just collect my costumes from the cow house, then I'll set off.'

'I'll walk there with you,' Lilian said.

It seemed to Bobby then that a look passed between Mary and her sister; a subtle one that she might almost have missed, but it was there all the same. As if the two had some secret they were sharing.

'What was that all about?' she asked Lilian while she gathered up her two costumes – her rag dress and bridal ballgown – at the cottage.

'What?'

'That look I saw you give Mary.' Bobby frowned. 'You didn't tell her about the baby, surely?'

'Of course not.' Lilian shook her head. 'I can never get anything past you, can I?'

'Well, what is it then?'

'Nothing bad, I promise. Just a surprise for later.'

Bobby laughed. 'Not another one. Those girls really are in danger of being spoilt completely rotten.'

'This one isn't for them,' Lilian said. 'At least – but I've already said too much. All will be revealed.'

–

It was a difficult walk to Sumner House. The snow was a good six inches now, and reaching the stately home was like hiking through the alps. Bobby was glad she had had the sense to change into her sturdiest boots and walking trousers before setting out, regardless of any teasing she was likely to receive from Ernie King.

'Oh, I do hope everyone can make it,' she murmured to Lilian as they finally stood outside the door to the big house, waiting for the matron to let them in.

She need not have worried, however. It took more than a fall of snow to deter Dalesfolk from having a good time on Christmas Day. When Bobby and Lilian were shown into the ward, they discovered the place was already packed to the rafters with people drying off as they waited for the afternoon's entertainment to begin.

The room looked spectacularly theatrical. The beds had been rearranged where possible to give the bedbound men the best view of the stage, pushed back against the wall to create more room for the rest of the audience. Chairs lined the walls on each side, where the parents and guardians now sat, and so far around forty children – both village natives and evacuees – sat cross-legged on the floor, chattering noisily with one another about the presents they had received that morning. Bobby recognised a couple of them. Tommy Zielinski was there, of course, being minded by Mrs Hobbes while his mother performed, and she spotted Florrie's friend Louis Butcher among a group of children from the school. The tea they were to have afterwards had been laid out in the old library, which usually served as a common room and mess hall for the patients here who were able to be mobile.

Several of the patients and hospital staff were to be involved today, some on stage and some off. One patient was already mounted on a ladder, waiting to operate the spotlight for them, while a doctor who was to act as stage manager stood by the pulley system that would open and close the starlight curtains. One of the nurses sat in a chair by the stage with a copy of the script, ready to act as the prompter. The pianist, another patient, played jolly Christmas tunes at his instrument to entertain the audience while they waited.

Topsy came forward to grab Bobby as soon as she saw her.

'Birdy, you must get changed as soon as you can,' she said sternly. 'You're terribly late.'

Bobby looked at her watch. 'I suppose I am a little late, but there's still half an hour. There's a lot of snow out there, Topsy.'

'Go and get into your costume, quickly. Teddy is in charge of wardrobe until Mary arrives. Where is she?'

'She said she wouldn't be far behind us,' Lilian said. 'She had to get the children ready.'

Again, Bobby was sure she saw a look pass between her sister and Topsy. There seemed to be some conspiracy between the women of Silverdale: one she had been deliberately excluded from.

'Oh yes. I forgot she had people to bring,' Topsy said vaguely. 'Lilian, you may go sit with the parents, unless you'd rather hop into bed with an airman. I don't suppose he'd mind.'

'I'm sure he wouldn't, but I think I had better stay respectably in mixed company,' Lilian said, smiling.

'Now you,' Topsy said, folding her arms at Bobby. 'Go on, into the dressing room with you and no dawdling. You are the star, you know.'

Bobby smiled. 'Happy Christmas, Topsy.'

'Never mind that. Off you go, lickety-split.'

Bobby almost saluted, but she managed to restrain herself. She found Teddy guarding the door of the cast dressing room, wearing his Baron Hardup jacket.

'Oh, wonderful. Are you joining us on stage again, Teddy?' she said.

'Yes, although I am sorely out of practice. Jack did not really wish to have a role, however, and I believe I can remember all my lines.' He smiled at her. 'I hope my fiancée was not too bossy with you. She is very much the director today.'

'She was, but I find it rather adorable when she gets that way.' Bobby smiled too. 'That was a very proud "my fiancée" then.'

'I am a very proud man, and even more so when I can instead say "my wife". All that makes me sad is that my family in Poland will not be at our wedding, or even know

370

of the match. But perhaps the day is not too far away that I might see them again to tell them.' He grasped her hand. 'And all our happiness is thanks to you, Bobby. I ought to have listened to you before, but all men are foolish and stubborn, whether Polish or English. I am no different from the rest of my kind.'

'You don't still have doubts?'

'I have many worries about our future together, but now I know my Topsy can be happy with no one but me, they shrink to the size of troublesome mice and I try to pay them no more mind.' He nodded to the dressing room door. 'But my fiancée regards us crossly for chattering when you ought to be putting on your dress. You had better go in. There are two screens, one horizontal and one vertical, to divide the room in half and spare our modesties. The ladies change on the right.'

—

It felt odd that after so many weeks of rehearsing, struggling for costumes and backdrops, painting props and scenery, learning lines and dances and songs, the pantomime performance seemed to rush by in a blur.

All Bobby's worries about what could go wrong disappeared as she threw herself into her role. There was something different about performing to an audience of children. Yes, they had had small audiences before – the airmen at the hospital had already seen the dress rehearsal, as had Lilian – but here were people who really lost themselves in the story. In the magic.

These were people who believed that she was Cinderella, although her rag dress was nothing but old dusters and cheesecloth. They believed that Sandy and Archie were not men but Lavvy and Clot, the Ugly Sisters, as they showed their bloomers and comically fell on their bottoms. They believed that Laura Bailey's magic wand, a knitting needle with a silver ribbon tied to the end, really had the power to make a coach out of a pumpkin. It didn't matter to the children that Cinderella's kitchen – the backcloth so ably painted by Jolka and Mary – was a combination of cheap paint and tent canvas, or that Baron Hardup's shabby, ancient tailcoat was the same one worn every year by the Master of Ceremonies at the village fete. To the children the story was as real as Father Christmas, and they ooohed and aaahed, shouted and laughed as loudly as any audience at a big city theatre.

It felt like no time at all until the first act was drawing to a close and they were nearly at the interval. The last scene before they took a fifteen-minute break for tea and biscuits was the one in which Cinderella emerged triumphantly into the ballroom in her enchanted gown, fleeing just as the clock struck midnight.

Mary had now arrived and taken over wardrobe duties. She was helping Bobby with her hair and make-up in the dressing room ready for the big scene.

'There we are,' she said, dabbing a little rouge on each cheek. 'Now you're perfect.'

'Thank you, Mary.' Bobby stood up and took a deep breath. 'Just this scene before the interval. Do you think everyone is enjoying it?'

'I don't think you'd find a more appreciative audience at Drury Lane.' She smiled down at Bobby's dress. 'You're as pretty as a picture, Bobby. Just as bonny as the real Cinderella.'

She laughed. 'Don't be daft.'

'You are. Now don't let yourself be distracted when you get on stage, will you?'

'Distracted by what?'

Mary gave her an enigmatic smile. 'You'll see.'

Bobby left and crept around the backcloth into the stage right wings. Archie and Sandy were behind the screen too, waiting for their entrance cue. On stage just in front of her was Ernie King as Buttons, acting as the Master of Ceremonies for the ball.

Archie grinned at her. 'Good luck, old girl,' he whispered, before Ernie announced 'Lavinia and Clotilda Hardup' and he and Sandy marched on stage arm in arm.

All right. Now even Archie was acting oddly. What was going on around here that Bobby didn't know about? Had they set up some trick to play on her as a Christmas jape, to make the children laugh all the louder when she fell on her face on stage? It was exactly the sort of thing Ernie might think up, although she couldn't imagine why Lilian or Mary would be complicit in humiliating her.

'A mysterious and beautiful stranger!' Ernie–Buttons announced, which was Bobby's cue to enter. She did so, summoning the lofty and poised demeanour she had nurtured during rehearsals – one that was somewhat undermined by her Bradford accent, but no one in Silverdale was likely to notice that.

'Who is that beauty?' Jolka said to the girl playing Dandini.

'I could not say, sire.'

'She looks like the girl I met in the forest, with whom I fell so deeply in love. I must dance with her.'

Bobby had been subtly scanning the stage area for signs of booby traps, in case her fellow cast members really did have a trick ready to spring on her, but nothing seemed amiss. She couldn't really see beyond the boundary of the stage while the spotlight was on her, blinded by its light as she was. However, as its operator turned it to highlight Jolka as Prince Charming, Bobby was able to see the audience.

That was when she spotted him. Charlie. He wasn't sitting with the parents but was cross-legged on the floor in his RAF uniform, with Florrie and Jessica cuddled up to him on each side. He was staring at her rapt.

Bobby felt her heart leap, and she only barely stifled an audible gasp. In fact she wasn't sure she had stifled it, but since she was supposed to have just caught sight of the man of her dreams on stage as well as off it, the audience would hopefully assume this was all part of the performance.

'I have never seen a woman more beautiful,' Jolka said, bowing to her. 'I would very much like to have you in my arms for the next dance.'

Bobby gaped for a moment, so thrown by Charlie's unexpected appearance that she lost her line.

'Arms and heart,' Ernie muttered from behind her, whose memory for lines made him as good as the prompter. She flashed him a look of gratitude.

'You may have me in your arms and in your heart, your highness, for as long as you would care to keep me there,' she said demurely to Jolka, curtseying in return, and the two began their waltz. It was Bobby's favourite dance of the pantomime, since with Jolka leading she didn't need to remember any of the steps.

As soon as the clock struck midnight and she had fled the ballroom, shaking loose her glass slipper on the way, the curtains fell and Bobby hurried out of the wings to seek Charlie. He had anticipated her, and was already on his feet by the door. She almost knocked him back through the frame as she threw herself into his arms.

Charlie laughed. 'Steady on, Cinders.'

'Oh, I could kill you, surprising me like that when I was on stage! You awful, beautiful man. What on earth are you doing here?'

'Let's go somewhere more private, shall we? Otherwise there are going to be a lot of confused children wondering when Cinderella became such a good-time girl as to be juggling two sweethearts at once.'

'We can go into the library where the tea is to be.'

She took his hand, holding it tight as if he might suddenly disappear again, and led him there.

'My God, you're a sight for sore eyes,' he said softly when they were alone, looking down at her dress. 'You're beautiful, Bobby. Absolutely beautiful.'

She blushed. 'Mary made it for me.'

'I suppose it would do terrible things to your lipstick if I kissed you, wouldn't it?'

'It would, but do it anyhow. You're worth a fresh coat.'

He smiled and took her in his arms for a kiss.

'Well,' he said breathlessly when they broke apart. 'This isn't the shy girl who greeted me the last time I was on leave.'

'I've missed you so much, Charlie. You are staying, aren't you?'

'Until the 30th, if you can bear me that long.'

'Oh, I should like that very much,' she said, nestling against him. 'Nearly a whole week together! But tell me how it happened. You said all leave was cancelled.'

'And so it was, until yesterday. We had an unexpected visit from some brass, who turned up with no warning to check on conditions at the camp. When they heard that some of the men there hadn't had home leave in over six months, they reinstated Christmas leave for all but essential personnel.'

'Bram too?'

'Bram too. He's going home to be with his parents in London.'

'And… Hunt?'

'I got the impression the senior officers who inspected us were far from happy with him,' Charlie said with a grim smile. 'He had a face like a depressed bulldog afterwards. I'm wondering if he'll still be there when we go back, or if they'll find some excuse to put him out to pasture. I can't think why they suddenly decided to inspect us though, and on Christmas Eve.'

Bobby smiled. 'It's a mystery.'

He held her back to look into her face, lifting an eyebrow. 'This wasn't anything to do with you, was it?'

'I can't say for sure but I sincerely hope so.'

'What did you do, Bobby?'

'I'll tell you another time. I have to be on stage in five minutes. Anyhow, it isn't important as long as I've got you here for Christmas after all.' She looked up at him. 'Mary knew you were coming, didn't she?'

'Yes, I sent her a telegram yesterday morning. I told her to keep it a secret from you if she could and I'd try to be here in time for your pantomime. I almost thought I wouldn't make it when I saw the snow, but then I thought about my beautiful girl and strode out into the desolate wastes with a song in my heart and ice in my socks.'

'You are an idiot,' Bobby said, laughing.

'Am I not your Prince Charming?'

'You are, but you're an idiot as well. I do love you, Charlie.'

'Bobby...' He looked into her eyes, his expression soft. 'You promised me the last time I saw you that you'd think about something for me.'

'Yes.'

'Well?'

'Topsy and Teddy are engaged,' she said dreamily. 'They're to be married next month.'

'Are they? Wonderful.'

'It is rather wonderful, isn't it? I've been thinking about weddings a lot recently. We seem to have had engagements being made and broken all over the place.'

'As thrilled as I am for Topsy and Teddy, Bobby, it's a wife for myself that I'm more interested in.' He ran one hand over her hip. 'I'd love to see you just as you are now,' he said quietly. 'Standing at my side in church while I promise to love you and make you happy always. Will you?'

Bobby rested her head against his chest. 'Yes, Charlie.'

'Before I go in February?'

'If it's possible.'

He tilted her face up to kiss her. 'Then I promise I'll spend every day of the rest of my life trying to deserve you.'

Chapter 33

It seemed only a blink later that Christmas Day, to which so much had been building, was coming to an end.

The pantomime had been a big success, with the audience cheering themselves hoarse as the final curtain fell. Already there was enthusiastic talk by the organisers about writing a *Dick Whittington* script for Christmas 1942. The school choir had sung their song and then the children had played party games like Murder and Hide-and-Seek until it was time for tea, the airmen smiling mistily at the young ones' cries of delight as they thought of their own children far away.

After the games the children had had a slap-up feed of rabbit paste sandwiches, hot sausage rolls, sugared apple rings and fairy cakes with chocolate icing, with lemonade to drink. Each child went home with a slice of Christmas cake and a little toy: a carved doll or pennywhistle made by the men at the hospital, or a toy plane courtesy of the Canadian airmen, who had requisitioned some of the metal models used in their training. All agreed it had been 'wizard', the most wonderful Christmas ever, and it would be one in the eye for Hitler if he knew about it. Florrie even announced importantly to the others that she intended to write and inform him of it, so the Führer should know how British children cocked a rebellious snook in Germany's direction in spite of his silly old war.

Charlie had been much in demand when they had arrived back at Moorside after the festivities.

'You must sit by me, Uncle Charlie, and see the new tricks Ace has learned,' Florrie informed him imperiously.

'No, by me, and hear the story of how I was lost in the woods with Henrietta,' Jessie said.

Charlie raised an eyebrow at Bobby. 'Lost in the woods?'

Bobby smiled. 'On Christmas Eve, no less. But I mustn't say a word on the subject or Jessie will never forgive me. I don't include nearly enough lions and tigers when I tell it, she says.'

'I think Uncle Charlie would rather like to sit by Bobby this evening,' Mary said with a smile. 'But he has something to give you both first, I believe.'

The squeals of joy and delight when the children set eyes on the beautiful dolls' house Charlie had crafted for them were so loud as to even have Ace joining in with an excited singsong howl of his own. Bobby was sure she saw a tear in her fiancé's eye as the two little girls threw themselves at him for a hug.

The appreciation of this magnificent gift was given all the time it deserved. Every perfectly decorated little room was explored; every piece of furniture taken out and cooed over before it was replaced carefully in its right position; every doll and toy soldier that Reg had made and Mary had dressed given a name and character to suit them. The adults smiled as they watched the innocent play of the little girls, who had created an elaborate domestic life for the house's doll inhabitants before the evening was out.

That evening, playing Rummy for farthings and listening to gramophone records with Charlie in their midst once again, it felt like the family circle was complete. As much as Bobby would have liked some time alone with her fiancé to discuss everything they had to discuss – Charlie's imminent mobilisation, and the wedding day she had finally agreed to name – she knew that could wait for another evening. That night she was happy just to be in her lover's company, surrounded by the people she held most dear and knowing everyone she cared about was safe. Worries about her sister's condition and Charlie's preparations to join the fight could be put away until Boxing Day.

Florrie sat between her and Charlie on the settee as bedtime approached, with Jessie claiming a place on Charlie's other side. He stretched one arm over the back of the settee to brush against Bobby's shoulder, however, keeping her close to him.

'What was your favourite bit of Christmas, Jessie?' Florrie asked her sister sleepily.

'Our dolls' house, definitely,' Jessie said, giving the little building on the carpet a worshipful glance. 'Oh, but the pantomime was smashing too though. I told everyone who was there from school that you were our friend, Bobby. You were so pretty in your frock. I didn't know you could be so pretty.'

Bobby laughed. 'Thank you. I think.'

'I liked when we went down the big hill on the toboggan Dad sent,' Florrie said with a yawn. 'It was like him being here, sort of. But I liked when I beat Louis at Murder too. Bobby, what was your favourite bit?'

Bobby smiled at Charlie, and reached up to press the hand on her shoulder. 'I think anyone may guess mine.'

'It really has been a wonderful Christmas, hasn't it?' Lilian said. And everyone agreed once again that in spite of the hardships of war, it had indeed been one of the best Christmases they could remember.

–

Lilian slept fast at her side that night, but Bobby couldn't sleep. Too many things had happened in the last few days for her mind to be still. She wondered if Charlie, too, lay awake in the little box room at Moorside, thinking of her. It wouldn't be long now until he could lie in her arms at night when he came home on leave. What that would mean for her job and their future she wasn't yet sure, but after everything she had experienced over the past few months, she no longer felt she could wave him off to the fight without first making him truly hers.

After once more trying and failing to fall asleep, she got quietly out of bed and tiptoed into the parlour, where she lit a candle. Then she hunted out her notebook. She still had an article she had promised Reg to deliver, although perhaps it might not be quite what he was expecting.

Bobby kept her pen poised for a long time before she began, thinking over the last few months. She thought of Topsy and Teddy, so different in background, temperament and circumstances, but with a love that had managed to transcend all obstacles. She thought of Bram, the young refugee hounded and bullied by the man responsible for his care purely because of his faith. She thought of Archie, grieving for a lover whose existence he could never acknowledge because society judged their feelings for one another to be unnatural. And she thought of the London evacuees in the village, the Canadian airmen, Piotr and Jolka, and all the friends she had made here from different parts of the country and the globe. Then she began to write.

Many hard things are said about our race in these troubled times. It is difficult to remember, when we open our morning newspaper to find out what terrible events had occurred the day before, that there can be warm and tender feelings among our fellow men. We curse the Germans as we queue for eggs and sausages, we curse our politicians when new items are added, regular as clockwork, to the ration, and sometimes we even curse our friends, who have helped themselves to the last of our butter ration over afternoon tea or taken the final oxtail from under the butcher's counter.

War can make us bitter, turning our anger on friends and enemies alike. We forget our nobler qualities, because we are tired and hungry and exhausted by conflict. Who would not be war-weary, after two years of rationing, shortages, blackouts, bombs, evacuations, and loved ones in danger far from home? But we must not allow ourselves to forget, because those nobler qualities are what set us apart from animals and make us the higher lifeform on our planet. And we all have these nobler qualities — yes, I even include the Germans in that. War may test these qualities, but it can also bring them to the fore in a way nothing in peacetime can do.

'What?' I hear you scoff. 'Surely not. War brings nothing to us except misery and deprivation.' Well, it certainly brings those things: I don't think there is a person in Great Britain, or in the world, who would attempt to deny that. But today, which is Christmas Day, I was in a room

filled with people sitting companionably together who – before this war began – had never so much as imagined the existence of the other. Children from our capital city, two hundred miles away from us in distance and even further in life experience, sat side by side with farmers' children from the heart of the Yorkshire Dales. Wary of each other when the evacuees first arrived, today I saw them comparing toys and sharing cakes, laughing together at the same jokes as they watched our village pantomime. Servicemen from Europe and the Commonwealth mingled with their English counterparts, sharing a smoke and some talk of the progress of the war. Sweethearts kissed and made plans for weddings that, were it not for this war, would never have occurred.

I'm sure we all wish the war to end tomorrow, but that is no reason we shouldn't embrace some of the happier changes it has made in our communities: the friends it has brought to us who we would otherwise never have met, and the worlds outside our own we have been privileged to take a glimpse into. We are reminded, on this day above all others, that we must not let bitterness overrule everything that is good and generous in our souls simply because we are hungry and tired.

And above all, we must remember that we ought to rejoice in our differences just as we do in what makes us alike, for our differences, too, can bind us together. What unites us above all is that we are people – imperfect, flawed, but striving to do better and be better than our baser urges would have us be. And it is through this unity that we will be able to rise above the forces of darkness which are at this moment seeking to dominate this world, and bring tolerance, peace and brotherhood back to all our fellow men.

'Not bad, that, lass,' Reg grunted when Bobby floated to her newly reinstated desk on the 3rd of January to begin work again. She had left her article on his desk for him, and he had clearly just finished reading it. 'Bit on the saccharine side, but folk go for that stuff at Christmas. At any rate, I appreciate the sentiment. It'll do for next December's number – if, God forbid, there's still a war on then.'

Bobby didn't answer. She sank into her chair with the letter she had received that morning still gripped in her hand, staring at nothing.

'Listen, lass, I was having a talk with the missus yesterday eve and I reckon I've been a stubborn old goat about thee and our Charlie getting wed,' he went on, full of affability after a week of good food and good cheer. 'That is to say, Mary reckons I've been a stubborn old goat and I wasn't allowed to get a word in to say otherwise. Still, happen she might be right.'

Reg paused to allow her a space to speak, but when no answer came he carried on.

'Charlie says you two are wanting to be wed before he flies out, and I can understand why. Man wants a wife to come home to when he's on leave, and a girl who's engaged shouldn't be left on her own long without a wedding ring on her finger. Happen I were too hasty when I said I'd made up my mind about letting you go from the mag after you married. With Charlie away you've no house to keep except for you and your dad, and until there's a bairn to consider then there's no reason you can't keep working for me as before. Mind, it'll be another matter when the war ends, or if ye two start a family. But for now, I'm happy to keep you on as a married woman while Charlie's out in the fight.'

He paused, but again no answer came.

'Might even have a new position for you,' he said. 'Didn't I tell you there could be something else for you here with "editor" in the title one day? I've been thinking we could use another reporter on *The Tyke*. I'm not able to get out and about as I once was and it'll be cheaper than relying on freelancers to fill the mag, just as long as we can find someone who'll work for the money. I'll set you to train them up and give you the title Deputy Editor – provisionally, mind, till I've seen how you get on. How's that?'

Bobby stirred. 'Deputy Editor?'

'Aye, I reckon you've got the makings of one in you.' He frowned. 'Summat up this morning, lass? Can't seem to get a word out of you.'

'It's… this letter,' Bobby murmured. 'It came for me in today's post.'

Reg glanced at it. 'What is it then? Bad news?'

'It's… Reg, I've been called up.'

A letter from Betty

Hello, and thank you for choosing to read *A Wartime Christmas in the Dales*. I hope you have enjoyed this third visit to Silverdale as much as I enjoyed writing it.

In this story, Bobby Bancroft wrestles once again with the challenges faced by an ambitious young woman trying to find her place in the world against the backdrop of a war-weary Britain. As the Christmas of 1941 approaches and the tide of the war starts to turn, the glimmer of a better future finally begins to emerge – but as Bobby knows only too well, with her airman fiancé Charlie preparing to join the fight, that future will come at a cost.

I'd absolutely love to hear your thoughts on this book in a review. These are invaluable not only for letting authors know how their story affected you, but also for helping other readers to choose their next read and discover new writers. Just a few words can make a big difference.

If you would like to find out more about me and my books you can do so via my website or social media pages, which can be found under my other pen name of Mary Jayne Baker:

Facebook: /MaryJayneWrites
Twitter: @MaryJayneBaker

Instagram: @MaryJayneBaker
Web: www.maryjaynebaker.co.uk

Thank you again for choosing *A Wartime Christmas in the Dales.*
   Best wishes,
   Betty

Acknowledgments

Huge thanks as always to my brilliant editor at Hera, Keshini Naidoo, and the rest of the team at Hera and Canelo for their hard work on this book. Thanks also go to my agent Hannah Todd at Madeleine Milburn Agency for her support.